I0703863

Lockhardt Sound

Heather O'Brien

LOCKHARDT SOUND

American Pie
Words and Music by Don McLean
Copyright © 1971, 1972 BENNY BIRD CO., INC.
Copyright Renewed
All Rights Controlled and Administered by SONGS OF UNIVERSAL, INC.
All Rights Reserved   Used by Permission
Reprinted by permission of Hal Leonard Corporation LLC

Sometimes I Feel Like a Motherless Child
Traditional (circa 1899)
Public Domain

Fifth edition 2025
(Previously published as *The Ties That Bind*)
[First edition 2001 | Second edition 2010|
Third edition 2018 | Fourth edition 2023]

Published in Fernley, Nevada – USA by *Word Rites Media*

eBook ISBN: 978-1-962501-03-3
Paperback ISBN: 978-1-962501-02-6
Hardback ISBN: 978-1-962501-01-9

Library of Congress Control Number: 2025904158

Cover by Warren Design

The Music is Murder saga

Lockhardt Sound

A Fate Worse Than Fame

Ballad of Someday

Hit Makers

Feels Like the End

Betrayer's Lullaby

High Water or Hell

To learn more, visit: www.booksbyheather.com.

ACKNOWLEDGMENTS

I would like to thank the following people for their love and support.

My husband, my children, my grandchildren, and the previous generations of my family, all of whom have made me who I am.

My utmost affection to: Erin, Tracy, Marci, Lisa, Cherie, Jana, Mike, Becky, Kim, Sheila, David, Skip, Bob, Charlie, Jama, Rhona, my pals at UHC, and all who believed it was possible to slay this beast.

Melissa Osborne, my personal wine consultant.

Mostly, I thank God, to Whom I am grateful for every blessing in my life.

Deepest gratitude must be given to my Beta readers:
Erin Adams, Emily Conner, Rose Ferraro, Heidi Leifson White, Larry Moore, Christina Naughton, Hugh Pitt, Ryan Rayston, and Kim Timperio.

This book would be incomplete without the help of those who selflessly gave their time, expertise, and technical assistance:

Dr. Emma Lew (Dade County Medical Examiner's office)
Trevore Fletcher (Criteria Recording Studios)
Sergeant Craig Leveen (Coral Gables Police Department)
Penny McCrea (the *Miami Herald*)
Doctors Phillips, Granovsky, Leff, and Krafcik (Sutter Medical Group)
Jacob Bunton (Lynam, Adler)

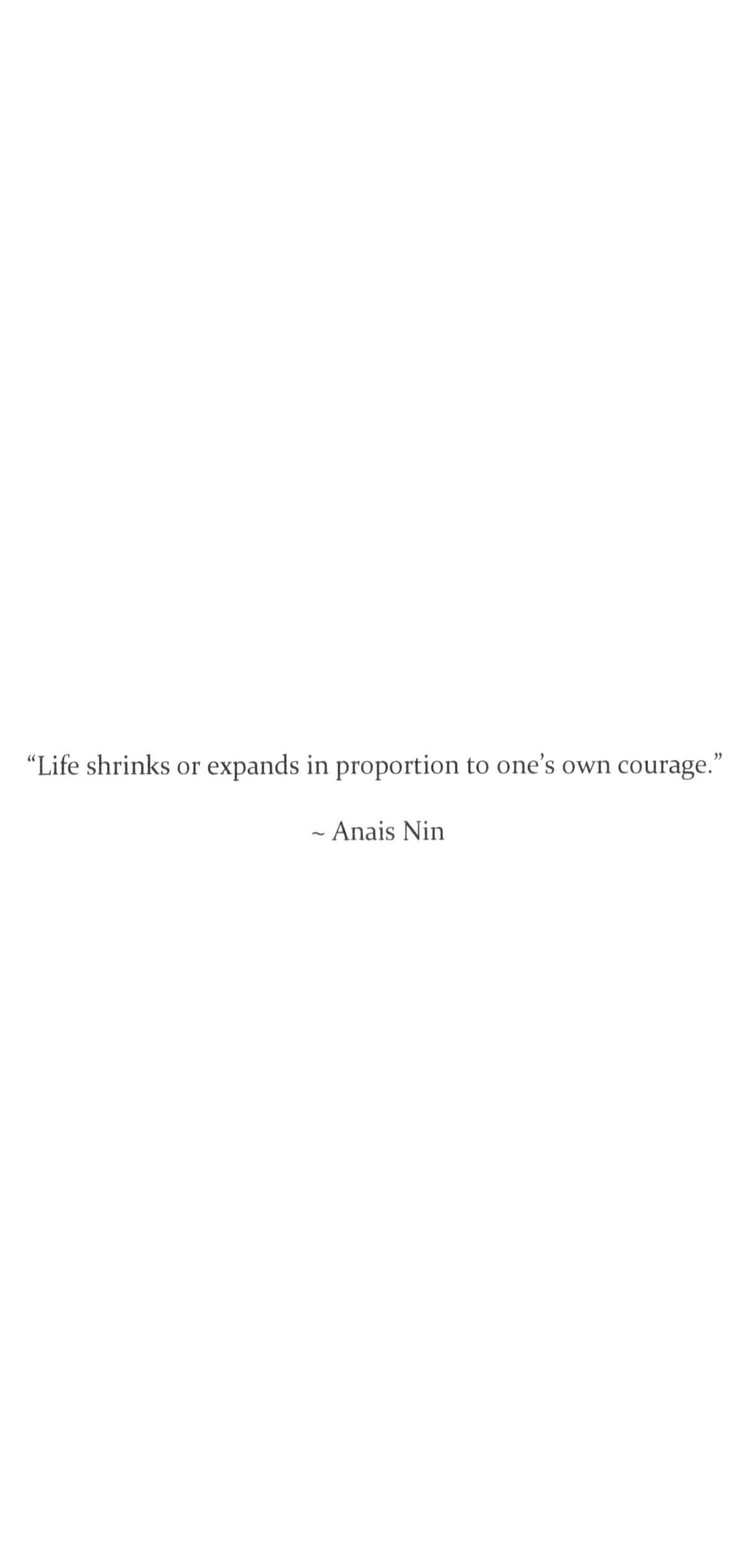

"Life shrinks or expands in proportion to one's own courage."

~ Anais Nin

For Andy

CHAPTER 1

I F NOT FOR THE CHICKEN soup, Jordan Grant's entire day would have been different. He would have stayed at the television studio to sign post-interview autographs. He would have been prepared for Mo McDaniel's notorious "gotcha" questions, designed to make him look insecure and naïve. He might have never found out. And he would have looked forward to dinner with Ginny.

Above all, Jordan wanted the one thing fame and money could not buy: a heart that mirrored his own. A love to die for. But for now, he had made his decision. The more he chewed on it, the better it tasted.

His only regret? The six months it had taken to come to his senses. Sure, he had heard the rumors. But gossip was an occupational hazard—particularly in this town. So he had dismissed the reports, passing them off as another example of the press doing what they did worst.

"You should've been more careful, Gin," he muttered, tightening his grip on the steering wheel until the color drained from his knuckles.

Under reasonable scrutiny, her alibis would have dissolved like sugar in a steaming cup of Earl Grey. The occasional migraine. Working hours that would have sent TV crew unions protesting. Meetings with her agent at suspicious hours because "I'm *busy*, Jordan—when else do I have the time?"

Perhaps Mo McDaniel was right. Perhaps he was naïve. Maybe he should feel foolish. Instead, he vacillated between anger at her cheating and relief that it would end. Tonight.

He navigated his convertible toward Malibu as if on autopilot. Warm wind skirred through his hair as he cruised north on Highway 1. Disjointed recollections—good and bad—gusted through his head like the curving rows of inky clouds before a coming cyclone.

He had declined having a car pick him up earlier, much to the frustration of his agent.

"What's the point of being a rock star if you won't act the part?" Bill had urged, as he always did.

"I'm not a rock star," Jordan had playfully insisted, as he always did.

"Your fans disagree. So does your publicist, the media, distributors, promoters, recording studios, Lockhardt Sound...need I go on?"

"You left out my *entourage*."

"You don't have an entourage."

"So, I probably don't need a car."

Bill Taft had hung up with a disapproving harrumph. As he always did.

Jordan rolled his shoulders and adjusted himself into the hand-sewn leather seat. The high noon sun beat down upon his lap, his forehead, and the top of his head. Not a cloud in sight. He regretted not grabbing a hat.

To his left, beachgoers sunbathed, frolicked along the strand, or waded out into the Pacific. It was late spring. A perfect day for a drive. A nice break from a hectic schedule, and a welcome pause from recent events. June was a month commonly associated with graduations and weddings. Beginnings. But not tonight. Not for him.

The last four months had left him physically and mentally spent. Japan, Germany, Australia, his native England, and finally back to the States. Sometimes, he struggled to maintain the obligatory smile. But that famous Grant smile had brought him success every bit as much as his voice. Jameson had drilled this fact into his mind.

It had also brought him Ginny.

On some level, Jordan dreaded confronting her. Hollywood's reigning princess would doubtless claw like a street cat once confronted. Defensive aggression, they called it. He hoped Ginny would maintain her decorum long enough to get through dinner. That she would consider both their reputations. Or at least hers.

The upside of his preoccupation with her infidelity? It had made today's show almost bearable. Though anxious, his decision to uncouple their coupling had brought unexpected relief. He had answered questions with wit and candor, charming both host and audience.

"So, tell us about *Umbra*," Maureen "Mo" McDaniel had said. "I listened to it on the way in this morning. People say it's your best so far. I'd have to agree."

The crowd cheered and applauded, shouting Jordan's name.

He flashed a nervous smile at the frenzied audience, mindful of the common "tells" that gave him away. No rubbing his hands along his pantlegs. Or crossing and uncrossing his legs. He lifted his chin at his host. "Thanks, Mo. Of the three, it's my favorite. I even co-wrote a couple of the songs."

"Talent sure runs in your family. How's Ben?"

"I think he's started writing the next album."

"Already? Wow."

"I'm hoping to get down to Miami soon to work on some ideas we've thrown about, but I still have a few weeks for *Umbra*'s publicity campaign."

The crowd's whooping and catcalling increased.

The thought of those few more weeks had dimmed his polished interview smile. Harsh lights. Cameras. Talk shows. Photo shoots. He detested the lot. For him, it was all about the music. His professional persona could not run more contrary to who Jordan Grant really was.

"You returned from Europe a few days ago. Did you manage to spend any time with your parents while you were in England? Or meet up with Chris—isn't he over there?"

He nodded. "Mum and Dad met me in London while I was there. Never saw Chris, though. Mirage was in Madrid. We tried to meet up in Paris but, conflicting schedules and all. Their tour's winding down. I'll see him sometime next month."

"And what about Ginny Stevens?" Mo had sidled up close, batting her artificially taught eyelids at him as if to wheedle out some juicy scandal. A chorus of whistles sounded from the men, and a few women, at the mention of the actress.

Jordan's cheeks had flushed, instantly annoying him.

Mo turned to her audience, a victorious grin stretched ear-to-ear. "There it is, girls. Isn't he *cute*?" She touched his arm in mock sympathy as the predominantly female audience squealed with delight. "Forgive me, Jordan. I couldn't resist."

However baffling, Jordan Grant's public shyness endeared him to his fans. Teenaged girls swooned for the blond pop idol who blushed whenever asked about his love life.

The taping consumed most of the morning. And his patience.

Of course, the interview looked different in his head than what the cameras filmed. To offset the irritation of Mo McDaniel's probing questions, he had fantasized about how the interview might have unfolded had he the freedom to face her interrogation with honesty instead of measured, restrained talking points.

"So, Jordan," Mo would have asked, "how's Chris?"

"Chris and Mirage are still touring Europe. I would've seen him while I was there if he'd taken time out of shagging every groupie at his concerts."

"And Ginny? It's been six months now. Any wedding bells in your future?"

"Funny you should ask, Mo. I rang to see her when I returned, but she was sick."

"What a shame. Nothing serious, I hope."

"She'll be fine. Actually, I cooked her some homemade chicken soup."

"You cook?"

"I cook for my son all the time."

"Your son?" Mo would have gasped. "You have a son?"

"Mm-hmm. Chase. I'm not supposed to tell anyone about him. It's in my contract. Jameson Lockhardt insisted. He'd hate to have my being a grown man with a school-age son ruin my image as a perpetually boyish 'sex

symbol.' I mean, what teenager wants to hang posters of someone's dad on their bedroom walls?"

"S-so, are you...married, too?"

"Nope, never married. Too busy raising my son."

"What about Chase's mother? Where is she?"

"Dead."

"Dead?" Mo would have cringed, wondering how she had lost her upbeat interview with pop music's biggest celebrity.

"I watched her die giving birth to my son."

"I...I'm so sorry. Does Ginny know about Chase?"

"Of course. But they're not close. She doesn't much like children."

"Oh, um, okay. Is, uh, Chase home in Malibu right now?"

"No. He finished kindergarten last week. He's in Miami with Ben and his wife. I miss him. Of course, I could spend more time with him if I didn't have to do these sodding talk shows and public appearances and run all over the world smiling my famous rock star smile. But we all have to pay the bills, don't we?"

"I see."

"So anyway, I fixed Ginny some homemade soup earlier this week. I'd been booked for a signing here locally, but it was canceled due to some problem with the venue. A broken pipe in the loo or something—which was fine with me. Anyway, I drove all the way to Bel Air to deliver this soup. And then the funniest thing happened."

"What?" Mo would have asked, eager for an upturn in conversation.

"She walked out her front door with Matt Kincaid."

"The actor?"

"That's him."

"He was visiting?"

"I wouldn't exactly call it 'visiting.' She was wearing the house robe I gave her for her birthday two months ago. This blue silky thing she'd fancied."

"No!"

"Yes! She walked him to his car and kissed him goodbye. He grabbed her bum and she giggled before he finally got in his car and drove away."

"My goodness," Mo would say. "Did you confront her?"

"I'm having dinner with her tonight to break it off. Good thing this show won't air for another couple of weeks, huh?"

During the interview—the *real* one—Jordan had grown agitated as the memory of Ginny's betrayal invaded his mind. Mo McDaniel assailed him with questions about his public and private life. His sole source of relief came while performing a track off *Umbra*. At least while he sang, he could put everything else out of his mind.

His relief was short-lived. Mere yards beyond the studio's electronically controlled gates he encountered the ever-changing, though never-vanishing, group of young girls who stalked his every move. The announcement of his appearance on the *Mo McDaniel Show* had drawn fans from across the greater Los Angeles area to the Burbank studio, each hopeful for a glimpse, a picture, a conversation…a marriage proposal.

"Bloody summer vacation," Jordan had muttered as he motored through the coterie. His Jaguar's leaping cat hood ornament provided little by way of a barrier. For a moment, he regretted rejecting Bill Taft's suggestion of a driver.

The crowd erupted into a screaming frenzy as Jordan pressed the button to close his convertible top. The roof rose and unfolded rapidly enough to isolate him from the throng of teenagers sprinting toward his car. Security kept them at bay while he navigated through the animated mob, flashing a gracious smile as he turned onto West Alameda Avenue. The gates had narrowly avoided trapping one young girl's arm as they closed.

The commute back to Malibu took longer than usual, thanks to a couple of ill-timed road construction projects. Beach traffic caused further delays. But as always, Jordan endured. Soon, he would be able to change into shorts and a T-shirt. Maybe take a dip in the pool, if he had time. The thought of having to change again in a few hours to meet Ginny drained him on several levels.

In fairness, they had little in common. Ginny enjoyed dressing up. He preferred casual attire. She enjoyed the nightlife. He preferred the beach. She attended awards shows. He never attended—even when he knew in advance he had won. Their problems were a matter of incompatibility as much as infidelity. He should have known it would not last.

His brothers did.

Both Chris and Ben had warned him at one time or another, but he had discarded their advice. They had babied him his whole life.

"Not exactly marriage material," Ben had commented. "Chase will want brothers and sisters. Is that what Ginny wants?"

"It hasn't come up yet. It's still new. I don't want to scare her off."

"If it scares her off, at least you'll know."

Jordan had dismissed the notion—not due to any confidence in Ginny, but because Jordan doubted he could ever be half the man Ben was anyway.

Chris, on the other hand, had encouraged the relationship at first.

"She's exactly what you need," he had said. "Someone to draw you out. Give you something worth blushing about. I mean, c'mon. You don't smoke, no drugs, little drink. Not much point in being a pop star if nothing pops, is there?"

But lately, even Chris had voiced suspicions.

Tabloids routinely portrayed Ginny's smiling visage arm-in-arm with Hollywood notables. Bachelors, as well as men who had lost any claim to bachelorhood. One rag had even issued a picture of her with Chris at some New York gala. A gala neither of them had attended. Jordan ignored tabloid news. Especially if it involved his brother. Chris's reputation was legend. One Jordan had witnessed first-hand at a young age. Still, he trusted his brother.

Bottom line: Jordan wanted more—and less—than Ginny could offer. He wanted to raise his son, make music, and settle down with someone who loved him for himself.

If anything, Jordan Grant was an *anti*-rock star. Ginny, on the other hand, lusted for celebrity like an addict.

Or a whore.

He rattled his head, surprised at the profanity of his inner voice.

To complicate matters, Ginny had started dropping hints. Marriage-type hints. Jordan did not envision his actress/girlfriend in that role.

The tension in his shoulders eased as he motored through the gate of his Malibu property. Days like today, he valued his community's tight rein on the paparazzi and fans who seemed forever more skillful in their attempts to sneak onto his private beach or scale his fence.

The second he walked through the door, he dropped his keys onto the entry table next to a stack of mail and kicked off his Bass penny loafers. Out of habit, he cocked his head and listened for Chase's infectious laughter. When he heard nothing, he opened his mouth to call for him, then stopped. His eyes darted across the empty living room, dining room, and stairs. Silence enveloped him, save the distant rumble of a passing airplane.

He flattened his lips, dipped his head, snatched up the mail, and strode into the kitchen, cursing the obligations that had prevented him from accompanying his son to Florida.

Umbra was the classic blessing-curse scenario for the twenty-eight-year-old. It had cemented the success of his first two multi-platinum albums. But the mark stamped on the annals of music like a branding iron on cowhide had resulted in unmanageable demands on his time.

Since February, Jordan had signed so many autograph books, headshots, album covers, and cassette and CD inserts with indelible markers, his left hand threatened to remain permanently curled in position.

After tonight, though, he had four days before his next commitment.

He intended to spend most of that time sleeping—alone.

The indicator light on his answering machine blinked red. He dropped the mail on the kitchen counter and pressed "play" before pulling loose his tie and untucking his shirt. The robotic voice announced three messages.

"I guess you're not back yet," Ben said. "Ring us when you can. Cheryl took Chase shopping today for a new life jacket. Quite the waterbug, your son. I took the boys out on the boat yesterday. He tried to jump off the side."

Jordan hitched his breath and jerked his head toward the machine.

"No worries. I caught him mid-jump."

He exhaled, then grabbed a glass from the cupboard.

"Anyway, I've been working on some songs for the next album."

"Let's get over *Umbra* first, buddy." Jordan pulled open the refrigerator door and grabbed a bottle of apple juice.

"Another reason you should move out here. It'd be easier to work if we were closer. Chase agrees. Tell your father, Chase..."

"Come to Mimami, Daddy!" Chase's small voice cheered into the telephone. "I love you! Hey, gimme that back, Kyle! It's mine!"

Jordan smiled sincerely for the first time all day as he listened to his son argue with his cousin before the call ended. From what he deduced, Ben's youngest had helped himself to Chase's rubber dolphin—a solemn offense amongst post-kindergarten boys.

The second message was from Nancy Chambers. "Mr. Lockhardt wants to discuss your itinerary. Better prepare yourself, Jordan. He's making tour-talk again. Call me back."

He grabbed a pen and note paper from a drawer and scribbled a reminder to call Bill Taft to schedule a call with Jameson, who was notorious for dealing directly with artists—not their agents. An annoying habit Jordan had grown accustomed to during his time with LSI. Chris had never even bothered with an agent. He had dealt with Jameson, and Lockhardt Sound, his entire fifteen years in the business.

Another tour. Bigger than the last one, if he knew Jameson. Gotta sell those units.

He gulped his juice, then dropped his head back and stared at the ceiling. Hopefully, it would not eat into Chase's summer vacation next year. Fall and winter tours generally involved fewer dates and were more tolerable. So far, he had avoided a full-blown world tour. But he was a headliner now. An all-season commodity. Son or no son, his life was not his own.

His jaw set as the last message played.

"Hello, my darling," Ginny cooed, her voice invading the sanctity of his home.

"Hello, whore," he spat, easing into the term. He leaned against the counter and finished his drink.

"Calling to confirm dinner tonight. I'll have to meet you there, though. I have an appointment at six."

"I bet you do."

"You sounded so mysterious when you called last night. I can't *wait* to find out what's been going on in that adorable head of yours."

"Me too."

"Hope the show went well today. I'm sure Mo loved you. They all do, you know. Oops! Gotta run. Love ya. Ciao!"

Jordan closed his eyes and inhaled a deep breath through his nostrils.

It was going to be a long night.

***

"BMG," Marci called out in her most professional tone of voice.

Farin stuffed the first envelope, then set it down, unsealed, atop the rose-colored carpet and to her right. "Check."

Marci checked BMG's name off the yellow legal pad with a red marker. She crossed her legs beneath her. "EMI."

"Check."

Head down, she peered at her best friend. A slight smile brushed her lips. "Lockhardt."

"*Yes.*" Farin stuffed this particular envelope with exaggerated care before placing it to her left.

"Polydor."

"Check."

"Sony."

"Check."

"Universal."

"Check."

"Warner Brothers."

"Got it." Farin surveyed the six envelopes to her right, then picked up the single package to her left and kissed it for luck. "Now all I have to do is run these over to Donovan's office. He'll put the cover letter together and mail them off next week."

Marci dropped the legal pad and marker, then stood to stretch her arms and legs. "You're nervous. Don't be."

"When I told him I went ahead and picked up the CDs, he laughed. He said even though I saved him a trip across town, he's not cutting his commission." Farin lay back onto the living room floor and stared at the ceiling, the package addressed to Lockhardt Sound resting across her chest.

Marci inspected her hands and wrinkled her nose. She disappeared into the bathroom, then returned wiping her hands on her jeans. "I'd hate to see you disappointed. You read the trades."

"I know, I know. They're not signing anyone right now. But if I could get on with LSI, I'd have it made."

"You've said that since we were thirteen." Marci fastened her hair with one of the two clips she retrieved from the bathroom, then motioned for Farin to sit up. She secured Farin's mass of auburn curls into the second clip. "You're obsessed."

Farin adjusted the clip a touch, then stood and cleared the clutter in the center of their living room. "I have to try."

"You know, the other day I read about the way Lockhardt treats—"

"You and those stupid magazines."

"They have to get those stories from somewhere."

Farin regarded her friend. They stared at one another in that wordless language they had shared since childhood. She stepped forward and embraced her. "Thank you."

Marci squeezed her tight. "No problem."

She pulled away, cleared her throat, and assessed the room. "It's your week to dust. I'll vacuum. Wanna flip for the toilet?"

"Nice try. Bathroom's all yours. I've got the kitchen this week."

For twenty years, Marci Williams and Farin O'Conner's close friendship had defied all logic. Mainly because they disagreed. About everything. As children, it was the color of their treehouse walls. Farin hated pink. It clashed with her hair. Marci, on the other hand, could not have cared less if their treehouse contained a wired music system with a drop cord painstakingly strung from the back yard all the way into the O'Conner home.

Later, it was after-school activities, lipstick colors, clothes, music, and boys. Lately, it was the debate over the division of household responsibilities.

The one thing they had always agreed upon was their strong affection for one another. In the end, that point mattered most.

"When are you planning to drop those tapes by Donovan's office?"

"I was hoping to do it today..."

"You're not sticking me with the whole apartment."

Farin's shoulders slumped.

"Let's just get it done and then I'll ride with you."

With an exaggerated sigh of resignation, Farin turned on her bare heel and trudged down the hall.

Marci loaded the dishwasher, then procured rubber gloves and cleanser from the under-sink cabinet. Minutes later, Rick Astley's "Together Forever" blared from the direction of the bathroom. Farin could do nothing in her life without a Top 40 background track.

The girls had met in the spring of 1968, before kindergarten. The O'Conner family had relocated from Seattle to Santa Barbara. Farin's father, Kelley, had moved his young family to California to open a law firm with Marci's father, Joseph Williams, a friend from law school. The O'Conners lived blocks from the Santa Barbara Pier. For years, their summers were spent vacationing together in the Cayman Islands, Yosemite, Cancun, and Disney World.

The girls were as inseparable as their parents. Blessed with brains and beauty. To their mutual confusion, people often mistook them for sisters. From the day they met, they were the biggest part of each other's lives.

Especially after everything unraveled. They had not corrected a stranger's assumption that they were related since they were ten years old.

Only in high school did they confront the possibility that their individual life paths might not include the obvious presence of the other. Farin had dreams. She would be a singer with platinum-selling records and thousands of admiring fans. And LSI would be her label.

"We're out of Windex. And paper towels."

Marci propped the mop against the counter and pushed a loosened strand of dark hair out of her face. "Put 'em on the list. You done already?"

"No." Farin sucked in her cheeks and glanced at the palms of her hands. "I still have the toilet and the floor to do. But the Comet's eating my flesh. I'm gonna lose the skin on my hands."

Marci inspected Farin's hands. "Use gloves. You know the drill."

Farin headed back to complete her chore. "*Drill* is right."

A lighthearted squeal emanated from down the hall when Billy Ocean's "Get Outta My Dreams, Get into My Car" came on the radio. Marci chuckled and grabbed the mop.

The single part of Farin's dreams Marci could share was the part about admiring fans. She was Farin's biggest. She supported her in every decision she made relating to her career—even the one that separated them. When Farin had announced her plan to leave Santa Barbara after graduation, Marci had cheered her on. The day after the girls had received their high school diplomas, Farin bid the Williamses a bittersweet goodbye and headed for Los Angeles. Marci stayed behind, opting to earn her bachelor's degree in Business Management at the local university.

Years went by. Farin struggled for her big break; Marci struggled with her grades. Farin played open mic nights, weddings, hotels, amateur nights, and an endless number of dive bars, singing with more than her fair share of fledgling bands. Marci formed study groups, wrote essays, battled test anxiety, and earned her degree. At first, they spoke every day. Then, weekly. But as life moved forward, they did too.

Lonely and professionally frustrated, Farin almost packed up and left LA, which would have broken her vow to never return home. Marci fared better back in Santa Barbara. She went into banking. Moved into her own apartment. Bought a brand new 1986 Chrysler LeBaron.

"I need you," Farin cried into the phone one night.

Soon after, Marci told her parents she had arranged a transfer from the Santa Barbara branch of Bank of America to Glendale. Farin found them a two-bedroom apartment and renewed her commitment to her career.

Three months ago, Farin decided she had waited long enough to become an overnight sensation. She dipped into the hefty trust fund her beloved father had left her and pressured her agent to find a decent studio. She recorded three songs: a Joni Mitchell cover, and two original songs written by the drummer from her last band. Now, her fate rested in Donovan Reed's hands.

Marci's eyes sparkled as she entered the bathroom where Farin crouched, scrubbing the toilet bowl. "I have an idea."

"A maid?" Farin stood, pitched the sponge into the sink, and flushed.

"You can hire us each a maid when you're rich and famous. Until then, you'll have to sweat with the rest of us peasants." She fingered a strand of curls that had freed itself from the clip. "Maybe a hairdresser, too."

Farin tucked the hair back into her unruly mane, then rubbed absently at her hairline. "What's your idea?"

"Dinner."

"*Dinner*?" Farin clapped her hands against her cheeks. "What's that?"

Marci folded her arms and arched a single brow. "My treat."

"Yeah?" Farin brightened.

"It's a milestone, right? We should celebrate. I'll make reservations while you shower."

"You shower first."

"You take longer."

"You always accuse me of using up all the hot water."

"Your hair takes longer to dry."

"But I make up for it because it takes me less time to do my makeup."

Marci raised her hands in surrender. "Fine. I'll shower first, then while you're in the shower, I'll make reservations."

Farin lifted her chin and shot her a satisfied smile.

"But don't wear the black dress. It's June. Add some color to your life."

"What're you wearing?" Farin asked.

"Pink," they said in unison, laughing.

CHAPTER 2

GINNY STRODE INTO LE DOME with a perfected promenade and an equally polished smile. Across the street from the Sunset Boulevard establishment, fans beckoned her with shouts and animated, full-arm waves. Paparazzi documented her every move with rapid-fire clicks of their cameras. She passed them with the usual, fleeting wave. Only on special occasions were photographers allowed within several yards of this well-known hub of the elite. This was not one of those nights. Yet.

As she stepped inside, all eyes fell upon the long-legged blonde. Crystal blue eyes sparkled in the dim, artificial light as she drew her sunglasses down the bridge of her celestial nose, accentuating her dramatic entrance. Her hair rested in large, impeccably pinned curls above her shoulders. The slit of her royal blue, backless evening dress stopped at center thigh. Matching three-inch stilettos stabbed the marble-tiled entrance like ice picks. A string of cultured freshwater pearls with matching drop earrings and a three-karat blue diamond cluster ring—which only tonight did she move from her left ring finger to her right—completed the ensemble.

Restaurant patrons yet to secure a table heard the clicking and whining of cameras as the doors closed behind her, the equipment popping and flashing outside like strobe lights as she disappeared inside. Ginny scanned the room, made her inquiry with the maître d', then headed for the bar.

To the uninitiated, Le Dome's exterior appeared little more than a hole in the wall amid Sunset Boulevard's flashy, filthy commercial district. Inside, the restaurant buzzed with the wealthy, well-known clientele tourists longed to encounter during a visit to one of the most famous, and infamous, cities in America.

Jordan sat upon a barstool near the back, shoulders slumped, nursing a single malt scotch on the rocks. The murmuring crowd, clinking glasses, and the intermittent bussing of tables only half-registered in his mind as he contemplated the chore ahead of him. Ginny did not take rejection well.

The hullabaloo accompanying her arrival alerted him to her approach before she entered his line of vision. When he spotted her, he finished his drink in a mighty gulp and waved in her direction.

She kissed his cheek and slid onto the stool beside him. "Sorry I'm late."

"What kept you?" he asked with more accusation than curiosity. He chastised himself for the remark. He had plenty of time.

"Last-minute rewrite for tomorrow's show." She fluttered a delicate hand toward the bartender. "We had to re-shoot the last five minutes."

Jordan lowered his head and tuned out Ginny's incessant chattering, scrutinizing her every move through narrowed, distrusting eyes. She placed her handbag atop the bar. Fingered her pearls. Inspected her manicure. Glimpsed herself in the mirror hanging on the wall to Jordan's right. Pouted to accentuate her red lips as she tilted her head first left, then right.

"Sorry about that," the bartender said upon her arrival. "We got swamped there for a sec."

Ginny eyed her up, then down, a look of manufactured disinterest on her face. "And you're telling us this *because*—?"

Crimson cheeks replaced the bartender's genial smile. "I wanted you to know I wasn't ignoring you, Miss Stevens."

Ginny leveled an icy stare upon her. "That's *Ms.*, dear."

"Sorry, *Ms.* Stevens."

"You're fine," Jordan interjected. "It's crowded for a Thursday, isn't it?"

Her eyes darted his way, then back to Ginny. "What can I get you, Ms. Stevens?"

"I think," Ginny blew out an exaggerated breath and glanced at the ceiling, tapping her chin with the tip of a finger, "I'll have a white wine spritzer."

The woman nodded, then asked Jordan, "Another scotch, sir?"

"Thank you, Miss…" He scooted to the edge of the stool and leaned in to read the girl's name tag. "Jayma. What a lovely name."

"Thank you, Mr. Grant." She dipped her chin, tucked a strand of fine, pearl-blonde hair behind her ear, then hurried off to fill their order.

"You always do that," Ginny spat with an indignant shoulder roll.

He propped an elbow onto the bar and faced her slowly, jaw fixed. "Do what?"

Something in his tone warned her off. She pushed out her lower lip and, in her whiniest little-girl-who-lost-her-kitten voice, said, "You always flirt with inferiors."

"I wasn't flirting. You were rude."

Ginny scoffed. "They shouldn't even be talking to us, Jordan. They're the help."

"How are they supposed to 'help' if they don't speak?"

"She'll want an autograph."

"Which I'll gladly give her."

"Hmph."

It was not all her fault. In his late teens, Jordan had admired Ginny Stevens on the BBC's broadcast of the American show, *Texas Tea*, which portrayed her as the lovable, dutiful, if strong-willed, wife of oil tycoon Tim Bryant. Her character, Chrissy, had single-handedly won American hearts, catapulting *Texas Tea* to the number one-rated series on primetime television. Jordan developed a crush on Chrissy Bryant and the actress who portrayed her.

Years later, after finding his own celebrity, the two met backstage on the CBS set of *This Evening with David Johnson*. That encounter eight months ago had left him starstruck. Two months of campaigning for her affections paid off. For the first time in his short career, he had used his status to his own benefit. And for the first time, he lived to regret it.

He learned the hard lesson other Hollywood newbies had before him. Like too many in their business, Ginny was a calculating opportunist. But Jordan had been naïve. Either way, the fantasy failed to live up to the reality. Ginny Stevens was no Chrissy Bryant.

"Remember, Jorie," his mum had cautioned him as a boy, "Wishes granted bring unexpected consequences."

Lynda Grant was rarely wrong. Jordan had come to the recent and somewhat pessimistic belief that every silver lining hides a cloud.

They finished their drinks with little discussion. A host ushered them to the main dining area's center table. Chin high, Ginny strutted like a Tennessee Walker past other patrons gawking or waving her way. Jordan strode more directly to their table. As the host handed over their menus, Ginny stood beside her chair and glared at Jordan, an expectant expression painting her flawlessly powdered face. Before she could protest the discourtesy, the host moved behind her and pulled out her chair.

She swept the folds of her dress beneath her to sit down. "Thank you," she snapped, eyebrow raised at Jordan as she jutted her chin toward their host.

***

Marci and Farin finished their appetizer as their entrées arrived. They had dined at Le Dome only once before, the night Marci had moved down from Santa Barbara. Farin had treated her to a celebratory dinner. Tonight, they had another reason to celebrate.

Champagne glass aloft, Marci straightened in her chair.

Farin smiled and followed suit.

"It's your turn," she said simply and sincerely.

"It *is* my turn," Farin agreed with a clink of their flutes.

The girls sipped their bubbly with an instinctive understanding of this juncture in their lives. This time, things would change. For the better.

"Why do I feel like I'm about to lose you again?" Marci asked. "I'm excited for you, but—"

"But you don't like change. Don't be silly. You'll never get rid of me."

Farin's affinity for music had made itself apparent the first time the girls played together in the still-unpacked O'Conner home a week after the move. Farin's mother, Beth, had suggested Marci come over and bring her new doll, which Marci proudly toted upstairs to Farin's attic playroom. One step inside the room had given Marci a glimpse into what would, years later, become the platform from which Farin would jump into adulthood.

The sloped attic walls had received more attention than any other room in the house. They showcased an array of torn out magazine posters of Joni Mitchell, Davy Jones, Bobby Sherman, Sonny and Cher, the Beatles, and the Beach Boys. A Kenner Close'n Play Phonograph sat on a stool in the corner. Marci had found Farin rummaging through her 45s, searching for Jefferson Airplane's "Somebody to Love," a gift from her father for her birthday some months back.

Marci wrinkled her nose at the driving beat. "What's that?"

"It's music." Farin squinted at her new friend. "Don't you have music in California?"

Marci pulled at the ruffles of her pink dress.

The girls stared at one another, sizing each other up. Slowly, Marci raised her arm to show Farin the doll she clutched in her hand. The doll had golden curls, bright blue eyes that resembled Marci's, and wore a beautiful wedding dress and veil. "Wanna play?"

"Sure." Farin changed the record player, then disappeared behind an old trifold partition. As the first few notes of "Respect" by Aretha Franklin played, she emerged from her hiding place. She crawled on the floor and held her own doll out in front of her, strutting the toy ahead of her in time with the music. The eleven-inch-high figure sported a sparkling rhinestone gown and dark curly hair painstakingly sprayed into place. It resembled no doll Marci had ever seen. Farin had taped half a Q-tip to its hand as a makeshift microphone.

Marci's eyes had grown twice their normal size as Farin sang along and made the doll dance. She sounded pretty, but Marci did not understand the music. Something about giving someone some money had been all she could make out. Marci watched nonetheless, riveted to her seat on the attic floorboards, as Farin sang the whole song by heart. Once finished, Marci and her doll cheered like a crowd in a stadium.

Farin and her doll bowed in appreciation of their adoring fans.

When the impromptu concert ended, the girls sat together on the shag rug that lay before Farin's three-story doll house.

"Gosh, Farin, you sing really good."

"My daddy says I'm gonna be famous someday—like Janis Joplin."

"Who?"

Farin scampered to her feet and returned to her record player. She replaced Aretha with "The Rain, the Park and Other Things" by the Cowsills.

When the dolls finally went down for their nap, Marci had busied herself setting up Farin's tea set, trying to ignore the noise coming from the small phonograph. Her mother had never sung those kinds of songs to her.

"You okay?" Farin waved her hand to get her friend's attention.

Blinking, Marci rattled her head. "Sorry. I suddenly had this image of you and Q-tip Barbie."

Farin cocked her head and frowned.

Marci did not know why this particular memory stood out in her mind. She had watched Farin perform countless times. Tonight though, things felt different. Like something had ended while something else had begun. She wished she could wrap up this evening and present it to Farin as a talisman against darker times. There had been many.

Tonight, Farin sat before her confident and self-assured. She held the grieving child at bay. A rarity for the woman who still suffered cruelly fifteen years after her father's death.

Farin set down her glass and picked up her fork. "Our waiter was checking you out."

Marci bobbed a shoulder. "You said I look like cotton candy."

"I was kidding. You look great."

"But you still wore the black. You promised."

"I didn't promise," Farin argued around a forkful of linguini. "Besides, I haven't done laundry."

"Soon, it won't matter. You'll have dozens of replacements."

Farin glanced down and inspected her dress. "I don't know. Maybe I'll keep this one out of spite."

"I remember the day you got it."

"*Everyone* remembers that day." Farin's smile vanished as she skewered a shrimp.

"Your mom was so mad. I never understood her problem with black clothes, did you?" Marci glanced up and saw Farin scowling at her plate, forked poised over her pasta, rubbing her hairline with her fingertips as she did when anxious or lost in thought. "Uh...did you leave a message for Donovan?"

The now of the question brought her back. "I told him I'd bring the CDs by on Monday."

"We could have done it on the way here if you hadn't spent so much time on your hair."

A mischievous smile flickered across her lips.

When their waiter returned to clear their plates, he scrutinized Marci with approving eyes. Farin noticed the subtle compliment register on her friend's face.

"Will there be anything else?" he asked. "Coffee? Dessert?"

Marci motioned to Farin. "How about you?"

"You want dessert?"

A second server appeared, holding a tray display of sugary pastries. Marci flattened a hand against her stomach. "I couldn't."

They agreed to an after-dinner coffee. Their waiter disappeared to procure their requests and prepare the check.

Farin reached for her purse. "You sure you want to get this? Seriously…"

"Don't you dare. It's on me."

Farin scanned the room as she enjoyed her steaming beverage. The freshly ground coffee tasted rich and bold, filling her middle with warmth. She absorbed the splendor of the restaurant's French décor and the lyrical laughter of other diners. Numerous celebrities dotted the crowd, enjoying their anonymity as much as their meals.

Marci gasped and leaned forward. "Did you see who just sat down at the next table?"

So much for anonymity.

Farin tilted her head to the side. "I'd hoped we'd skip this part. Who?"

***

"They're stalling the contract," Ginny complained. "Those tight-fisted so-and-sos don't want to give me my due. They think I don't know I'm the only thing holding that show together. Without me, it'd get canceled so fast it'd leave a sucking vortex the size of Texas in the lineup."

Jordan wondered whether to tell her before or after they ate. The picture of Matt Kincaid cupping Ginny's posterior and planting a passionate kiss on her lips looped in his mind like a broken film reel.

"So then the writers said, 'Oh, Ginny, you pulled off that scene like a pro.' A 'pro?' Was there ever a question?"

Her nonstop self-praise grated on him like a burlap shirt. He propped his elbow on the table, stone-faced, his eyes picking out her subtle imperfections. Imperfections he felt astonished not to have noticed before tonight. Thinning skin. Faint wrinkles on her hands. Her once-lithe fingers appeared more bony than slender.

"So Bob tells me I should do the shower scene naked—as in, like, *really* naked. What a pig. It's primetime! What's the most the audience would see? My bare back? Does he think I joined SAG yesterday?"

The fine lines beneath her eyes stood out more than anything. Of course, she did have seven years on him. He hoped he would look better than this at thirty-five. Years of stage makeup had taken its toll. Ironically, stage makeup was probably one of the only things saving her career.

"I'm not going to go nude so Bob can get his rocks off peeking at my privates." She paused and took a breath, then glanced around the room. "I wish our waiter would get back here with the appetizers. I'm starving. Aren't you?"

She reached across the table and touched his forearm. He shivered at the contact.

"Poor baby. I bet you haven't eaten all day."

"I had some chicken soup left over from earlier in the week."

"You need to get a real meal under your belt. I have a feeling you're gonna need your energy later." She winked.

"Do you?"

"Anyway, where was I? Oh, yeah. You know how Tim got shot last season? Well, the writers got a directive from the producers because it spiked the ratings. So anyway, point is, they're talking about shooting *me!* They're actually thinking about shooting Chrissy and dragging it out over fall sweeps. Can you imagine shooting me?"

"I think it's an excellent notion."

"Me getting shot?"

"What? Oh, no, of course not. The cliffhanger idea. It worked last time."

"Well," she countered with a haughty shake of her head, "I can't imagine being laid out in bed for possibly weeks."

"I can." He willed away a sneer.

"Oh, really?" Ginny's brows shot up then arched seductively. She sipped her spritzer, then set down the glass with feline care.

Jordan leaned back in his seat. "Gin, we need to talk."

Ginny Stevens splayed her fingers atop the spotless white linen tablecloth, her ring finger conspicuously exposed. "We do?"

***

"Kinda snappy, isn't she? 'Does he think I joined SAG yesterday?' I'd heard she was a prima donna, but wow!" Marci's eyes shown wide with disgust and avid fascination, like a spectator at a carnival freak show.

"You shouldn't be eavesdropping on their conversation."

"I can't help it. She's so loud," Marci defended, the picture of innocence, her voice pitched in a stage whisper intended only for Farin's ears.

Farin snuck a peek at their table. "Isn't that Jordan Grant with her?"

"Cute, huh?"

Farin lifted the cloth napkin from her lap, dabbed the corners of her lips, then placed it on the table and grabbed her black handbag. "You ready? I need to get out of this dress."

Marci drifted inconspicuously toward the table, craning her neck and leaning over further and further until Farin feared she would fall out of her chair and into Jordan Grant's lap.

"Sit up," Farin whisper-scolded. "What are you doing? Are you nuts?"

All at once, Marci's eyes widened. She righted herself in her chair. "Oh my gosh!"

"*What*?!" Ginny squawked.

Every Le Dome staff member froze in place. Every dining patron halted their meal and conversation. All heads turned, and all eyes rested, on the couple at the center table.

Ginny never even noticed.

Jordan held his hands out, palms down. "C'mon, Gin. Don't make a scene."

She bolted from her seat and towered over him, her perfect body wrapped in royal blue, eyes ablaze with hell's fury. In that moment, Jordan realized his plan had backfired. He imagined tomorrow's headlines.

"You're dumping *ME*? Do you realize who I *am*?"

"Sit down," he urged. "We can be civil about it, you know? I mean, if I can, you certainly can, right?"

Marci straightened in her seat, reveling in the melodrama playing out before her and the rest of the small crowd. She repositioned her chair in short scoots for a better view of the show. "Think Le Dome serves popcorn?" she whispered to Farin against the back of her hand.

Obviously, Jordan Grant had brought Ginny Stevens here tonight to end their six-month relationship. Marci had read about the actress' indiscretions. If anything, she admired Jordan for handling the woman's escapades so calmly. Marci would never put up with an unfaithful partner. Still, she could not help but admire Ginny's tenacity. She faced Jordan, chin raised, as if prepared for battle. Her lips did not tremble. Her hands did not shake. Her eyes did not water.

"Let's go," Farin pressed.

Marci's lips widened in sheer joy. Eyes fixed on the scene unfolding beside them, she whispered, "Are you kidding? I wouldn't miss this for all the tea in Texas!"

Farin lowered her head and rubbed her hairline with her fingertips.

"Civil?" Ginny howled, throwing her napkin onto the table. "You want *civil*? You drag me here under false pretenses and then tell me it's over? How 'civil' is that?"

"False pretenses?" Jordan's eyes narrowed beneath his creased brow. He opened his mouth to speak, then clamped it shut. The louder she protested, the more self-conscious he felt. This was worse than stage fright. It felt cheap. "No one needs to know our problems. Let's go someplace private and talk."

Ginny folded her arms. "What's the matter, big man? Think you can bring me here and use a bunch of strangers as a shield in order to avoid the fallout?"

"I rather thought you'd consider your reputation." Jordan sat back and let his arms fall casually at his sides. She was right. He had hoped the public setting would act as a buffer between them. Another hard lesson learned from Ginny Stevens. "You're a beautiful woman, Gin. Best not to wash our dirty linen in public."

Ginny stomped a Stiletto. "Speak *English*, Jordan! It's nineteen eighty-eight! The British Invasion ended years ago!"

He twirled his finger toward their waiter for the check. "I won't sit here while you make a scene. You'll leave with me now so we can sort this bloody thing out or I'll go alone. Your call, love. Either way, it's over."

With a rageful glint, Ginny pursed her lips. She shot a warning glare at their approaching waiter, stopping him in his tracks, then leveled an icy stare back at Jordan. She stabbed the air as she seethed, "Nobody dumps me, Mister Rock Star. I've got news for you. You're a flash in the pan. I've had a career since before you booked your first gig."

Jordan's eyes met hers, half-begging and half-warning her to stop. "This is getting out of hand. Let's be adults here."

"Adults? Adults don't send personally signed headshots to teenaged girls. Child molesters do. Here's a riddle for ya. What has ten thousand legs and no body hair? Can you guess? *Can you?!* The audience at a Jordan Grant concert, that's what!"

"Enough."

"You know what teenaged girls are, you English prick? They're fickle. Next year, they won't even remember your name. And *I'll* have a three-movie deal with Paramount!"

Though he tried, he could not grind his teeth fast enough to choke back his ready retort. "Keep shagging the right people and you might."

When the implications registered, Ginny stood aghast.

Jordan raised an eyebrow. "Shall I name names?" He gestured over his shoulder to the table in the far corner, where Matt Kincaid dined with one of the producers of his show.

All at once, Ginny became aware of the dozens of eyes watching her. Matt Kincaid stole a glance at her, as if pleading she not drag him into the scandal, then averted his eyes back to his dinner companions. She realized she had never gained the upper hand in this battle. Jordan knew. Worse, she had dropped her public façade long enough to present Jordan with the satisfaction that he knew she knew as well.

She weighed her options. Deny the accusation and play upon the public's sympathy? Cry and play upon their emotions?

No.

Ginny Stevens buckled for no man. Jordan was supposed to propose tonight. She had stopped by three jewelry stores today to peruse diamond engagement rings, inspecting each at length until settling upon the one she intended to make him buy her. Instead, he had ambushed and humiliated her. He did not deserve the tears she could easily manufacture.

In the end, Ginny determined to take Polonius's advice: be true to yourself.

She snatched her bag off the table, then clutched the stem of her wineglass, which she had barely touched. "Fuck you," she seethed, tossing its contents at him. The wineglass rolled from her fingers onto the table.

Ginny stomped toward the exit without a backward glance.

Jordan had ducked to prevent the drink from dousing his shirt. A droplet or two caught him, but a sudden squeal from behind him realized his fears. He swung around to find two women seated at the table directly in the spritzer's flight path.

The first, a brunette in a pink strapless gown, covered her mouth with her hand. Her shocked amusement riddled him with embarrassment. He made a mental note to send a letter of apology to Le Dome's management. If only he could personally apologize to each of their patrons. The brunette's contained laughter died in the space of his attention.

Her dinner companion, a redhead in a black cocktail gown, deepened his embarrassment to remorse. From the moisture cutting jagged swatches in her makeup, to her limp hair, to the small puddle in her lap absorbing into the fabric of her dress, the redhead had caught every drop of spritzer he had dodged to miss. He deflated at the sight. Why had he chosen to break up with Ginny Stevens in front of the entire world?

Waiters rushed to the table as the sensationalism of the confrontation quelled. They brought additional napkins and cleared the table. The woman leaned forward to avoid her hair dripping onto the floor.

As they bustled around her, the woman in pink edged her seat over to assist. "Are you okay?"

"Help me stop dripping enough so I can go to the ladies' room." Farin touched a fresh napkin to her face. Her cheeks flushed as all eyes shifted from Ginny Stevens to her. Damp-haired and mascara-splotched was not the image she hoped to display to a captive audience.

Marci flattened her lips as she assisted the waiters fussing over her. "That...was...*amazing*," she giggled, separately emphasizing each word.

"Yeah. Amazing."

"Pardon me," a British voice interrupted her humiliation.

They looked up in unison to find Jordan Grant hovering tableside.

"My name's Jordan. I couldn't be more embarrassed to meet you under these circumstances."

Marci dropped the napkin. She sprang to her feet and shot out her hand. "Marci Williams."

He refocused his attention away from the young and—he began to notice—beautiful woman who looked like she had gone for a dip in his backyard pool. Her face grew crimson as Le Dome staff scurried about them to erase the ordeal. He shook the brunette's hand, offering an apologetic, "Hello, Marci."

Marci nudged Farin's leg with her foot. Her thrilled smile never left her face.

Farin stared at Jordan in abject humiliation.

He wince-smiled an apologetic, "Hello."

"Hi."

Marci interjected, "This is Farin."

Jordan nodded. "Farin. Is there anything I can do?"

She rapidly shook her head. "I-I'm all right."

He held up a finger. The wait staff immediately retreated, carrying the table linen. He removed his dinner jacket, then lifted it her way as if seeking permission to place it around her shoulders. Marci watched with open-mouthed fascination.

"Really, Farin, I'm so sorry."

She did not protest as he draped the jacket over her shoulders. She pulled the lapels closed around her. "Thank you."

"Listen, anything I can do. I'll pay for the dry cleaning. Or I'll buy you a new dress."

The reality of the moment slowly registered in Farin's mind. Jordan Grant stood beside her, swaying foot-to-foot, as embarrassed and uncertain as she. The same Jordan Grant who was with Lockhardt Sound. Her stomach fluttered. "Mr. Grant—"

"Jordan," he said. "Please."

She swallowed hard. "Jordan, I'm...really. I just need to clean up a bit."

"At least let me pay for dinner."

"That won't be—"

"Done!" Marci exclaimed like an auctioneer confirming a closing bid.

Farin slit her eyes at her friend. Marci grinned unrepentantly.

"Very well." Jordan straightened his stance. "Consider tonight my treat, for what it's worth. If there's anything else I can do, please let me know."

"No," Farin repeated. "Nothing at all Mr. Gr...uh...Jordan. I need to go clean up."

Jordan gave them a curt nod. "See you in the bar, then."

Marci led her to the restroom to freshen up. Farin watched over her shoulder as Jordan approach the hostess desk. She wondered why he asked them to meet him in the bar. Then, it hit her.

Of course. He wants his jacket back.

CHAPTER 3

FOR TWENTY YEARS, DONOVAN REED had represented the finest and worst in the business. Funny how last year's best often turned into this year's worst. Not so funny how too many of his clients fell into the latter group. But these things had a way of cycling. Instinct told him he would soon experience an upswing. And he knew exactly who would make it happen.

Donovan's lack of punctuality was as legend as it was frustrating. Those who knew him best scheduled meetings hours or days ahead, then gave him a false start time to offset his tardiness. Today, he ambled into his office before noon. His secretary considered it a good sign.

He stood beside her, tapping his foot, as she finished her phone call.

At last, she pulled off her headset. "I told you not to hover."

"How's the itinerary for the day?"

"You missed your nine o'clock. Shocker, I know. I rescheduled it for two." She handed him a stack of opened mail. "Farin O'Conner dropped her demos off earlier. I put them on your desk with the letters."

"They're done already?"

"What else have I got to do with my morning?"

He held up his hands in mock surrender. "Anything else?"

Cher clicked her tongue. "Calls. The usual."

"Have you had lunch yet?"

"I think I'll do something crazy today and go at noon."

Donovan ignored the sarcasm and strolled into his office. His desk lay bare save the small stack of CD mailers and letterhead documents. Mostly, he conducted business from scribbled notes he jotted into an overflowing three-ring organizer, though he rarely paid attention to details such as dates and times. He dropped the mail atop the desk and wandered out to the little kitchenette. He grabbed a cup of black coffee, and then carefully sipped it down as he returned to his office.

Leaning back in his chair, he propped his feet atop his desk and sifted through the mail. The bills he stuffed into his organizer for later consideration. Most of his attention went to the dozens of headshots and query letters from potential clients. He studied each at length, then stacked them up for Cher to handle. If they sounded interesting, she would schedule an appointment. If not, she would send the standard rejection letter.

"Midget. Had parts in three major motion pictures. Attended Barnum and Bailey Clown College. Agent just died...blah, blah, blah." He put that one in the appointment stack.

"Drive a nail into my own forehead with a hammer." Reject.

He carried the sorted letters out to Cher, who gave directions to their office on Wilshire through her headset. With nods and shakes of his head, he gestured which stack was a go, which a no-go. She nodded her understanding without pausing her telephonic soliloquy. He whistled as he strolled back to his office.

Hunched forward in his chair, he signed the bottom of each of Farin O'Conner's query letters with a Montblanc pen, then matched them up to the pre-addressed CD mailers. Once finished, he had a stack of six sealed mailers and one extra letter. Confused, he rifled back through the stack, double-checking the recipients before returning to the reception area.

He caught Cher closing up for lunch. "Before you go, could you track down Farin O'Conner for me?"

She gave him a dry look, dropped her bag, pulled Farin's card from her Rolodex, and dialed the number. Donovan shuffled back to his desk. A moment later, she buzzed him. "She's on three. I'm going now."

"Farin, babe, can ya hear me?" he said into the speakerphone.

"Loud and clear."

Odd, he thought. She sounded as if she had expected his call. "Well, hey, I got your demos."

"Did you listen to them? Are they okay?

"They're great! Cher and I've been listening to 'em all morning. I'm sure we'll see some action real quick."

"Awesome. I appreciate all you're doing."

"Look, babe. You sure the studio gave you all seven CDs? I just wrote a whiz-bang query and noticed one's missing."

She paused. "You're not missing anything."

"Uh, yeah...I am. I got six CDs here, but I don't have one for LSI."

"Right."

"You don't understand." He spoke with animated hands, pointing as if she could see him. "I got a query sitting right here for Samantha Drake. When she hears this tape, you're a shoe-in."

"We're not querying LSI," she replied flatly.

He wrinkled his forehead and sank into his seat. "Farin, I realize the word on the street says LSI isn't signing right now, but Sam'll give it a listen. I talked to her personally. You said you wanted this. I can bag it for you. What gives?"

"Nothing. I changed my mind about LSI."

"H-hang on. Let's think about this a sec. You've got a rock-solid demo—"

"So, someone else should pick me up, right?"

Donovan frowned. Every time he varied his schedule, something went haywire. Tomorrow, he would not leave the house until mid-afternoon.

"But...why?" he asked in utter disbelief.

The line fell silent a beat. "I have my reasons."

Seconds of dead air passed before Donovan realized Farin did not intend to share those reasons. The abrupt change troubled him. He had never pegged her for the type who would sabotage her own success, but maybe he was wrong. He hoped not. She was good. Better than good. He counted on her to take him with her all the way to the top. "That's it then?"

"Let me know when you hear something."

"Count on it," he answered as Farin O'Conner, his brightest prospect, hung up.

***

"Mr. Grant?"

The voice floated into Chris's awareness as if from a great distance. Mirage had ended their tour in Frankfurt, Germany a little over forty-eight hours ago. Exhausted from the three-month European tour, the band of four men and one outrageous, outspoken woman had dragged their spent bodies aboard their chartered airplane for the long flight back to New York. Instead of taking a day to rest between flights, Chris had opted to continue on to Miami. He had passed out the entire last leg of the trip, and again the minute he stumbled into the limo LSI had arranged to meet him at Miami International.

"Mr. Grant? Sir?"

Having found him, sleep would not so easily loosen its grip. During the cross-Atlantic portion of their flight, his internal clock never grasped which circadian rhythm to follow from minute to minute, resulting in a fitful rest. He had alternated between mumbled conversations with his equally-spent bandmates and watching a badly edited in-flight movie Elliot had scored. A French art film that had originally opened at Cannes. Other than his friend and bass player's contribution, its most redeeming quality appeared not to be the misspelled subtitles.

"Sir?"

With a start and an indrawn breath, Chris bolted up and opened his bloodshot eyes.

"Sorry to wake you, sir," the chauffeur said. "We're here."

"Right." Chris blinked groggy eyes as he scooted to exit the vehicle.

"I've already unloaded your bags."

Chris nodded. "Sorry, mate. I've forgotten your name."

"Charles," the man reminded him.

"Right, right," Chris said absently. "Cheers."

Chris slid him one of several one-hundred-dollar bills he had obtained at the International Exchange Bank near the baggage claim area at Kennedy last night, then staggered up the wide front steps of Ben and Cheryl's three-story mansion. Ben waited at the front door, arms crossed, head cocked, a thinly-masked look of disapproval on his bearded face.

"Hi, honey, I'm home." He slid his sunglasses from the bridge of his nose to the top of his head and offered an ambivalent smile.

"Nobody dresses like that in real life, you know. What did you do, fall out of a leather tree?"

"Grand seeing you too, old man."

Ben began hefting Chris's luggage into the foyer. "You couldn't have left some of this back in New York?"

Chris looked up, left, then right, sweeping the stuccoed pillars and arches of the estate with slanted eyes. "I know, I know. Space is a real problem."

"How was the tour?"

"Exhausting. But Faith didn't cause too much trouble this time. We only had to bail her out once, in Amsterdam, so I judge it a success."

A crooked grin found Ben's face. He chuckled again, this time in earnest. "What'd she do this time?"

"She snuck out of the hotel the night we rolled in and did a little sightseeing in the Red-Light District."

Ben set the last bag in the marbled entryway. He paused as Chris's news registered. An image of Faith Peterson, Mirage's untamed keyboardist, formed in his mind. "But prostitution's legal in Amsterdam, and softer drugs are tolerated."

Chris yawned and stretched. "We're talking about Faith."

He grunted, then motioned him into the kitchen for tea.

The moment Chris stopped using both legs to fight gravity, he fought the urge to fall back asleep. He collapsed with a groan into the nearest kitchen chair as Ben filled the kettle. "What time is it?"

"Two."

"What day is it?"

"Friday."

"Ah."

They spoke in periodic bursts of banal pleasantries, restricting their exchange to industry matters. MCA Records had bought Motown. Mötley Crüe's manager, Don McGhee, had been sentenced to five years' probation for drug smuggling. Céline Dion, a French-Canadian singer representing Switzerland, had just won the Eurovision Song Contest. Michael Jackson's "Dirty Diana" had broken the record for most consecutive charting singles off an album. And Sonny Bono was now mayor of Palm Springs, California.

Chris withered at the table, thumbs hooked on his belt loops, his glassy eyes peering into nothing, while Ben leaned against the kitchen counter, arms folded, staring at the stove. They existed in a state of familiar, if intangible, discomfort. Apart from their blood, looks, and similar professions, Chris had little in common with Ben or Jordan.

"Any idea when you'll start recording again?"

"We'll meet with Jameson once I'm back in New York."

More silence followed.

Fatigue aside, Chris relished the fast-paced lifestyle his fame demanded. His brothers kept more to themselves and their family. Ben and Cheryl had their blissful, ten-year marriage. Jordan had tried to make a life with Chase's mother before she died in childbirth. Both had children; he did not. In fact, he had not dated the same woman for more than, he could guess, a couple of weeks in his entire life. Some called him a rogue. But Chris preferred the gentler term "short attention span."

When the teapot whistled, Ben prepared their cups and placed one in front of Chris before sitting opposite him. "I talked to Jordan earlier."

Chris blew cool air at the hot liquid.

"You should ring him. Let him know when you'll be bringing Chase back."

"I'll ring him later."

Ben clicked his tongue. "Right."

Chris finished his cup faster than he should have. The liquid burned his tongue, throat, and the roof of his mouth. He was eager to trade their strained conversation for the privacy of the guest bedroom Cheryl made up for him on his rare visits. She always situated him on the second floor, far from the third-floor master suite. He enjoyed his solitude, if not in his everyday life, then certainly while visiting family.

He slid the cup across the table, then dropped his head on his extended arm. "I'm knackered. Think I'll go upstairs and have a kip. I'd hoped to catch the boys. Where is everyone?"

The front door opened before Ben could answer. With a sound like a cattle stampede, three young boys trampled across the living room, down the hallway, and toward the kitchen.

"Uncle Chris!" Their cheers overlapped one another as they nearly tackled him backward onto the floor. "Uncle Chris! Uncle Chris!"

Cheryl Grant arrived next, purse hooked over her forearm, sunglasses in hand. She mouthed a wide-eyed and welcoming, "You're here!" over the boys' chatter, set her things on the kitchen counter, then caught her husband's eye. Ben stood to greet her. She moved into his embrace and gave him a quick kiss.

"How was the show?" Ben asked.

"To be honest, I think the lads enjoyed the popcorn and candy more than the film." She rested her head on his chest and looked at her brother-in-law. "How was the flight?"

"I slept on the plane here and there." His nephews climbed him like a ladder, each vying for his attention.

"You look completely done in. Boys, give Uncle Chris some space now."

"Come outside and play, Uncle Chris," Ben's eldest son, Derek, beckoned as he pulled at his right arm.

Kyle pulled at his left. "Yeah, come play out back with us."

Chase, the youngest of the three, had climbed onto his uncle's lap. He played with the zippers and snaps on Chris's leather jacket. "Let's go swimming."

"You heard your mother," Ben scolded as Cheryl stepped away from the embrace. "Let Uncle Chris relax, understand? You too, Chase."

Chris ruffled Chase's straw-blond hair. He smiled for the first time since his arrival. "It's okay."

Chase made a face. He waved his hand in front of his nose. "You smell."

"I imagine so. Uncle Chris needs a shower."

"Guess what?"

"Tell me."

"I'm six."

He gave Chase a quick tickle. "I know you are. I sent you a present, remember?"

"A guitar!"

"Aye," Cheryl said, her tone thick with motherly disapproval. "You certainly did. We've grown familiar with the sound of that guitar, haven't we?"

Chris chuckled.

"My birthday's next week," Derek chimed in. "Are you gonna be here, Uncle Chris?"

"Afraid not, mate. I've got to take your cousin home to California." Seeing the disappointment manifest itself on his oldest nephew's features, he added, "Not to worry, though. I've got something special picked out for you."

"Nothing pornographic, I hope," Ben muttered.

"What's por...porgo...what's that word mean?" seven-year-old Kyle asked.

"It means Mum's going to spank your dad in a minute," Cheryl said.

Chris waggled his eyebrows. "Something like that."

Cheryl snorted. "You're incorrigible."

Chase reached up and pulled Chris's sunglasses off the top of his head and tried them on.

Cheryl studied Chris's pale skin and bloodshot eyes. "When's the last time you had a decent meal?"

"Whenever I was here last. You're the best cook I know, other than Mum."

"Lads, let Uncle Chris be. He needs to shower and have a rest."

"Outside, boys," Ben instructed.

The young trio grumbled their protests as they made their way to the back yard with all the dejection of scolded puppies. Shoulders slumped. Downcast eyes.

Pursing their lips to stifle smiles, the adults watched them depart. Cheryl grimaced when the French doors slammed shut.

Chris craned his neck to watch them through the sheers. "Can you remember being that young?"

Ben split the curtains with his hand, glancing outside to ensure the boys found some nondestructive way to occupy their time.

Cheryl opened the refrigerator door and pulled out a large, lidded bowl. She set it on the butcherblock near the sink. "You two speak for yourselves."

"They're good boys," Chris said.

"Aye, perfect gentlemen. Noo, upstairs before we have to carry you. Go on."

Chris stood with a moan and grabbed his empty teacup. He shuffled toward the stairs, depositing the porcelain vessel in the sink as he passed. Ben followed behind while Cheryl brought up the rear.

In the foyer, the three squabbled over who would carry what. An electronic chirp filled the air around them, ending the debate. Cheryl and Ben watched, luggage clutched and straps draped across their shoulders, as Chris unzipped his carryon to retrieve a bulky cellular telephone.

"Hello?"

Ben proceeded up the curved staircase. He knew that greeting all too well. The greeting that signaled Chris would throw off family for another casual encounter.

Cheryl remained at the foot of the stairs, politely waiting for Chris to end the call. She hefted the weight of a duffel bag to stop its strap from slipping off her shoulder.

"Well, hello," Chris's tone dropped to a sonorous baritone.

Ben stopped halfway up the steps as the echo of Chris's voice reached his ears. He turned and watched his brother a moment, tempted to drop the bags on the steps where he stood. *Let the games begin.*

Chris wrestled the receiver between his shoulder and his ear as he picked up the two overnight bags left in the foyer and started up the stairs, a devilish grin stretched across his lips. "You are a bad girl, aren't you?" He growled seductively. "Oh really? I'd like to see that."

Ben caught his wife's patient yet irritated expression as Chris moved past him.

Cheryl marched upstairs behind him. "Does this mean he won't be joining us for dinner tonight? I marinated chicken. I knew I shouldn't have marinated the chicken."

Sarcasm saturated Ben's voice. "We both know he'll eat the bloody chicken. He'll be starved when he comes in tonight."

Chris's fiendish laughter echoed down the stairs from the second floor. "I'll be there at seven. We'll order in. No, of course not. I'm sure what you're wearing is fine. It's not like I'll be seeing it long. Oh—and make sure you've a razor on hand." Another devilish snicker escaped his lips. "No-no, not for me."

Ben and Cheryl reached the guest room as the conversation ended. Chris tossed his cell and jacket onto the queen-size bed. "I'm afraid I won't be joining you for dinner," he announced.

"I gathered," Ben said.

"The boys'll be disappointed you're not here," Cheryl said.

"I'll make it up to them. We'll take the boat out tomorrow. You mind, Ben?"

Ben hefted two large bags of luggage onto the bed. "Ring Jordan before you leave."

Chris stood straight, kicked his heels together, and saluted.

Cheryl dropped the duffel bag next to the suitcases. "It hasn't even been an hour and you two are at it. You'll both have to do better. At least for the boys' sakes. Now, Ben. Did you tell him?"

Ben's eyes remained fixed on his younger brother as Chris snatched up his cell. "Not yet."

Chris's fingers froze over the keypad. "Tell me what?"

"Jorie's finally broken up—"

"—with Ginny." His lips curled into a lighthearted smile, temporarily dropping the chip on his shoulder. He side-eyed Ben. "I heard. Front page. About time, eh? Sodding wench."

"There's more," Cheryl chirped. "He's seeing someone new."

Chris cocked his head. "So soon?"

"He says she's lovely."

"That's bloody fantastic. I'd expected him to brood for weeks. Anyone we know?"

"He met her at the restaurant the night he gave ol' Ginny the what-for."

"Perhaps there's hope for him after all."

Before leaving him alone to make his call, Cheryl made sure Chris had fresh towels. Ben confirmed he had a key because "I'm not waiting up for you."

Chris regarded them as he would his parents. He thanked Cheryl for the towels. Yes, he had a key. No, he did not need anything else. Except a nap, a shower, and to head back out as soon as possible.

He walked them to the door, cell phone in hand. As promised, he dialed the Malibu number and pressed the send key. Jordan answered on the third ring.

"Heya." Chris barked out a laugh. "I hear congratulations are in order."

"You at Ben's?"

"I am. I'll return your son in a few days."

"How was the tour?"

Chris groaned. "You know how it is. I'll relay the highlights when I get there. Now tell me, what's this about some new bird? The press is mad over Chrissy Bryant's well running dry at Le Dome. Was she as wicked as the reports?"

"Let's say I've learned you don't tell someone you don't want to see them anymore in a quiet restaurant."

"I could've told you that." Chris sat on the bed and kicked off his shoes. "So, who's this new girl Ben and Cheryl are on about?"

"She's amazing. I can't wait for you to meet her. When are you coming?"

"Let's see." Chris sprawled backward onto the bed next to his luggage. "Today's Friday? I'm thinking Monday. That way I've got the weekend."

"I'll have them over next weekend then. Barbecue okay? I'm certain the girls will want to meet you."

Chris sat up. "Girls? Jordan, did you start a harem?"

"I can't believe you'd even suggest—oh wait, yes I can."

"I was about to congratulate you."

"I was referring to her girlfriend."

"Girlfriend?" Chris enjoyed the mental image but decided against sharing.

"Roommate," Jordan clarified. "I'll have them both over. Marci's a gem."

"Count Chase and I in. I hate to cut this short but if I don't get in the shower soon, Ben'll be up here with a can of Lysol or some awful thing. I'll ring you tomorrow. I'm taking the boys out on the boat. You can talk to Chase."

"And I'll get the grill out this week to make sure it's clean."

"Before you go, is the nanny about? What was her name again?"

Jordan paused. "Nicole?"

"*Nicole*! That's it!"

"I had her take her vacation while Chase was away."

"Let her know I'm coming in?"

"Not bloody likely. It took me a month to calm her down last time you were here."

Chris disliked the change in his brother's tone, but decided battling one sibling was enough for the day. "Fine. I'll find another distraction."

CHAPTER 4

TWO WEEKS LATER

A HEAVY WHITE FOG CLUNG *to the Santa Barbara streets like the thick strings of a spider's web in an abandoned farmhouse. The coastal air, icy and dense, smelled of salt and seaweed. Glowing street lamps cast muted halos of mist, dotting the city streets. In the black of night, it seemed impossible that the freshness and life of spring would replace the gloomy murk in a matter of hours.*

Farin searched every doorway, every shadow along the empty street. Her white silk nightgown wafted and curled around her tiny ankles. A brass barrette secured her long mane of auburn curls. Her eyes narrowed as she continued on, barefoot, searching every inch of the dark night.

As if from out of nowhere, music suffused the air. She could not quite place the oddly familiar tune.

"Daddy!" she called with longing and despair. "Where are you?"

She walked on, out of the safety of her neighborhood, past the shopping mall, and into the business district. The music's volume increased, guiding her path. Her mother would reprimand her for wandering off alone, especially so late at night. Her father would scold her for leaving her bed and wandering out into the darkness. But she did not care. She had to find him.

He had missed dinner earlier, not that his absence alone should worry her. An important lawyer, long hours were a natural part of his job. He had explained this to Farin many times, and she knew her daddy only wanted the best for her and her mother. Still, the looming feeling that something terrible had occurred clung to her thoughts as the mist clung to the buildings, the ground, and the night. She could feel it. She had to find him and bring him home.

Just when she thought she might collapse from the chill of the impenetrable salty air, a blinking red light came into her line of vision from far off in the distance. Faint at first, the image grew brighter as she approached. The beat of drums and guitar strains grew louder as well. Farin recognized the blinking red beacon as the rear turn-signal light of their family station wagon. She looked around, confused, then headed toward the driver's door.

Fear gripped her as she came alongside the vehicle. She made out the buckled front end of the brown station wagon, its heavy steel wrapped snugly around the passenger's side of a smaller vehicle. Thick, warm steam floated up from beneath the hood of the car, the pressure causing a sinister hiss. The radio played, casting "American Pie" into the still night air.

... drove my Chevy to the levy but the levy was dry ...

"Daddy!" Farin cried, a forlorn yelp the likes of which only a ten-year-old could produce. The quiet, eerie scene frightened her beyond explanation. Nothing rumbled or stirred from her father's car or from the smaller vehicle. She heard no moan, no cry for help, nothing but the maddening hiss of the engine and the strains of music from the radio.

... and something touched me deep inside the day...the music...died ...

She walked slowly, almost paralyzed, toward the driver's door, afraid of what she might see. Since she heard no sound but the radio, he must not be inside. Maybe he had abandoned the car to look for help. Maybe she had passed him in the fog as he went to search for a pay phone from which to call the police or her mother. Yes, that had to be it. He was on the telephone at that exact moment.

All at once, she felt desperate to run back the way she had come. He would worry if he called and she was not at home in bed. But despite the rattlings of her young mind, she drew closer, pulled by a force so strong she nearly stumbled as she reached the driver's front door.

Inside the car, hunched over the steering wheel, sat the crumpled, lifeless form of Kelley O'Conner.

***

At 4:30 Thursday afternoon, Farin sat cross-legged on the overstuffed couch with its bright floral print, clicking her left ring finger against her thumbnail. Breaking the barrier between nightmare and reality had been the usual violent thrust. She cursed herself for falling asleep. Sleep brought no comfort, provided no solace from the agony in her heart. An onslaught of tormenting images, past and present, raced through her mind's eye. The horrifying dream, a legacy attached to her soul, lingered at the forefront of her consciousness.

Quiet permeated the apartment. Dim light drew soft shadows against the pastel colors of the living room in stark contrast to the gloomy sunlight streaming through the window.

She surveyed her surroundings, unsure of the details of the past hour since sleep had released her, shoving her back to present. She remembered the dampness of her face and hair, her sweat-soaked sheets adhering to her naked body. The elapsed time between then and now was a mystery.

The only distinguishable sound echoed from Mrs. Hanson's television down the hall. The muffled drone of Oprah and her audience occasionally invaded the silence. A Doctor Somebody gave advice on how to cope with the loss of a loved one. Farin stared at her front door, tempted to race out into the hall, pound on the deaf old widow's door, and demand she change the channel or at least turn down the volume.

She wondered if Jordan had his television on. If he watched Oprah. A ridiculous thought. His schedule left him little time to watch television, especially talk shows...especially today.

July in Los Angeles was usually warmer and less gloomy. Outside, the gray day was stuffy and overcast. A lazy, humid breeze stirred the birch trees outside the open second-floor windows. They had not run the air conditioner in days.

She raked her curls with slender fingers, padding uneasily into the kitchen in search of something to calm her nerves. Breakfast dishes filled the sink. She had neglected to wash them earlier.

A half-consumed bottle of vodka sat on a freshly papered cupboard shelf. Vodka would not have been her first choice. Then again, she had never developed much of a taste for alcohol. That was her mother's department.

"*No!*" she demanded of the empty room. She fused her eyelids, willing the images from her mind. No more living in the past. Marci would be home soon. Farin determined her spirits would improve by the time she walked in the door.

Hands trembling, she grabbed the vodka and took an eager drink. She winced, then covered her mouth with her hand as the liquor burned her stomach. A few careful sips later, she could almost stand the taste without gagging.

She returned to the cheery living room of their cheery garden apartment, shut the blinds against the smog-filtered sunlight, and dug into an end table drawer for a book of matches. One by one, she lit the candles spread around the living room. In the flickering light, she plopped down squarely in the middle of the thick, plush carpet. Then, she made her decision.

She could not bear to go back to Jordan's tomorrow for the memorial.

"I know you're upset," Marci had said that morning. "But there's more, Farin. I know you. What happened last night?"

Farin had waved off the question but she suspected Marci left for work unconvinced. More questions would undoubtedly follow tonight during dinner. Dinner she had forgotten until now she had promised to make.

Marci had always been the insightful one. The one who did not crumble like week-old bread with each crisis in her life. Farin's Rock of

Gibraltar. For the last four days, Farin had again tested the limits of their friendship. During agonized phone calls, Marci had encouraged her not to blame herself for Chase's death. Only Marci knew and understood the truth haunting her.

The echo of Mrs. Hanson's television blared in her ears. "...and above all, remember it takes time to heal. It's okay to grieve."

She took a swill from her bottle, resisting the urge to hurl it at the wall. If only that senile old woman would change the channel.

Desperate to silence the tormenting echoes assaulting the apartment like the mournful wail of a ghost, she trudged into her room, grabbed a cassette tape off her nightstand, and hurried back to the living room. She loaded it into the stereo, then turned the volume up high enough to drown out Dr. Somebody. As the music began, she shut her eyes, held her breath a beat, then exhaled.

Inside, Farin screamed. She screamed from the depth of her being—begging, pleading, praying for her mind to shut off. But she had lost count of unanswered prayers long before today. Fusing her eyes, she tilted her head back and gulped the clear alcohol.

The telephone rang. Another violent shove back into reality. She went to the kitchen, eyed the apparatus suspiciously, then picked up.

The cadence of Jordan's accent soothed her. Less than twenty-four hours had passed since she left his place. It felt longer. Though she had initially welcomed the break, she longed for him. They had spent little time apart since Le Dome. Before the accident, Marci had started teasing her, accusing her of moving out one article of clothing at a time.

She slid into a kitchen chair, balanced the phone between her shoulder and her ear, and picked at a loose corner of the bottle's label. "How are you? Did you sleep?"

His voice broke as he replied. "Some. I wish you were here. Please reconsider, love—about dinner tonight and about tomorrow."

"Jordan, I—"

"I know I keep pestering you about it. I'm trying to understand."

"It's not that I don't want to be there."

"Then say yes."

"You need your family, and they need you. Your parents flew halfway around the world. They're distraught. The last thing they need is a stranger in their midst. You and me? It's only been—"

"It's been forty-two days." He cleared his throat. "What of it?"

"They don't know me from—"

"No one cares about that. Besides, Chase would..."

She dropped her head onto her hand and massaged her temple.

"Ben took Mum and Dad to a hotel after you left. Mum couldn't bear to stay. Too many reminders."

She tried to concoct better excuses—anything to spare her the agony of the memorial—but the vodka haze clouded her brain. "What if they think I'm not good enough for you?"

"You don't believe that. Besides, they know how you tried to…how much Chase…Bloody hell, Farin. I *want* you here. Don't make me beg."

His words settled like marble in her middle. Her absence tomorrow would be nothing less than a selfish abandonment. But neither longing nor guilt could override her fear.

As she attempted to explain, a new voice—a stronger, more controlled voice—came on the line. "I couldn't let him go on. Don't know how he'll make it tomorrow as it is."

She sniffed and raised an eyebrow. "Ben?"

"Guess again," the voice teased at the other end of the line.

Her body tensed and straightened in the chair. The vodka bottle teetered as she placed it on the kitchen table.

He spoke in a slow, hypnotic lull. "I need to know about tomorrow. Like we discussed, Jameson'll be here. I'll spend the majority of my time with him. He's flying back right after the memorial."

"I…I don't know."

"You can't still be upset about last night."

The guilty stirring between her thighs both compelled and repulsed her. Like every verbal exchange she had with Chris. His unwavering attention had been evident from the moment they met—the day Chase died.

At first, she accused herself of misinterpreting his signals. But Marci had noticed, too, and tried to warn her. Farin had blamed her friend for planting the ridiculous seed in her head, accusing her of reading too many gossip magazines. Eventually, the seed had taken root.

She nursed another drink from her bottle.

"Jordan's beside himself. Don't you want to comfort him in his hour of need?"

His condescension irritated her. "Of course I do."

"Then be here tomorrow. Say two-ish? Ta."

He hung up.

***

Marci ran late. Her recent promotion had resulted in countless meetings, and Los Angeles traffic always left something to be desired. She had spent an hour traveling less than four miles, her LeBaron sandwiched between a Mack truck and a Mercedes Benz.

Instead of cursing the commute, she used it to prepare for whatever might greet her at home. Yes, Jordan's loss was unspeakable. Yes, Marci felt horrible for him. But she was selfish enough to worry more about her best friend. The tragedy had ushered an all too familiar darkness back into Farin's life.

Marci suppressed her own feelings about the accident, yet the scene looped in her mind. Farin hovering over Chase's tiny body, desperate to breathe life back into his lungs. Chris holding Jordan back as he screamed and fought against him.

She rattled her head as she turned left at Mountain Street and motored toward Verdugo, trying to cast the memory from her consciousness. Farin had been a wreck these last few days. Then again, she had been a wreck the larger portion of the last fifteen years.

Pulling into the covered space in their apartment complex, she blew out a breath and loosened her shoulders. She would not let Farin down. She would be strong. One of them had to be.

A brief struggle with keys ensued as she balanced the two heavy bags in her arms. She had stopped for Chinese on the way home, figuring Farin would forget to cook.

Two steps inside the door confirmed her suspicions.

Lit candles veneered their inner sanctum with flickering golden light and shadow. It looked like midnight mass at the Catholic church down the street. Only, instead of an organ hymn, "Rhyme and Reason" blasted from the stereo. An uncapped, empty vodka bottle lay sideways on the oak coffee table. And Farin O'Conner, Warner Brother's newest discovery, sat zombie-like in the center of the living room—drunk.

Farin swayed to-and-fro, as if adrift in a tiny craft on an ungentle sea. Judging from her distant, glassy glaze, she was. Her hair hung in unkempt spirals, framing her blank, tear-streaked face. The plain white T-shirt she wore was inside out.

In her left hand, Farin clutched a tattered snapshot of her and her father, the last one ever taken. Marci knew it well. It was she who had taken it the weekend before their annual Memorial Day camping trip to Yosemite.

"I won't ask how your day went." She headed straight for the kitchen. "Your dad's John Denver tape gives you away."

Farin sat up with a start, then stretched to press the stop button on the cassette player. She squinted at the VCR clock display. "You're home late."

Marci set the bags down on the table and dropped her keys beside them, then doubled back to the living room. She switched on a lamp and blew out the candles. "If I'd known what I'd find when I got here, I might have stayed at the office. Anyway, I brought Chinese. Consider it a bribe. Maybe if you eat enough moo shu pork you'll fill me in."

Farin untangled her legs from beneath her and stumbled to her feet. "I know I've been difficult."

"It's not that. It's just, you've been gone and calling me for moral support. I'm not good over the phone."

"Sorry."

"Have you talked to Jordan?"

"A couple of times. He's not so good."

"Well, maybe after tomorrow he'll start rebuilding his life." Marci opened the blinds and stared outside. Somberly, she asked, "What time's the funeral?"

"Noon. I have to be there at two."

Marci beckoned her into the kitchen to help organize the food. "When you got home last night, you said you weren't going."

"I know. But when I talked to Jordan today, he was so…sad. Then Chris got on the phone. I sorta promised I'd help coordinate things at the house."

And there it was. Farin did not need to say another word. The lousy snake. "Be careful."

Farin plunked down into a kitchen chair. "Don't start in again about what you've read in those stupid magazines."

Marci dug through the utensil drawer, procured a set of tongs, then shut the drawer with a hip-thrust. "The stress of the last few days…it's too much. We know where that leads."

Farin tapped her fingers atop the table. "Well, I'm going."

Marci scoffed under her breath. "Of course."

"It makes sense. Jameson Lockhardt's coming. Chris'll be with him most the day. With Ben and Cheryl trying to keep their parents from falling apart, Jordan needs help dealing with things."

"And you think you're in any shape to do that?"

Farin stood in a huff, snatched the plates, dropped them on the table, then doubled back to pour two iced teas. "What am I supposed to do? Bail?"

Marci sat down and broke apart a set of chopsticks, rubbing them together like a boy scout trying to spark a flame. She took her frustration out on her food. "If you go, you'll end up in your dark place again. We try to keep you away from the dark place, remember?"

Farin pushed the food around her plate with her fork.

"Not hungry?"

"I have a headache."

"Vodka does that."

"So does the inquisition."

Marci lifted her right shoulder.

"I'm not a child, Marce."

Marci chased a mouthful of fried rice with her iced tea. "Look. I'm on your side. There's just something about him I don't trust."

"Yeah. It's called the *National Enquirer*. Honestly, Marci, how can such an intelligent individual put such credence in unfounded, unsubstantiated crap?"

They finished their meal in silence. They had had this conversation a million times over the years. Different topics, same outcome.

The muffled sound of a studio audience's hearty laughter assaulted Farin's ears. She considered calling the building manager and making a complaint against Mrs. Hanson. Every part of her longed to be with Jordan.

Marci stood and grabbed her plate. She gestured Farin's way. "You done?"

She nodded.

"I'll get the dishes."

Farin returned to the living room and peered out the window. Not a star in sight through the smoggy sky. Maybe she should have gone to Jordan's for dinner tonight after all. Malibu was beautiful at night.

Memories of her home in Santa Barbara flooded her senses. The pacifying roar of the waves a mere two blocks away. Her parents tucking her into crisp linen sheets. Wispy tendrils of pipe tobacco sending up that distinctive aroma she had once associated with the word "home." She closed her eyes and drew in a deep breath, recalling the scent of cherry and whiskey casings, savoring the temporary disruption to the melancholy of the day.

"I miss you, Daddy," she whispered. "Please take care of Chase."

Most often, Farin felt removed from the rest of the world. Unable to participate beyond the surface level of human interaction. Apart and alone, even in crowds. The concept of "normal?" It eluded her. She was frozen somewhere beneath the waters of time, thrashing and pummeling against the ice surrounding her, frantic to break through, desperate to reach the shores of peace and clarity.

Only music transcended the mired complexities of her soul. More than a sacred space. It was where her father still lived. A beacon of light amongst the empty darkness threatening to strangle her.

Farin believed in God. Still, she did not understand how He could bear to watch His creation suffer. Chase had turned six last month. How could Jordan continue to live without his only son? How could he endure the vile things the tabloids said about the circumstances surrounding the accident? How would he avoid falling into the same frozen waters she had plunged heart-first into fifteen years ago?

She left the window and curled up in a ball on the large flowered sofa, admonishing herself for harboring so many adolescent questions at the age of twenty-five. The idea of showing up at Jordan's tomorrow and confronting all the black-clad strangers terrified her. It was too soon. But she had to try.

Marci emerged with strong black coffee, some ibuprofen, and a friendly smile. "Truce." She motioned for Farin to sit up. "You know me. I mother."

"You do mother."

"But in a good way."

"In the best way." Farin accepted the hot beverage as Marci settled in beside her. "But you always forget the cream and sugar."

Friends again, they discussed happier subjects between sips. Sometime during their conversation, Mrs. Hanson shut off her television and went to bed. Farin relaxed at the abrupt absence of background distraction.

"I miss our treehouse," Marci said.

Farin grinned at the recollection. "I miss the stereo."

"Remember when that wire shorted out and the fire started?"

"We almost burned the place down." She snickered.

"And your mom running out with the fire extinguisher?"

"She didn't know how to use it."

"And then, when she figured it out, she lost control and sprayed fire retardant everywhere!" Marci laughed so hard she had to set her cup down to avoid spilling her drink.

They reminisced long after the coffee ran out. About summer vacations. Road trips. Museums. Sleepovers. Disneyland. At one point, they felt so full of life, they believed anything was possible.

"I thought we'd grow up and change the world," Marci said.

"You wanted to work with our dads." Farin's smile temporarily faded. "You were gonna go to law school and—"

"—and you were going to marry Shaun Cassidy!"

Her eyes twinkled at the memory. "He was so *cute*! Whatever happened to him?"

"He was on *Matlock* a few months ago, remember?"

"That's right!"

"You know, if you substitute his brown eyes for green, he looks a little like Jordan."

"You think?"

"*Totally.*"

The would-be siblings retired close to midnight. Farin's head had cleared. Her stomach was full. She could not wait to see Jordan. Tomorrow, she would try again. She would be strong for him, and she would continue to swim for the shore.

As she lay back in her freshly changed bed and punched her pillows into place, a flash of her earlier nightmare threatened to send her head back into darkness. She scrambled to think of something, anything, to kill the monsters in her mind. At first, she thought of Jordan, but could only see his sad face. Worse was the sound of his voice, broken and defeated, on the telephone earlier. It was good Chris had taken the telephone when he had.

Chris.

His voice stole into her thoughts. No outward emotion. No sign of grief. Farin envied his self-control. If only she could be—or appear to be—more like him in that respect. He exuded all the strength and courage she lacked.

Of course, Chris was no blond pop idol like Jordan. His features were darker, more European. Slender like a baseball player, with a certain swagger in his walk that seemed at all times deliberate and choreographed. Like his smirk, a lopsided twisting of his lips that claimed to know more about her than she did about herself. And those dark eyes. Soulful. Deep. Penetrating. They had tunneled canyons inside her last night as she tried to leave.

Something intangible had passed between them. Something curious. Something Marci would disapprove of had Farin dared mention it.

All at once, Farin could not stop the forbidden thoughts rising within her. She needed respite from the darkness of her dreams. How she longed for peace, even for one night. Even if it came from Chris.

She lay back slowly in her bed, closed her eyes, and began tracing the firm shape of her full breasts and the smooth curves of her body while reflecting on the night before.

She had woken up yesterday morning as she had for weeks—wrapped in Jordan's arms. The sound of gentle snoring in her ear comforted her. Despite her bladder's protests, she stayed in bed to avoid waking him.

Only three days since the accident, he had struggled for meaningful rest. She had stayed with him, cooking for him and Chris, managing condolence deliveries of food and flowers, and assisting with funeral arrangements. She had accompanied Jordan to pick out Chase's casket—a small white coffin with white crepe interior and brass handles and fittings. It upset her, but she did not complain. Jordan had not noticed, and she had not told him, that the pristine walls of his beautiful home had started closing in on her.

Details of their romance swirled in her mind as she lay there, watching rays of light against his bedroom wall descend in concert with the sunrise. Jordan's arrival in her life had come as unexpectedly as Ginny Steven's drink in her face. From that first night, he had swept her into what felt like a fairytale romance—flowers, whispered endearments, sunset walks along the beach, and endless nights of lovemaking.

She spent their time apart with Donovan, reviewing contract negotiations with Warner Brothers, who had wasted no time contacting him after hearing her demo tape. Jordan had continued the *Umbra* publicity campaign. They had fallen into a routine that outpaced their budding courtship.

Then, tragedy had struck. Time stopped, yet simultaneously accelerated, like the high frequency spin of tires in a burnout.

In six weeks, she had gone from humiliated restaurant spritzer-magnet, to romantic cliché, to...*what*?

A triplet of knocks at the door had drawn her out of bed. She glanced over her shoulder as she padded across the room, relieved her movements had not disturbed Jordan—and that she could finally use the restroom.

She cracked open the door bare inches, self-conscious over her bedhead and day-old makeup as she gave Chris a furtive glance.

"He awake?" he whispered.

Her hand shot up to cover her mouth. She shook her head and whispered back, "We still have a couple of hours, right?"

"Why are you covering your mouth?"

"Morning breath."

The hint of a smile played at the corners of his mouth. "I arranged for a car to pick everyone up. The press would eat us alive right now. Let's let him sleep."

The day had passed slowly, with tearful reunions as first Ben and crew, and then their parents, arrived. Despite their welcoming embraces during the introductions, Farin felt partitioned off. Their blind acceptance felt like a garrote around her neck.

Lynda Grant wrapped fragile arms around her, her cheek warm and moist from undried tears as it pressed against hers. "Jorie's gone on about you for weeks, dear. You're lovely. Isn't she, George? Just...love—"

George guided his grieving wife to the sofa and asked one of the grandkids to get her some water.

Farin remained in the entryway as the family assembled in the living room as a single unit, as if each member had reserved seating. George and Lynda huddled on one side of the U-shaped sectional, Derek and Kyle both hovering in their orbit, ever ready to comfort them. Jordan took his regular spot, opposite them. Ben and Cheryl settled in at the foot. Chris stood, odd man out, arm propped atop the fireplace mantle. Once the players had assumed their places, the full weight of the sad occasion had hit her.

I'm sorry I couldn't save Chase.

She slipped into the kitchen to organize a snack, hoping to make herself useful and invisible so they could grieve in peace. As she put the kettle on the stove, Cheryl joined her.

She passed dozens of cellophane-wrapped condolence platters on her way to the cupboard. "All this food. You two will be nibbling on crackers for months."

"I opened the ones with fruit so they won't spoil too quickly. And there are casseroles in the fridge from some of the neighbors."

Cheryl extracted cups and saucers, then clasped the edge of the counter with both hands, lowering her head. Almost immediately, she righted herself, raising her chin. "I'll sort the tea, pet. You should be with Jorie."

"I-I thought I'd give him some time with his family."

"People in the middle of a storm pray for sunlight, Farin. Go...*shine*."

Jordan had mentioned his sister-in-law had won the Miss Glasgow title in her native Scotland before marrying Ben. Even in the midst of unbearable sorrow, she carried herself with the grace one might expect of a beauty-queen-turned-millionaire's-wife.

Her soft blue eyes propelled Farin out the kitchen's swinging doors and into the living room, where she sat beside Jordan. He adjusted himself on the sofa to drape his arm around her as if she belonged there—her own reserved seat.

No matter how she tried, she could not shine.

Hours crawled by. Lynda's intermittent sobs bested her husband's, sons', and grandsons' attempts to comfort her. Through tea, dinner, and after-dinner brandies. When Jordan excused himself to wash his hands, Farin followed.

"I'm gonna head home."

He reached for her. "Why?"

"It wouldn't be right for me to stay. Not tonight. Besides, I've been cycling the same clothes for days."

Elevated voices erupted from the living room, curtailing any attempt to change her mind. By the time they returned, the back door had slammed shut, Derek and Kyle had disappeared upstairs, and Cheryl stood, arms crossed, before her husband. She turned on her heel to sit beside her mother-in-law and hush her tears.

"What in bloody hell is going on?" Jordan asked.

Jaw clenched, Ben turned away. "Nothing."

"What 'nothing' this time?"

Cheryl scowled at Ben. "Your brothers disagree about tomorrow's guest list."

Farin went to Cheryl and Lynda to say her goodbyes. Between meeting Jordan's entire family under the gravest of circumstances and the growing tightness in her chest, she could think of nothing but getting out the front door.

Jordan walked her to the entryway. He took her in his arms. "I wish you'd stay."

She buried her face in the nape of his neck, taking in his scent and the warmth of his skin. The image of Chase's small body floating face down in the swimming pool flashed in her mind.

She pulled away, cupped his cheek, and declined his offer to walk her to her car. "Promise me you'll try to sleep."

The night breeze filled her lungs as she made good her escape. She exhaled the tension of the last three days as she approached her little blue Celica at the end of the clean, white pavement beyond Chris's rented Mercedes and Jordan's Jaguar.

Images of the accident bludgeoned her, so detailed she had to wipe her eyes to make out her keys.

Not now! Please let me make it home first.

"Going somewhere?"

She turned with a start, searching the shadows through blurry eyes until she spotted a tall, lanky silhouette leaning against the garage door. He ambled forward out of the shadows, his eyes fixed on hers, daring her to look away.

She trembled as he drew near, his wavy hair dancing in the night breeze. "I thought you'd gone down to the beach or something."

"Do I frighten you?"

She turned away, unable to match his gaze.

He chuckled as if he had won some ground, as if it mattered. "You're not leaving?"

She chin-pointed toward the house. "What happened in there?"

"My brother and I have very different definitions of loyalty."

"I'm not following."

"No worries. Don't you want to see what Ben and I do for an encore?"

She folded her arms and looked down at the cement. "Think I'll pass."

He rested an arm atop her car, eyeing her bottom to top. "The moonlight becomes you."

"*Excuse* me?"

"You've been here for days, Farin. Don't pretend you haven't noticed me staring at you."

She stepped back, bumping into her car. "This isn't appro—"

He tsk-tsk'd her, shaking his head in mock concern. "But such a worrier. How long have you and Jordan been seeing each other?"

She fidgeted with her keyring. "About six weeks."

Chris glanced up at the star-filled sky. "Six weeks? I was in Spain about then."

He edged closer, spouting hackneyed come-on lines. Yet what he lacked in originality he more than made up for in intensity. His eyes locked in on hers, as if seeking to put her in a trance. As desperate as she was to leave, she had found it nearly impossible to open her car door.

As Farin recalled their encounter, her fingers slid from her breasts to the growing moisture between her thighs. She had found her respite from the ugly reality of the last few days. Nothing would come of the events of the night before. Her relationship with Jordan satisfied her.

But tonight, in the privacy of her own room, her own thoughts, she could not stop herself—did not want to stop herself—from indulging a harmless fantasy. In her imagination, she surrendered to Chris's strength and passion. He banished her monsters, however temporarily.

CHAPTER 5

FARIN'S THROAT TIGHTENED AS SHE neared the beach house. After turning back five times along the way, her conscience won out. A promise was a promise—no matter who she had made it to. A glance at her cassette player's clock display told her Chase's young body would be laid to rest soon. No backing out now.

She glimpsed the sun worshippers enjoying the beach as she drove north on Highway 1. KIIS FM played an up-tempo mix of summer hits, programmed for teens and tourists. She heard Poison, INXS, and Midnight Oil. At the intro to Pebbles's "Mercedes Boy," she flipped off the radio.

Last Sunday, she and Marci had driven this same route on the way to meet Jordan's son and brother for the first time. Nervous excitement had peppered their conversation along the way. Would Chase like her? Would they bond? And what about Chris?

Marci spent the drive reassuring her over meeting Jordan's son; the other half, she relayed salacious tabloid accounts of Chris's playboy escapades.

"Either you've got a secret crush on him or you're a proxy reporter for one of your magazines. I don't care which. Be nice today."

Marci adjusted her seat back and propped her feet upon Farin's dash. "It'll be fine."

"Maybe I should've brought Chase a present—a toy or something."

"He's a kid, not a dog. Besides, it's Malibu. I doubt he's lacking toys."

Jordan's home appeared small, almost quaint, compared to the spacious mansions dotting the Pacific coast. Still, it had a subtle charm. The breathtaking precision of the landscaping, groomed grass, flowers, trees, and shrubs distinguished it amongst larger homes with less land.

Jordan jogged out to welcome them as they pulled up. Inside, he gave a quick tour of the house so Marci could get her bearings, then ushered them out back to meet his family.

Farin spotted Chase playing in a sandbox across the yard against the back fence. The resemblance to his father struck her, from his golden locks and tanned skin to his charismatic smile.

"Chase! Come on, son. We have guests."

The boy halted the overriding task of filling his buckets with sand and scampered cheerfully toward his father, who scooped him up into his arms.

"This is Miss Farin. And this is her friend, Miss Marci."

Chase wriggled out of his father's arms, stood tall, and bowed deeply as if having rehearsed the movement all day. "Nice to meet you, Miss, and you, Miss." He straightened proudly, pleased with himself as he extended a tiny hand to each of them in turn. He glanced up at his father as if for approval. Jordan winked in reply.

Farin knelt down. "I'm happy to finally meet you, Chase. Your dad talks about you all the time."

"He didn't tell you I was building you a sandcastle, did he?" he whispered conspiratorially. "It's a secret!"

"Oh—well, no he didn't. But I bet you're the best castle-builder in Malibu."

He beamed at the praise. "Wanna help with the towers?"

"Not now, son. The ladies only just arrived."

"But Dad, if she's gonna be our girlfriend, she has to play with me, too, right?"

Crouched at Chase's side, she squinted up at Jordan. "He's right. It's only fair."

"But don't you want the ladies to meet your uncle?"

He shrugged. "Uncle Ben told Aunt Cheryl he *always* meets the ladies."

Marci stifled a giggle.

From outside their line of vision, Chris rushed over and scooped Chase into his arms, roaring and tickling his sides. Chase squealed, "Stop! Put me down!"

Chris flipped him over, hanging him by his ankles. "What's the magic word?"

Chase squirmed, nearly kicking his uncle's sunglasses off his face. "Please!"

"Nope! Try again."

"Daddy, make him put me down!"

"Tell him, buddy! You know it!" Jordan urged.

"What is it, then?" Chris pressed, swinging him side to side. "Come on, now."

"*Coda!*" Chase shrieked at last, chortling breathlessly.

Jordan and Chris laughed and cheered his victory as Chris righted him on the lawn.

"*Coda?*" Marci chuckled. "Zeppelin?"

With a cheeky wink, Chris stepped forward, hand extended. "I'm Chris."

She accepted his hand. "Marci. Why *Coda?*"

Chris nodded down at his nephew. "Go on, then. Tell her."

"It came out the year I was born," he replied as if he had answered the question a hundred times before. "Daddy, can we go swimming now?"

"Soon, son. We still have to get our guests something to drink and start the grill."

"Okay." His smile faded as he trudged back to his sand box.

Jordan slipped his arm around Farin's waist and addressed his brother. "And this is Farin. Farin, this is my brother, Chris."

As he took her hand, she felt Marci's eyes upon her.

Time dissolved. In the halted seconds between handshake and greeting, she took a full inventory—tall, shirtless, barefoot, playful with his nephew while aloof toward his brother. Dark sunglasses rendered it impossible to see, let alone read, his eyes. She hoped no one noticed the tremble in her voice when she said hello. Moreover, she hoped she mistook what felt like a jolt of electricity pass between them.

Jordan suggested they make themselves comfortable while he finished prepping the grill. They settled into thick-cushioned chairs around a glass-top patio table while Chris procured drinks.

Farin grabbed the sides of her chair and blew air through her puckered lips, her eyes flickering with unease. Marci shook her head, incredulous.

Upon his return, Chris sat opposite her. He sipped bourbon on the rocks, his glasses still masking his gaze. She cursed the echoes of Marci's warnings, blaming them for her heightened sensitivity. Of *course* he was not staring at her.

They had made small talk while Jordan championed the grill, declining all offers of assistance. Chris participated little, a mere voyeur as Farin and Marci discussed their lifelong friendship and Jordan relayed accounts of his ongoing publicity campaign.

Soon, only ice remained in his glass.

"You heading in for a refill?" Jordan asked.

Chris nodded.

"Great. Help me with the kabobs. We're all ready, here."

When the men left to collect the skewers of shrimp, steak, and vegetables, Marci whirled around and elbow-nudged Farin. "What are you doing?"

"What?"

"Chris!"

"What about him?"

"This little staring contest you've got going on?"

Farin scoffed. "Please."

Jordan glimpsed Chase out of the corner of his eye upon his return. The child had climbed to the top of the diving board and had inched out toward the edge.

He dashed up the ladder in a flash and grabbed his son, who twitched at the sudden attention. "Chase, how many times have I told you not to climb up here? It's very, *very* dangerous."

Alarmed, the small boy hugged his father's neck until they returned to solid ground. "But I want to go swimming."

Farin and Marci hurried to Jordan's side. "Is he okay?" Marci asked.

"He loves climbing this bloody thing. I've warned him repeatedly. I may end up having to take it down."

Farin felt blood surge to her face. "I'm sorry, Jordan. I should've paid closer attention."

He gave her shoulder a tender squeeze, then carried his son over to the table. "I want you to sit here, son, and think about what you did."

Chris sauntered out of the house with another round of drinks. "I told him earlier about playing near the pool."

"It's his newest fascination. He's been wanting to learn to dive since he watched you."

Chris tossed back half his drink. "He's growing up. You can't keep him under your thumb forever. What you need to do is get someone over for lessons." He leaned across to his nephew, who gazed longingly at the semi-complete sandcastle at the far end of the yard. "Master Chase! What-say you and I have Miss Nicole find you a swim instructor tomorrow? Then you can swim with your dad and me."

"Cool!" He wrung his hands with excitement as he wiggled in his chair. "Then I can dive and hold my breath and float!"

Chris shot an I-told-you-so glance at his brother.

Jordan walked off to tend the grill. "I still think he's too young."

"You and I swam like fish at his age—even younger."

Once Chase was off the hook, Farin and Marci helped him complete his castle while Jordan and Chris prepared dinner. Later, they ate, and laughed, and discussed music, art, and the Magic Kingdom. Quite the Goofy fan, Chase made the girls promise to come with him and his father next month for a visit.

"You come too, Uncle Chris."

"Oh, I'm invited?"

"Of course! You're Uncle Chris."

"Can't argue that logic. Let's see how it goes, okay?"

"Okay." Chase nodded, satisfied with the non-binding agreement.

The women had insisted on handling the dishes. Farin washed and Marci dried.

"Admit it," Farin gloated. "You were wrong. It's been a perfect day."

Marci dried freshly washed silverware with a dish towel. "I'm reserving judgment. I saw how you two looked at each other."

"It was...nothing. He's harmless. A bit charming. Not *Jordan* charming, but still."

Marci bobbed her shoulders.

Farin handed over a dripping clean plate, then grabbed a saucepan. "The only reason I reacted that way when I met him was because *you* built him up."

"You may be genuinely unaware of the looks he's given you, but I'm not. Besides, he thinks you're using Jordan."

Farin stopped mid-scrub, her hands dropping into the soapy water.

"He thinks you're using him to get ahead in your career."

"Would I have given up the chance to send LSI my demo if I was trying to get something from Jordan?"

"You don't have to convince me, Farin. It's that weasel I'm referring to. Either he's coming onto you because he has no respect for his brother, or he's trying to protect him by testing you out."

She dug through the water for the saucepan and resumed scrubbing. "What *is* it with you? You're so determined to hate him, I think even *he* feels it. At least get to know him. I was hoping you two would hit it off."

"Wea-sel," Marci sing-songed, folding the dishtowel to access the drier side.

"Think what you want, but I'm happy. Jordan's perfect. Chase is a doll. I signed my contract Friday afternoon. Things are good."

"Well, if Chris thinks you need to break into the business on your back, he's wrong. He was a nobody once, too."

Farin's jaw slacked. She turned her head, smiling at the barb despite herself. "Thanks a lot!"

Marci dipped the tips of her fingers in the soapy dishwater and flicked them at Farin. "You know what I mean!"

The summer sky had faded to gray with the sun's descent. Stars peeked through the twilight in the east as orange and pink hues synthesized the waning light to the west. The cool, gentle breeze they had enjoyed earlier now brought a chill to the air. Pleased she had thought ahead, Farin went back outside to retrieve the sweater she had left on her chair.

As she approached the table, she saw Chase's still figure floating face down in the deep end of the pool.

"*Jordan*! *No!*" The cry bubbled up out of her before she dove into the pool.

Details of the following hour vanished into a blurry, nightmarish haze. She pulled Chase from the pool and performed CPR while a shocked Marci called 911.

Jordan and Chris, who had left the back yard long enough to relocate the cooling grill, rushed back out to the patio to find Farin soaked to the skin and hovering over the still form of Jordan's only child.

Chris held his brother in a full Nelson as Farin continued her lifesaving attempts. Jordan cursed himself for never having learned CPR. They watched helplessly as she listened for breathing, checked for a pulse, and pumped the small boy's chest, desperate to get oxygen into his tiny body.

"Chase, Daddy's here! I'm right here, son. You'll be okay."

The ambulance had arrived in minutes. Jordan looked on, powerless to help as Chase lay limp and breathless upon the pool's hardscape surround. Paramedics took over from Farin, who trembled beside him on her hands and knees, her clothes and hair dripping. Jordan stood frozen in place as his son's skin turned a sickening blue. The paramedics lifted Chase onto a gurney and into the back of an ambulance. They waved Jordan inside to accompany them to the hospital.

Chris grabbed Jordan's keys from inside. He tossed them to Marci and gestured for Farin to take the front passenger's seat. He climbed in back and maintained communication with the local hospital via his cell phone as Marci blazed a trail behind the ambulance. When Chase's condition deteriorated en route, dispatch informed Chris that he and Jordan would be life-flighted to Cedars-Sinai Medical Center in Los Angeles.

"He has to make it," Chris demanded, lips tight with determination. He jerked his head at Marci. "Can't you drive any faster?"

"Unless this car sprouts wings so we can keep up with the helicopter, this is the best I can do!"

Farin dipped her head and massaged her forehead with two fingers. "Let's not fight."

Chris called the hospital. "Yes. I need the Emergency Room, please."

Traffic had been kind for a Sunday evening, but it still took forty-five minutes to drive over Highway 10 and onto Beverly Boulevard, where the large hospital loomed like an ominous barrier before them. Marci and Farin dropped Chris off at the emergency room entrance and then parked in the visitor's lot.

As Marci killed the engine and removed the keys, photographers and reporters assembled outside the emergency room doors. The women watched in disbelief as a camera-toting crowd inched their way as close as hospital security would allow. They pitched camp and waited for news about Jordan, Chris, and the mysterious commotion that had brought the two megastars to the hospital that evening.

Farin gasped, an appalled witness to the scene unfolding before them. "How did they know we're here?"

Marci unfastened her seatbelt. "This is your fantasy, not mine. Nothing in the world would be worth this to me. I mean, I love reading about this stuff. But living it? No thanks."

They fought their way through the paparazzi, talked their way past security, and hastened through the emergency room doors. The quiet waiting room cut a stark comparison to the frenzied scene outside. They found Chris in an otherwise unoccupied bank of seats near the back.

Marci scanned the room. "Have you seen Jordan yet?"

He looked at her with bloodshot eyes, his voice barely audible. "He'll be okay," he said as if to convince himself more than her or anyone else. "Any minute now, Jordan will bring news."

An hour ticked by with no word. Finally, a doctor in green scrubs pushed through the doors. He pulled his scrub cap from his head as he approached. The three huddled together, stunned, all too certain of the news they were about to hear. The doctor confirmed their identity, then said, "I'm sorry. The boy didn't survive."

Marci gasped, covering her mouth with her hand. Chris shot up and disappeared through the doors from which the physician had emerged. Farin sat paralyzed, staring at the hospital floor, speechless.

Jordan did not surface right away. The staff did their best to comfort him, offering him all the time he needed to say goodbye to his son. They moved them all into an unoccupied room to give them privacy, as well as to allow the hospital staff to resume their duties with minimal public disturbance.

A triage nurse assessed Farin for shock. The hospital chaplain met with Jordan in Chase's room. Police were summoned—at first to question those present at the time of the incident and then to block off the hospital parking lot. They ensured the removal of camera equipment so that, when Jordan and company departed, they could do so without the crowd mobbing or crushing them.

Finally, Jordan joined them, his ashen face swollen and tearstained. He breathed heavy and slow. His eyes had deepened to seafoam green. He locked his brother in an embrace. The two men sobbed openly, unashamed that Farin, Marci, and a few hospital staff standing by in case they needed anything, witnessed the scene.

Farin watched, curiously detached. Her own memories rose like vampires at dusk. She wished she could do or say something to ease his pain, yet refrained from comforting him. She knew all too well what inconsolable felt like.

Jordan came to her at last. He held her in his arms, quaking with sobs. She patted his back, unable to think of one word that could change, alter, or ease the cruel reality he faced.

They had known each other such a short time. She had no right to be there with him now. And yet, she could scarcely abandon him.

A nurse slipped into the room and touched Jordan's arm. "I'm sorry Mr. Grant, but there are some forms we need you to fill out. I hate to ask. It shouldn't take long."

Jordan pulled away from their embrace. He sniffed and cleared his throat, nodded at the nurse, then followed her out the door.

"I'm gonna get some coffee," Marci said. "Anyone know how Jordan takes his?"

"Tea," Chris said, no trace of emotion in his voice.

"I'm sorry?"

"He drinks tea."

"Right. Well, Farin, do you want coffee? Or...you, Chris? Anything?"

Chris shook his head.

"I'm good," Farin said.

"You wanna come with?"

"I...I should probably stay."

Marci nodded. "Be right back."

When she left, Chris brushed Farin's shoulder, motioning her outside.

She hitched a thumb at the door. "I need to be here."

"He'll be awhile."

"What about Marci?"

"Don't you need some fresh air?"

She hesitated, but agreed. It felt as if the walls would collapse around her.

They exited through the emergency room entrance, relieved to discover the press had been pushed back.

"Look," Chris began, "I hate to put you out, but our family's scattered about here, or Florida, or England. I'll have to contact everyone and arrange for them to fly out. Also, I'll need to handle Lockhardt." He paused a moment and looked down. "And then there's the funeral."

Farin looked down and away. "If there's anything I can do..."

He brushed her arm again. This time, his fingers lingered in a gentle embrace behind her bicep. "I'd like to spare Jordan as much as possible."

She swiped her fingers beneath her eyes. "I know how it feels to lie awake at night missing someone you love. My dad died when I was ten."

Uttering the most personal detail of her life to a virtual stranger felt somehow liberating. Then all at once, her knees gave out.

Chris dashed to catch her before she fell. As he pulled her up, she began to weep. He steadied and held her as photographers clicked their cameras and journalists shouted questions, flashes and voices overlapping from behind the constructed barrier. She rested her head on his shoulder, knowing she should pull away but grateful for the temporary comfort.

"We should get Jordan out of here. I don't know—it's all so unbelievable, so sudden."

"That's the way it always happens," she said. "Without warning."

They stood together long enough for Farin to collect herself. This was

Jordan's grief, Jordan's time. It would not do for her to compound the problem by bringing up her own past.

When she had moved out of Chris's arms, he released his embrace with some hesitation.

Farin spotted security guards dispersing a small crowd as she neared Jordan's driveway. Most wore black. Many held bouquets of flowers. All were teenage girls. They swarmed her car, clamoring for her to stop and collect their offerings, begging her to deliver them to their grieving idol. Frustrated as the fans slipped by and around them, the guards nodded apologetically and signaled they would deal with the issue.

Jordan had warned about the possible consequences of mingling with fans. No matter how well-intentioned they appeared, he had learned the hard way it was better to maintain barriers. Today, Farin made an exception.

She stopped her Celica outside the gate and rolled down her window to address security. "It's okay. I'll take care of it."

The girls shouted over one another, thanking her, crying, and promising to leave right away.

She collected as many bouquets as she could carry. "I'll make sure Jordan gets these, but you have to go before security calls for back-up." Once back behind the wheel, she drove through the gate and parked near the Eastland Catering van. She ducked around back amid the echoes of their thank-yous.

Two days ago, the media had blown the lid off "Lockhardt Sound's biggest secret." The press exposed the hidden life of Jordan Grant and the young son he had kept secret throughout his career. Papers splashed photographs of the tiny boy all over their front pages. It had sickened the Grant family. Rumor had it, Jameson Lockhardt had taken the breach of confidence personally. He wanted someone's career. The question was, whose?

"My goodness, Farin!" A familiar, if effeminate, voice chuckled playfully in the kitchen. "Did you knock over a florist on your way over?"

She peeked over her armful of flowers. "Dale!"

Farin O'Conner and Dale Eastland went back years. They had played together during Farin's nightclub period. Around the time Farin decided to start recording, Dale realized his growing disillusionment with the business and traded in his bass for the chance to start a catering business.

Dale cleared a space on the counter for Farin to place the mound of flowers, then wrapped his arms around her and pulled her into his thin, strong embrace. "How're you holding up?"

"Ask me in a couple of hours."

He pulled back, kissed her cheek, and leveled his knowing, indigo orbs at her. "You can do this."

With a nervous nod, she searched his eyes. "I've missed you."

He tweaked her nose with a gentle finger, then turned back to prep the hors d'oeuvres. "I nearly fell over when you called me for this gig!"

"I needed the best and I hear you're it. I was surprised, though. I knew you'd left the business, but this? Isn't it a bit...? Oh, I don't know."

"Obvious? Forget it, doll. I came out of that closet the day I plucked my last bass string. Think of it as closing one door and opening another. Especially after losing so many friends over the last few years..."

Farin touched his forearm.

He covered her hand with his own and squeezed. A momentary sadness enveloped them, then evaporated. "Anyway, things couldn't be better! Now all I need is some sweet, young thing with a clean bill of health to share it with! Hand me that knife over there on the counter, will you?"

They caught up on the latest industry gossip as they bustled about the kitchen. Farin searched for flower vases while Dale arranged trays of lunch meats, veggies, salads, and assorted breads.

"What about *you*? Jordan Grant? And I was thrilled to hear about your Warner Brothers deal. It's about time. You always were in a different league than the rest of us."

Farin accepted Dale's cheerful, if biased, admiration even as the sound of cars arriving outside distracted her from her floral arranging.

Dale planted a delicate hand on his hip. "What's the problem?"

She glanced over her shoulder. "What do you mean?"

"You know what I mean. Those sad dark eyes. The shaking hands—"

She glanced down at her open palms.

"Uh-huh. See? I know you. I was there, remember? Fixing your makeup before you went on the night of the ten-year anniversary of your dad's death? And that was five years ago." His voice softened. "I hate to see you still stuck in your past, is all. It's morbid. And, as your friend, let me assure you it won't help that man of yours a bit. You're stronger than this, doll. I know it."

Farin willed her trembling fingers to cooperate as she cut back the stems on the last few flowers and arranged them in the final vase.

"Shouldn't you go and see if Jordan's here yet?"

"In a minute. I don't want these flowers to die."

Dale tapped his lips with an index finger, studying the finished trays, then touched up the garnish. "I hear Jameson Lockhardt's making an appearance today. No irony there, huh?"

"I've already signed with Warner." She attempted to assist with the food, but Dale shooed her away. "And anyway, I changed my mind about

LSI. I don't want any misunderstandings with Jordan. I can do this on my own. Besides, you know Lockhardt's reputation."

"Can't disagree with you there. Still, after all those years you set your sights on him, you must be curious."

Farin gently fingered the soft velvet petals of a vaseful of forget-me-nots. "Not anymore."

"I don't know who you think you're talking to. If I had a dollar for every conversation you and I had about—"

"That was before."

"Before Jordan?"

"Partly. But he's told me things. Things I didn't know."

Dale turned to her, wide-eyed. "Like...?"

But all at once, Jordan was beside her.

Her heart ached at this sight of his drawn face and tear-swollen eyes. How she longed to ease his pain. And how well she understood it.

"I'm so glad you're here," he whispered, wrapping her up in an embrace. When he pulled away, he took her hand in his. "I hate crowds. And today, I don't know how much I can take."

Farin glanced at Dale, then at the swinging kitchen doors, then back to Jordan. "I'll be right beside you. But...before we go in," she motioned to the counter behind her. "I stopped on the way in. I couldn't help it. These are from the girls out front."

He pursed his lips, then swallowed. "They're lovely. But Farin—"

She held a finger to his lips and shushed him. "It won't happen again. You need to know how much your fans love you, especially today."

Jordan kissed her fingertips. "C'mon. Let's get this over with."

Farin let him lead her out of the kitchen. She looked back at Dale as she left. With a wink and a nod, he mouthed a silent, "You can do this."

Mourners filed in and out of the house, a slowly undulating sea of black, rising and falling as they gorged themselves on free food and liquor. They crashed like the tide against Jordan's white leather furniture and soft blue surroundings in the tremendous sunken living room. Jordan's darling boy had played upon the same carpet these strangers now trampled in their attempts to mourn his passing.

Heat washed over Farin, its intensity so strong she feared she might faint. A group of mourners whisked Jordan away, drawing him into grudging conversation. She wanted to follow along, to stand beside him as she had told him she would. Instead, she felt absent. In her mind, she was somewhere else. Another city. Another house.

A similar scene had played out that day in her childhood home. A well-respected and successful attorney, Kelley O'Conner's many friends and associates had come to offer condolences to Farin and her mother.

But Farin feared the houseful of sad-faced strangers who, one-by-one, leaned down to her, smiling their brave smiles while insisting, "Everything will be all right." Most of the afternoon, she huddled close to her mother, clutching fistfuls of her dress. Emotionally, she had been younger than her ten years. Until three days before, she had lived a sheltered existence. Her parents, particularly her father, had been her entire world.

"Hello, young lady." The greeting came from the smiling face of a fat, golden-haired man with a funny voice. He smelled of alcohol and spearmint mouthwash. "I'm sorry about your father. I know you're sad and confused right now. But it'll get better. Sometimes accidents happen."

As she had reached up to accept his veiny, outstretched hand, her mother had said some cross words she did not understand and had ushered her away.

Kelley O'Conner died in a drunk driving accident. The underage driver of the other vehicle, James Wellingham, was not arrested. He served no time. Farin did not know why. The golden-haired man had explained, simply, that accidents happen. His words had not brought her an ounce of comfort.

Now, mere days ago, six-year-old Chase Grant had drowned in his father's pool. The words again echoed in her brain. *Sometimes accidents happen.* The random unfairness made a kind of sense. Yet still, no comfort.

Cheryl approached her with a glass of white wine, which she gratefully accepted. "It's good to see you."

"Why do I keep feeling like an intruder?"

"Och! Don't think on it. No one else feels that way. Particularly our Jorie." She stepped back and gave her the once-over. "And don't you look lovely."

There was something comforting about the warm Scottish burr in Cheryl's voice. Not too thick an accent. Americanized, but distinctive. She displayed none of the outward grief the family had two nights before. Save Jordan, it appeared their family had spent their tears in private. Now, they would project strength for the rest of the world.

Farin sipped her wine, visually scanning the room. "I haven't seen George and Lynda."

"Ben drove Mum and Dad back to the hotel after the funeral. The boys stayed with them. Mum's so upset, Dad's afraid she won't make the flight tomorrow. It's better this way. She's said her goodbyes."

Farin glimpsed Jordan near the fireplace, centered in a crowd of suited men holding lowball glasses of bourbon. Every so often, he nodded graciously or rubbed his brow. When he caught her staring, he attempted a brief smile. "I wish Jordan didn't have to be here."

"He'll be fine. Our Jorie's a strong man when he needs to be."

She stuck close to Cheryl throughout the afternoon. Four glasses of Chardonnay later, she began to relax. Mostly, because she had yet to run into Chris.

"He should be here with the family instead of out in Lockhardt's limo, discussing business," Cheryl complained as they grazed the buffet. "Ah well, at least with him preoccupied, he won't be tweaking Ben's nose."

Whatever the reason, Chris's absence suited Farin just fine.

Jordan returned to her at last. Cheryl squeezed Farin's hand, then slipped away to find her husband.

"You can't be doing half as well as you're trying to make everyone think."

He rubbed the back of his neck. "If I hear one more person tell me how 'truly sorry' they are, I think I'll go mad."

"Have you eaten anything? Do you want me to fix you a plate?"

"I'm not hungry. I'm not anything. I—"

He took her hand and led her away from the crowd. Farin glanced back over her shoulder, searching for Cheryl as if she were a buoy. But Cheryl was nowhere in sight.

Jordan led her up the stairs, down the hall, and into the master suite. He locked the door behind them, then took her in his arms.

"I don't want to talk, Farin. I don't want to hear those people in my head. They didn't know my son. They're not here for Chase. They're here for me or Chris or Ben. And not because they care—but because of who we are."

Farin searched his eyes. "What can I do?"

"I don't want to be a grieving father anymore," he said, his voice breaking. "Or a son, or a brother, or a celebrity. I want to be *me*. I want to believe something good still exists in this world. That I have even one good reason to wake up tomorrow. I want...I want my son back."

Tears spilled down Farin's eyes as she held him close. Distantly, she heard herself say, "I want him back, too."

Jordan drew back and kissed her. Soft at first, then with a sense of urgency.

He did so want her in his life. It took courage to stand by him the way she had, tangled into the web of his life, his family, and his obligations so soon into their relationship. The tragedy of the last few days had made him feel as if he had known her a lifetime. She was the one salvation in his life since the accident. He thanked God he had found her.

Jordan unbuttoned her fine linen suit, then slid off her jacket, pleased to find only a silk camisole beneath. She neither questioned nor objected as he undressed her, garment by garment, kissing her scented skin from the nape of her neck to the tips of her toes.

It felt wrong on some level to be there, shunning the houseful of guests, abandoning their thoughts and sorrow for a retreat into each other. Did they not have a responsibility to exhibit their grief to everyone downstairs? Would making it public somehow wash it away?

No.

He lowered her onto his bed, knowing everything he needed in that moment lay before him. Farin's breath against his cheek, her arms around him, her arched back, felt truer than anything he had ever known.

In the afterglow, he buried his head in the softness of her chest and wept. Everything he had defined himself by now lie in the ground. "What would I have done if I hadn't found you?"

Farin held him closer and stroked his hair. "I'm here, Jordan. I'm not going anywhere."

CHAPTER 6

ARIN AND JORDAN TARRIED AWHILE before returning downstairs. They knew they would be missed if they vanished too long.

"At least the crowd's thinned," Jordan observed.

"I should probably check on Dale."

He kissed her fingertips, then disappeared into the sea of black.

On her way to the kitchen, she saw Chase's nanny sitting alone near the bay window, shoulders slumped, legs crossed, examining her open palms. She was a whisp of a young thing with an air of innocence about her. Every so often, she swiped tears from her eyes.

She looked lost. Farin sensed it immediately. Nicole had not only lost Chase, who Jordan said she loved. She had lost her job as well.

"You okay?" Farin asked, stopping as she passed.

Nicole looked up. Farin could not discern whether the sudden attention embarrassed her. "I'm okay."

"Everyone's telling Jordan how sorry they are. Seems they should be saying that to you, too."

She tucked a few renegade tendrils of thin, tawny hair behind her ear. "I'm getting ready to leave, anyway. I was hoping to see Chris before I go."

Farin's stomach flipped. "I think he's out front somewhere."

Nicole thanked her, then stood and hurried for the door.

Dale held his hands up as Farin entered the kitchen. "I can't do dinner, so don't ask." He consulted his watch. "It's almost six. I was supposed to leave at five."

Farin plucked a grape off one of the remaining serving trays and popped it in her mouth. "If you hadn't stocked the bar so well, everyone would probably be gone by now."

"No doubt. In any case, I've sent everyone else home. Maybe they'll get the hint."

"I hope so."

Dale picked up one of the two trays. "Grab that last one and follow me. I hate to rush, but I've got a date."

Farin followed behind him. "Anyone I know?"

He did a quick sashay. "He's a chef at L'Restaurant. I'm trying to poach him away to come work for me. It's nothing definite, you understand, but we did exchange some promising looks. His interview's tonight and the champagne's on ice!"

Farin helped clear the clutter and collect the empty trays. She wondered if Nicole had found Chris. She sort of hoped not.

"How 'bout you, doll? How're you holding up?" Dale asked.

"I'm okay."

"And Jordan?"

"Making it. That's about as good as it gets today."

"He's lucky to have you, you know."

Farin reached for his forearm. "I'm glad you're here."

He winked before returning to the kitchen. "I'm glad you called."

She finished dressing the table, then peered into the living room. Cheryl stood next to Ben, chatting with someone Farin did not recognize. Jordan stood nearby in a cluster of similar strangers, his face lined in grief.

As she considered interrupting and rescuing him, she was overcome by the feeling of being watched. Her eyes flitted around the living room, then the hallway. Everyone seemed immersed in banal conversation. When she turned around, she spotted Chris at the bay window near Nicole's vacated chair. He fixed his gaze upon her, admiring her almost insolently.

To Chris's right stood a man. Correction—*the* man.

The man who had graced the cover of every trade magazine she had ever read. The man with the commanding presence. Not a wrinkle in his black Armani suit. Not a smudge on his highly polished Italian leather shoes. Farin would have known him anywhere. Until six weeks ago, she would have given anything to sing him one song.

This was Robert Jameson Lockhardt, Senior.

In person, he was larger than life. A towering figure with a staunch, round frame. His hawk-like eyes, keen and steely blue, absorbed every detail of his surroundings. A maze of character lines etched across his coarse, serious features, though he did not strike Farin as someone who often laughed or smiled. He was attractive, in an intimidating sort of way. Impeccably groomed with white-blond hair, side-parted and age-thinned. He emitted confidence, wealth, vigor, and success.

Standing before the music industry's most controversial mega-mogul, close enough to smell notes of bergamot and iris in his cologne, made her wonder. Had she made a mistake pulling LSI's copy of her demo?

But Jameson Lockhardt was more than a legend; he was infamous. Over the years, she had heard whispers of chart manipulations and payola schemes. An unusually high rate of employee turnover. The rumors intrigued her.

In recent days, Jordan had hinted at similar scandals. He both admired and despised Jameson for his tactics, and dealt cautiously with the genius who had forged his career.

Farin watched him as if nailed in place, mesmerized as he scrutinized the roomful of people with narrowed eyes, a martini in his hand and an obscure sneer on his face.

"Hasn't anyone ever told you it's rude to stare?"

She spun around to find Chris beside her.

"I see you made it."

Her body stiffened. "Nicole was looking for you."

His telltale grin teased the corner of his mouth as he reached past her to the table for a snack. "She found me."

As he brushed by her, she closed her eyes to savor the heady mix of musk and the natural scent of his skin. Last night's fantasy flashed in her mind.

She caught herself and mouthed a voiceless reprimand. Turning to leave, she bumped the corner of the dining room table with her hip. She winced in pain, then cursed under her breath.

"You okay?" Chris reached for her.

She jerked away. "I'm fine."

He dipped his chin and stared up at her, lips sucked in. "Do all men disturb you, Farin? Or just me?"

Irritated more at her clumsiness than the accuracy of Chris's perception, she half-limped, half-stomped away.

When Jordan saw Jameson Lockhardt marching toward him, he was both relieved and apprehensive. He recognized the flat intensity of his stare. And, while the subsequent summons to follow the old man outside to talk enabled Jordan to break away from the small group holding him conversationally hostage, Jordan doubted he had the strength to endure what promised to be an exhausting exchange.

Jameson had offered his condolences earlier. Time for business.

"*Umbra* debuted at number two six weeks ago," he began before Jordan had so much as taken a seat at the patio table. Jameson chose to stand, as usual, as if he did his best thinking on his feet. "It occasionally hits number one, then drops back." He lifted his palms, as if waiting for Jordan's verbal participation.

Jordan fixed a rueful stare at the diving board.

"Number two's not bad, by lesser standards. Your single's up five notches. That's good, but not great. Richard Marx dropped to number three this week. He, D'Arby, and Winwood are all falling. They're the ones we're watching."

"And Def Leppard's at number one." Jordan blew out an exasperated breath, willing his focus away from the pool. "I follow the charts."

Jameson waved him off. "Not your genre. But yes, that damn song's been on the chart for weeks. Maybe you need a one-armed drummer of your own."

Jordan slumped back into his chair, hoping the suggestion was a joke. "I gather we're releasing another single?"

The old man folded his arms across his chest and stroked his bald chin. He stared off into the middle distance. "It's not about issuing a new release. It's choosing the right track. Listeners are all over the place right now. We've got Ziggy Marley, Midnight Oil, and Debbie Gibson...all on the same chart a month ago. Bloody eighties. Bobby's scheduled a focus group to determine our strategy. I'd wager LSI it'll be a ballad. Probably your title track. Those birds cream for your ballads."

Jordan stood and gave a half-hearted nod as he turned to go back inside. "Have Bobby call Bill when he decides. I need the time off anyway."

Jameson dropped his arms and scowled. "Time off?"

"A couple of weeks or so, yeah."

"This is no time to weaken under personal tragedy. You need to bury yourself in your work!"

"I buried my *son*, today!" Jordan cleared his throat as the reality of his own words found him. He moved his hands to his hips. "I'm taking some time."

Jameson held up a large, authoritative hand. "This isn't a negotiation. You'll have your itinerary Monday." He left Jordan grieving and dumbstruck as he pulled open the sliding glass door and stomped down the hallway, nearly knocking Farin over in his haste.

She flattened herself against a wall. "Excuse me."

Lockhardt huffed and continued at pace.

Jordan sat, elbows on knees, with his back to the pool. She dragged a chair over to sit beside him but he pulled her onto his lap, tucking his face into her chest. She stroked his hair. Comforting him made her feel strong for a change.

Her momentary doubt over whether she had erred in withholding her demo evaporated as Jordan relayed the brief conversation. "What sort of monster would demand you resume your schedule so soon?"

"I have no choice."

"Everyone has a choice."

He drew her in and lay his forehead against her shoulder. "Lockhardt can end a career with a phone call, Farin. It wouldn't be the first time."

She rested her head atop his.

They sat in silence for a long time. Finally, he moved her off his lap and stood up. "I've had enough. I want these people out of my house."

He slipped off to compose himself while Farin helped Dale clean up in the kitchen. When finished, Dale packed and loaded his equipment, then climbed into the Eastland Catering van and rolled down the window. "You did it, doll," he said. "You got through the day. I'm proud of you."

Farin kissed his cheek. "I'm not the one I'm worried about, to be honest."

"Well, he made it too. By the skin of his teeth maybe, but he did it. Now go. I'll see you soon."

She sent him off with a warm embrace and a promise to meet soon for lunch.

Back inside, she beelined to the dining room to clear the buffet table of leftover plates, napkins, and glasses. In the living room, Cheryl thanked the last of the mourners as they filed out the front door.

It made sense now why Ben had been upset about Jameson flying in from New York. Ben saw through him, unlike Chris, with his obvious loyalty to Lockhardt. Lockhardt had only exacerbated Jordan's grief.

"One for the road," demanded a throaty British accent from behind her. "Martini. Dry. No olives. Make it a double."

Farin whirled around. Jameson loomed before her, holding an empty glass. She bristled at his presence. Her knee-jerk reaction was to defend Jordan's position. Then, all at once, things felt different.

His expensive cologne and menacing demeanor fogged her senses. Worse, for all her righteous anger, she lacked experience with men of his stature. His presence dwarfed her, though she nearly met his glassy-eyed gaze in her heels.

Her nose wrinkled as she caught a whiff of his many prior double-martinis-dry-no-olives.

He shoved the empty glass her way. "Are you deaf?"

"I—I don't know how…" she mumbled, embarrassment besting her anger. Her cheeks grew hot. "Maybe I can catch someone before they leave."

Jameson peered into Farin's dark eyes. A flicker of recognition registered across his rugged face. "My dear girl, I don't give a two-penny damn what you do. All…I want…is a *drink*!" He slammed the glass atop her armful of trash and marched toward the living room.

Farin froze a beat, her parted lips moving and mute. But as the stench of bergamot and gin evaporated in his wake, she reclaimed her abandoned anger. Unlike Jordan, Jameson Lockhardt could take nothing from her.

She found him and returned the glass. "Mr. Lockhardt, I don't work for Jordan, and I certainly don't work for you. If you want another drink, go to the bar. You may intimidate everyone else around you, but I don't have to take it." Heart pounding, she retreated to the kitchen to discard the trash.

It took less than thirty seconds to regret her assertiveness. She hung her head and held onto the sink. "What have I done?"

The crowd departed, only family remained amongst the post-memorial service clutter of the living room when Jameson emerged, arms flailing about him. "Get her out of this house!"

Chris leaned against the fireplace mantel, loosening his tie. "What now?"

Jordan sank into the sofa and dropped his head back.

Chris tossed his tie onto the coffee table. He stretched and yawned as Jameson explained the egregious offense in great detail.

"Then, she just walked off!" Jameson pointed at the kitchen door.

"Would you like *me* to get you a martini?" Chris gestured to Cheryl. "Is the staff gone?"

Her gaze flicked upward.

He raised his arms in exaggerated fashion. "Can someone *please* get us a bloody martini?"

Jameson inhaled a huge, indignant breath. "I will *not* be mocked!"

"—or, we could go out for a martini," Chris suggested, palm up.

Jordan stood with a resolute grunt and left to find Farin. Details mattered nothing to him. He needed peace.

Jameson's eyes narrowed to lethal slits. "Who. Is. She?"

Chris cocked his head. "Who's who?"

"The girl!"

"Oh yes, the *girl*! She's Jordan's girl, actually." He raised the back of his hand to the side of his mouth, wrinkled his nose, and whispered, "It's new."

"Is she in the business?"

"Just signed with Warner Brothers."

"So, she's new."

"Brand new. New to Jordan. New to the business. Just...*new*."

"Solo artist?"

"I believe so, yes."

"Who's her agent?"

Chris glanced past Cheryl at Ben.

Ben lifted his shoulders and shook his head.

Chris looked back at Jameson. "I'm afraid that's all I got. We only met her a few days ago."

Jameson's tone simmered to a resentful growl. "What's her name?"

"Farin." He looked to Ben for confirmation. "Farin...O'Conner?"

Ben nodded.

The old man blanched. He steadied himself against the sofa. "What did you say?"

An odd silence befell the family. Chris and Ben traded curious glances. "You know her?"

His eyes darted sightlessly around the room, as if reviewing the brief biography. "Warner signed her?"

"So, you *do* know her," Chris pushed.

"Of course not!" Jameson stormed around from the back of the sofa, unbuttoned his suit jacket, dropped onto a cushion, and crossed one weighty leg over the other.

Chris watched as Lockhardt rubbed his pantlegs with trembling hands.

In the kitchen, Jordan made his plea to no avail.

"I'm sorry," Farin protested. "If an apology's due, it should be his."

Jordan rubbed his temple. "That's unlikely."

"Should I go?"

"Of course not!"

"Maybe we should let things calm down. It's been such a long day."

Chris swaggered into the kitchen, chest puffed out. He crossed his arms atop the butcher block, brows arched, and announced, "Jameson wants to see you."

Farin inched closer to Jordan. "I won't apologize."

"On the contrary." Chris reached past Jordan, grasped Farin's forearm, and pulled her forward. "He wants to meet you. *Formally.* A proper introduction."

Jordan followed behind, praying for the nightmare to end.

As they approached, Jameson rose from the sofa with all the congeniality of a campaigning politician. He took Farin's hand and gently kissed the tips of her fingers. "Forgive me, Miss O'Conner. My short temper too often gets the better of me. I'm sure you understand. It's been a dreadful day."

She stared in fearful uncertainty as the others exchanged puzzled glances.

"Now." Jameson sat back down and patted the cushion beside him. "Chris says you recently signed with Warner Brothers. Did you send anything to LSI?"

Farin remained standing. She jutted her chin in feigned confidence as she wondered if Jameson might know, through Donovan's LSI contact, that Donovan Reed represented her.

Jameson fixed his gin-pickled gaze upon her. "Audition for me."

All around them, shocked breaths were taken and held. Jordan and Chris faced each other, open-mouthed. LSI had long since been considered the most difficult label in the industry with which to land a contract. Jameson had not personally conducted an audition in years.

"No thank you," she said. Inside, her stomach churned.

Jameson paused, lips puckered beneath his scrunched brow, gauging her sincerity. "I'll leave my card. You can call me tomorrow."

Farin's toes curled. Weeks ago, she would have given her firstborn for such an opportunity. Had she not begged Donovan to make it happen?

The insanity of dismissing her life's dream did not escape her, but she refused to back down. Jordan or no Jordan, Farin no longer romanticized Lockhardt Sound. Something about the man frightened her. Out of the corner of her eye, she saw Ben give her a curt nod of encouragement.

"You realize," Lockhardt continued, "I could prosper you in ways you could scarcely imagine."

She shifted her weight to one leg. "Money isn't everything."

Jameson's booming laughter pierced the silence enveloping the room. "Is that so? Well, experience tells me everyone has a price."

"I'm not for sale, Mr. Lockhardt. Thank you anyway for your kind offer."

CHAPTER 7

CHRIS STOOD ON THE SIDELINES of Jordan's living room, unobtrusive as he beheld the Lockhardt-O'Conner Show. He could not decide which of them fascinated him more—Jameson's near-begging for Farin to join LSI, or Farin's obstinate refusal which, by his estimation, amounted to career suicide. No *Twilight Zone* episode was more entertaining.

All he knew was that Farin was more than beautiful. More than intelligent. She was a tempest—headstrong, alive. And his next mission in life was not his next album, as Jameson might expect, but to make Farin O'Conner pant and sweat beneath his sheets.

He eyed her salaciously, even as he endeavored to will away the gut-punch of their initial meeting and the subsequent events of that fateful day. Even before the accident, the day had not gone as Jordan had planned. Farin's friend had launched an attack on his philandering lifestyle. Jordan had cautioned him to be on his best behavior. Though conformity had never been his strong suit, he had tried to behave.

Jordan had cornered him as they cleared the grill. "Why're you trying to destroy my evening?"

"You never said she's a singer," Chris had argued back. "Does Ben know? If so, he didn't tell me. Sheds a certain light on things, doesn't it? C'mon, mate, a *singer*?"

"What of it?" Jordan snapped.

"I met this little tart once. Grand at first, before I discovered she was only after a leg up—and not my leg, I'm afraid."

Jordan coughed out an irritated chuckle.

"Laugh now, but be bloody careful."

"If Farin wanted help, I'd help her. I even offered. She said no."

Chris had refrained from further warnings as they wheeled the grill near the garage to cool. "Does she have any sisters?" he asked half-seriously.

"What about Marci?"

Chris scoffed. "Not my type."

"Every woman's your type."

"Not this one. She'd sooner rip my head off."

"I thought you liked the rough stuff!"

Farin's scream had cut through their banter, changing their lives in an instant. The ambulance, the hospital, Chase's death, Farin's reaction—

That was it.

If Chris could identify the one moment that awakened him to the wonder of Jordan's girlfriend, it was her reaction to the devastating news. Farin had collapsed into his arms outside the ER. He had comforted and held her. She had needed him. And he was there.

He stood before her now, entranced as her visage seared into his brain. The full curve of her hips stirred him. Ample, teardrop-shaped breasts. Long legs, taut muscles. Wavy, coppery curls. Those full, sensuous lips. The narrow slant of her chocolate, almond-shaped eyes.

Chris memorized every detail. He would stow the image in his mind and ferry it home to New York with him. He would hold it, caress it. He would sleep beside it at night. Wake beside it each morning. He would hunger and thirst for it.

And he would be back. Oh, yes. He would have her, even if only once. She would come willingly, wanting him as he wanted her.

After making his failed bid, Jameson tendered his goodbyes. Lockhardt rarely experienced defeat. It appeared to have left him as bewildered as he was angry.

Chris walked him to his waiting limousine, silent at first. "She's something else, isn't she?" he said at last.

"You're smitten," Jameson spat with barefaced disapproval.

He barked out an unconvincing laugh, burying his hands in his trouser pockets. "She's Jordan's girl."

"Remember that." He paused before lowering himself through the open door. "And back off, ya prat."

The admonition took him aback. Throughout their long association, they had developed a near-familial bond. Jameson saw him as a rebel, a label Chris rather enjoyed.

The uncharacteristic chastisement wounded him. He smiled against the reprimand. "You've always enjoyed a good conquest."

"Not this one, Chris."

He cocked his head, squinting in curiosity.

"I mean it. Leave...her...be." His index finger stabbed into Chris's chest three times, punctuating each word before he lowered himself into the car.

Chris shut the door and stepped back, then watched Jameson's limousine drive past the security gate and through the small crowd of fans who still lingered, whistling and beckoning for Chris's attention. For the first time since joining LSI, Jameson had reproved him like a child. But more than the simple scolding unsettled Chris. Farin's presence had disturbed the music mogul. But why?

Upstairs, Cheryl and Farin dallied in Jordan's master bathroom, primping like schoolgirls. "You've won my husband over, you know. Neither Chris nor Jorie ever stood up to that old windbag before."

"Temporary insanity." Farin watched Cheryl comb her long, ash blonde hair with a silver-plated hairbrush. Her mother used to have hair like Cheryl's, but darker, almost black. Her father spent entire evenings brushing it as they watched television.

Two weeks after his death, she had it cut above her shoulders. She never grew it back.

Downstairs, Ben poured three snifters of Hennessey for his brothers and himself. In the welcome silence of the early evening, they congregated in the living room, a family again, and removed their public masks.

Chris ruminated over Jameson's ominous warnings. He sipped his liquor and, for once, kept his peace.

Ben's eyes flitted back and forth between his brothers, his brows knitted in concern. Their feelings for each other ran deep, yet the surface was a storm. As the oldest, it fell to him to still the white-capped tension and make his family whole.

Troubling images assaulted Jordan's racing mind, each more disturbing than the last. He wanted to destroy, break, and tear something until his hands bled.

They sat in silence, nursing their drinks. Ben stretched his legs toward the coffee table and crossed them at the ankles.

"Well, one of us should say it," Chris said at last, his voice saturated with anxiety and discontent. "Either of you care to guess what's up with the old man?" He leaned forward and rested his elbows on his knees as if expecting his brothers to huddle up.

"I couldn't care less about the Lockhardts," Ben said. "All I know is, every drop of sweat from that man's brow hits the music industry and ripples out to some effect on my family."

"I've never seen him behave so strangely."

Jordan dropped his head onto the back of the sofa and closed his eyes.

Ben gave Chris a questioning glance. "I noticed, too. Jordan? Did you drop Farin's name with Jameson?"

Eyes fixed on the ceiling, Jordan shook his head. "I offered. She said no."

"Have you ever seen him so...?" Chris searched for the appropriate word. "I don't know. It was all rather bizarre, wasn't it?"

On that point, they agreed. Jordan dropped out of the conversation except to offer a token nod, shake of his head, or grunt as appropriate. Ben and Chris sat on either side of him, talking around him and unsuccessfully coaxing him to participate. They concocted explanations to account for the bewildering congeniality Jameson Lockhardt had shown Farin.

"He acted like he knew her," Chris insisted.

"But how?" Ben asked.

"You're both being ridiculous," Jordan told them.

Ben chuckled, twirling his rocks glass in his hand. "Farin sure did put him in his place, though, didn't she?"

A knock at the front door pulled the would-be sleuths away from their suppositions.

Jordan groaned. "Whoever it is, make them go away."

"I'll get it." Ben patted Jordan's knee, then set down his drink and went to the entryway. When he opened the door, he blinked twice.

"Hello, Ben," Ginny Stevens greeted. She held a black silk handkerchief beneath her black lace veil to dry invisible tears. "I'm here to be with Jordan."

Stunned speechless, Ben reflexively stood aside as Ginny swept past him.

She looked pale and tragic as she crossed the living room in a ceremonious stroll. Bedecked in black from head to heel, she hid her platinum tresses neatly beneath an Audrey Hepburn-inspired *Chapeu du Matin*. Her makeup, heavy and flawless, accentuated her sparkling blue eyes.

"Darling!" She threw herself into Jordan's arms as he and Chris stood. "Don't worry. I'm here now."

Bemused, Chris adopted an Elvis lip curl and glanced at his older brother. Ben downed his brandy, then sidled up to Chris and whispered, "Might want to pop upstairs and warn the ladies. I'd like to avoid a row."

Chris nodded. "Brilliant idea."

Jordan unlocked Ginny's arms from his neck and stepped back. "What are you doing here?"

She dropped her black leather handbag on the cocktail table and removed her gloves one finger at a time. "I'd have been here sooner, but I had to rearrange my schedule. And, of course, I had to go shopping."

"We're through, Gin. It's been weeks since—"

Ginny plopped down on the sofa. "Really, Jordan. You made your point. Don't worry. We'll work things out."

Ben watched the scene play out before him, an audience of one. He almost felt sorry for Ginny. If she did not remove herself from the premises—and soon—Jordan would not be held accountable for his actions.

Chris found the women in the master bathroom. He greeted them with a smug grin, stretching his arms and resting them high against the door jamb. He caught Cheryl's attention. "An old 'friend' of Jordan's just arrived."

Her eyes flickered in understanding. She collected her things and replaced them in her travel bag. When finished, she squeezed Farin's arm and excused herself, ducking beneath Chris's arms as she left.

Oblivious to their traded glances and verbal shorthand, Farin stood primping in the bathroom mirror. "I'll be down in a sec." She fluffed, then sprayed, her curls.

Chris watched her, transfixed. When Farin turned to leave, their eyes met and held.

"Excuse me." She ducked beneath the barricade of his limbs.

He grabbed her upper arms and pulled her close. "We need to talk."

She struggled against him. "What are you doing?"

"Let's go have a drink somewhere."

"You're insane," Farin whisper-shouted.

He pulled her closer, his breath hot on her cheek. "You're trembling."

"Stop!" She wrenched free, shoving Chris back onto Jordan's unmade California King. She spun around to leave, but stopped short when she found Ben standing at the bedroom door, arms akimbo.

Chris clambered up and hastened away, avoiding his brother's stare.

"All right, then?" Ben asked after his brother's departure.

Farin nodded. "I don't know how to...explain—"

"I know my brother, Farin. But are *you* okay?"

She smoothed her pantsuit with trembling hands. "I'm fine. I'd hate for Jordan to think—"

Ben touched her shoulder. "There's nothing to say to Jordan. As for Chris...I can speak to him."

She studied him with grateful eyes. A handsome man, strapping and tall. A kind man. He had Jordan's warm green eyes and Chris's dark wavy hair, only shorter and combed back over his head. Laugh lines and subtle crow's feet filled what of his face peeked out from around his fully-bearded and mustached face, something she found curious for a man who lived in Florida. Somehow, she felt safe around him. "I can take care of myself."

He nodded, giving her a lopsided grin. "Anyone who can handle Jameson Lockhardt the way you did can handle my brother."

"Besides, Jordan said he's leaving soon, so..."

He sucked his teeth. "Look, the reason I came up—actually, the reason I sent Chris up—was to tell you..." His voice trailed off, then came back sharp. "Ginny's here. I thought you should know."

She stared down at the floor. "Are she and Jordan...?"

A bark of laughter escaped him. "No, kid, nothing like that. He's trying to get her to shove off. I don't think she's drunk, but she's quite stubborn."

Ginny rested on the sofa, legs crossed casually as Jordan encouraged her to accept their fate and leave.

"Matt and I are done, darling. I've told him. No sense in prolonging the inevitable. There're reporters outside your gate right now. We can go out, hand in hand, and it'll be all over."

"It *is* over. That's what I keep saying. The cheating doesn't really matter anymore, does it? We grew apart long before the split. You know that. Don't make me say something to hurt you. Not today. I'm not up for it."

She sighed in exaggerated fashion, addressing him as if he were four. "Jordan, you couldn't possibly hurt me." She took a relaxed sip of her drink—which she had helped herself to amidst Jordan's maddening diatribe about their failed relationship. "You love me."

"I *never* said I loved you."

"You know as well as I do not all men come right out and say it." She uncrossed her legs and leaned forward, reaching for his hand and giving it a sympathetic squeeze. "Give yourself time, honey. The words will come."

Jordan snatched his hand away. "It's over, Gin. Accept it. Stop acting as if I proposed!"

The barb struck a nerve. So much so, she almost lost her composure. She rose and glowered at him, setting her jaw as if restraining herself until she could vocalize her thoughts without emotion. "I won't leave you at a time like this. I have to be here to comfort you."

Cheryl had planted herself near the bottom of the stairs, arms crossed, not wanting to intrude, but Ginny's comment prompted a cynical burst of air from her lips. "Aye. You've been here ten minutes, and that's the first mention you've made of this foul day."

Slack-jawed, Ginny spun around to address Cheryl. She clutched her chest. "Are you suggesting—?"

"I'm seeing someone else," Jordan blurted out, as much to his own surprise as hers. "I didn't want to hurt you, Gin, but you've left me no choice."

Ginny's jaw dropped. Out of the corner of her eye, she caught sight of Ben descending Jordan's staircase beside a woman she did not recognize. As they reached the bottom floor, she sneered and scrutinized the redhead. "You must be joking." She coughed out a cynical laugh. "*That?*"

Farin raised an eyebrow as she reached Jordan's waiting embrace.

In a furious sweep, Ginny collected her handbag, gloves, and hat off the cocktail table, then stomped past the couple and toward the door. She stopped long enough to whisper into Jordan's ear, "You'll regret this someday, Jordan Grant, and you'll *beg* me to come back."

"Thanks for stopping by." Chris waggled his fingers as she crossed the room.

"Screw you, Chris."

"Ah, love, I'll screw many, but never a slag like you."

She exited the house, leaving the front door open. She marched to her car amid a hail of clicking and snapping cameras.

Cheryl shut the door as Ben visually scanned the living room. The house fell quiet, feeling suddenly empty and enormous. The full impact of their interminable day hit him squarely in the chest. He knew Jordan had reached his limit and been forced well beyond it.

Childish laughter that had once filled the air of the beach house had vanished like smoke. Chase Grant had made these walls a home for Jordan and filled them with joy. The weeks and months ahead saddened Ben. "You've got to get out of California, little brother. Out of this house. Come to Florida. You need your family."

Jordan raised his hands to his waist, blew out a long breath, and stared down at the floor.

"Think about it. You'll go mad in this place without Chase. All the memories...all the history...Hollywood's never been for you. It's Lockhardt's *image* of you."

He raked his hands through his hair. "I'll think about it," he promised in a cracked whisper.

"It makes sense," Ben urged.

"Can I get through this day first?" He headed for the back door.

Ben reached out his hand, but Cheryl moved between them as Jordan passed by. "Let him go."

He opened his mouth to protest, but she shook her head. "You can't live their lives for them."

Chris cast his eyes in Farin's direction, then lifted his chin toward the back door. "Going after him, then?"

"Not yet," Cheryl said. "Jorie needs a minute. The day's caught up to him. The best way we can help him is to get his home in order."

The mourners had left the house in unsurprisingly bad condition. Stacks of dishes, soiled napkins, and full ashtrays littered the living and dining areas.

While Ben and Chris cleared the living room, Cheryl aired out the house, and Farin resumed picking up in the dining room. Sadness lingered in their midst, mingling with the stale odor of tobacco, coffee, food, and alcohol.

Chase Grant's small body had been laid to rest. They had performed all the customary rituals: the funeral, the interment, and the memorial service. As they cleaned, no one voiced their shared thought: the casket had looked incomprehensibly small, wrong—like a cruel joke.

Farin piled dirty plates onto the buffet table, which Ben promised to break down once they finished. She dragged the kitchen garbage can in to more efficiently dispose of used cocktail napkins and various debris.

Glancing over her shoulder toward the living room, she mused over the sight before her. Ben, Cheryl, and Chris worked in unison, operating in a sort of choreographed groove, understanding each other's gestures and one-word sentences. Such a different scene than the lives portrayed in magazines or on television. The fantasy of celebrity insisted life was a song and dance. Never would a star lift a finger in tiresome endeavors or shatter under personal tragedy.

The scene Farin witnessed stood in stark contrast to the myth created by publicity agents and peddled by their media co-conspirators. There were no false smiles here, no power trips. Ben was right. The Grants were not their glamorous personas. They preferred each other's company to the glitter of fame. Above all else, they were a family.

Flowers of every type and every arrangement adorned the foyer in blues, reds, whites, yellows, and oranges. Wreaths and bouquets of carnations and roses, lilies and a stunning array of exotic creations crowded tables and shelves throughout the living and dining areas. Tomorrow, she and Cheryl would gather them up and relocate them to little Chase's gravesite.

As she dragged the garbage can back to the kitchen, she noticed the most unique bouquet of all resting on the dining room table.

Its deep green stems were thick and strong. Short, yellow crowns. Long, slender leaves. A hearty contrast to more elaborate, fragile, arrangements. The golden petals reminded Farin of her bright, sunny kitchen back in Glendale. Marci had insisted they decorate with what she described as "optimistic colors."

Farin wondered how Marci's day had gone.

"These are lovely," she said aloud, to no one in particular. "Daffodils, right?"

Cheryl temporarily ceased wiping down the large square coffee table and looked her way. "They're from Jorie's agent, I think. I'm not sure what they are." She resumed her task as she called out, "Oi, Chris. You're the expert. What are those?"

"Expert?" Farin glanced his way and frowned doubtfully. "Let me guess. You started your career as a florist."

Chris set down the vacuum he had procured from the laundry room and moved toward her, scanning the room to gauge their privacy. He leaned in close and stole a whiff of her hair.

She jerked her head away.

He righted himself but kept his tone low. "Let's say I'm adept at finding appropriate gifts for appropriate occasions. I enjoy the senses...*all* the senses: the sight of a beautiful woman; the smell of her; the sound of her sighs when I take her; her taste...the first touch that builds anticipation." He took and placed her hand in the middle of his chest. "Can you feel it?"

Farin felt his heartbeat through his untucked dress shirt. Again, she recalled the previous night's indulgence into fantasy.

Chris Grant had something. A quality she could not label. Attractive, but unlike Jordan or Ben. He bordered on skinny and walked with a pronounced swagger that simultaneously sickened and drew her in with its confidence. He unsettled her. She disliked him. Or maybe she disliked the effect he had on her.

Her voice quavered as she whispered, "Stop." She wriggled to extricate her hand from his.

He held her steady, ignoring the tepid plea. "Our senses evoke emotions. Flowers symbolize these emotions. From as far back as the Victorian era, they've been assigned distinct meanings. Take these jonquils." He fingered the soft, golden petals with his free hand. "They have dual meaning, actually. The first? Sympathy. An apt choice for such an occasion."

Farin swallowed hard. "And the second...?"

He dislodged one of the yellow buds from the arrangement and handed it to her, his bold, sensuous smile victorious. "Desire. Also an apt choice for such an occasion."

Eyes wide, she drew back her chin. He had said it. Out loud.

She backed up, turned, then hurried out the back door.

Cheryl whirled around and walked toward the kitchen as the back door closed. "What's wrong?"

From the living room, Ben shot him an acrimonious frown.

Chris knelt down and retrieved the discarded jonquil. He threaded the stem through the lapel of his suit jacket and shrugged.

***

After restoring the house, Ben and Cheryl took in the sun's slow descent into the Pacific. They watched Farin join Jordan on the beach. Such a lovely girl. Clearly, Jordan was falling in love with her. It reassured Ben to see them together in the twilight, arm-in-arm, as the tide came in.

A perfect couple, he thought. *Sometimes, you know.*

His little brother needed someone special, particularly now. Still, he wished Jordan would leave Los Angeles.

Memories of their childhood in Bledlow, England lived vividly in Ben's mind. The Grants were a close family. Even Chris, the rebel of their clan. As the years passed, their lives had grown complicated. They existed thousands of miles from one another. Chris in New York. Jordan in

California. He in Miami. If the events of this last week had proven anything, it was that they still needed each other. Ben wanted his brothers back.

Six months, he decided. It might take longer to convince Chris, but six months would allow plenty of time to convince Jordan he belonged with the people who loved him.

CHAPTER 8

"*D*ADDY!" *FARIN CRIED. SHE BALLED up her tiny, ten-year-old fists and raced away from the wreckage in the center of the intersection. The eerie stillness of the scene frightened her. No one stirred from her father's car, or from the small black Porsche. No moan or cry for help floated on the murky night air, nothing but the maddening hiss of steam and the last strains of American Pie from the station wagon's still-playing radio. The sight of her father, lifeless and bloody, shook her to her core.*

She could not hear the man who pursued her now, but she felt him racing up behind her. She did not want to turn around or think what would happen if he caught her. His face was cloaked by the thick fog.

> ... and I knew if I had my chance
> ... that I could make those people dance
> ... and maybe they'd be happy for a while ...

The melody faded as she ran past the pier toward her home. When she stopped to catch her breath, she did not look behind her. She sensed the man still followed, still pursued her. As she gasped to fill her lungs with oxygen, she felt her fingernails being ripped off her fingers. The pain stabbed at her. Something warm and wet filled her hands. Looking down, she saw the blood.

***

Marci rose early Saturday morning—a rare occurrence. She yawned, executed her morning bathroom ritual, then wrapped an afghan around her shoulders despite the relative warmth. Shuffling into the kitchen to start a pot of coffee, she heard stirring in Farin's room.

She swiped the breakfast nook's window curtains and peeked out at the sun cresting the Verdugo Hills to the east. The first weekend of August. The weather forecast remained the same today as it had for days: hot and humid. No relief in sight. She had tired of the heat and longed for rain.

She grabbed two mugs from the cupboard and plunked them down atop the counter, then sat and waited for the pot to finish brewing.

It was no use. Neither of them could deny the nightmares had returned. The same nightly torment Farin had suffered since age ten. Tearful screams had cheated them both out of yet another night's sleep. The time had come for an intervention.

Marci yawned again. She stretched her arms wide to shrug off the loss of sleep, then snatched the afghan before it slipped from her shoulders onto the floor.

Soon, Farin joined her. She sulked into the kitchen, head low, and slid into a chair. "Sorry."

"It's okay." Marci filled their mugs, then doctored them to perfection. "You need to get back into therapy. They're getting worse. At first, it was the accident. Now, you've got the guy who killed your dad coming after you like some maniac. Maybe Dr. Logan can help."

"Logan's a quack," Farin snapped, avoiding Marci's eyes. She picked at a frayed corner of the kitchen tablecloth. "Five months and all he came up with was that I had some 'father-fixation' preventing me from committing to men. I loved my dad. I'd give anything to have him back. But honestly, a father fixation?"

Marci delivered Farin's coffee, then doubled back to the fridge. "Maybe you're confusing the guy who killed your dad with Chris. That Wellingham guy took your dad away and, when Chris started coming on to you, you were afraid he'd take you away from Jordan. It's symbolic. I read all about symbolism in last week's issue—"

"Nice try." Farin picked up and blew on her mug. "Chris wasn't anything serious. And anyway, he's back in New York. End of story."

Marci retrieved eggs, cheese, and some veggies, then shut the refrigerator with a side-thrust of her hip. "We're out of sausage."

"That's fine. I'm gonna take a shower before breakfast, though. Jordan's flying back today. I'm picking him up at the airport." She rose and stretched, then left the kitchen with her mug.

And that was another thing, Marci thought. She switched on a burner with an irritated flick of her wrist. It was not her place to tell Jordan how screwed up his girlfriend really was. He had called a couple of weeks ago before leaving for New York after spending a horrendous night trying to calm Farin down after one of her nightmares.

Marci had struggled to explain. "It's a mess. I don't know what to say."

"If something's going on, I should know, shouldn't I?"

"They started when she moved in with my family. Maybe before."

"She said her father died when she was young. I guess I didn't realize how bad it was for her."

"Her mom started drinking, which made things worse. It got ugly. They rarely talk now."

Jordan had expressed concern and asked how he might help.

"I'm not sure anyone can. She's gone to a shrink. And for a while, things got better. But when Dr. Logan started digging into her past, she stopped going."

"Too close?"

"Honestly, Jordan? I don't think she wants to get better."

"Why not? It's no way to live, is it?"

"It's like she feels this is all she has left of him. She doesn't want to let go."

Jordan had not responded.

"So now you know. The only question is, can you deal with it?"

"Are you asking me if I plan to walk away?"

"She's my best friend."

"I'm not going anywhere," he had assured. "I wish I could do something."

It comforted Marci to feel that she had an ally where Farin was concerned. Farin had hit the bull's eye. Even better, she had yet to run away. Usually, she ran. She had run from every relationship she had ever had.

Farin returned to the kitchen, combing out her wet curls. "I forgot to ask. Has Donovan called back yet?"

"Nope." Marci slid a perfect omelet onto a plate, then sprinkled a pinch of cheese on top.

"I've been leaving messages. He hasn't called to discuss my schedule. I wonder what's up."

"Who cares? The contracts are signed and sealed. The hard part's over. Be patient."

***

Farin used the spare key Jordan had insisted on giving her. She spent the day fixing up the beach house. This included prepping a roasted chicken dinner for two. Although they both knew she could never match his culinary skills, he would appreciate the effort.

The last month had dragged along as the *Umbra* campaign wound down. Each day rose as a vulgar challenge. But Jameson had been right after all. Over time, Jordan's passion for his work distracted him from his grief. She had heard gradual improvement each night as they chatted on the telephone before bed.

Tonight would be exquisite—nice meal, soft music, and a moonlight stroll. She yearned for autumn. How wonderful it would feel to stretch out beside him in front of a crackling fire. Never had she felt so content with a man. Every day with Jordan filled her with happiness and music, whether or not they even saw each other. Life was good. Despite the nightmares.

Soon, she hoped, she would find the courage to utter the three words she had never said to a man in her life.

***

Chris peered out from the balcony of his Manhattan penthouse at the street, the rooftops, and the park. The hot August night hovered sticky and humid over New York City. Though close to midnight, its congested traffic had barely thinned. Street noise and distant sirens continued unabated in the city that never sleeps.

He fingered a fat joint of green bud in one hand and suspended a snifter of well-aged Courvoisier in the other. His thoughts roamed as he sipped the liquor. The haunting echo of a lone clarinet played a jazzy rendition of "Rhapsody in Blue," the sound wafted casually from the street, or perhaps from the window of a nearby resident. It was difficult at times to distinguish the direction from which the many noises of this towering metropolis originated.

The city lights emitted an eerie, amber glow as he looked out over Central Park. New York never really darkened. He drew in a long, deep hit of his joint as the familiar smell of pollution mixed with the essence of life below. The smoke expanded in his lungs until he fought the urge to cough.

How could Ben suggest he leave this mysterious, magical existence? What could Florida offer him? It was too bright. Too exposed. In Manhattan, he could be anyone. He could sequester himself in his room like a recluse or join the anonymous masses wandering around below. Whatever whim or fantasy, it lived in the city.

Of course, there was one fantasy inhabiting his heart that had not journeyed to New York—yet.

The ample-bosomed brunette he had brought home hours earlier purred from his open balcony doors. "Coming back to bed?"

He turned to see her poised seductively against the frame. He would have called her by her name if he could remember it. She stood wrapped in one of his silk sheets, her thick hair mussed from their earlier encounter. One of the most beautiful girls he had ever seen...that night.

She padded across the balcony on bare feet, then crouched beside him, slipping her hand inside his robe to fondle his manhood while planting warm, inviting kisses down his neck. As always, he rose to the occasion. When she began to stroke him rhythmically, he grunted in appreciation.

"Fancy a bit more, eh?" He drew down the sheet and pulled her soft, creamy nakedness to him. "I'll be in straightaway." He moved his tongue smoothly, slowly, along the curve of her lips, then down to her hardened nipples. It drove her mad. But to him? Sex was as natural as breathing. There was nothing erotic or even sensual about foreplay. He had mastered the physical act of sex and knew exactly what women wanted.

"Come soon," she whispered with breathy eagerness as she stood and headed back inside.

He exhaled a stream of pungent smoke. His thoughts turned to the one fantasy forever on the perimeter, always out of reach. Since his return from California, he had thought of little else. Some nights, he would lie awake for hours, anguished and tortured at the thought of making Farin surrender her magnificent loveliness to him. Her public response may have looked less than promising, but her eyes had betrayed her.

Those dark, magnetic eyes told him everything. Farin fooled herself with a man like Jordan. Baby Brother might be kind and loving, but she would tire of that eventually. In her eyes, Chris saw fire, pain, and an aching passion. Jordan could never understand such things, but Chris knew in the depths of his being that one day, he would have the ravishing beauty in his bed.

***

Farin waited two weeks for Donovan to contact her before trying again—in person. She had left countless messages complaining she should have heard something by now. His lack of response, coupled with Lockhardt's bid for her demo at Chase's memorial, left her paranoid. Something had happened. She needed to know what.

"Maybe it's your contract," Marci had proffered one night as they watched a late movie and munched on heavily buttered popcorn.

But it was not. Farin had confronted Donovan's secretary earlier that afternoon. "The contract's fine," Cher had said. She mentioned something about negotiations but, "I can't say more than that. You know how he gets."

Marci retrieved a napkin from the coffee table, wiped her greasy fingers, and leaned back into the couch. "Maybe you should call your lawyer. And oh—your mom called today."

Farin glowered at the television screen. She swallowed her iced tea in a distasteful gulp. "Drunk?"

"She's lonely, Farin. You never call her. And like it or not, you're all she has left."

"She has her booze," Farin spat, her tone as hard and frigid as the ice filling her tumbler.

"She's still your mother."

Marci had never understood. She and her mother had an entirely different relationship.

The doorbell rang. Marci hopped up to answer—probably grateful for a conversational pause even at the late hour.

Marci hated feeling stuck between Farin and her mother. She loved them both, but also pitied them. She had said so before.

"You may not wanna hear it, but you're just like her. Both stuck in your grief. Maybe you two should pull together instead of ripping each other apart."

"I'm done with her."

"That breaks my heart. For both of you."

"Don't ever feel sorry for me, Marci."

Farin had heard it all before. She had had a bellyful of it.

The frumpy but pleasant widow from down the hall stood at the front door in a tattered blue bathrobe, curlers in her hair, holding out a big bouquet of flowers. "Sorry to bother you girls so late," she rasped, exhaling cigarette smoke through her nose. "These came for Farin earlier today. You two wasn't in so the guy left 'em with me."

Farin nudged past Marci for the bouquet and searched for a card. "Thank you, Mrs. Hanson."

"What do we owe you for the tip?" Marci asked.

"No tip." The woman shook her head as if they were crazy. "No card neither."

Farin continued rummaging through the bouquet after the woman left. "Jordan always sends a card."

"It probably fell out." Marci took the arrangement into the kitchen for some water. "Where do you want them? They'd look great in here. The yellows match perfectly."

"And he usually sends white roses," Farin called after her, musing over the sunny buds. She had taken a rose from every bouquet he sent and pressed it in the family Bible, along with its card. The Bible nearly overflowed with them now.

Then, it dawned on her.

She stomped into the kitchen and reached for the vase. "Gimme these. I'm throwing them out."

"Why? The smoke? I'm sure they'll air out."

Farin began shoving the flowers into the garbage disposal in the sink, blossoms first. "It's not the smoke. It's Chris."

"What?"

"Chase's memorial?"

Marci's brows arched, then rounded into a scowl. She turned on the water for Farin. "Weasel!"

Farin hit the switch. She watched with satisfaction as the stems sticking up through the rubber shield spun like straws in a doodle bug hole.

Marci grabbed a wooden spoon and reached in front of Farin to shove more of the bouquet down into the disposal as Farin added fresh blossoms from the remains of the arrangement. "End of story, huh?"

She shot her friend a guarded look, then hit the switch again.

Farin arrived at Donovan Reed's office at ten the next morning, foolishly believing he might have dragged himself in by then. She sipped coffee with Cher until noon, and even manned the phones while Cher broke for lunch.

"You sure you don't wanna come with?"

"I'm fine here, thanks. Besides, I don't want to chance missing him if he peeks that fat, round face of his in for a second."

By the time Donovan arrived at two, Farin had reached her limit. She stalked him into his office, then stood squarely in front of him as he lowered his portly frame calmly, even happily, behind his black lacquered desk.

"Don't tell me you didn't get my messages. I've already talked to Cher."

"Whoa, now! Why the hostility, babe? I was just coming in to call you!" He unbuttoned the ill-fitting jacket of his cheap beige suit.

She folded her arms and stared at the plump balding hippie with the long gray ponytail. "In six years, you've never steered me wrong, Donovan. But you're a terrible liar."

He dropped his organizer atop his desk and pressed the button on his intercom. "Cher, hold my calls, please."

A grunt of laughter came across the speaker. "You got it."

Farin planted her hands on the desk and leaned forward, peering into his close-set eyes. "It's September. I was supposed to start recording in August. Who exactly do you work for?"

He waved his hands before him. "Okay. You got me. Take a seat, okay? Have some coffee. You take cream and sugar, right?" He reached toward the intercom once more.

Farin straightened and crossed her arms. "Now, Donovan."

"Your contract's been bought out. Isn't that great?" A self-satisfied smile stretched across his bloated face. "They were, shall we say, persistent. We just finished all the haggling and negotiations. It's supposed to be a surprise, babe! Lighten up! The details would've bored you, trust me. I mean, I had to deal with Warner Brothers, then—"

"What do you mean, bought out?" She studied Donovan's enthusiastic expression, stupefied. "What have you done? Why am I hearing about this after the fact? And why do you look so happy?"

"We'll all come out of this smiling, Farin. Even *you*. He offered a lot more than the Warner deal." Donovan stood and crossed his desk, beaming. He wrapped a congratulatory arm around her. "All things considered, he could be taking an awfully big risk—uh, no offense."

When his initial pitch fell flat, he disengaged, stepped back, and waved a placating hand before her. "He went *nuts* over your demo tape!"

Farin rubbed her forehead with the ball of her hand. "Who's 'he'?"

Donovan looked her in the eye—with gusto—and proudly proclaimed, "Jameson Lockhardt! *Himself!*"

***

Jordan had suffered a long day. The morning was a protracted interview with *Entertainment Weekly*, the afternoon passing in misery taping a guest appearance on yet another afternoon talk show. *Umbra* had become a blockbuster. Tour plans had finalized. His responsibilities now shifted from promoting an album to hyping an upcoming tour and preparing for life on the road.

Just as well.

The relocation seeds Ben had planted had slowly taken root. Jordan longed to wake up whole again, without finding himself wandering sleepily into his son's empty room so they could prepare for the day.

Farin's dramatic arrival that evening did nothing to ease his weariness. She entered mumbling something about firing her agent and booking a flight to New York. "Six years!" she shouted, repeatedly.

She stormed into the living room, performed her regular ritual of kicking off her shoes, then began treading angrily back and forth in front of the fireplace.

Jordan watched her pace, his head spinning at the stream of consciousness only she could follow. "Let's talk this out before you go booking any flights." He patted the couch, beckoning her to join him. "We're *sure* Donovan knew not to approach LSI?"

Furious and frustrated, she refused a seat. "I talked to him right after you and I met. He called me, wondering where the CD was. He was all, 'I can bag it for you, babe!' I told him it was no mistake and *not to send it off.*"

Jameson's reaction to meeting Farin stole into his mind. The news made a strange sort of sense, on some level. Outward appearances aside, Jordan had long suspected Lockhardt Sound meant more to the old man than dollars and cents. His genius and instinct were legend, yet it seemed as if he hid behind his empire for something personal. How or why this might include Farin, he could not guess. "Has he contacted you yet?"

Wild-eyed, she sucked her teeth. "I can't work with him, Jordan. He bought me like a piece of prime beef!"

He thought a long time. She stared down at him as if waiting for him to impart wisdom he could not offer. Instinct told him she was right to worry. It also told him it was pointless to try to talk her out of confronting the old man. "How long will you be in New York?"

Her eyes softened with gratitude. "Four days, tops."

He blew the tension out through his lips, satisfied her anger had subsided. But before he could get up to pour them each a glass of wine, her temper resurfaced. "Donovan was with me for six years, Jordan. *Six years!*"

He leaned back into the sofa and rested his arm along the back. "You're right. Jameson's insensitive and manipulative. Donovan should've told you. But it's nothing personal, Farin. Betrayal's the rule in this business, not the exception."

She spun around and glared at him like a tigress protecting a cub, or a kill. Dangerous, almost deadly, and quite passionate. Jordan stirred in the face of her menacing beauty even as she railed, "That's why I only work with people I trust! Six *years*, Jordan!"

He watched as she resumed pacing, this time pounding her fists against her thighs. In the end, he got up and procured the wine. She needed to calm down. And he was getting hungry.

"I'd go with you," he said after coaxing her to take a seat. "My schedule's full. Why don't I ring Chris? He has plenty of room—and the old man's ear. I hate to have you running around New York alone."

She froze, mid-sip, swallowed, then stared down at her painted toenails. Her voice softened. "It's a quick trip. I'll be fine in a hotel."

"He wouldn't mind. He might not even be there."

"It wouldn't feel right. We're basically strangers."

"After all we've been through? My family loves you."

A doubtful scoff escaped her pursed lips. "I'd rather not."

Jordan set down his wineglass and wrapped his arms around her. He inhaled the familiar sweet scent of her skin.

Every day, he fell deeper.

New York would be perfect. It would give him time to find the appropriate token. When she returned, he would ask. It might be too soon to propose, but he knew they should at least be living together.

Despite his lifelong desire to find a woman with whom to share his life, he had never felt this way. Not with Kim. Not with Ginny.

Farin was the one. The only one.

She cuddled into him, nestling her cheek against his neck. "Don't be mad about the trip, Jordan. Or about my not wanting to stay with Chris."

He tilted her face up to his. "Come back soon. I miss you already." He left out the all-important "I love you" that had never followed but soon would.

As if from nowhere, Farin had become everything to him: lover, friend, companion, and confidante. Yet, if he told her too soon, she—and others— might worry his grief over Chase had birthed his love for her. He needed to be sure, himself, that this was not the case.

For this reason alone, he would wait until she returned from New York. With her business concluded and her worries gone, they would be free to decide the next step of their journey.

Perhaps he would give Chris a call anyway. It never hurt to have friends nearby when in a new, unfamiliar place.

CHAPTER 9

A FEW SECONDS AFTER CHRIS opened his eyes, he remembered he lay thousands of miles from Malibu. Sleepy images of tangled limbs, of skin-on-skin, of lustful cries begging him to take her again and again, receded like ebb tide.

He reached beside him to ensure he was alone, then turned his head to stare sullenly at the bedside clock. An empty Crown Royal bottle lay overturned atop his nightstand, partially obscuring his view. The glowing red numbers of the clock's digital display read 5:43 AM. Try as he might, he could not fall back asleep. He had dreamt of Farin, again. It had woken him, again.

He cursed his weary, aching soul as he recalled the vow he had made to himself before returning to New York two months ago. He had sworn he would take her image home with him. Mission accomplished. In his mind's eye, he saw her as clearly as if she lay there beside him. The sweetness of the vision stirred him. As usual, he had come out of his dream in a high state of arousal.

Chris tossed aside his bedcovers and rose to put on the kettle. The torture of waking up each morning with an insistent, throbbing, near-painful erection frustrated him. In the last six weeks, he had bedded a record number of women, hoping to satiate his lust. But instead, it had focused his libidinous obsession to agonizing clarity. It ruled him, now, as if he were its slave.

Padding toward the bathroom for his newest morning ritual of a cold shower, he looked down with disgust at his engorged length.

Enough was enough. One short meeting with Jameson from now, Mirage would start their first real vacation in three years. No tours, late night recording sessions, or planned personal appearances. The break would enable him to pay his dear baby brother a visit.

He shivered in the cool water as he stepped into the shower stall and pulled shut the door. He shot a lewd, toothy grin through the clear glass at the full-length mirror hanging on the far wall, wagging his eyebrows as he sang, "Ca-li-for-nia, here I come…"

***

"I'm here to see Mr. Lockhardt," Farin announced to the plain but sharp-dressed receptionist outside LSI's executive offices.

The woman raised her right index finger, then dropped the telephone line when the call she transferred connected. "He's in a meeting. Do you have an appointment?"

"I didn't have time to call."

The thin brunette studied Farin, her drab brown eyes magnified behind bottle-cap glasses. Deadpan, she pushed her thick spectacles up the bridge of her nose. "Mr. Lockhardt sees no one without an appointment."

"He'll see me. Tell him Farin O'Conner's here."

She tilted her head. "You'll need an appointment."

Farin peered past the woman and down the long hallway. Nameplates shaped like gold records were mounted to the left of several doors. The office at the far end of the corridor had a larger version than the others. Though unable to make out the inscription from this distance, she suspected it was her final destination.

She moved past the desk, toward the hallway. "Thanks anyway. I'll find him myself."

With impressive alacrity, the receptionist bolted up to intercept Farin's near-sprint down the hall. "You can't go back there, Miss O'Conner! Don't make me call security."

Farin halted a pace from trampling the woman. She bore down into her close-set eyes. "I'm going to see Mr. Lockhardt today—with or without your help."

***

Jameson poised himself, mouth open, to reprimand his receptionist when she buzzed his office. That was, until she announced Farin's unexpected arrival.

At the mention of her name, Chris white-knuckled the armrests of his chair. The timing could not have been better had he planned it.

Jameson stabbed his intercom. "Of course, I'll see her," he barked into the speakerphone. "Send her in immediately."

Chris vacated the chair facing his mentor's desk. He relocated himself against the office's side windowsill, just out of sight. Though feigning nonchalance, his blood coursed his veins like racecars on the Silverstone speedway.

"Don't you have a vacation to start?" Jameson grumbled with disgust.

"It's started, so stop bossing me around." He fixed his eyes on the door. "What on Earth is she doing here?"

"It's none of your concern."

A triplet of knocks preceded Farin's entrance.

Jameson stood, breaking into a wide smile. "My dear! What a pleasant surprise! You should've told me you were coming. I'd have sent my plane for you."

Chris watched from the windowsill, gobsmacked as the old man extended his arm in welcome, then crossed the room to close the door behind her. An encore performance of the congeniality he had witnessed at the memorial. In fifteen years, he had never seen Jameson treat another person with such warmth. Or any warmth, for that matter.

Farin slid the pouch of her crossbody purse around from her hip to her middle and held it tight. "Sorry to barge in on you. We should probably talk."

"I couldn't agree more," Jameson called over his shoulder. He gestured to Chris's vacated seat. "Make yourself comfortable."

Her eyes flitted left, then right, as she lowered herself to sit sideways in the seat. She clutched her bag in her lap and scanned the office.

A grin hitched the corner of Chris's mouth. He gaped at her like a perched cat waiting for a bird to be freed from its cage. Finally, their eyes met. He lifted and wiggled his fingers in a mocking imitation of a friendly greeting.

Her eyes widened above her parted lips.

Head cocked, he leered at her in an almost antic way, then returned to normal, as if nothing had happened. "How've you been?"

"Fine."

"Is Jordan about?"

She repositioned herself to face Jameson's desk. "Why?"

"If he were, I'd think he'd have accompanied you to this…'meeting,' you said?"

She lifted the strap over her head and placed her handbag in the chair beside her.

"Yes, *our* meeting." Jameson's booming voice scythed the rising tension. "I'll see you out, Chris."

As the two men stepped into the hallway, Farin fused her eyes and struggled to steady her nerves. Whatever determination had impelled her to fly from LA to New York to confront Jameson Lockhardt wavered. Somewhere in the hallway, she realized a face-to-face with the man she had so resolutely put in his place two months ago could backfire.

Chris's presence had further shifted her off her axis. He knew she was here—alone.

She sank into the tufted wingback and tried to relax. As she waited, she studied his immense office. Elegant in all its mahogany and leather furnishings; tasteful in rich greens and burgundy décor. It had a museum-like vibe, with a nod toward modern technology. From sophisticated and obviously expensive computers, stereo equipment, and electronic devices, to the framed da Vinci sketches and Diego Velazquez paintings hanging upon his veneered cherrywood walls, an aura of omnipotence filled its space.

For the second time since meeting Lockhardt, Farin asked herself, *what have I done?*

In the hallway, a conversation ensued in hushed, angry whispers.

Jameson lapsed into his more familiar disposition. He stabbed the air. "I told you to back off."

"What's the problem?"

"I see the way you look at her."

"She's a grown woman! What's with the Jekyll and Hyde routine? At Jordan's, *here...*"

Lethal fire shot from Jameson's slitted eyes. Jaw clamped shut, he snarled, "Stop trying to solve whatever dime-store mystery you've cocked up in your addled brain. And forget about the girl. If you wanted her that badly, we both know you could have her—despite her common sense. But to what end? If you have the witless urge to steal a woman away from another man, go ahead. But not your own brother's."

Chris's upper lip twitched as Jameson's arrows hit their target.

The old man clasped Chris's shoulder with a meaty, wrinkled hand. "That way lies madness, son, I assure you."

In the end, Chris stormed from the LSI offices, bitter and confused. Again with the chastisement. Jameson had been more like a father to him than his real dad. Now, he was shutting him out.

As he crossed the lobby floor and approached his waiting limo, he rid his mind of all things Lockhardt and formulated his next move.

Farin stood as Jameson returned, having regained some of the resolve that brought her to New York in the first place. "You bought out my contract."

"And paid handsomely for it, I might add." Jameson eased himself into his chair.

"Mr. Lockhardt—"

"Please." He held up a large, beringed hand. "Call me Jameson."

"*Mr. Lockhardt*, I'm not sure why you're doing this, but I have no intention of signing with Lockhardt Sound."

His lips curled into a sinister, if polite, smile. "Please, call me Jameson."

Something in his patient tone contradicted his level stare. His eyes focused on her with unyielding obduracy, rendering her small and bare.

She swallowed hard.

"Have you discussed this with Mr. Reed?"

"I fired Mr. Reed."

"I see." Jameson rested his clasped hands atop his mahogany desk. Had he worn a clerical collar, one could have mistaken him for a priest at prayer. "Why are you so against signing with LSI?"

"I told you. I'm not for sale like one of your works of art." Farin waved toward the wall.

Jameson nodded, the epitome of understanding. "As I told *you* before, I can make you a star."

"I'll make myself successful."

His nostrils flared above tightened lips to suppress a chuckle.

The condescension spurred her on. She scooted to the edge of her seat, tapping the tip of a finger atop his desk as she spoke. "It's *my* talent and *my* voice, not some company. And even if that weren't the case, are you suggesting Warner Brothers couldn't make me successful?"

"They could, indeed." He rocked backward. "But they won't. You'll find their offer permanently rescinded."

Her features blanched as she sank back. "So...if I don't sign with you, you'll make it impossible for me to sign with anyone else?"

His blank, unrepentant stare went through her.

She opened her mouth to respond, but the words evaporated. Maybe she should have made the man's martini, after all. "How could you?"

"Simple. You're a complete unknown." When Farin did not counter, he continued. "I confess, your reticence confuses me. A thousand young singers like you would sell their grandmothers for what I'm offering. What is it? Jordan?"

She lowered her head.

"Perhaps you underestimate him. Or the relationship."

She shot him a direct look. "You know *nothing* about—"

He chuckled. "That's better."

Jameson had not felt such exhilaration in years. Much to the frustration of his A&R department, LSI had not signed a new act in ages. He had seen no need. But Farin would sign. Today. And she would have things easier than most. He would see to it.

Watching her wrestle with the reality of their situation, he recalled what an insolent child she had been and how much she had changed. She resembled her mother, in both personality and appearance.

"But why *me*, Mr. Lockhardt?"

He rolled his chair back a few inches and crossed his legs. "There are only two things you'll ever need to know about me, Farin. I'm very smart, and I'm *very* rich."

She scoffed. "You left out humble."

Jameson grinned, enjoying their exchange. Maybe he needed to try a different approach. Then again, maybe she had best despise him for the time being. "Such gumption from a girl with no success could work—for *or* against you. Now, I realize you may have heard some rather dire stories about me. I'd wager most of them are true. But the facts speak for themselves. Jordan, Chris, and all their peers here at LSI—each of them got exactly what they wanted. And in record time, if you'll pardon the pun."

She rolled a shoulder.

"Do you think we'd be here today if I hadn't checked you out? That Mr. Reed didn't fill me in during our negotiations? I know what dues you've paid. The club years. The disappointments. The near misses. I also know your dream was to sign with LSI. With *me*. What I don't know is, what changed?"

Farin's leg bounced as she thought of her father, and of Jordan, and her long journey to this moment. Jameson was right. She was stubborn. How could she argue? Lockhardt Sound had risen amidst the ashes of a hundred failed labels.

Still, one issue remained.

"You treat people like workhorses, Mr. Lockhardt. The way you treated Jordan at Chase's memorial? It was heartbreaking. And I'm not an animal."

"It's *Jameson*." He rested an elbow on the arm of his chair and rubbed his chin. "I'm a businessman, not an entertainer. If the success of *your* company relied on a few dozen musical geniuses and their assorted egos, you'd be wise to kick them in the seat of their trousers now and then. The fruits of their achievements are easily spoiled. If I didn't keep at them, they'd rest on past and present successes and then wake up one day wondering what happened to it all. And I'd be broke. Fame and fortune are much harder to maintain than they are to achieve."

His words entranced her. For the next twenty minutes, he defended his questionable reputation. He spoke with passion and eloquence, pacing his office with a powerful, calculated gait, punctuating his words to convey a lyricism that made her feel like nothing existed outside his doors. When he finished, she felt she understood the logic behind his actions.

And all at once, she felt she understood Jameson Lockhardt as well.

This was no monster. Granted, his methods bordered on tyrannical but, in his mind, the end justified the means. He aimed to succeed. Had she not considered similar ulterior motives when she had first recognized Jordan at Le Dome?

In this respect, Jameson's attitude mirrored her father's—the attorney, the breadwinner, the husband, the head of the O'Conner household. Farin's father had worked hard for his practice, his home, his family...

"I'm afraid I may have misjudged you."

Jameson waved off the apology, but she detected an overwhelming sense of satisfaction settle upon him. "I take it we have an agreement, then?"

She gave him a sheepish nod.

"Brilliant. We'll book studio time straightaway. For now, you should meet a couple of people."

The cloud inside Farin's mind cleared as Jameson exited the office, as if he had released her from a spell. The impact of firing Donovan struck her. Had she made the right decision? Had he given her a choice?

In any case, Jordan would enjoy this turn of events. He had never said it outright, but she suspected he liked the idea of her being with LSI. Maybe he thought it would bring them closer—as if that were possible.

Jameson returned with another distinguished older man in tow. "This is my attorney, Ross Alexander. He'll be drawing up your contract."

In one hand, Ross grasped a pen and notepad. He extended the other in greeting. "It's a pleasure to finally meet you, Miss O'Conner."

She stood and shook his hand, noting the scent of fresh soap and woody cologne. A handsome man of average height. Somewhat shorter than Jameson, and leaner. He had tan, taught skin instead of the fleshy jowls that reinforced Jameson's stuffy appearance, and kind eyes etched with the faintest of crow's feet. His hair, dark and thick and peppered silver, was meticulously sprayed in place.

Ross took the empty seat to Farin's left. For the next hour, they talked around her, chatting about arrangements and preliminary plans until she felt invisible and out of her depth.

"And call Taft." Jameson pointed at his colleague. "Tell him I'm sending Farin his way."

"I thought—"

He shook his head. "Reed's out. Bill's a better fit, anyway."

Farin's ears perked at the name. Bill Taft was Jordan's agent.

At last, Jameson checked his watch. "I'd planned on showing you the building but I'm afraid the rest of my day is full. I've already missed a couple of meetings."

"I-I'm sorry, Mr. Lock—"

He eyeballed her, this time with a hint of whimsy.

She blushed beneath his unspoken admonition. "Jameson."

"You do need to meet the head of A-and-R before you go." He glanced at Ross.

"She's down on seven with Bobby," Ross said matter-of-factly, scribbling notes on his legal pad.

Jameson paused, then growled, "I know."

Ross looked up, eyes wide with understanding. "She should be right up."

The room fell still. For a moment, Farin grew uneasy again.

When Jameson turned back to her, he was again the genial host.

"There's one last issue we need to discuss before you leave. I think you should consider changing your name."

The color drained from Farin's face.

He held up his hand. "Your last name. It's common in this business."

She scraped her upper teeth against her bottom lip. Her name. She had never considered changing her name. It was her father's name.

There came a knock at the door. Seconds later, a serious-looking woman entered the room as if she owned it. Marching forward at a self-possessing pace, her high heels shortened her gait, causing only the slightest sway to her thin hips. Not a single wrinkle in her tailored, skin-tight pencil skirt and jacket.

Farin straightened in her chair.

She wore her shiny black hair in a severe crop. Shoulder-length. No layers. Straight bangs. Like model Tania Coleridge in George Michael's "Father Figure" video. Tall. Broad shoulders. Much about her gave the impression of feigned masculinity, as if indulging a feminine side might leave a negative impression with male counterparts. She was stunning.

Jameson and Ross stood as she approached. Farin stood as well.

"This is Samantha Drake, my head of A-and-R. Sam, this is Farin O'Conner, LSI's newest acquisition."

Samantha Drake. Even the name was impressive.

Unlike Ross, Samantha made no attempt to shake Farin's hand. She offered a curt nod and a quick "hello."

Farin managed a nervous smile.

"We're discussing a name change. Any suggestions?"

Samantha propped herself on the corner of the desk, crossed her ankles, and stared straight through her. "First or last?"

"Last."

"What do you have so far?" She scrutinized Farin from curls to cleavage to her bow flat heels, squinting as if concentrating all her energy on the task at hand.

"I threw it out right before you arrived."

Samantha Drake's lips protruded slightly as she studied Farin, and Farin could only guess what she saw. Over the course of her fledgling career, others had voiced various observations: "a looker," "curvaceous," "thin, but not model thin," "bedroom eyes." Once, a semi-hurtful judgment of "lacking exceptional qualities—vulnerable, approachable yet dynamic. A disarming sexual aura offset by a distinctive innocence, a sadness of some kind."

Farin shifted her weight from one foot to the other, willing away ghostly echoes of past scrutiny.

With a slow shake of her head, Samantha reached her verdict. "In truth, Jameson, I see no good reason for a change. It suits her."

Farin exhaled in relief.

But when Jameson caught Samantha's eye, she pivoted. "Then again...we-uh...can always do better. What was her mother's maiden name?"

Farin knitted her brows. "S-St. John, but I really don't think—"

"St. John," Samantha echoed, tapping her chin with a manicured finger. She adopted a look of intense contemplation as if envisioning the public, the magazine and record covers, the posters, the marquees.

Farin sensed an edge to Samantha Drake's short, unfriendly disposition. Jameson had likely breached LSI protocol by signing an artist without A&R's input. Perhaps some irritation lay beneath the surface.

Samantha hopped off the desk and smoothed her skirt. "St. John works."

"Agreed." Ross resumed his note-taking.

"Brilliant." A vague smile crept across Jameson's lips. "Farin St. John it is."

Farin collapsed into her chair as if physically struck. The idea of changing her name—particularly to anything having to do with her mother—repulsed her.

Still, over the course of the last couple of hours, she had adopted a strange and sudden loyalty to Jameson. He had the experience. He had the people. All she had was a voice and a dream.

Jameson propped his elbow on his desk and motioned to her, palm up. "No objections, I trust."

"I guess not, if you really think it's necessary."

He looked at Ross. "Register that here in Manhattan as well as LA. Go with whoever gets it done first."

"Good as done," Ross said, making additional notes.

With that, Jameson announced his business with Ross and Samantha had concluded. He walked them to his office door, thanking them for their time, then returned for some final words with Farin.

"Things will start happening quickly. It's the nature of this business. But let me leave you with this, my dear..." His mood darkened as he approached her. He took her hand and held it with both of his own. "Stick with me. You'll have the *world*. That's a promise, Farin. And I don't make promises lightly."

She stared into his aging eyes, overcome with their intensity. "Thank you, sir. Again, I'm sorry for—"

"I ask only two things in return. One, never see anyone at LSI on a romantic basis—except for Jordan, of course."

She blushed beneath downcast eyes.

"Two, use your new name from this moment on, without exception. This is who you *are* now. Your life changed today. Forever."

Farin's heart raced, fascinated and frightened by his assurances. Their eyes locked and, had she not known it an absurd notion, she would have sworn he had tried to hypnotize her.

A young man barreled into the office, startling them both. "Sorry to bust in on you Dad, but have you seen Sam? Her secretary said she was with you."

For a fleeting second, Jameson appeared to unravel. Eyes wide, a reflexive shake of the head, then immediately back to his normal, abrasive persona. "Didn't Nancy explain I was in a meeting and not to be disturbed?"

The young man tucked his head. "I didn't ask."

"Remember to do so in the future. In the meantime, come meet our new star. Farin St. John, this is my son, Robert Jameson Lockhardt, Jr."

"Bobby." He traipsed forward, hand extended. His baby blues sparkled as he smiled. His father's eyes, decades younger and almost childlike. And friendlier than she would have imagined any offspring of Jameson's.

Bobby looked more California than New York. GQ-handsome with such flawless features, he appeared almost plain. He had a surfer's frame. Tall and slender. As if he spent his summers at the beach instead of the board room.

As they shook hands, she noticed a flash of crimson in his cheeks.

"Sam didn't tell me we'd signed someone new," he said.

"A-and-R didn't bring her in. I did."

Bobby nodded, still smiling and shaking her hand. "Then where did my father find such a lovely lady?" he charmed, brash and awkward like a schoolboy.

"Through Jordan," Jameson cut in. "They've been dating for months."

Bobby dropped her hand and stepped back. He pushed thick strands of blond hair out of his face.

After the sometimes-odd exchanges she had witnessed between Jameson and the LSI staff, Farin was ready to leave. Jameson was right. Her life had changed today. She needed to decompress. Moreover, she needed to get back to the hotel and call Jordan.

She shook Bobby's hand again before he left, then turned to Jameson. "I should go. You're busy and I've more than overstayed my welcome. Thank you, Jameson, for everything. I'm glad we settled our misunderstanding. I'm honored to be with LSI."

Jameson escorted Farin to the elevator. Her calling him by his first name did not escape him. Just as she had not escaped him after all these years.

He waited until the elevator arrived, then said goodbye. "Bill Taft will have your contract before close of business. I'll let him know how eager we are to get you into the studio. How long will you be in New York?"

Before considering the impropriety of her actions, she rushed out of the elevator, gave him a spontaneous hug, then stepped backward into the cab and pressed the button for the lobby floor. "I leave Wednesday afternoon. If you need me, I'm at the Plaza!"

***

Farin felt delirious as the elevator descended twenty-five floors to the lobby, stopping only twice along the way. Hours ago, she had arrived in a fury, ready to tell Jameson Lockhardt to go to hell and take his company with him. His reputation had colored her perception of him much the same way those trashy tabloids had colored Marci's opinion of Chris.

But she had been wrong about Jameson. She understood him now. She could not wait to get back to her room and call Jordan with the news.

As she made her way through the crowded lobby, a beautiful amazon of a woman dressed in chauffeur garb headed toward her. "Excuse me, Miss O'Conner." She motioned toward the glass doors. "Chris Grant's outside in the car. He'd like a moment of your time."

Farin peeked past the woman. A long white Mercedes limousine sat parked in the loading zone outside the glass doors. "What does he want?"

She turned and headed for the doors. "Please follow me."

The back door of the limousine opened as they approached.

Her lips compressed as she lunged past the driver and slammed the door shut. Seconds later, the moonroof rolled back.

Chris poked his head out, a knowing smirk across his face. "Now why did you do that?"

"What are you still doing here?"

He sprawled his elbows on either side of the car roof. "I live here. New York's my city, remember?"

"Leave me alone." She marched toward the corner to hail a taxicab, but called over her shoulder. "I'd have to be crazy to get into an enclosed space with you."

Chris exited the vehicle and jogged after her, excited by the thrill of the chase. "C'mon. Get in so we can have a chat. What are you afraid I'll do?"

"I wouldn't venture a guess."

He caught up with her at the corner and clasped her arm. "I'll take you to lunch, maybe show you around a bit. You said you were here alone."

She spun around, meeting his dark, tempting orbs with her own. "So what if I am? I don't trust you."

He let her arm drop as he towered over her, his tone deepening. "Are you sure it's *me* you don't trust?"

Their eyes deadlocked. He tilted his head to the side without breaking eye contact, and Farin knew she would look away first.

She turned to hail a taxi.

"Well?" he persisted.

Chris felt himself stir. The evidence pressed painfully against the fly of his jeans. Her unwillingness to look him in the eye spurred him on. He did so love a challenge, and all-too rarely found one.

As she stood defiant on the dirty New York City street corner, jaw set, eyes slit, waving her arms to flag down a cab, he considered his options. If he let her go now, he might not have another chance.

Seeing no alternative, he picked her up, tossed her over his shoulder, and hoofed back toward the limousine.

"Put me down, Chris! I mean it! *Now!*" Her face reddened in anger and embarrassment.

He exhibited no sign of exertion as he carried her. "Maybe if we spend some time together you won't be so afraid of me."

"Me? Afraid? Of *you*?" Farin laughed.

Bystanders pointed and gawked at the scene, some recognizing Chris and calling out his name. Some pulled out cameras and snapped pictures.

Farin struggled against him. She tried to kick herself loose but nearly lost a shoe. At one point, she raised her hand off his back, to strike him, but quickly put it back down to maintain her balance.

As he toted her through the rubbernecking crowd, the thought of her occupying his bed consumed him. He gauged her weight and imagined picking her up, moving her, and positioning her just so. How many times had he dreamed of being locked in a passionate kiss with this woman he now held, albeit unwillingly, in his arms?

Chris deposited Farin in the back seat, careful not to hit her head on the doorframe in the process. She slid across the leather seat to the opposite side to make good her escape, but encountered an elaborate bar and entertainment center—no door. He gripped her forearm and dropped into the seat beside her, closing the door to the onlookers who pressed ever closer.

The short workout left him mildly winded. "Lose the attitude, Farin. I won't hurt you."

"You won't hurt me, but you'll kidnap me?" She struggled to get past him and out of the car. "Let me out of here!"

He released her but extended his arms outward to block the exit. "Promise you'll have dinner with me."

"No."

"It's only dinner."

"*No.* Let me out of here."

His face registered a hint of genuine hurt. For the first time since they had met, he looked unsure of himself. "Bloody hell, Farin. What have I done that's so awful you won't have dinner with me?"

She collapsed into the seat and stared up at the cream-colored headliner, wondering if she could climb out through the moonroof. "I'm your brother's girlfriend, that's why. It would be *wrong*, that's why!"

He snapped his fingers, then pointed at her. "Speaking of Jordan, I checked my messages. He asked me to look after you. Wanna hear it?"

In that moment, Farin knew she had been outmaneuvered. Jordan had called anyway. He probably figured he was helping.

She considered telling Chris she hated and wanted nothing to do with him—but there were two problems with that. Firstly, it might create tension between him and Jordan. That would mean tension between Jordan and herself and possibly other members of the family.

Secondly, she did not *hate* Chris. He had on several occasions now rid her nights of the monsters that stalked her, though he could never know it.

Still, he made her feel unsettled. Vulnerable. She admitted they generated friction, though for her part, the attraction was harmless. The only person who took it seriously sat before her, eager and expectant.

Chris had put her in an impossible situation. Truth told, Jordan had, too.

The weight of an endless day pressed upon her like the crowd of onlookers who now surrounded the limousine, laughing and shouting and trying to see inside the tinted glass. She was too anxious to get back to her room to resist any longer. What reasonable excuse did she have? Besides, if she got out of his car now, she risked getting crushed. She resented feeling so powerless.

She faced him, expressionless. "I suppose we're eating at your place."

Chris hit the limo door twice, then relaxed into the fine leather seat. Immediately, the car was in motion, maneuvering through the crowd and then weaving into Sixth Avenue's congested traffic. He instructed his chauffeur to stop at the Plaza before taking him home.

His smile returned, as did the mischievous glint in his eyes. He lowered his voice to address his captive. "My place? Well, if you insist."

CHAPTER 10

THE LIMOUSINE RETURNED TO THE Plaza at seven sharp. According to the message waiting for her upon exiting the shower earlier, Chris would remain home to prepare their meal. This left her free to worry about the coming evening in solitude as the car motored toward West 74th Street. She was not so naïve as to miss the calculated move. She wondered if Chris had ever played chess.

Realizing the futility of over-thinking the situation, she engaged the entertainment system and surfed unfamiliar channels. She found a country station, then classical, then oldies. A Don McLean song filled the car.

> *... well, I know that you're in love with him*
> *... 'cause I saw you dancing in the gym*
> *... you both kicked off your shoes ...*

With a shudder, she rotated the dial. A jazz station sent her back into her seat. She listened trance-like to its soothing sounds. Before long, her unspoken favorite, Billie Holiday, filled the back of the limousine with a soulful masterpiece. She closed her eyes and banished every other thought as the melody moved through and around her.

> *... Sometimes I feel like a motherless child ...*

Her father had often told her she had started singing before she could even speak. He had owned an impressive collection of vinyl records and cassettes, an eclectic mix of jazz, blues, folk, rock, country, and even classical works.

> *... Sometimes I feel like a motherless child ...*

Bare weeks after her husband's death, an intoxicated Beth O'Conner attempted to destroy the entire collection. Three Beatles albums, some Elvis 45s, and several other pieces were lost in the emotional explosion before young Farin pleaded tearfully with her mother to let her move them upstairs into the attic. From then on, they were her most valued treasures.

> *... Sometimes I feel like a motherless child ...*

Soon, Farin hoped, her music would find its own admirers. She had spent years pursuing the dream her father had inspired within her. Now, Jameson Lockhardt would make her dream a reality. He had promised.

How she wished she could share her good news with her dad. Maybe somehow, he knew. He must. He had been her biggest fan.

... A long, long way from my home ...

Farin observed the liveliness of tourist traffic on dirty streets amid the bright lights of the city outside the limo's tinted glass. There was no point worrying. She had committed to dinner. Besides, nothing Chris could throw her way could spoil her triumphant day.

With the release of a cleansing breath, she rested her head back on the seat and let her arms fall limp to either side of her. Her left hand brushed against something on the seat near the bar. Looking down, she noticed a small black velvet box tied with a red satin ribbon. No card accompanied the box. Instinctively, she knew this, too, was by design. No card. Like the jonquils.

She glanced up to see if the blonde Amazon driver was spying through the rearview mirror, then untied the ribbon with shaky hands. Inside the box, she found a red satin pouch. Within the pouch, she discovered a perfect, loose, two-karat round sapphire.

Farin rolled the gem in the palm of her hand, captivated by the reflection of city lights bouncing off its intricately cut planes while the rhythmic jazz stylings of Miles Davis worked miracles on her nerves.

She replaced the stone, then dropped the box into her purse. An odd gift from an odd man, unlike the tropical flowers that had arrived earlier at her room. Bobby Lockhardt had sent them, along with a card that read, *Welcome to Lockhardt Sound. Much success, Bobby.*

But unlike the flowers, Farin could not accept the sapphire. It did intrigue and, she hated to admit, arouse her. Was there some deep symbolism attached to the gem, as with the jonquils? Dare she ask?

Another move in Chris's dangerous chess game. Dropping the gift into her purse—however temporarily—might be misconstrued as participation. Had she, however unwittingly, played along?

She should have declined dinner. Maybe Marci was right. Maybe she should go back to Dr. Logan. No matter her dedication to Jordan, only a fool would deny she was flirting with temptation. How long could she pretend Chris did not pull at her like a beggar to a crust of bread?

But no. Jordan was everything she wanted. At last, she had found the security she longed for. She had fallen in love. All Chris offered was a lie in the face of reality.

Farin knew reality all too well. Sadly, Jordan knew this reality, too. She would no sooner betray her love for him than she would take her own life.

***

The pilot announced the Boeing 727's final descent into JFK Airport. Jordan poised his hands to unbuckle his seatbelt, drawing a soft giggle from the woman beside him in First Class.

"Nervous flier?" she asked.

He relaxed his hands onto his lap. "I'm surprising someone," he confessed.

"A woman, I take it?"

His cheeks warmed. "I'd wanted to come with her, but I had some conflicts with my schedule."

"So did you resolve your conflicts or ditch them altogether?"

"They're sorted."

"I'm sure she'll appreciate the gesture. What woman wouldn't be swept off her feet by such a surprise?"

That morning, he had woken to a feeling of impending doom. After a careful inspection of his surroundings, everything seemed fine. A glimpse of the silver-framed photograph on his nightstand, of Farin smiling on his arm at a recent charity event, solved the mystery. It was she. Specifically, her absence. Still, he could not shake the feeling that something sinister had occurred or waited.

Only once before had he felt such dread—the day Kim died. Jordan had waited outside the delivery room clothed in hospital garb, shoved out moments before by doctors and staff running into and out of the cramped space. Peering in through the small window, he had watched with incomprehensible horror as she called his name, screaming, reaching toward the glass until they sedated her.

In the end, they had sedated him as well.

"How long have you and your girlfriend been together?" his seatmate asked.

Jordan peered through the portal window at the illuminated skyline. "A few months."

"And already chasing her across the country? It must be love."

Love. Jordan had never been in love before. In fact, he had not dated more than a couple other girls before Kim. But two years into their courtship came the announcement of her pregnancy, which had prompted the marriage proposal she ultimately declined. It never occurred to him they were too dissimilar to make a life together.

But Kim had known. Jordan had found and read her journal one miserable, lonely night. A night when Chase woke him every hour with mewled and fretted cries. In it, he read what she had never told him. She had planned to end their relationship before learning of her pregnancy.

"How long are you two staying?" his seatmate asked.

He gave her a coy side-eye. "You're not a reporter, are you?"

She dared to touch his hand. An innocent, reflexive gesture. "No. Your secret's safe with me, I promise."

Recovering from Kim's death took time. To complicate matters, he had an infant to care for. A child forever hungry, dirty, sleepy, or sick. At twenty-two, Jordan was barely a man himself. Even so, he needed to make some decisions for his life.

Ben's career had exploded long before then. His chart-topping compositions were among the most successful songs of the 1970s. He had relocated from London to a mansion in Key Biscayne, a tropical paradise off Miami's coast, with Cheryl, three-year-old Derek, and yearling, Kyle. They urged Jordan to bring Chase and live with them in their newfound Eden, but he had opted to stay home with Mum and Dad.

Likewise, Chris had achieved meteoric success with Mirage. They were nine years into their association with LSI when Chase came into Jordan's life. Uncle Chris had relocated as well, moving to Manhattan to stay close to the LSI offices.

In New York, Chris had every starry-eyed groupie he could ever want, and he wanted them all. Tales of women parading themselves in and out of his bedroom like a revolving door had staggered Jordan.

The plane touched down, its breaks causing passengers to pitch forward in unison as tires screeched across the runway.

"So, is your girlfriend in show business, too? Would I know her name?"

"She's a singer. Here to sign her contract."

"How exciting! Gonna take her out to celebrate?"

Jordan had always wanted to find the right woman to settle down with and raise a family. Though his might seem an idealistic dream in a so-called enlightened age, he had wanted it as long as he could remember. But as days stretched into months, Jordan's immediate task involved creating a secure life for his son.

Music was an obvious vocational choice. Their father had been a thriving band leader. Their mother, a successful dancer before family eclipsed career. Coupled with his older brothers' popularity in their chosen fields, Jordan's choice made sense. The family consensus was, his Billy J. Kramer-meets-Phil Collins voice and heartthrob good looks would bring him success.

"Let me help you with that." Jordan yanked the woman's carry-on from the overhead bin, which coach passengers had monopolized in the hope of grabbing their bags as close to the exit as possible.

She thanked him. "Who says chivalry's dead?"

With nothing but a fledgling band and a near-debilitating case of public shyness, Jordan had sung his way through the UK club circuit, leaving Chase in his parents' capable hands. Each time a gig turned sour or an opportunity failed to materialize, thoughts of Chase spurred on his efforts.

One night, a club owner in Wales had tried to stiff them. Jordan lost his temper for the first time in his life. He grabbed the man by his lapels and flung him backwards into the bar, towering over him. Bouncers rushed in to assist, but something in Jordan's eyes stopped them in their tracks. When he glared back down at the Welsher, he whispered through gritted teeth, "You'll pay us now, mate, one way or another."

That night marked the end of a long year of dues-paying in Great Britain. From there, they migrated to Ibiza, Spain and then, Australia. But six months with little success found them defeated and England-bound, their proverbial tails tucked between their legs.

During Jordan's absence, Chase had grown into someone he scarcely recognized. Eighteen months old now, Jordan had missed his first step. Mum had let Chase talk on the telephone the few brief calls Jordan could afford. The boy had babbled and bubbled into the line. Nonetheless, Jordan had missed Chase's first word.

If his parents ever worried that he seemed rudderless during the time he took to reacquaint himself with his boy, they said nothing. Meanwhile, Jordan spoke often with his brothers in the States. They urged him to cross the Atlantic and try his luck in America.

Finally, Jordan made the call that changed his life. "If you're serious, I'm ready," he told Chris.

The rest, as the cliché went, was history. Jameson flew Jordan over and began working with him straightaway. Ben came to Jordan's aid, relinquishing most other commitments to concentrate on his baby brother's career. A year later, Jordan topped billboard charts around the world.

For all his irascibility and impossible expectations, Jameson had made it happen for him. Now, if Farin would let him, he would do the same for her.

"I wonder what's taking so long," the woman said.

Jordan craned his neck toward the front of the queue. "I've no idea."

She shifted her weight from one leg to the other.

"Are you meeting someone here, too?"

"Nothing romantic on my end, I'm afraid. Just business."

Air travel reminded him of endless, trans-Atlantic flights. Notably, his trip to England to retrieve his son. He had arrived in front of his childhood home driving the exact new luxury car his father had talked about for a year.

George Grant loved Cadillacs. When Jordan had arrived in Bledlow driving that year's Seville, Dad sounded more interested in the car than his youngest son. "This must have cost a fortune, what with import tax and European modifications."

"It's not mine. I'm only borrowing it while I'm here."

When the time came to leave, Jordan asked his father to drive them to the airport. "You can return the Caddie to the owner for me."

"Is it far, Jorie?" Mum had asked. "Should I follow?"

"The owner will get you back home, but come along for the drive."

The entire way to Heathrow, Dad discussed the car's various specs. He acted like a child in a toy store with a thousand-pound note.

From the passenger seat, Mum had said, "I love these leather seats."

"Listen to that engine," Dad had said. "Instead of going to a six-cylinder engine, they took the four-point-one-liter v-eight and turned it sideways to bolt it to a four-speed overdrive automatic transaxle!"

"Look at all the gadgets on the dashboard! Is that a cassette player?"

Dad had regarded her, incredulous. "Driver information center. Gives you the engine readouts and fuel economy. This beauty's front-wheel drive and has automatic overdrive transmission! Did you know that? Its independent suspension uses MacPherson struts in the front, a transverse fiberglass leaf spring in the rear, and an electronic level control. The power-assisted rack-and-pinion steering makes it a cinch to maneuver—"

"Oh, George!" Mum flipped down the visor. "The mirror has little lights all around it!"

"It's a third-generation model, you understand. They took off over forty-two centimeters in length and lightened 'er up by three-hundred, seventeen pounds," Dad had said in amazement. "Smooth and steady! I can't feel a single bump in the road!"

At Heathrow, Jordan's father helped him unload the luggage from the trunk. Mum wept and cradled Chase as if she would never see him again. They made small talk as they escorted him to the gate.

Never a demonstrative man, his father had clasped his shoulder and shook his hand. "You make the lot, now, son. All you little pikers are finally out from underfoot. Maybe I'll take your mum on a second honeymoon."

Mum had giggled. She batted at her husband's arm, then turned to

Jordan. "Oh, Jorie, do ring us and let us talk to Chase. And meet a nice girl. You don't take care of yourself."

When their flight was announced, Jordan had hugged his parents. His dad pushed him away and both men wiped their eyes a bit.

"So where does that magnificent marvel of modern engineering go, then?"

Jordan handed him the vehicle's title. "The details are all right here."

His father stared open-mouthed at the typed print that bore his own name and address. "What? How?"

Mum went to his side. When she read the title, her eyes bulged.

"Thanks, Dad, Mum. I hope I can be half as good with Chase as you've been with all of us." With that, he and his son had boarded the plane.

"Okay, here we go," the woman said as the queue began inching forward.

"Finally," Jordan said.

"It was nice talking with you."

"You too."

"I almost wish I was flying back with you," she said as they strolled up the jet bridge. "I'm dying to know how she reacts when she sees you!"

Jordan habitually surprised those he loved. He could not wait to get to the Plaza. Farin had entered his life like an answered prayer. For months, they had shared their lives and his bed. A bed he had realized this morning felt lonely without her.

She was his dream come true. He had fallen in love with her. And tonight, he would make sure she knew it.

***

Chris said nothing. Instead, he moved aside, bowed, and extended an arm in a grand flourish as he opened the door.

Farin stepped inside. Her eyes darted about the foyer, searching for some visual ground upon which she might anchor her attention. "I'm here, as promised. Something smells good."

"Do you like duck?"

"Never had it."

He looked her over with hungry eyes. "A night for firsts. My favorite."

She tucked her hair behind her ear, set her purse on the entryway table, then shed her coat. He moved to assist, then hovered behind her.

"You smell good," he said. "Much better than the duck."

When she turned to take her coat, he held it tight. Somewhere between the prolonged nearness and the intoxicating allure of his cologne, her heart began thumping. Always hypnotic aromas with him. Always breaching her personal space.

She tossed her head, slid out of her shoes, and surrendered the jacket, wandering barefoot into his lair. "You and Jameson must use the same interior decorator."

He hung up her coat, then joined her. "I suppose we share certain tastes."

His place looked nothing like she had expected, whatever that might have been. Contrived more sensibly than one might expect from such an infamous playboy. Victorian in fashion. Antiques and collectibles perched and peeked out ostentatiously from floor to walls to ceiling. Classical music filled the air. It made her feel regal. And underdressed.

Well, until Chris opened his mouth.

He offered her a seat on his Louis V sofa. "Dinner's almost done. Fancy a drink? I have an eighty-two Château Margaux breathing in the kitchen. Unless you prefer something...harder?"

His tongue poked at the inside of his cheek, stifling a smile as he traipsed off to procure her drink, seemingly satisfied with her inability to relax. The lust-fueled fantasies she employed to slay her nightmares toyed with her mind, leaving her guilt-ridden and uncomfortable, like the sofa upon which she dithered, awaiting his return. Her thoughts turned to LA.

"You didn't talk to Jordan this afternoon, did you?" she asked when he returned with two glasses of Bordeaux.

"Why? Trouble in Dreamland?" When she accepted the wine, his finger brushed her hand.

"Chris, please don't—"

"Make yourself at home. I'll meet you in the dining room." He strolled, glass in hand, back to the kitchen.

Farin watched him retreat, then glimpsed the formal dining table far across the penthouse. Unlit taper candles and two place settings occupied its space, which would effortlessly accommodate a dozen people. She wondered if Chris entertained much, or whether he hosted orgies.

One thing was certain. It was useless—and dangerous—to stay.

She set her wineglass on the coffee table, then stood up. As an afterthought, she snatched the glass back up, downed its contents, then tiptoed toward the foyer.

It was unfair that Jordan was stuck thousands of miles away while Chris inhabited her line of sight, a virile, vital man. Jordan should be celebrating her good news with her, not Chris.

She slid into her flats and collected her coat and purse. Garlic, wine, and musk filled her nostrils. Her stomach wambled, protesting its empty state. She had not eaten since breakfast.

"Where are you going?" Chris hurried over, a desperate edge to his voice.

She twirled around, sifting her hair with trembling fingers, still unable to meet his gaze. "This was a bad idea."

"Don't go. Everything's ready."

"I have to."

He reached out but did not make contact. "I'm sorry. I know I made you uncomfortable. Please, stay and eat."

She bit her lip and tried to steady her pulse.

"You can't blame me for finding you so attractive."

She grasped and yanked the doorknob.

He caught her arm. "No-no. I'll stop."

Her head spun as he closed the distance between them. Why did he stand so close? She heard his breathing quicken, or was it hers? If she had only made it out the door.

"It's just dinner."

"Promise?"

"Whatever you what."

"Okay. But I'm leaving as soon as we're done." She abhorred the tremor in her voice. Even more, she hated the cocky expression on his face that told her he had heard it.

Chris pulled out her chair, lit the candles, then sat opposite her at the head of his cherrywood dining table. They ate in cacophonous silence.

He tried not to stare. Not to fawn over her perfection in the flickering candlelight. Not to revel in her frequent hip-shifts and shoulder rolls as she devoured her meal with equal parts gusto and nervosity. He longed to see the glow of her naked body in the dimness of his bedroom. She had stayed for dinner. Certainly, she would stay for more.

"When's your flight back?"

"Wednesday. Bill Taft's already scheduled a meeting for Friday. I don't know. Everything's happening so fast."

"I actually know Bill. Well, I've met him."

"Jameson says he's the right fit. I guess we'll see."

Chris spoke between mouthfuls and occasional sips of wine. "I still can't believe Jameson signed you. And you say he's having you change your name?"

Farin nodded, savoring the roast duck, red potatoes, and fresh asparagus tips. "Yeah, well. That's the one problem I have. I like my name."

"What did Jordan say about it?" he asked coolly.

"I had to leave a message. He's been busy with tour prep."

Chris opened his mouth, then stopped short, rattling his head as he chuckled low and quiet.

"What?"

"Nothing."

She furrowed her brow. "Tell me."

He dabbed the corner of his mouth with his napkin. "It's curious you two haven't moved in together yet. Frankly, I'm surprised Jordan hasn't proposed. He's mad about you. He's told the whole family."

Farin skewered a forkful of asparagus. "That's none of your business."

"But supposing he did ask?"

"We've never discussed it, if you must know." She dropped her fork onto her plate, then pushed it away. "And since you asked, I'm a little curious myself. Why are you so interested in my personal life?"

His gaze locked upon her as if through the crosshairs of a sight. He leaned forward. "Do you really want to know?"

She paled, then swallowed hard.

And, bullseye.

He pushed back his plate as well. Dinner was over. Time to move on to the next course.

***

When Jordan reached the Plaza Hotel and found Farin away, he called home to check his messages. Chris had invited her out to dinner. Good. He had hoped they would get a chance to see each other.

Since learning of Farin's lack of family, he had hoped to share his own as a surrogate. She had already grown close to Ben and Cheryl, both of whom she now spoke with on a regular basis. She had even accompanied him not too long ago for a weekend getaway in Florida. Maybe after this visit she would develop a better relationship with Chris as well.

He dug into his front pocket and pulled out his keychain. Fortunately, he still had the house key Chris gave him a couple years back. He had failed to return it.

Perfect. He would go over and wait for them to return from dinner. Then, if they felt up to it, they could all go out and celebrate Farin's good news.

He removed the key from the chain, popped it into his trouser pocket, left the keychain on the hotel desk next to the phone, then called the front desk to arrange for a taxi.

***

Chris rose from his chair and ambled her way. "You want answers? I'll tell you whatever you want to know. Where should we start?"

Farin looked down and away as he propped himself against the table before her. Every cell in her body pulsated. Red wine, duck, asparagus, and red potatoes churned in her stomach. She wondered what Jordan might be doing at this moment, three thousand miles away from Chris's penthouse.

He inched closer. "Well?"

She sprang from her chair and double-stepped toward the door. "I have to go. You said you'd understand."

He called after her. "Is that what I said?"

"Thanks for dinner. It was great."

"No dessert?"

She snatched her purse off the cocktail table without breaking stride.

Chris followed, close on her heel. "Why don't you say it?"

She hastened to the door, then stopped short, as if an afterthought. Plunging a shaking hand into her purse, she felt around until she found the gift box. She stretched out her hand, averting her eyes. "Here. I can't accept this."

"What are you so afraid of?"

She yanked open the door. "I told you before. I'm not afraid."

"You were lying before...and you're lying now." He reached around her and pushed the door closed, then turned the lock. A moment later, his hands were on her upper arms, pulling her to him. "Your heart's racing. Can you feel mine?"

She fused her eyes. Maybe by doing so, she could shut out the stirring he evoked in the deepest part of her being. She tried to think of Jordan, but all resolution faded into a pale blur at the feel of Chris's hot breath on her neck.

"I've wanted you since the first moment I saw you," he growled.

"Let me go, Chris. This is wrong."

"Tell me you want me."

He pulled her closer. She felt his arousal against her, and the heat igniting between her own legs. "I...I love Jordan."

"But you want *me*." He drew her in, pressing his eager mouth to hers.

She struggled against him at first, pushing the palms of her opened hands against his shoulders. She moved her neck back and side-to-side to escape his arms and the impact of his kiss.

For a split second, he considered releasing her. He had promised himself she would come willingly into his arms. He was Chris Grant. Never had he forced a woman into his bed. Never had he needed to. Farin's resistance baffled and frustrated him. Had he been wrong about her?

Then, almost imperceptibly, he felt her abandoned the fight. Her hands relaxed. The tension in her arms eased. She clutched a handful of his hair and kissed him hard.

The shift galvanized his resolve. All the days, all the weeks, all the months of lying alone in his bed at night, or next to some woman he cared so little for it amounted to the same thing. Those nights were over now.

Suddenly, the door before them opened. Farin's eyes widened in horror as she tore away from his embrace. Her mouth dropped open in panic.

Jordan stood before them, his hands still on the key and doorknob. He blinked unbelievingly at Farin, then Chris, then back to Farin. Stunned with realization, his face flushed. His eyes grew cold. A vein popped out in his neck and another in his forehead.

Before either of them could utter a word, Jordan stormed away from the scene, leaving the key in the lock and slamming the door behind him.

Chris clenched his jaw. He stepped away, opened the door, and retrieved the abandoned key from the lock. He studied it, vaguely recalling having given it to Jordan some time back. How ironic that he had chosen this night to use it the first time.

He tucked the key into his pocket, then returned to Farin. Reaching out, he asked, "Where were we?"

Aghast, Farin slapped him across the face and fled.

CHAPTER 11

For two weeks, Marci witnessed Farin rip herself to shreds. Mostly, Farin stayed in her room. Marci heard the sobs through her friend's locked door.

"Do you need me?"

"Go away."

"Farin, please let me help."

But no amount of coaxing worked. She refused to leave the house, or her room, except for studio sessions. Even then, their brief interactions resulted in bickering over trivial matters. As penance for her sin, Farin neither ate nor slept, and she declined all telephone calls.

Yes, the calls. Beth O'Conner's occasional attempts to connect with her only child had increased tenfold. The woman sounded worse than ever. Marci now worried for Beth's emotional *and* physical wellbeing.

Marci had watched Beth's steady decline from loving wife and mother to bitter alcoholic following Kelley's death. Initially, Farin had remained loyal to her surviving parent. She overlooked the fact that her own mother no longer got out of bed to prepare lunches or drive her to school. Farin assumed every household chore she could manage.

When school counselors had grown concerned about her home life, Farin blamed herself for her sudden lack of attention to personal hygiene. No one but Marci saw the occasional bruises. Farin had sworn her to secrecy on the honor of their friendship.

But soon, Farin could no longer convince school authorities the O'Conner home still provided a safe and nurturing environment for a child of ten. Pale and undernourished, her spirit had withered.

Resentment sprung up between mother and daughter. Farin withdrew from the world. Within six months of Kelley O'Conner's death, Farin had moved in with Marci's family to avoid the inevitable. Joseph Williams received word that Family Court Services planned to intervene.

Years apart had not reconciled them. While many in their Santa Barbara community pitied the poor widow who had succumbed to despair and grief, Farin suffered the betrayal of her mother's virtual abandonment. In the end, Farin left Santa Barbara to pursue her dreams, swearing to never look back.

Since then, Marci had become a reluctant mediator, relaying news of Farin's career to Beth, who still longed to be part of her life.

Curiously, when Marci had shared the good news that Farin had signed a contract with Lockhardt Sound, Beth had become incensed. An indiscernible rant had ensued. Beth's alcoholic cravings were all she had left. Local liquor stores had become pseudo-beneficiaries of her portion of her husband's life insurance and their once-hefty savings. Soon, Marci's father had confided, the bank would take the house.

Marci feared that losing her childhood home would destroy Farin. Kelley O'Conner's ghost still inhabited its space. After everything Farin had done to maintain her father's memory, this might be the fatal blow.

Worse than Beth's uptick in communication, another caller had added to Farin's misery.

"She doesn't want to talk to you, you weasel. *Ever.* Leave her alone."

"You certainly dislike me, don't you?" Chris had grumbled, no hint of regret in his tone.

"I guess money and celebrity aren't everything, huh?"

"Is that so?"

She hung up. The man was impossible.

Each time the phone rang, Marci grew wearier. The turning point came when Bill Taft called on a business matter.

"I'll see if she's in, Bill. Hold on a sec."

Marci marched to Farin's door, closed her eyes, and drew in a deep breath. She tested the doorknob, then exhaled, relieved to find it unlocked.

Inside, Farin lay atop her bed, curled up with a pillow. Cheap Trick's "The Flame" played on her cassette player. She stared at the far wall and did not give Marci as much as a glance before demanding, "Get out."

"Bill Taft's on the phone."

"Take a message."

"It's business, Farin. Hasn't the self-pity lasted long enough?"

Farin's nostrils flared. She jerked herself out of bed, stabbed the "stop" button on the player, then stomped down the hallway, vowing to have another line installed so she could take future calls in her room.

Bill Taft was a friendly, supportive man, like Donovan before him. But unlike Donovan, Bill was a competent, punctual professional. On days like today, those qualities irritated her.

Somehow, Farin had shelved her situation with Jordan long enough to meet Bill upon returning from New York. A bespectacled, rotund forty-something with bad skin and capped teeth, he wore a constant smile. The contrast of his Polo shirts, khakis, and convivial nature against Jameson's more fastidious, suited pomposity made theirs a curious association.

Farin snatched the receiver off the kitchen table, dreading the idea of waxing happy when her life had gone off a cliff.

"Our first official business call! So, first things first—how are you?"

She studied her reflection in the kitchen window as the afternoon sun cast a mirror-like reflection over the glass. Her hair sat wrecked and stringy atop her head. Days-old makeup applied before her last studio session smeared across her face. She had not changed clothes in days. "Never felt better."

"Awesome! Listen, I know it's short notice, but Lockhardt Junior's flying in next week. It's publicity time. He's scheduled a photo shoot."

Pictures. Just what she needed.

She made note of the pertinent details, then ended the call as soon as she could. When she turned to go back to her room, Marci stood in the kitchen doorway, arms crossed, blocking her way.

"You're not going back to bed."

"Oh really?"

Marci pointed to the kitchen chairs. "We need to talk."

"About what?"

"Last time I checked, I wasn't your secretary."

"Then don't be."

"Fine. The machine can take the calls. You can sort through the messages yourself."

"Whatever."

Marci collapse into a kitchen chair, her face contorted in disgust. "You need to decide, Farin. You need to decide what's more important—your career or your love life."

"All this about phone calls?"

"It's beyond phone calls. But, okay. Chris, I understand, but your *agent*? And your mother's tried to reach you for weeks."

"Why? You tell her everything going on in my life anyway."

"You know what? You seemed happy for a while—*truly* happy. Can't you call Jordan and explain things the way you explained them to me?"

Farin's eyes arched in sadness above quivering lips. "Because there's a For Sale sign hanging on his gate. He's gone and it's my fault. You can't blame it all on Chris. We both know what would've happened if Jordan hadn't walked in on us."

"Have you tried Cheryl or Ben?"

"I can't drag them into this." She sank sorrowfully into the chair opposite Marci and dropped her head atop her folded arms.

"You can't beat yourself up forever. It was just a kiss."

Farin glanced up at her. "Was it?"

***

Bobby Lockhardt was an ideal, albeit unanticipated, diversion. They met for a lengthy photo session in West Hollywood on Thursday afternoon. It started out slow, but Bobby's magnetism soon had Farin feeling refreshed, bright, and almost winsome.

"Remember, you're a pop star! What's this face? Are we going goth? Where's makeup?"

The pressure was enormous, despite having done a dozen previous photo shoots over the years.

"You're *selling*! Don't scare away the fans! Show me those pearly whites!"

When Farin realized the photographer had grown agitated with Bobby's backseat direction, she laughed despite herself.

"That's my girl!"

Dinner at Spago was an unexpected extension to their day, and not an unwelcome one. It permitted her to get to know Bobby better. He made a handsome, distinguished escort.

She sipped champagne, ordered lobster, and they laughed over appetizers. The more champagne he poured, the more she relaxed.

"I don't get it. How is it you don't have a girlfriend? You could have anyone! You're smart, attentive—"

He raised his highball and gave her a sideways glance. "Charming."

She touched her flute to his glass. "Charming, yes."

"And sensitive, Farin. I'm very sensitive."

She laughed until her sides ached. "So...? What's the deal?"

She had answered his questions about her life, avoiding those pertaining to her father or her situation with Jordan. Now, it was his turn.

"What's it like working for your dad?"

He smoothed his tie against his chest. "Now-now, we agreed. Family's off limits."

"Okay." She nested her chin into her open palm and glanced upward in thought. "What do you want most in life?"

He dodged the inquiry. When she pressed him, his mood shifted. His captivating smile faded to a nebulous expression she could not label.

"C'mon," she urged as he poured the last of the champagne into her flute and signaled their waiter for another bottle.

"I have no personal life," he stated matter-of-factly. "What I want most is to show my dad LSI will be fine when he retires. In case you haven't noticed, he's not getting any younger. A personal life doesn't fit into my schedule."

"But aren't you lonely?"

He shrugged, redirecting his focus to his salad.

"I mean, you're a nice guy. You can't work your whole life with nothing to show for it. Don't you want to get married? Have kids?" Farin considered her words. Somehow, she could not picture Jameson Lockhardt bouncing a brood of toddlers on his knee.

Bobby laid his fork against his plate, tines down. The ease of their earlier conversation died, as if a black cloud had settled over their table.

For a while, he stared at her. Farin could not discern the unspoken warning his blue eyes held. The hair on the back of her neck stood on end.

When the waiter served their entrees, she offered the man a weak smile, grateful for the interruption, but said nothing. She squeezed a lemon slice over her lobster.

"I'll have something to show for my life," Bobby said at last. "I'll have the most important thing—the only thing. I'll have LSI. But I didn't fly out here to talk about me. You're the reason for this visit."

As he spoke, Farin noticed a subtle twitching of his left eye. Almost a wink, but not. It shut his lids, drawing up his cheek in a spasm. It distorted his smoothly handsome features, making them appear oddly twisted. Seconds later, it subsided.

She regretted upsetting him. Facial tic aside, he was a perfect gentleman. He opened doors for her, pulled out her chair, ordered her meal. Mostly, he kept her mind off her troubles.

As they enjoyed an after-dinner coffee, Ginny Stevens glided into the restaurant. Her arrival sent Farin back in her seat, and back to Le Dome. But tonight, there was no paparazzi, no camera flashes, and no reporters firing questions at her machine-gun style.

Unfortunately, Ginny noticed Farin as well.

As always, the actress dressed in the finest silk and draped her hand on the arm of one of the most eligible men in the country. Her attractive escort looked askance at Farin and Bobby. Farin recognized him as the prominent plastic surgeon Marci had pointed out in one of her magazines. Tabloids claimed he had proposed. A stolen glance at Ginny's left hand revealed no sign of an engagement ring.

Ginny Stevens's career had plummeted since the network killed off Chrissy Bryant. They had gone ahead with the plan to have Chrissy shot. For several episodes, Chrissy lay in a hospital bed, hooked up to an array of tubing and faux monitors. Ginny had complained between takes about her character's lack of lines. The director explained coma patients did not speak.

Weeks later, much to Ginny's surprise, the monitors flat-lined. Now, *Texas Tea*'s Tim Bryant had an old flame comforting him over Chrissy's unexpected death.

Rumor had it Ginny had burned a bridge. She had not worked since.

"Is this the flavor of the week?" she spat in Farin's direction, head high as the host escorted her and her date to their table.

The accusation sent Farin's mind anew to the For Sale sign in Malibu. She endeavored to ignore the snide comment. A tall order.

The women exchanged acid glances. Farin straightened in her chair and glared into the actress's cold steel eyes. Never would she buckle publicly, no matter what transpired in her private life.

Her eyes narrowed in mock curiosity. She inspected the details of Ginny's near-perfect features, then turned to Ginny's escort, running the underside of her hand along her own jaw line. "You missed a spot."

A certain satisfaction rose within her as Ginny and her date retreated to their table, but the mood passed as fresh remorse engulfed her.

Bobby laughed as they retreated in an indignant huff. "Aw, c'mon Ginny. Don't go away mad..." Turning back to Farin, he added more quietly, "...just go away."

Farin picked up her napkin and dabbed at her eyes.

"Hey." Bobby scooted close and touched her shoulder. "What's wrong?"

She shook her head.

"I was only having fun. I didn't mean to embarrass you."

Farin sniffed. "You didn't."

Then, the floodgates opened. Unable to stop herself, she divulged the entire account of her would-be tryst with Chris Grant.

When the waiter passed, Bobby stopped him and ordered her a whiskey.

He listened intently, scoffing, shaking his head, and widening his eyes in all the appropriate places. Shushing and calming her as she released weeks of guilty pain.

"Maybe we should move this session to the limo," he suggested when they had started attracting the attention of fellow diners. "I'm happy to hear you out, but this isn't exactly my area of expertise."

"I don't know what to do," she continued, folding her napkin for the umpteenth time and dabbing her eyes.

He signaled for the check. "Let's figure it out elsewhere. You belong to LSI now. This isn't the sorta press we're after."

Farin got to the part about the For Sale sign as they climbed inside the limousine. With that, she dissolved into a crying jag.

"Chris Grant." Bobby wrapped an awkward arm around her. "I could've told you he's bad news. On the upside, I think I can help. I know for a fact Jordan's in Florida."

Her cries ceased.

He reached inside his suit jacket and retrieved a blue silk handkerchief, then handed it over. "He's shooting a video in New York next week. You should fly back with me Sunday. It'd give you guys a chance to talk."

Through moist, mascara-smeared eyes, Farin smiled sincerely for the first time in weeks. She accepted the handkerchief, then crouched down to fix her face in the mirror behind the bar. "Bobby Lockhardt, you just became my favorite person in the world."

***

Ben called the night Farin packed for her trip. He kept the conversation light, at first. Cheryl and the boys were fine. He had made progress on Jordan's next album. He congratulated her on her contract and apologized for not having called sooner. But once Farin told him she knew Jordan's current whereabouts, his demeanor changed.

"I wasn't surprised. I told you—I know my brother."

She clamped the phone between her ear and shoulder as she hefted her packed suitcase off her bed. "I tried to leave."

"And probably bruised his ego in the process. He's been this way since puberty. Hell, maybe before."

She sat on the edge of her bed, hanging on his every word. "If you know all this, why doesn't Jordan? He *moved*, Ben."

"He knows, Farin. And I've tried to talk to him. He's too busy being angry and hurt to think. Yes, leaving California was impulsive. But it was the right thing to do. It's not you. Chase dying like that...it shattered him. He sees this as another loss."

The hope sustaining her since Bobby's invitation to accompany him back home waned. "Bobby Lockhardt's flying me to New York tomorrow. I know Jordan's there. I have to see him."

A pause filled the line. "I don't know if he's ready yet, kid."

Ben's warning stung, but Farin envied Jordan and Chris having someone so loyal to protect them.

When their call ended, Farin left her room in search of Marci. She owed her friend an apology.

***

Jordan arrived at the Greenwich Village studios an hour early. Anything was better than pacing his Plaza Hotel suite.

Shortly after checking in last night, Chris had called him, claiming to want to make peace. Jordan refused an invitation to dinner.

"I'm moving," Chris announced before he could hang up in his ear.

"Brilliant," Jordan spat. "Back to England, I hope."

"Ben was right."

"Ben's always right. What's your point?"

"I'm moving to Key Biscayne. I've already bought the house. We all need to be closer."

Jordan almost hung up anyway.

"Don't blame Farin, mate. It was me. Let me make things right."

Hearing her name on his brother's lips enraged him. He slammed down the phone, then rang the front desk to hold further calls.

Make things right?

Chris was the family playboy. The black sheep. Fine. Everyone knew his track record with women. But Jordan had never expected Chris to pursue *his* woman. Nor had he expected his woman would let herself be caught.

Jordan's fury did not end at Chris's door, however. Or even Farin's. The responsibility lay squarely with him. *He* had pushed them together. *He* suggested she call Chris. *He* asked his brother to watch over her. His eagerness for Farin to bond with his family had led them all to this dark place.

Even still, he had seen them—the way they looked at each other. There she had stood, wrapped in Chris's arms, no hint of reservation on her face. Her fingers had clutched Chris's hair.

Chris had claimed fault, but Farin could have left. She *should* have left.

Jordan glanced at his watch and, seeing it was time to get to makeup, headed down the long corridor behind the set. Time to pull himself together. His losses had mounted over the months. He would not add his career to the tally.

As he passed the back door, he saw her.

Followed closely by Bobby Lockhardt, her pale face and the black circles under her eyes stunned him as much as her unanticipated presence. His anger collided with genuine concern. She looked as miserable as he felt, and as beautiful as ever.

***

The combination of stress and hangover made Bobby's tour unbearable. Instead of marveling at the behind-the-scenes peek at the Lockhardt production studios—studios she would doubtless utilize herself one day soon—she squinted through bleary eyes, searching for any sign of Jordan.

Since the photo shoot, Farin and Bobby had spent little time apart. He accompanied her to her recording sessions. They met early for breakfast, had lunch, went shopping, dined and danced at the hottest clubs in LA well into early morning hours, only to repeat the cycle hours later. It was bottomless champagne for her; vodka and lime for him, with "enough soda to make it fizz." But unlike her, Bobby suffered no outward effects.

Her plan to sleep on the flight had failed, leaving her as exhausted as she was determined.

"For lunch, I'm treating you to the best hot dog in the city," he announced as his tour ended. "That is, if you and Jordan aren't making up in his dressing room by then."

"If only it were that easy."

"It'll cure what ails you." He nudged her arm and inclined his chin toward a group of people near Jordan's set.

Nausea bubbled up inside her belly as she turned and saw him. He stood with Samantha Drake. At first, she thought he saw her, too, but he turned his attention back to their conversation.

Bobby called out, "Sam! There you are!"

Farin's head throbbed. She needed caffeine. And aspirin.

Bobby strode toward Samantha as if something urgent weighed on his mind. He dragged Farin along beside him.

Samantha spared him a casual glance, then held up a finger to finish her conversation.

He would not be ignored. "I need to discuss this new development. I just got back from LA. We need to get you up to speed!"

"What are you talking about?"

He regarded her with an incredulous jaw-drop. "You haven't heard?" He glanced to his left. "Hey, Jordan. How's it going?"

Jordan set his jaw and focused on Samantha.

"Bobby, what are you talking about? No one informed me—"

"Let's go back to the office. We need Ross." Bobby linked his arm in hers and marched off.

"But Jordan's shoot—"

He waved a hand in the air. "Psh! He'll be fine. He's a pro. Done it a million times."

Samantha continued her verbal protest as Bobby led her off the set.

Engulfed in silence despite the bustling set, Farin and Jordan looked cautiously at one another. She wanted to rush into his arms, but his censuring glare warned her off.

She managed a faint "hi," fearing she might vomit.

Jordan crossed his arms.

"Surprised to see me?"

"Not particularly. You're with LSI now."

Her heart sank as he turned to leave. "Wait, Jordan...please?"

He stared through her. "I can't do this right now."

"Please. I flew all the way out here to talk to you." She reached for him but he jerked away.

Jordan sprouted a mocking smile. "Then I guess your trip's as futile as the one I made to see you."

She lowered her head. "I deserve that."

"Yes. You do." He disappeared down the corridor without a backward glance.

***

"Pride," Bobby said around a mouthful of hot dog as they strolled along Sixth Avenue, intermingling with the bustling noonday crowd of business professionals procuring their lunch. "He'll come around."

The gray, windy day mirrored Farin's disposition as they trudged along. Fall had finally arrived...so close to the holidays and so far from the brief contentment of June.

"I talked to my dad," Bobby continued, picking at the crumbs in the paper hot dog bun tray. "He said you should follow him to Florida."

"What?" She stopped short, suspending the steady flow of pedestrians. They grumbled and protested as they passed.

"He said Jordan's still grieving Chase and probably doesn't know what the hell's good for him right now."

"You told Jameson about this?"

He gave her an innocent shrug. "He asked about you."

Farin peered beyond the crowd with sightless eyes, conflicted at Bobby's indiscretion.

"You really made an impression on him. I'm almost jealous. Here I thought I was an only child." He chuckled, then fake-punched her shoulder.

She stared back at him, unamused.

He gathered their trash, tossed it into a nearby receptacle, then swiped his hands. "Anyway, if you decide to do it—move, that is—he said to let him know."

"I can't...*move.*" She tucked a strand of curls behind her ear, toying with the idea nonetheless.

"You said you loved him."

"I do."

For the second time since they met, Bobby's mood made a dark, ominous shift. His smile vanished. His tone adopted the same air of mystery she had felt crawl under her skin at Spago. "Sometimes you have to make sacrifices for the people you love."

"Have you ever been in love, Bobby Lockhardt?" She elbowed him, lips curled into a coy smile. "Is that why you're telling me all this?"

Bobby's face tensed. Again, his left eye spasmed. "No. But if I ever am, nothing will come between us—least of all three thousand miles of land."

Farin said little as they returned. Her head no longer ached. Rather, it raced as she pondered Jameson's suggestion and Bobby's strange response to her query. Why the troubled reaction? Had his parents' separation many years earlier traumatized him? Could she abandon Marci to follow Jordan across the country? Did Jordan even want her anymore?

She marched back to the studio, resolved to work it out, shoot or no shoot. But when they arrived, the set was quiet and near-empty. Jordan was nowhere to be seen.

Two dancers gossiped on the sidelines about an injury. Fearing the worst, she searched the dressing rooms. Jordan occupied the last room to the right. He sat on a worn, cream-colored sofa, his head buried in his hands.

He looked up when she walked in. "What are you doing here?"

"Can we talk? I heard there was a setback."

Jordan searched her eyes. "What's there to talk about?"

"Well...us."

He scoffed bitterly, leaned back, and combed his fingers through his hair. "*Us*?" he echoed.

"If you'd let me explain—"

"I'm not blind." He fused his jaw.

"I didn't even want to be there! I wanted to be with *you*."

"So what? Now you're Stephen Stills? Love the one you're with?"

Farin rubbed her left arm. "I'm sorry."

Jordan made no move to comfort her. He stared at the floor as the image of them together gut-punched him. Was this anything less than an encore performance of Ginny's betrayal? Still, was he prepared to let her go—to end it?

"Five minutes," he said.

He listened to her heartfelt apologies, livid as she relayed the details of Chris's subtle manipulations. Despite himself, he believed her. But before he reached for her, blindly forgiving all, he hesitated. "I know what I saw, Farin."

Her arms flailed in frustration and regret. "Nothing happened! I left right after you did. I went to try to find you! I don't want him, Jordan—I want *you*. I'm glad you walked in when you did. I love you!"

Jordan flew to his feet. They faced each other, both shocked and hushed at the unplanned declaration. Guilty tears welled in her eyes. He remained still, deflated, jaw clenched in stubborn resistance.

She sobbed into her hands. "I'm sorry. I can't bear standing here and not having you hold me. It can't end like this, can it?"

His body quaked as her words bored into him. "I need time, Farin. This doesn't stop because you're sad and sorry. I don't know what to think, or feel. Maybe we can have dinner tonight. For now, you need to leave. I can't do my job with you here."

She lunged forward and threw her arms around his neck. Body-wracking sobs escaped her as she buried her head in the nape of his neck. "I'm so sorry."

Jordan's eyes fused shut. He wanted to block out her nearness. He did not want to feel her touch. The touch that drove him from Los Angeles. The touch that woke him at night, calling her name and reaching beside him only to find cold pillows and empty sheets.

He stood motionless, arms flapping at his sides as he defied his longing to reach around and return the embrace. His conscious mind demanded he push her away.

But in the end, his will faltered. He wrapped her in his arms. "I do love you, Farin. I should have told you sooner. I should have realized sooner."

***

Farin sat on her bed, her damp hair wrapped turban-like in a towel. Her eyes flitted intermittently between the television and the task at hand. Since signing with LSI, she no longer watched MTV for entertainment— she studied it for research.

The folds of her plush hotel robe parted as she drew up one leg to access her toenails. She twisted lengthwise the long length of toilet paper she had procured from the bathroom and wove it between her toes as she sang along with "Groovy Kind of Love."

The idea of meeting Jordan for dinner left her nervous, but hopeful. Dozens of possible scenarios, good and bad, scurried through her mind. She grabbed the remote from beside her and increased the volume. Maybe Phil Collins's amplified voice would drive away her fears.

If Jordan did not want her back, he would have never suggested they meet.

She rummaged through the few nail polish bottles she had thrown into her bag, decided on a shade of red, then shook the bottle of Avon Single Stroke. Nineteen eighty-eight might be the year of fuchsia, but the popular color did nothing but clash with her hair.

Besides, red looked best with her black dress. The same dress she had worn the night they met. The same dress her mother hated. More like a crutch than a habit, it was her default evening wear. She had purchased it the day before she had left Santa Barbara for Los Angeles—primarily out of spite.

"When I die, don't let anyone come to my funeral in black," her mother had slurred more than stated during a drunken, stream-of-consciousness rant. "Promise me."

Farin gnawed absently at the inside of her cheek as she inspected her finished toenails, then hobbled into the bathroom, tissue still woven between her toes, to do her hair and makeup before painting her fingernails. She unwrapped the towel from around her head, then shook out her coppery ringlets. What would it be tonight? Banked curls? Loose and wild?

Banked curls with a barrette won out. Understated. Timeless.

An hour later, she was ready to walk out the door...forty-five minutes early.

She sat back down on the bed, her limbs spread and splayed to allow extra time for the polish to dry, and stared from the television to the bedside clock, then back again. Anita Baker's "Giving You the Best That I Got" ended and Rod Stewart's "Forever Young" began.

A curly-haired youngster sat upon Stewart's lap as the singer rocked and sang to him. They sat in the back of a pickup truck, watching rural America disappear before them.

Farin glanced down at her attire as a wave of guilt and longing swept over her. She missed her dad. And, on some level, she missed her mother. At least the mother Beth had been before the accident. In Farin's mind, she imagined Beth scolding her for her choice of attire.

"With all the bright colors and exciting options out there these days? Honestly, Farin! How many times have I told you—any girl under the age of thirty who wears black is ill-bred and loose!"

Her parents had disagreed over this point, notably when Farin was eight. The O'Conners and the Williamses had taken a cruise to the Bahamas that spring, and had participated in a formal dinner their first night at sea. As had been Kelley's habit, he enjoyed surprising Farin with gifts. That night was no exception. As they readied themselves for their evening, he had presented her with a large, beautifully wrapped box.

Her eyes had expanded with glee. "What is it?"

"Only one way to find out," he had said with a loving smile.

She opened the box with care, squealing as she drew back the red tissue paper concealing a beautiful black and white lace dress. She leapt around the stateroom in excitement, dancing and twirling as she held it to her.

Her father nodded at the box. "Look again. You missed something."

With exaggerated care, Farin arranged the gown on her stateroom bed, then sifted through the tissue to discover a black and white beaded hair clip. "I'm gonna look like a star tonight!" She rushed into his arms, wrapped her thin limbs around his neck, and held her cheek to his, giggling as he rubbed his stubble teasingly against the softness of her skin. "Thank you, Daddy!"

Beth appeared wearing a similar if more adult version of the dress.

Her mother had looked stunning that night. The dress had hugged her hourglass figure. When she walked, she moved with a soft grace that made other men sit up and take notice. But despite that grace and beauty, Farin had heard Beth admonish Kelley for buying such a dark dress for a child.

"It's a formal dinner," he had chided, handsome and impressive in his tuxedo. "Do you honestly think one evening dress'll corrupt her?"

He took Beth into his strong, muscular arms. Then, he straightened his posture and swept her around the compact space, dancing and humming and nibbling at her neck.

A softness blanketed Beth's exquisite features as she smiled, then giggled. "Don't you start with me, Kelley O'Conner."

She had tried to remain serious as he hummed "Let Me Call You Sweetheart" into her ear. "Children should be children. Why not something red? Or green? Why black? She's only eight!"

Kelley braced his wife's back and dipped her low, kissing her lips as he lifted her back up without missing a step. "Hush now," he sang to the melody. He finished the dance with another grand dip.

Farin rushed in from the restroom, beaming with excitement. Her parents gasped at the sight of her. She stretched out a delicate hand, the beaded clip resting in her palm. "Mommy, will you put my hair up?"

"You look like a princess." Her father gave her mother a side-eye, then nodded with delight when she smiled in concession.

Beth jutted her chin in mock stubbornness as she brushed Farin's long curls and fastened the clip, the tresses spilling down her back. "We'll let this be an exception then, won't we? It's too late to have you change. You do look beautiful, sweetheart. Now give me a kiss and let's go. You don't want to keep Marci waiting."

Farin had not thought of this memory in ages. She would never forget the way her parents looked that night. Such love. Such happiness for so many years. She still had the ensemble tucked away in her hope chest back at the house in Santa Barbara. Unless her mother had destroyed it like she tried to destroy her father's records.

When it was time to go, Farin stood up, shut off the TV in the middle of the Escape Club's "Wild, Wild West," and scrutinized herself in the hall mirror while stepping into her shoes. She smoothed down her dress. It had no lace. No matching beaded clip suspended her curls out of her face. It would not be as easy as waltzing Jordan around the restaurant, humming in his ear.

Things had been easy at eight.

***

The restaurant Jordan chose mesmerized Farin. A chandelier hung high off the middle of its domed ceiling. A center wall boasted recessed black-and-white circus-themed sketches backlit with golden light. The exterior wall consisted almost entirely of arched glass decked out with pleated window treatments. The enormity of the space engulfed them, while the low lighting and lush black and gold upholstery of their intimate booth guarded their privacy.

They made small talk over dinner, as if ignoring their problem would solve it. Jordan noticed how stunning Farin looked and how hard she tried to make the evening special. She kept their conversation lively, sparkling at his every word. For his part, he felt frozen somewhere between renewed passion and first-time jitters.

"But where do we go from here?" she asked as the waiter delivered their entrées. "I can't bear going back without you."

"It's not that simple. I need to know how you feel about Chris, and what we're going to do about it."

Her brilliant smile dimmed. "But it *is* simple. I won't see him again."

Jordan stared at his plate. "He's my brother."

"Things would be fine if he'd leave me alone."

"I love you, Farin, but we can't have a three-way rivalry. Frankly, I'm more concerned with the way you feel about him."

"There's nothing between Chris and me except what's in his mind. Please, Jordan, we *can* work this out, can't we?"

He took her hand, placing a tender kiss on her fingertips. "There's an entire country separating us now."

"You haven't sold the beach house yet. You could come back—"

His lips flattened into a sad frown as he slowly shook his head. "I needed to get out of LA. I didn't even realize it until I left, but Ben was right."

Her voice quivered. "Then what can we do?"

Jordan touched his wineglass to hers. "We're going to finish our dinner. Then we're going back to my room and I'm going to make love to you until the sun rises tomorrow morning. The last thing I want to do while we're together is worry about what we're going to do while we're apart."

Later, Farin lay distracted in thought. She had hoped Jordan would change his mind. Bobby's words echoed in her mind as she considered Jameson's recommendation.

He caressed her back, burying himself in the softness of her body. "You okay?"

"I can't relax."

"What's the problem?"

"Geography."

He rolled onto his back and stared up at the ceiling. Instinct told him not to send her back to LA without some kind of commitment. She needed it. In truth, so did he. "What if you move to Florida?"

She rolled her head across the pillow and stared at him, lips parted.

He touched her face. "This is a problem we can solve."

Hours later, Jordan watched Farin sleep, a peaceful radiance emanating from her as he stroked her hair. Perhaps tonight, the nightmares would not come.

However unplanned, this would be the true test. Chris had expressed remorse. So had she. Should he have mentioned his brother's impending move? Would it influence her decision either way?

As he buried his head beside hers, he hoped she meant what she had said about wanting him only. They would all find out soon enough.

CHAPTER 12

CHRIS CHECKED THE PENTHOUSE TO ensure the packing proceeded as planned. His bandmates had volunteered to help, though they disagreed with his decision. The movers he had hired to drive his rented moving truck to Florida would arrive first thing tomorrow and head south. An odd choice, for sure. Normally, he would have shipped his car and let professionals load his belongings, then flown down to Miami. Instead, he had decided he did not trust strangers looking through his things. Besides, he needed the two days' drive. It would give him a chance to sort his mind.

He had thought non-stop since that ill-fated evening. About his life. His future. His nature. He experienced regret for the first time in his thirty-two years. Not that Farin had been with him, but that they had been interrupted before he could seal the deal. Though his brother's pain brought him no pleasure, Chris considered it a matter of collateral damage.

Disturbingly, Chris had found himself impotent ever since. The condition so horrified him, he had consulted a specialist. Fortunately, it was nothing physical. There was another explanation. But now, not only could Chris not get Farin out of his mind, he could no longer drown his insatiable thirst in other women.

He had predicted her refusal to take his calls. No worries there. He had patience. For now, he would move south, acclimate himself to sun and sand, rebuild his broken relationship with his family...and wait.

Stopping at the bathroom, Chris found the door locked. He pounded a couple of times. "Oi! Who's in the loo?"

"Elliot," came his bass player's quiet voice.

"Pinch it off, mate. I need to whiz."

A crash from the direction of the kitchen caught his attention, but before he could investigate, Todd Dalton and Lance Turner shoved past him with his king size bed frame. "Careful, now. I don't want a lorry full of broken goods."

"Some of us actually worked for a living before Mirage, remember?" Lance chuckled. "Dalton Furniture would've been nothin' without their delivery boys, yeah?"

Mirage's thirty-four-year-old drummer was the oldest member of the band, but he refused to grow up. His baby face let him pass for a man in his twenties. He liked fast cars, rugby, and junk food. Lance was not particularly interested in women—unless of course they liked fast cars, rugby, and junk food.

When the second crash sounded, Chris dashed around his friends and into the kitchen. He found his keyboardist on her hands and knees, facing the wall, picking up shards, slivers, and chunks of broken glass.

"Nice view," he teased, his voice low and suggestive. "Why are you smashing my crystal?"

She jerked her head back at him, jade eyes aflame. "Remind me again why you didn't hire packers. Why'd you drag all of us in on it?"

"I wanted some quality time before I go." He smirked.

She made a face, then resumed searching for broken glass. Now and then, she paused to pinch off smaller splinters from the palms of her fingerless black leather gloves. "Miami's a fucking two-and-a-half-hour plane ride away. We'll see each other...at the office or something. We'll have coffee."

Faith Peterson was the only female, the only Yank, and the last to join Mirage. A spicy, redheaded ball of fire, she stood five-seven in her four-inch spiked boots. The public had never seen her without her trademark black leather wardrobe she had a body tailor-made to fit—from her black leather trench coat to her black leather string bikini. And it was not the least bit uncommon to see her sporting both at the same time.

Miss Peterson often lied about her age—not to appear younger than her thirty-three years, but older. Older men drew her in like a rabbit to a snare, something about which her bandmates reveled in heckling her. She disregarded personal boundaries, swore like a man when provoked, and was an unmerciful cocktease. Both Chris and lead singer Todd Dalton had learned this the...well, hard way.

Wicked ways aside, however, Faith was both fierce and loyal to her cohorts and would do anything for them. She would miss Chris more than he knew. More than she would ever admit.

She stood up, dumped the broken glass into the garbage, clapped and dusted off her gloves, then continued packing. "Housework sucks. You should stay here in New York instead of moving to Florida to piss off your family."

He chortled at the barb. "What's that supposed to mean?"

"Everyone knows you're chasing that new girl, Farin whatshername. You think if you stick close enough to Jordan, you'll be able to steal her."

His smile vanished.

Faith grinned triumphantly, a single brow twitching upward.

"I don't chase bird. I don't have to. And I'm not chasing Farin. Besides, women are off limits from now on. I'm giving them up and concentrating on my family."

She scoffed into her gloved palm. "The day you give up women is the day I walk through Central Park to St. Thomas Cathedral in a pink fucking polyester Sunday dress."

"Careful. I might hold you to that."

"You're not fooling any of us with this 'good boy' shit. You don't care about anyone or anything but your dick—that includes your family. You've got a massive hard-on for that chick and you'll do whatever it takes to get her. And while we're on the subject, let me give you some advice..."

"I already have a mum, Faith."

She cupped his face and peered up at him. "Jordan's one of the few men I respect. What you're doing stinks. Find someone more available. Hell, find a dozen! Go down to the backstage door at the Garden. You've done it enough."

He removed her hands and placed them at her sides. "You don't know a thing about this, and I've neither the time nor the inclination to explain."

Todd and Lance returned from the truck, beads of sweat dotting their foreheads. Todd headed for the bathroom while Lance checked the near-empty refrigerator for a beer. "Did any of the dishes make it into the carton or did she smash the bloody lot?"

She ignored the barb. "Did Chris tell you he's giving up women?"

Lance spun around and shot Chris a quizzical look. "I thought you were after that new girl."

Faith folded her arms across her chest and raised her shoulders.

Chris visually inventoried the room. "Where's Elliot? I haven't seen him in about an hour."

"The loo," Todd complained as he rejoined the others.

Lance handed him a beer. "I thought I saw him take his bass in with him."

"Did you hear Chris is giving up women?" Lance asked Todd.

He gulped his beer, then belched. "Why?"

"You're making more out of this than it is," Chris assured them amidst their laughter. "Are we about through?"

"Everything's loaded but the cartons in here," said Todd.

Faith grabbed the last beer and started down the hall. "I'll go get El."

Lance called after her. "He hates when you do that."

Moments later, Faith called for the others to join them in the bathroom. "We have the first song for our next record."

Lance arrived first. "Is that what you were doing in here, El?"

Publicly, Elliot Lawrence was an enigma. He had little to say and, seemingly, no past or present. What he did have was an innate understanding and appreciation for music, often composing entire albums in his sleep. He penned most of Mirage's songs. Recently, he had begun moonlighting, creating musical scores for major motion pictures. He was the indispensable talent behind Mirage.

"You pick the strangest places to write." Chris lifted his hand to his hips.

Elliot shrugged and tossed back his dark hair. "Acoustics. Wanna hear it?"

"I need the room first, mate," Chris said. A few moments later, the band reassembled.

Faith scowled and play-fanned the air. "What've you been eating?"

He elbowed her. "Stop it."

Elliot hummed and began to pluck his unamplified instrument. The group listened intently. The song moved a little slower, had a more romantic feel than they usually played, but it was solid, with a great beat, nice rhythm, and hot lyrics. It had definite potential.

When he played it a second time at Lance's behest, they all joined in. Lance slid his drumsticks out of his back pocket and drummed rhythmically on the bathroom counter. Todd played air guitar. Faith moved her head to the melody, harmonizing with Elliot's lyrics.

Chris bobbed his head, jaw fixed, studying them in turn. They had made it out of the armpits of show business virtually unscathed, together so long, they were like family. In fact, he had never felt this close to anyone in his own family.

But maybe that would change. He had to try. Of course, he might never get them all into one bathroom for a sing-along, but he might be able to bridge the gap between them. Bridging the miles seemed like a good first step.

Chris retrieved his guitar from his otherwise empty bedroom and rejoined the others. Elliot played the song a third time as Chris worked out the chords. A new song had been born in a now-vacant Manhattan penthouse.

Damn, he loved show business.

***

Ross Alexander rubbed his weary eyes as he lowered himself into his usual seat on the worn, tapestry-woven sofa set against the wall to the left of Jameson's desk. Their secret, after-hours meetings had become routine over the last two weeks. It was close to midnight, and Halloween to boot. Even his understanding wife had voiced suspicions.

The coupling of a single desk lamp and the illumination of surrounding skyscrapers bathed Jameson's office in an amber, preternatural glow. Shadows on the wall gave sinister overtones to the classic paintings hanging mute in the room. Perhaps the day itself made the space feel more ominous than usual. Or perhaps the entire cloak-and-dagger routine wore on Ross's nerves. He wanted to go home.

As far as Ross was concerned, Jameson had taken the entire debt concept too far. If his old friend would tell Farin the truth instead of controlling her life, things might be simpler. Cleaner. Maybe they could reconcile.

But Jameson did not seek reconciliation. The affair ranged decades away from his professional persona. It clung to his person like a suit two sizes too small. If the truth went public, the news would slash like a jagged knife into the core of Jameson's private life and leave a permanent, bloody stain on Lockhardt Sound. Jameson sought absolution, not resolution.

The old man rocked gently in his chair as he watched Ross position, then reposition, himself upon the sofa. "Did you talk to your real estate friend?"

"Yes." Arm outstretched, Ross squinted at the notes he had scribbled on a piece of paper. He realized too late he had left his glasses in his jacket pocket back in his office. "He found a place close to Jordan's. It'll be ready on time."

"Splendid. And don't breathe a word of this to anyone—especially Bobby."

"Where is Bobby, anyway? I haven't seen him for a couple of days."

"He's in California with Farin."

Ross arced a concerned brow.

Jameson waved him off. "I know...they've grown quite close. She asked him down for some party she's having, so he took the jet out straightaway."

"I smell complications."

"The only problem would be if they became romantically involved. No, they're just friends."

"You're sure?"

"He's afraid of women, Ross. You know that."

Ross forced an unconvincing smile. "All bases covered, then, I guess."

"After all these years, everything's in place. My business...and my family. Nothing can go wrong now."

"You realize you should have had a stroke and died years ago, right?"

Jameson conceded the point with an indulgent chuckle.

"Have you checked in on Beth?"

A hint of sadness etched into the lines on Jameson's face. "She's the same. Maybe worse."

"And you've no help for her? Rehab?"

"How many times have *you* offered?" He shot up from behind his desk. "She's as stubborn as the day we first met."

"Has she said anything to Farin? If Beth finds out Farin signed with you, she could ruin your plans."

Jameson clasped his hands behind him and paced the floor between his desk and the floor-to-ceiling window, his figure shadow-like as it moved back and forth in the dim light. "Farin still refuses to speak with her."

"If that changes, Farin may feel entitled to a portion of LSI. And rightly, she probably is. That doesn't bother you?"

Jameson waved off the possibility without breaking his gait.

The old man had operated this game sub-rosa, like all his private affairs. He manipulated Farin and her mother like pawns. Beth O'Conner was a lifetime member in an exclusive club of those who could annihilate Jameson's empire with a whisper.

Since rediscovering Farin, Jameson had vacillated between relief and a renewed state of paranoia. Now, it was as if his old friend felt invincible. Giving Bobby the opportunity to get to know Farin? Reckless. If everything was finally in place, why tempt fate?

Ross opened his mouth to protest, then thought better of it. Josephine had voiced her displeasure when he called to let her know Jameson had summoned him to the office again.

He rose from the sofa and yawned into his hand. "Josephine will have me in the guest room if I don't get home soon. Looks like you've dodged yet another scandal. Another victory for Jameson Lockhardt. Hear, hear."

***

When word reached Beth O'Conner that her baby girl planned to move across the country, calls to the apartment became near-constant. Farin dodged them, at first. When that tactic failed, Marci campaigned for her to give in.

"Beth won't have your Florida number," she reasoned. "It could be the last time you talk to her."

So, she endured a final call. Seconds in, she regretted it.

Bitter, incoherent slurs bore into Farin's ears, depositing them atop an ever-present pile of emotional buckshot, which lay in her stomach. Each lead pebble represented a word, accusation, or hurtful memory accumulated over fifteen years.

"I can't talk now, Momma. I'm busy."

"Oh yes, yes you can. And you will." Beth hiccoughed, then swallowed.

Farin glanced at Marci, who hovered nearby for moral support, and signaled for privacy. When Marci left, she slid into a kitchen chair and rubbed her forehead with one hand, the other gripping the phone like a vise.

"So, you're moving away. Just like that. You weren't even gonna tell me you were leaving. He's whisking you off into his world."

Farin frowned. "What?"

"Oh, I know. *I* know. I know what he's doing. He's got you now."

"*Who?*"

"And I'm sure he'll make it up."

"You're making no sense," she snapped.

Beth snickered angrily. "Your career's *funny*. You're a funny girl. A stupid girl. No loyalty."

"Loyalty? Do we really want to talk about *loyalty*, Momma?"

"You shouldn't have done it, Farin. You sold out. That's what you did, you sold out! He doesn't care about you!"

Farin struggled to untangle the random threads of conversation. Was her mother angry about her signing with LSI? About her relationship with Jordan?

Eventually, Beth's derision gave way to sobs. "Please come home."

Farin swallowed hard and set her jaw.

"You have to know. I need to...show you. I loved him so m-m-much."

"You should go lay down, Momma."

"It's important."

Though curious at first, she knew the deal. Another ploy to get her to visit. Another empty promise to change. Another attempt to derail the train of freedom that would transport her from the muck of her past to the pristine, bright destination to which she finally held a ticket.

"Promise you'll see me before you leave."

"Remember when you showed up at our high school graduation, Momma? Remember standing up right in the middle of Janie Knott's valedictorian speech and screaming for me until she had to stop talking? And the whole school booing and yelling at you to sit down?"

Beth whimpered pitifully.

"And how Marci's parents tried to calm you down so they could watch us get our diplomas? Do you remember falling down the bleacher steps and breaking your arm?"

"I was so proud." She sniffed twice, then blew her nose.

"You humiliated me that day, Momma. Like you did for years. Like you're trying to do right now! I told you. I'll *never* go back to Santa Barbara. Not while you're alive. Why are you calling me? Why won't you leave me *alone*?"

"Hateful. You're *hateful*! Like him!"

"And you're drunk. As usual."

"You wanted what you'll get! You'll see. I'm not the enemy here! Your father—"

"Don't talk about my father! Daddy'd be sick in his soul to see what you've become! You're a pathetic, useless waste of oxygen! I *hate you*!" She slammed the receiver into the base of the phone.

Farin sulked in her room and did not resurface until Marci coaxed her out for the dinner she had prepared as a guilt offering.

She plated the meal as Farin grabbed their drinks. "Okay. Bad idea. Sorry."

"She's getting worse."

"I know."

"How dare she talk about my dad?"

"Well, it's done now. And I've made comfort food."

Farin thanked her as she slid a plate of roast chicken and potatoes with fresh green beans before her. It smelled delicious. If only her stomach were not tied in knots.

Marci ate in silence at first, pretending not to notice Farin pushing her food around her plate with her fork. "Wanna talk about the party? You love Halloween."

She rested her head upon her fist. "Jordan won't be here."

"But Dale's coming. He's even catering. And Bobby'll be here."

"True."

The thought eased her troubled mind. She and Bobby understood each other, somehow, though they had agreed certain topics—such as family— were strictly off limits. Like her, a certain sadness enveloped Bobby at times. That and his odd facial tic, which Farin tried to ignore.

At first, she had attributed his intermittent moodiness to all the alcohol they drank when they were together. Then, she discovered Bobby never even drank alcohol. His "vodka and lime with enough soda to make it fizz" was no more than club soda. She did not ask why he had lied about it. Something haunted him. She did not know what, but she understood it. And him.

***

Thanks in part to the glowing recommendations Jordan had given him after he catered Chase's memorial service, Eastland Catering had become the toast of Hollywood. His business had become so successful, he toyed with the idea of opening his own restaurant. And as a thank you, Dale had insisted on catering Marci's shindig. She accepted the food, but insisted Dale attend as a friend—*not* the help.

Marci had outdone herself decorating for the party. Cellophane balloons free-floated across their apartment ceiling, reflecting the dim lighting of the room, while ribbons of green, gold, and black curlicued from their necks. She set up a special table for Dale's culinary masterpieces and backed the furniture up to the walls, providing an area for dancing should anyone be so inclined. The radio played in the background. KIIS FM could not have sounded better had she programmed the playlist herself.

Despite the merry décor and attempts to appear cheerful, Farin's heart lay with Jordan, in Florida. It seemed Marci had invited her co-workers as filler to hide the fact they had few close friends besides each other. With the exception of Dale and Bobby, Farin's only hope of excitement rested with meeting Marci's new boyfriend, Dan, whom Marci expected any minute.

Dale, Bobby, and Farin huddled together for the most part, periodically attempting conversation outside their circle. Three hours in, Marci declared the night a failure. Farin's friends had little in common with Marci's crowd.

"I'm sorry, Farin. The four of us probably should've gone to a club."

"Nonsense!" Dale gave Marci's arm a tender squeeze. "It's gorgeous. And I've already called dibs on the sofa when I pass out from all the tequila! Bobby, you'll have to take the floor. Or the bathtub."

Bobby chuckled in the affirmative and lifted his club soda.

The anticipation of Dan's arrival visibly preoccupied Marci's thoughts. Farin spotted her checking her watch as she busied herself with hostess duties. She refused all offers of help, insisting she wanted to keep busy.

"So," Dale sing-songed, "when's this record of yours coming out?"

"Around Christmas." Farin shifted her weight to find a stance that did not mean agony for her feet. She hated wearing shoes, especially in her own home. Her heels nearly killed her. "That's why I put off the move until the first of the year. Well, that and this publicity campaign Bobby's put together to run me into the ground."

"You'll get down there just in time to say goodbye." Bobby sipped his drink. "Jordan'll be going on tour about then."

"It'll be okay. I'm booked solid anyway."

"Farin." Marci appeared from the kitchen carrying a tray of food. "Mr. Lockhardt's on the phone for you."

Farin and Bobby looked at their watches, then each other, and shrugged.

Dale stepped forward. "Marci, let me help you."

She shooed him away. "This is your night off. If you really want to help, do something to liven up this dud."

He winked her way. "*Liven* as in engage with your friends? Or do we want the police called? Tell me what I'm working with, here."

Bobby followed Farin into her room to take the call. She kicked off her shoes and plopped down, sprawling across the bed while Bobby wandered around, surveying the space in an unobtrusive holding pattern.

Farin heard Marci pick up the kitchen extension. "I got it, Marce." When she hung up, the dull murmur of guests ceased. "Happy Halloween, Jameson. Did you go trick-or-treating?"

"I decided to take the year off. And you? Did any hobgoblins arrive on your doorstep?"

"About twenty or so. They do it early out here."

"How goes the party?"

Farin grabbed a loose curl and twirled it in her fingers. "Boring. Marci invited her banker friends. If it weren't for Bobby, I don't know what I'd do."

Out of the corner of her eye, she watched Bobby finger her knickknacks and bric-a-brac, read the authors and titles of her books, and study her music collection. He nodded every so often, complimenting her taste, as if fascinated with the objects and mementos with which she surrounded herself.

Jameson said, "I decided to call before I went home. Is the move still on?"

"Sure is! As soon as the record's released, I'll fly down to look for a place."

"Why don't I fly you down in the company jet? We'll discuss your summer tour."

She gasped. "A tour?"

"Did I not promise you the world, my dear?"

Bobby brightened at Farin's smiling face, giving her an enthusiastic thumbs up.

"We'll discuss it in more detail later. Shall I plan the trip?"

"It's too much," she cooed.

"Rubbish! Nothing's too much for my newest star!"

"You win. Are you headed home now? Even *you* need to sleep sometimes. I don't want you getting sick."

"Soon," he promised. "And oh! I have a housewarming present for you."

Farin stared at the ceiling, her lips lifting into a wide smile. "Really? I can't wait!"

Her eyes trailed down to the foot of her bed, where Bobby now stood, watching her and shaking his fists in a humorous poise as if to remind her Jameson had only one child. She rose from the bed and gave his arm a pinch. "Did you need to speak with Bobby? He's right here."

"Actually, I would if you don't mind."

Farin beckoned Bobby closer and handed over the telephone, sticking out her tongue as he took the receiver. Without a backward glance, she slid grudgingly back into her shoes and headed off toward the living room to continue her conversation with Dale.

Consequently, she did not see Bobby sprawl full-length atop her bed. She did not see his face fall into near-spasmodic tremors, or his eyes glaze over in what resembled temporary mania.

In the living room, Dale cheered Farin's announcement. "A tour? How exciting!" He gave her a congratulatory hug. "And speaking of exciting...notice the dancing tellers?" He swayed slightly as he gestured at the small crowd, who seemed to have finally loosened up.

"Impressive." Farin touched her fresh glass of wine to his empty shot glass.

Bobby scoffed as he returned. "Sounds great now, but wait. She'll start out feeling like she owns the world and come back feeling like she had to carry it on her shoulders."

Farin ignored Bobby's cynicism and turned to Marci. "Where's Dan? I thought he'd be here."

"So did I. He probably had to work late. He'll be here soon."

The phone rang again. Marci sprinted off to the kitchen.

Bobby snickered as he watched the bounce in her step. "Is that how all you women act when you're in love?"

"You should give it a try." Farin cut eyes at him.

His face grew troubled as it did every time she broached the subject. "I told you. I'm not into relationships. Even if I did, say, get married and have kids, it'd be for show. I'd never see them. I'm always working—even when I'm not in the office." He uncurled his index finger from around his glass to tap his temple. "It's always up here. My wife and children would never see or even know me." He set his drink next to a platter of meats and cheeses, then walked off toward the bathroom. "They wouldn't want to," he added under his breath.

Dale and Farin exchanged glances as he disappeared down the hall. Brow wrinkled, Dale touched his chest. "Jekyll and Hyde much?"

Farin watched Bobby's retreating form. "He gets like that when I mention women. I shouldn't have said anything."

"I guess not. Hmm." Dale twisted his lips sideways. "Do you think—?"

"I don't think so. Sorry, hon."

He feigned offense. "Not for *me*! Those Twinkie-types don't do anything for me."

"No?" Farin gave his arm a playful shove. "Two years ago? Muscle Beach? A certain Swede named—"

"Enough." Dale raised his chin. "I wonder if ol' Cai ever decided to get off that fence, or if it became permanently lodged up his—"

"Now-now," Farin scolded in a motherly tone. "Let's not shock the bankers."

She glanced down the hall again. It had never occurred to her that Bobby might have homosexual tendencies. Maybe Dale was onto something. While it did not matter to her, maybe Bobby struggled to admit it. Even to himself. It would make sense. The only woman Bobby ever seemed to spend any time with was her. Why else would he act so uncomfortable whenever they discussed relationships?

Then, she wondered if Bobby might be ill. For years now, AIDS had scared the hell out of everyone. Even Dale had curtailed his amorous activities and had become a one-man lover. Or maybe Bobby had diabetes. No drinking? And those sometimes-glassy eyes of his? Farin had read somewhere that diabetics could not drink because of the insulin they took or something. Whatever the case, she wished she could tell him she would understand no matter what. She would not reject him. But despite their fast friendship, it seemed soon for such an intimate conversation.

Marci returned before Bobby, her mood somber. "Dan's not coming. He thinks he's coming down with something, so he's going to bed. I'm beginning to wonder if you'll get to meet him before you leave for Miami."

"It's okay." She put a comforting hand on her shoulder. "You guys'll visit. Why don't you invite him for Thanksgiving?"

She shook her head. "His folks live over in Riverside. He'll be with them."

The telephone rang again. "I'll get it. You stay here. Looks like your colleagues are getting ready to call it a night. It must be past their bedtimes." Farin winked back at her friend as she hurried to the kitchen. She picked up the receiver and greeted, "Happy Halloween."

"You sound out of breath," came a familiar British voice.

Her heart leapt. "I didn't expect to hear from you so late. What's going on over there on the East Coast? Jameson called a few minutes ago, too."

"Mum and Dad flew over for the holidays. We're all here at Ben's for the kids' Halloween."

"How's it going?"

"It was hard on Mum when Derek and Kyle went out in their costumes."

"I'm sorry, Jordan. I wish I were there with you."

"How's the party?"

She slunk down into a kitchen chair and twirled the spiraled telephone cord around her pinky. "Marci's boyfriend got sick so he no-showed. Marci's bummed. That's about the most exciting thing going on. But when Jameson called, he said he's sending me out on tour this summer."

The news seemed to lift his mood. "I hope you'll be opening for me."

"We're gonna discuss it on the way to Miami. He's flying me out. He says he's got a housewarming present for me. Now all I need is the house."

"You have one."

She shut her eyes. "Jordan..."

"It was your idea to live separately, Farin, not mine. Maybe this time apart will change your mind."

"You said you understood."

"I'm trying."

She blamed his bitter tone on the weight of his day instead of any lingering resentment over her refusal to cohabitate. "You never said why you're calling so late. Is everything okay?"

"Ben and I've been in the studio working on a new song and decided to take a break. He's right here. Say hi while I grab some tea?"

Before she could respond, Ben greeted, "Hi, kid!"

"Happy Halloween. How's it going?"

"We can't wait until you're here. How's the record coming?"

"Good." She lowered her voice. "Ben, is Jordan okay?"

His voice lowered as well. "He misses you."

"That's it?

"They say the first year's the hardest. He's holding up better than I could. I don't know what I'd do if I lost my boys."

"I wish there was something I could do."

"There is. Finish that record of yours and get down here."

"I will."

"Anyway, Cheryl sends her love. The boys are busy making out their Christmas lists. Mind you, it starts earlier every year. They probably only have one or two Halloweens left in them, though. The novelty's wearing off. They want to go to parties with their friends. I doubt they'd have gone out at all this year if their uncle hadn't shown up dressed like a pirate to take them."

The phone cord unraveled from around her finger and fell away. "Chris is there?"

Ben hesitated. "Uh...yep."

"Why didn't Jordan tell me? How are things between them?"

"Distant."

"How long has he been there?"

"Not long."

The clipped responses irritated her. "There's obviously more."

"Jordan wants to tell you himself."

"Tell me what? Are they fighting?"

He blew air out into the line. "Look, it'll take time. Chris is making more of an effort than Jordan, if you can believe it. The other day, we were gonna take the boys sailing—planned everything around Jordan's schedule. It was all set. But then Jordan decided he couldn't do it and canceled at the last minute. Tonight's been really awkward. After Chris got back with the boys, he joined Jordan and I in the studio. They're either ready to kill each other or I don't know what."

She traced the scar along her hairline with her finger. "It's all my fault."

"They'll work it out. By the time you get down here, I'm sure it'll all be forgotten."

"By the time I get—?" Farin heard Jordan in the background and knew Ben dared say little more. "How long is Chris staying?"

Hastily, he said, "Here's Jordan again."

Farin stood and skidded her chair away using the back of her legs. "What aren't you telling me, Ben?"

But Jordan came back on the line. "Have a nice chat?"

"You didn't tell me Chris was there."

She waited for a response that did not come.

She moved her free hand to her hip. "I don't want to show up while he's still there. How long's he staying?"

"Permanently," he confessed at last.

Farin hooked the chair leg with her foot, dragged it back to her, then sat down.

"I didn't tell you because I didn't want it to influence your decision to move down here."

Her thoughts raced to envision a single scenario in which this turn of events did not end in disaster.

"Say something."

She struggled to find her voice.

"He swore he won't bother you again. And Farin, I believe him."

She rolled her eyes and scrunched her nose into a sneer. "I hope you're right."

"We love each other. That's all that matters. Just get here soon. We have a whole new life to start."

CHAPTER 13

FROM HER FIRST VISIT SOME months back, Farin had fallen in love with Miami. By day, she loved its vaulted palms swaying in the warm tropical breeze of an intermittently cloudy sky or afternoon storm. By night, she loved the Miami Beach clubs pulsating with life, dance, and calypso music. The sky was bluer, here. The sun was hotter. The food, tastier. Miami smelled of cocoa butter and better days. Moreover, it lay thousands of miles from the corner of State and Cabrillo back in Santa Barbara. Florida had assaulted Farin's every sense. A textbook paradise. And from that first trip on, she had known instinctively she would live there one day.

The first Thursday of 1989, that day arrived.

The longing of the past three months loitered in the pit of her stomach as Jameson's private jet landed at the Kendall-Tamiami Executive Airport in South Miami. It had been a long flight. And while they had touched on business matters during that time, Jameson had mostly stayed quiet. For this, he offered no explanation. Farin assumed he was a nervous flier.

When she stepped out into the late afternoon, she inhaled the salty, humid Atlantic air. Soon, she would lose herself in her lover's arms.

Jameson passed her his cell phone as they descended the steps and crossed the tarmac. "Let Jordan know I've delivered you safely."

She peeked over the rim of her Ray Bans, accepted the phone with an appreciative smile, then dialed Ben's number from memory.

"Aye, there she is!" Cheryl greeted. "I sent Jorie off to the store. He needed something to do. How close are you?"

"We just deplaned."

Cheryl clicked her tongue. "Perfect. Gives me time to finish in the kitchen. Lockhardt's welcome to stay if he's hungry."

The driver loaded their bags, then navigated the vehicle toward the village of Key Biscayne.

Jameson removed the handkerchief from the breast pocket of his suit jacket and mopped his brow.

Farin touched his forearm. "Ben says the humidity takes some getting used to."

"I won't be staying long enough to acclimate."

"Are you hungry? Cheryl's making dinner. She says there's plenty."

"Extend my apologies. I have meetings tomorrow. I'm flying back to New York right away."

As the car motored north along the Florida Turnpike, Jameson discussed at length Farin's newly released album, her ongoing publicity campaign, and plans for her summer concert tour opening for Ebony Suede. The details overwhelmed her. Today, all she wanted was Jordan.

She stared out the window at the scenery whizzing by them as he spoke. "I'll have a few days before I have to leave again, right?"

Jameson patted her knee. His face adopted a less severe expression. "This is what you said you wanted."

She sank back in her seat and nodded.

When they reached Key Biscayne, their driver turned left off Harbor Drive then snaked around onto Palmwood Lane. Jameson grew animated, at last the jovial, dear man she had grown to trust and admire—the Jameson Lockhardt who, Jordan insisted, did not exist except with her.

The car pulled into and parked upon the bricked driveway outside a lovely, white stuccoed two-story along the lane. Palms, ferns, fountains, and privacy hedges surrounded the property.

"I'd mentioned I had a housewarming gift for you," he said with a gruff voice. He gestured out the window. "This is it."

Aghast, Farin peered out the window at the ample lawn, exotic plants, and bright flowers planted in white window boxes. The house resembled a life-sized replica of the doll house she had loved so much as a child. Impossible. He could not have known.

She threw her arms around his neck and held him tight. "It's beautiful! You shouldn't have."

"It'll do until you and Jordan are married."

She hastened to exit the limousine, but he held up a hand to stop her. "You can see the inside later." He handed her the keys and signaled the driver to continue on. "Right now, we need to get you to Ben's."

Clutching the keys, Farin turned around and watched the house—*her* house—disappear from view. When it faded from sight, she settled back, blushing slightly. "Jordan and I haven't discussed marriage."

He barked out a hearty chuckle, as if he knew something she did not.

Farin dared to rest her head on his shoulder. Jameson freed his arm and draped it around her in an expression of what felt like protectiveness.

He had handled everything like a father would have. An increasingly familiar occurrence. As if he wanted to compensate for her lack of a father figure. An absurd notion since she had only mentioned it once in passing. Perhaps Jameson had wanted a daughter.

If she tried, she could almost picture her father sitting next to her now instead of Jameson. How he might look having aged these many years. His sharp, green eyes dulling and in need of readers. His kind, strong face losing its elasticity. His orange curls and bearded face peppered with gray.

She shook away the fantasy and leaned into Jameson's embrace as the residual pain ebbed and flowed. Kelley O'Conner was never coming back, would never age another day, and remained changeless in her memory. Now, she felt herself slipping into the security of Jameson's promises for her future as easily as she had slipped into his arm.

"Are you okay, my dear?"

Farin moved out of the embrace and plucked her dress into place. In one fluid movement, she again wrapped her arms around him. "Thank you...thank you for everything."

He patted her back. "If you insist on thanking me all the time, I'll stop doing nice things for you."

She drew away as the limousine rolled to a stop along Ben's circular driveway.

Jameson remained seated as the driver unloaded Farin's things. She kissed his cheek before she got out of the car, then hurried into the welcoming arms of Jordan's family. He did not so much as lower the window to exchange pleasantries before instructing the driver to head back to the airport. Why bother?

It had been a triumphant day. He was certain he had gained Farin's trust. Now, he could make up for everything—and Beth could do nothing to stop him. Stubborn old woman. She had accepted nothing from him, and now look at her.

Though shattered by loss, she had waxed strong at Kelley's funeral. She had refused his proposal outright, even as Ross tried to reason with her. At least she had demonstrated some self-control.

But that was many, many bottles, ago.

A part of him wished he could tell Farin the truth, but that possibility had come and gone ages ago. Not even Bobby knew. If his secrets ever became public knowledge, the media would ruin them all. Jameson could not risk it. And so, he would protect himself, his family, and his business by any method necessary. The house was only the beginning.

***

Ben's mansion nestled near Westwood on beautiful Harbor Drive, his backyard mere yards from Biscayne Bay. His expansive, immaculately-kept grounds sprawled out over an acre. A tall, thick iron fence with overgrown hedges helped maintain his family's privacy. Inside the heavy oak doors lay, in Farin's opinion, nothing short of a palace. Cheryl had painstakingly purchased only the finest furnishings for their home. Without Jordan standing nearby to remind her, it seemed unreal that she was becoming a part of this world of wealth and luxury. She had never chased money. Never gave it a thought. She had always seemed to have what she needed. Still, she stared, awestruck at her surroundings as Ben, Cheryl, and chatterboxes Derek and Kyle welcomed her inside.

Jordan and Farin's reunion was a happy, if busy, one. Cheryl had cooked a feast. They ate poolside, laughed, and danced into the night. Farin's single disappointment was when Chris arrived before dinner, apparently by invitation. But except a few well-chosen glares exchanged across the table, everything went fine.

As the night wore on, Jordan grew inpatient, wanting Farin to himself. "Let's go," he whispered as they slow-danced to Breathe's "How Can I Fall."

She lifted her cheek from his shoulder. "Cheryl worked so hard."

"I've shared you long enough. You say goodbye. I'll load your bags into the car."

The drive from Ben's place to Jordan's a few blocks away on Matheson took less than a minute. Encompassed by nearly two acres, its modern lines overlooked Harbor Point. A large stone wall built around the estate provided protection and beauty. It looked palatial compared to his Malibu home. Farin gasped at the sight of it.

Jordan moved her things inside while she embarked upon a self-guided tour. The bottom floor had two living areas, a den, kitchen, two bathrooms, a bedroom, and a two-story entryway. The top floor included dual master suites with a fireplace in each, vaulted ceilings, a reading room, and two additional bedrooms. However tasteful the décor, it lacked a woman's touch.

"What do you think?" he asked when he joined her in his master suite.

"It's...*big.*"

"I'm sure we'll figure out some way to fill the space."

She ignored the unsubtle hint. Tonight, they would not bicker over their living arrangements. Tonight, they had some making up to do.

The next month passed in a frantic blur. Jordan's tour loomed nearer by the day. Farin balanced publicity obligations while trying to acclimate to her new surroundings. Every time Jameson called with an update of her July tour, she thanked him again for her life-size doll house, despite his insistence she stop doing so.

"Do you like your garden?"

"Are you kidding? I only wish I didn't have to hire a gardener."

At times, she wandered from room to room, admiring her brightly decorated bedrooms. At the end of a busy day, she luxuriated in a hot bubble bath in the enormous, jetted tub in her master bedroom. When not in interviews, photo shoots, or taping guest appearances, she spent her time without Jordan sitting out back in her garden, enjoying the Florida sunshine.

"I've never lived alone," she would tell Marci on their daily calls.

"At least you finally have more than one bathroom."

"You mean now that I only need one?"

"More's better. Too bad you'll have to clean them, though, huh?"

"I miss you, Marce."

"I miss you, too."

For his part, Jordan often expressed his displeasure over their living arrangements.

"I'm here, aren't I?" she would argue.

"In my life, but not my home."

"We're together all the time. At least when we're both around."

As his frustration grew, he wondered if her hesitation was born from the need for a more solid commitment. Did she want marriage? He did not shrink from this notion. Over time, he had started recovering from the loss of his son. But with their busy schedules, there seemed no right time to ask the way he wanted, to properly set the mood and scene.

Maybe after they both finished touring.

***

Farin squeezed Jordan's hand as they crossed the tarmac toward his customized tour plane in February. Weeks ago, she had arrived at this airport to start their life together. Now, he was leaving, just as Bobby Lockhardt had said he would.

Despite the forthcoming months apart, she felt settled and safe. They had mended their past and were stronger than ever. She hated surrendering Jordan to the road.

"May will be here before you know it," Jordan promised.

She watched with downcast eyes as Jordan's luggage rolled up the conveyor belt for loading. His band was already onboard, gawking at them through porthole windows. When he turned to say goodbye, she slipped a slender hand around his neck, drew him close, and kissed him fully on the lips. "I miss you already."

He held her tight. "I'll call every night." He drew back at last, kissed her fingertips, then climbed the steep metal stairs.

"I love you!" she called after him, waving as the plane door closed.

Jordan sat halfway down the aisle of the craft and waved as the plane taxied toward the runway. "I love you," he mouthed back.

Her eyes misted as she returned to the car that had taken them to the airport. "Take me home," she instructed, sinking back into her seat. Her thoughts raced ahead to May.

This would not mark the last occasion that time and distance would work against them. Her own tour—her first tour—would begin in July. As those preparations continued, maybe her schedule would ease the loneliness of their separation.

"Time to focus on you," Jameson encouraged. "Without good health, your stamina will suffer."

This tour would justify Jameson's investment into her career. She would make Jordan proud. She would make the world love her.

The drive through downtown Miami, across the Causeway, and into Key Biscayne passed uneventfully. Farin willed herself to focus on happy thoughts.

Interviews, photo shoots, rehearsals, and strength training would occupy the next few months of Farin's life. Daily sessions with her physical trainer and her choreographer would become the norm, as would myriad meetings with Bill Taft, booking agents, promoters, and a host of people whose sole job was to make her look and sound her best. Jameson promised someone from LSI would accompany her on the road.

By the time the car dropped Farin home, her spirits had improved. It thrilled and frightened her to watch her dreams materialize. A year had passed since she had left her last band. She could not wait to get back on stage.

She strolled up to her front door, rummaging through her purse for her keyring. As she inserted the key into the lock, she glimpsed a ceramic vase filled with yellow jonquils sitting on her porch.

No card was attached.

Through slitted eyes, she surveyed her surroundings as if expecting him to jump out from behind one of her rose bushes. Seeing no one, she picked up the vase, took it around to the side of the house, and deposited it in the trash.

Damn that Chris Grant anyway.

***

Another clandestine meeting. More angry pacing. Ross had grown accustomed to it. Jameson had worn a pathway down the middle of his prized hand-woven area rug. If the old man did not drop dead from a stroke, Ross might soon have one himself. But in addition to today's usual agenda of all-things Farin St. John, Jameson had added another topic. Mirage had received some damaging publicity.

"He's slipping away," Jameson announced, his back to Ross as he beheld the view of the concrete and glass skyscrapers opposite his window.

"You're upset about the move. Look at it this way. Mirage finished their new album. Sam says it's fantastic. Maybe their best ever."

"He destroyed their bond by leaving New York."

Jameson failed to mention, though Ross knew, that Chris had also broken their personal bond.

"They don't connect. Not like before. Elliot's all but moved to LA. He's doing more film work. Faith's stuffing who knows what up her nose—"

Ross frowned. "You don't believe she's using?"

Jameson looked askance at him. "Those fools see him as their bloody leader. They always did. Now, he's abandoned them. Sixteen years, gone. And for what? I've always been fond of him, Ross, but this time he's gone too far."

Ross recognized Jameson's tone. The tone that said Jameson smelled blood. The tone that had preceded Jameson blueprinting the collapse of Ginny Stevens's career after learning she had leaked the Chase Grant story.

"Jordan's tour's been a success," Ross offered, approaching things in a logical manner. "Farin's on schedule. And then there's that new girl, Megan—what's her name? Price. Megan Price. As for Mirage, I'm sure they'll be fine. Chris is changing. Sam says he's writing more. Leaving women alone. Maybe he's growing up. Or maybe it's some sort of sabbatical. He's lived in the fast lane for—"

"Listen to yourself!" Jameson dropped heavily into his chair. "You've never made excuses. Least of all for Chris."

"And your perception hasn't been this clouded in over twenty years."

Jameson leveled angry eyes his way.

"Mirage is *your* band. Lockhardt Sound needs them."

"Not anymore."

Ross regarded his old friend. He could not recall the last time Jameson had called on him solely to resolve some legal issue. Or to have a drink. He was a lawyer, not an artist relations rep. It was *Sam's* job to mediate the interest of the label and the talent, not his. But Jameson trusted no one else with the details surrounding Farin's life and career.

What a pity her world meant enough to Jameson to concern himself with something as insignificant as bad publicity. Chris should have never become so entrenched in the life of Farin O'Conner.

Jameson stared at, then through, Ross before standing to resume his pacing. His gait grew more purposeful. "When's their contract up?"

Ross eyeballed him. "Not for a couple of years."

"Bury promotion on the new record. Push back the release as far as possible. Get me a meeting with their booking agent."

"You'd kill our profits over this? What about what it'll do to Faith?"

"They'll only play small venues—around the Miami area—approved by me personally. No more records, no more concerts. The boy wants to be in Florida? Let him stay in Florida, permanently. Let the rest of the group bear the inconvenience of going to him. Have Sam field their calls. Except for Chris. He can talk to me."

Ross's lips parted. "But they're the bedrock of Lockhardt Sound. The lost revenue alone—"

"Subject closed." Jameson sat down, visibly pleased with his decision.

"It's over, Ross. Mirage is finished."

A summary of two decades assaulted Ross's mind. What he knew. What Jameson had done. How he had assisted. "Need I mention...?"

Jameson ignored him. "There's one more thing. Farin needs someone to help her when I can't be there. Not only for the tour but as a permanent installment in her career. I don't want just anyone. I promised her someone before she's out on the road."

Ross stared at his old friend for long seconds.

Jameson gestured questioningly toward him, palms open.

He browsed the stack of files beside him. "Gimme a minute. Remember when I was simply head of Legal? I do."

"There can be no mistakes."

Ross nodded. He hated their present circumstance, but he understood it.

The office door flew open. "I'll go on tour with Farin!"

Both men jumped at Bobby's unexpected arrival, shocked as he bounded into the middle of the office, hair unkempt and clothes disheveled, as if he had pulled one too many all-nighters.

Jameson huffed. "How long have you been out there spying?"

"Long enough to hear you needed someone to work with Farin. I was coming up to give you this." He handed his father a folder. "It's the last few press releases for the tour. C'mon, Dad! I'm the obvious choice!"

Jameson cleared his throat. He peered at Ross as if urging him to say something.

Ross remained silent.

"I'm perfect for this gig and you know it," Bobby pressed, crossing the room to sit in the unoccupied chair facing his father's desk. He ticked off his reasons on his fingers. "We've established a good working relationship. I know her quirks. I have her ear..."

"You're the head of the publicity department," Jameson pointed out.

"Traveling with the artists might not be part of my stated duties, but who better to represent our interests—*your* interests—during her debut tour than me? We all know she's your new favorite, Dad. Who better than me to make sure she's treated that way?"

Indeed, Farin St. John was big news. Her first single, *Woman-Child*, had peaked at number seven on the charts. They anticipated her follow-up single, scheduled for release soon, would do even better. If nothing else, Farin had an ace up her sleeve: she dated the biggest solo commodity in the music business.

They could not have planned it better.

Jordan was "it," and even though he hated the mobs of screaming fans always there in steady supply, he endured. He endured the love notes affixed to gifts thrown on stage in the hopes of finding their way into his hands. He endured the crowd that rushed the stage in Madison, Wisconsin, and again in Colorado Springs. He endured slipping into his hotel rooms through kitchens and back entrances.

He endured the occasional security break, when some daring fan would infiltrate his suite disguised as room service or housekeeping. He endured waiting in the hallway of a New Jersey hotel, dripping wet and in a towel after a shower, while security guards removed a seventeen-year-old girl from his bed after she had managed to sneak in, having slid down to his balcony from a rope attached to the roof. He endured it all, not for personal glory, but for love of the music.

LSI profited mightily off Jordan Grant's continued endurance.

This had been his most successful tour to date. His last two albums had gone multi-platinum. Fan mail poured in. Heartbroken admirers demanded answers. Who was this Farin St. John? Where did she come from?

The time was perfect to unleash Farin onto the waiting public.

After three days of indecision, Bobby received a reluctant green light from his father and headed to Miami. Farin was overjoyed to have him on her team. He knew he had her trust and cooperation. Bobby would prove he could handle fast-paced, high-stress situations without fraying at the seams.

It had been a difficult road, but he had finally arrived. As Jameson's only child and sole heir to the Lockhardt millions, Bobby would show he could manage LSI properly after the old man retired.

This opportunity would put his father's mind, and his own, at ease. It would also position him close enough to make Farin see how much he cared for her—a secret he kept hidden from everyone.

***

After completing a successful, if draining, tour, Jordan returned the last week in May to disappointment. His ears rang for days after the last show, collateral damage from cacophonous music and screaming crowds. He loved the performances, hated the travel, but returned with an overall high from the road that quelled only at the realization that he and Farin would have little time together.

Once again, she refused to move in with him. This time with annoyance. He felt the sting of her rejection, even through his exhaustion, but told himself she must feel overwhelmed as her own departure loomed near.

Soon, Farin would leave for cities from which he had returned. He remembered what an incredible time he had had on his freshman tour. But those memories were of little solace when Farin left the second of June.

From Atlanta to Boston, then on to Detroit, Farin took America by storm. She even stole the fire from the tour's headlining act, Ebony Suede. A goddess on stage, critics rhapsodized over her show. Undeniably, the ravishing songstress favored ballads. Night after night, her audiences cried tears of longing, joy, and sadness. Her upbeat numbers bid the crowd out of their seats to dance and cheer her on. Farin radiated contentment and happiness, at ease and in control in front of thousands of strangers who paid to watch her strut confidently across the stage in her glitter and sequins.

Between songs, while her guitarist swapped out his instrument for one with unbroken strings or her back-up vocalists took greedy gulps from their water bottles, Farin engaged her audience with wit, humor, and charm. Reviewers penned Farin St. John's performance as a force to be reckoned with, and each night Bobby watched offstage, his cheering the loudest in the stadiums.

Backstage, a different story played out. The members of Ebony Suede resented Farin's staggering popularity. Radio stations and newspapers clamored for her attention above theirs. Sometimes, it was difficult to discern whether the fans came for her or for them. This was not the way things were supposed to happen. Their agents raged at each other on the phone. Bill Taft relinquished other responsibilities to accompany Farin and deal firsthand with Ebony Suede's management.

Ebony Suede further complained Farin had snubbed them from day one, preferring to go straight back to the hotel after each concert instead of partying with the performers, guests, and groupies backstage. She did not take drugs, she drank in moderation, and she feigned almost irritating innocence if any man so much as dared to come on to her—and they *all* did. Bobby spent much of his time ushering Farin out of an impending brawl with the members of the band.

In truth, he knew Ebony Suede misunderstood. Farin had prepared with great discipline for her performances. Her growing celebrity was another matter. No one foresaw the media latching onto her the way they had. She felt out of her element. Utterly alone despite all the people and circumstances swirling around her. Several times, she begged Bobby to call Jameson and arrange a surprise appearance for Jordan, claiming the fans would be beside themselves. Ebony Suede threatened to sue if Jordan Grant so much as flew up for a visit to his lovesick girlfriend.

Only Bobby saw the severity of Farin's preoccupation with missing Jordan. He never mentioned it to his father or Bill Taft. But each night before going on, as the tension grew backstage, Farin called Jordan from her dressing room. Many of these calls ended in tears. Soon, long odds wagered whether she would manage to get to makeup and back in time to go on. A couple of times, Bobby had arrived at Farin's hotel while she was in the bathroom, retching. He had asked her if she suffered stage fright, but he knew. Farin missed Jordan, plain and simple.

In all his life, Bobby had never seen anyone so intent on making a relationship work. Why, he wondered, did she try so hard? Surely she and Jordan had resolved the problems of last year.

Still, there was obviously something going on—with Farin and with the rest of LSI. A few times before Jordan's return, Bobby had come over to pick Farin up for rehearsal and had seen Chris parked across the street in his Porsche, stalking her house. Tabloids exposed Mirage's disintegration. They blamed Chris Grant's move to Miami on a personal battle he had with lead singer, Todd Dalton. Bobby knew this rumor held no validity.

The rags had a field day. They had Faith Peterson free-basing cocaine and living in mortal fear of AIDS. Drummer Lance Turner had reportedly hung up his sticks and hightailed it back to England to reunite with a mysterious gay lover. Bobby knew Lance was no more a homosexual than he. Only bass player Elliot Lawrence remained unscathed amid the myriad of rumors, probably because he rarely opened his mouth to anyone and never made a scene, public or otherwise.

Bobby was ecstatic when headlines dubbed Farin the princess of the media despite the rumblings of Ebony Suede, and despite the necessity to accept Bill Taft's assistance in dealing with their management. He prided himself on a job well done. His father would have to sit up and take notice. All across America, Farin's act received fervent acclaim.

But in stolen private moments, as the days and weeks passed, Farin teetered on the edge of emotional and physical exhaustion. The cutthroat aura backstage, the pressure of the press, the fans, and the constant travel began to show.

In Albuquerque, she requested a more thorough sound check due to the previous night's disaster—when her mic cable mysteriously failed after her second number. Bobby had sworn he and Bill would stand backstage during her performance, more mindful of the crew, but Farin made Bobby promise to pick her up early, nonetheless. When he arrived, Farin sat in her bathrobe on the edge of her bed, still in need of a shower.

"You said you'd be ready." Bobby sat down beside her. "You okay?"

A blank expression covered her face like a death mask. "How'd you get here so fast?"

"Honey, I talked to you an hour ago." He brushed her hair out of her face. "When was the last time you slept?"

Farin shook her head as if to clear her mind. She stood and teetered around the room on unsteady legs. "Where are we tonight?"

"New Mexico."

She nodded, then made her way back toward the bed. Two feet away, she stumbled, but Bobby caught her before she fell. "I'm sorry," she said.

"Tell me the truth, Farin. Are you okay?" He fixed concerned eyes on hers. "I'm gonna call Bill. We're canceling tonight."

"No!" Farin begged, struggling to right herself in his arms. "I'm okay. I promise."

"You're exhausted. You can't go on like this. Maybe we should pull you for the last leg, huh? It's not worth it. It's been a great tour, but you're running yourself into the ground."

"I need to eat something," she said more clearly. "I'll be fine. Really. What time is it?"

"You're fine on time, hon. But how's it gonna look when you collapse on stage tonight?" He took her face in his hands and gauged her focus. "Ebony Suede would be too pleased by that, wouldn't they?"

"I won't give them the satisfaction," she promised. "And Bill...I won't let him down. I won't let LSI down either, Bobby. I swear it. Order something for me while I shower? I need coffee, fresh fruit, some carbs...energy food, okay?"

"You got it." He did not mention the two untouched trays of previous orders outside her door. "You sure you're okay?" He picked up the handset to call room service.

Farin reappeared momentarily, brushing out her hair. "I feel like an idiot, Bobby."

He replaced the handset. "Why on earth would you feel like an idiot?"

"I didn't realize it would be this hard. I'm tired. This isn't anything like the touring I used to do. I figured entertaining a live audience would be the same regardless of the forum. But it's not."

"Of course it's not," he said gently. "You're doing fine. Better than fine. You're terrific."

"They're right, you know. They're totally out of my league."

Bobby scoffed and let a bark of laughter escape his flattened lips. "Would it make you feel better if I told you their new album nosedived this week? They fell five notches, right out of the top ten."

She padded back into the bathroom. "I hate all the competition. What a horrible thing to say. I don't wish them failure."

Bobby laid back on his elbows and smiled. He heard the shower engage and the shower door close. He raised his voice to call after her, "Would it make any difference if I told you you're at number three?"

From the next room, he heard an enthusiastic squeal. He laughed.

Tonight's performance would find a very up, very on, Farin St. John.

As the tour continued, they received updates on the exploding success of her first album. While in Portland, they got the news her album had gone gold. By Denver, it had reached platinum.

LSI's mailroom flooded with fan mail. Each success drove Farin further. She pushed harder, performed better, and stopped worrying about Ebony Suede's sour grapes. As her popularity skyrocketed, she ignored the toll it took on her freedom and her nerves.

It disappointed Farin that, while her public regarded her as a fresh, new talent with the world as her proverbial oyster, she remained the same person. She had hoped the transformation would encompass her internally as well as externally. For what felt like eons, Farin had endeavored to recreate herself, to forget her past, to see herself as strangers saw her— mask and all.

The one setback in the tour came when she arranged to meet with Marci during her stay in Los Angeles. That day, the realization that nothing in Farin's private life had changed hit home with full force. When Marci walked through the dressing room door for their private lunch, Farin blanched. From the dark circles under her eyes to her defeated gait, Marci Williams had never looked so miserable.

Convinced Dan Albright saw other women, but without proof and unable to bring herself to end the relationship, Marci felt trapped. Dan was verbally abusive. He would spend the holidays with his family in Riverside again this year, but still did not invite Marci to join him. Work had become her refuge.

Farin pleaded with Marci to come to Miami for a visit but Marci begged off, insisting she was too busy. She promised to try to make it the following year.

Before Marci left, she told Farin her mother had been hospitalized. Marci's parents had called an ambulance two days ago after finding Beth passed out in a pool of blood at the house, a half-empty whiskey bottle in her hand and several empties scattered about. The hospital had admitted her with the diagnosis of chronic cirrhosis of the liver. It looked bad.

"You have to see her," Marci urged.

Farin was indifferent. "We knew this would happen sooner or later. It's her own fault."

"Your mom could die, Farin."

She lowered her head, desperate to remember the mother who had raised her. Before the accident. Before the alcohol. Before the abandonment that sent Farin to live with Marci. Surely she felt *some* compassion for the woman who had given her life.

"I can't go back, Marce." Her voice was as icy as the lack of warmth she found in her heart. "As far as I'm concerned, my mother died years ago."

Farin said nothing to Bobby about the situation with her parents. Instead, she poured her conflicting emotions into her act. Her lifelong love for music had begun with lullabies and cradle songs sung to her by both her mother and father. Standing in the spotlight in Southern California, so close to home, brought something magical to the stage that evening.

Damn her mother anyway. And damn Ebony Suede. Tonight, she was no shrinking violet, content to trivialize her accomplishments on the road, in the press, and in the record stores. Farin gave an unprecedented performance that night and dedicated the entire show to her father.

"I love you, Daddy!" She lifted her face, closed her eyes, and pointed toward the ceiling as she sang an a cappella rendition of "Let Me Call You Sweetheart." The crowd roared their approval so loud, her amplified voice scarcely penetrated the sound. Bobby stood backstage, riveted.

That night, Bill Taft and Ebony Suede's management had it out once and for all. Bobby ushered Farin out of the chaos before the brawl ensued.

By noon the next day, Jameson Lockhardt had bailed all the principals out of jail. From then on, peace reigned supreme.

On the last night of the tour, Farin received an olive branch at her room two hours before she left for the auditorium. When Bobby simultaneously announced her second single had soared to number one on the charts, she accepted.

In the end, the press issued nothing but adulating reports. Everyone knew Farin St. John would have a long and rewarding career with millions of loyal, admiring fans.

But as triumphant as renowned celebrity Farin St. John felt, the only thing Farin O'Conner, the woman, wanted was to get back to Florida and the man she loved.

CHAPTER 14

J ORDAN AWAITED FARIN'S RETURN. HE had stopped by her house earlier that morning to ensure everything looked perfect, from the spotless hardwood floors to the correct amount of sunlight shining through the shutters and lace curtains. He picked white roses from her garden, which he left in a crystal vase on her oak dining room table with a card that read, "Congratulations! Call me. I can't wait to see you."

The noon hour found Jordan preparing a light lunch. Something to occupy his time. When the phone rang, he rushed to pick up, eager to hear her voice.

"Your boat or mine, little brother?"

His shoulders slumped. "I thought you were in New York today."

"They cancelled the big mystery meeting. El's still in LA working on some gig for Fox. It's hard getting us all together these days."

"I've heard the rumors. How's Faith?"

The line fell silent for a beat. "I don't think she's freebasing, but she's using. I've tried talking to her but she doesn't listen. You know Faith. As for the rest of us, rubbish. Besides, we've been around too long to start worrying about bad press. It'll blow over once the album's released. There'll probably be another tour. It's been a while. Maybe too long. Anyway, that should kill the gossip. Now answer up—your boat or mine?"

"Can't make it today, buddy. Farin's due home any minute. Rain check?"

Chris's marked pause at the mention of Farin's name went unnoticed. With a somber undertone, he asked, "How was the tour?"

"Brilliant! Even Jameson was surprised when Bobby told him what a natural she is on stage."

"Bobby? He's with her?"

"You hadn't heard?"

"So, young Prince Robert's come out from behind his posh little desk to romp across the country, eh? No, I hadn't heard. But you know how life on the road is. I can't picture Junior managing days without sleep, missed meals, total exhaustion, and pressure every minute. But at least his absence explains why they've delayed releasing our album."

Jordan heard the concern in his brother's voice. "Worried?"

"Curious," Chris said, suddenly far away. "I've tried ringing Samantha, but she never seems to be available to take my calls. Nor, I might add, does she return them."

"Ring Jameson direct. You two're mates."

"Not anymore. He's changed."

"Maybe the old man's finally coming to grips with the notion he can't live forever." Jordan checked his watch. "Anyway, I need to get going. Will I see you next week at Ben's?"

Chris chuckled. "For Cheryl's latest excuse to throw a family soiree? Sure. I'm in."

Farin gazed at the stars crowding the Miami sky. A mild, clear Florida evening enveloped and comforted her as she stepped off Jordan's back porch in the darkening twilight. Champagne glass in hand, she strolled onto the soft, cool grass. She spun around wistfully in her airy, gauze dress, the green blades tickling her bare feet. Standing again in familiar territory filled her with a rare sense of contentment. "This is so much better than spending the night in some crowded restaurant."

"I'd rather have you to myself, anyway." Jordan encircled her exquisite body in his embrace.

She turned to wrap her arms around his neck and snuggle into his chest. "I love when it's just you and me. The last thing I want to see tonight is a bunch of people."

"Tired of crowds?"

"You're the only crowd I want."

He kissed her neck, inhaling her scent.

"I've missed you."

Jordan pulled back enough to kiss her lips with an urgent warmth. A familiar ache rose within him at the thrill of her nearness. Soft fingertips glided up and down his back as he held her closer, his desire mounting.

Farin set her champagne glass on the patio table and snuggled into his embrace. Their hands and lips explored one another as they drew so close, they became one person. His fingers sifted through her liquid auburn ringlets as he kissed her deeper, her sighs of pleasure encouraging him, begging for his touch.

She took a deep, giggly breath. "Such a beautiful night."

"Let's go inside," he urged breathlessly, his lips lowering to the base of her neck, his palms massaging the fabric concealing her breasts.

"No," she whispered, her breath sultry and demanding. "Make love to me right here, Jordan. I need you inside me right now."

He lifted her dress off over her head and tossed it aside, then lowered her downy body onto a blanket of grass. The sea breeze whipped through the palms curving out over the yard. As he fingered one fine, supple breast, he found her nipple firm and taught. Such a beautiful body. So willing, so eager.

Farin cooed as he fondled and caressed the roundness of her breasts and the moist flesh between her thighs. She arched for his body, wanting him closer, until their bodies were one. She kissed his face and grabbed handfuls of his silky blond hair. "I love you."

How she had missed the tenderness of his touch, his mouth, his breath on her body. She gazed into his eyes as he traced the curve of her chin, her lips, the side of her face with his fingers.

"I want to make you happy, Farin."

Her tongue traced the length of his lips. She nibbled lightly at the corners of his mouth and felt his response against her thighs. "I am happy."

He rolled onto his back as she rose from beneath him and straddled his waist. She straightened her shoulders, displaying the loveliness of her body before him as if in offering. He fixed her eyes with his. She lifted his right hand and placed it on her breast, her curls spilling about her shoulders and chest. She rested her hand atop his, shadowing every touch, every caress. She guided his hand beneath hers slowly, down the length of her abdomen, down between her thighs. When his hand broke free of hers, she tossed her head back in pleasure at the feel of his fingers inside her.

Farin's hips slowly gyrated as Jordan caressed her, his excitement growing with her response. She moved forward, running her fingers through the thick hair on his chest and then lower, tracing a trail of wispy hair as if she had found a map to buried treasure.

They touched, caressed, kissed, and kneaded each other's bodies as if in a dance. Face-to-face, eye-to-eye, heart-to-heart, they gave and they took of each other. The many months apart, unable to partake of each other, had nearly driven them both mad with longing.

"My angel," Jordan sighed as they climaxed at last, holding tight to each other's bodies until elation subsided. "I love you so much."

Farin lingered until her heartbeat slowed, then repositioned herself across his lap. He fingered her long, sweat-dampened spiral curls. They watched the starlit sky in silence, communicating with soft caresses.

"Move in with me, Farin."

Her body tensed upon his. "Do we have to discuss this tonight?"

"It's foolish to live apart. We spend our free time together, anyway. And lately, that's not much. You've been in Miami almost a year now. We've been together what—three months of that time? It makes sense to eliminate one of the beds."

Farin stretched out her arm and snagged her purse hanging off a nearby lawn chair, then removed a black velvet box. For a moment, her mind lapsed to a similar box she had received some time ago. A box she had not yet managed to return. It remained hidden in her lingerie drawer.

"Here." She handed Jordan the box, then settled back atop his chest, resting her head on her outstretched arm as she met his gaze. "I picked this up on my travels."

Inside this velvet box was not a loose, two-karat sapphire intended to hypnotize its owner, but a gold chain with a miniature platinum CD pendant attached to it. *Umbra* was engraved in script lettering on its face, along with Jordan's name. The inscription on the back read, "Let us cast one shadow."

Jordan held it up for inspection. "It's lovely."

"It doesn't matter if we live together or not as long as we both know—*really* know—how we feel. Please understand. I love you."

Jordan untangled his body from hers, sat up, and fastened the chain around his neck. He hooked his hand around her neck and pulled her to him until their foreheads touched. "And I love you. Thank you for the gift. I'll wear it always."

***

By the evening of Ben's cocktail party, Farin felt rejuvenated. A few days' relaxation and a little praise from Jameson Lockhardt was all she had needed.

Down Deep in Love, her second single, had spent the last five weeks at number one on the Billboard Top 100. Truckloads of fan mail poured in, along with interview, photo, and guest appearance requests. Jordan's home, and her own, were now surrounded by a consistent throng of admirers and camera-toting reporters.

After an eight-year struggle, she was an overnight success.

Farin viewed her nationwide acclaim with exhilaration. Performing for thousands of cheering, smiling faces, looking out over an endless sea of flickering lighters held aloft, fans swaying to the resonance of her voice, had transported her high above her intimate, humble beginnings gigging Sunset Boulevard's filthy, smoke-filled clubs.

Standing center stage, she had drawn and drank from a bottomless well of adoration. The crowds cheered, cried, screamed, whistled, and applauded. It was as peaceful and potent as sitting in the center of the sun. At last, her every dream had come true.

Conversely, the closest she ever came to seeing sunlight was a set of amber gels suspended on a gantry high above the stage, neon strobe lights, and blinding, unforgiving spots. Her daylight hours were spent catnapping on a moving bus, rehearsing, or pulling sound checks in empty stadiums and auditoriums. Each night, she had surrendered every ounce of her power to the music. A sacrificial offering to the starving, screaming multitude.

Time now to refuel, regain her strength, and begin again.

Ben and Cheryl greeted her with happy chatter as she followed them into the kitchen. Ben thanked her for the bottle of wine she brought and opened it to breathe.

"You look rested," Cheryl said as she set her up with a starter glass from another bottle.

"How long until you're back in the studio?" Ben asked.

"Jameson and I negotiated some time off so Jordan and I can enjoy the holidays."

"If November's any indication, we're in for a warm holiday season," Cheryl chortled.

Farin sipped her wine. "Jordan should be here by now. We'd planned to meet half an hour ago. I guess we're both running late today."

Cheryl bustled around the stove, minding the hard hors d'oeuvres. "He's on an errand. It's habit, I'm afraid. Whenever I have the family over, it starts out with our Jorie heading off to get me this or that from the store."

They settled into the living room with their drinks.

Before she could ask after the boys, Chris emerged from the large sliding door with Kyle in tow.

She diverted her attention, first to her watch, then to a quick hug when Kyle raced over to greet her, and finally to Cheryl's discussion of her favorite Thanksgiving fixings.

"Seven years in America and I still haven't perfected a turkey."

"Best bird I've tasted," Ben said.

She swatted his arm. "Aye, and you've had so many comparisons."

Farin tapped her wineglass with the nail of her ring finger as Chris approached. She had known he would be here tonight. Jordan had said not to worry, that Chris had changed since the move from New York. She remained unconvinced.

Before the tour, Bobby had seen him sitting in his car outside her house on occasion. And there were a couple of jonquil deliveries, too. Nonetheless, he had kept his distance.

If nothing else, though, his appearance had changed. His hair fell longer now, shaggy and sun-lightened. Tanned skin. Toned, defined muscles. Florida had been good to him.

When she realized she was staring, she looked away.

He greeted her with friendly indifference. "Hello there."

"Hi," she said, as if they had not been locked in a breathless embrace the last time she had seen him. She became aware of her every movement, certain all eyes would monitor them for hints of impropriety.

Before either of them could utter another word, Kyle whisked his uncle off to play with him and Derek.

Jordan arrived minutes later and greeted her with a kiss, which righted her nerves. Maybe Jordan was right. Hopefully, whatever tension she and

Chris had shared had abandoned them.

He disappeared into the kitchen to unload the small bag of groceries, then returned with a glass of wine and sat beside her. "Waiting long?"

"I was late. Marci called as I was leaving. She's having trouble with that boyfriend of hers." Farin relayed snatches of the conversation, the pain in Marci's voice, the things she had said. "I'm worried about her."

He put his arm around her and relaxed back onto the sofa. "We'll think of some way to get her down here."

They relaxed into easy conversation, with Cheryl sneaking off in intervals to replenish trays of snacks or refresh drinks. They discussed the material Ben had written for Jordan's next album, the highs and lows of Kyle and Derek's school grades, recipes Cheryl hoped to try soon, and Farin's epic battle of the bands with Ebony Suede. Chris hovered in and out of the room and the conversation, ever dogged by Ben's sons.

Cheryl watched Chris chase them into the foyer and heard the echo of his roar as they ran screaming upstairs. "They'll sleep well tonight."

Ben gave her a wink. "They're boys. They always sleep well."

Jordan held Farin's hand. She gave it a gentle, understanding squeeze.

A crashing noise echoed down from the second floor, causing Cheryl to wince and sending Ben upstairs to spoil the fun. "Think I'll disappear into the kitchen now to check the brie," she said.

Farin rose to assist, but Jordan insisted on going instead. "You rest," he said, kissing her cheek. "I'll go."

"You always help," Farin called after him. "Cheryl's gonna think I'm rude—or lazy!"

Soon, Farin's bladder protested the three glasses of wine she had imbibed. On her way to the restroom, she heard the boys protest in unison their father's admonition. She grinned at the exchange.

When she finished her business, she found Chris perched against the wall in the hallway opposite the restroom door. The sight of him stopped her in her tracks. Notes of Indian sandalwood, lime, and lily filled her senses.

"I hear the tour went well. Congratulations."

She rubbed her bare arm. "Thanks."

They stood together a long, awkward moment. Farin reproached herself, unable to reconcile the pull his dark eyes had over her.

Chris Grant was a man. Nothing more. She had resisted far more charming men in her life. Truth told, Chris was not all that charming anyway. Most of his lines lacked originality.

Earlier, she believed she had finally dismissed him from her mind. She had even stopped using him as a crutch to slay the demons in her dreams. But now, a familiar ache near her center warned her to walk away. "I should get back." She brushed past him in search of the safe haven of Jordan's arms.

She refilled her wine glass with straight vodka, then added a touch of cranberry juice. When everyone reassembled in the living room to hear Ben relay with some humor the events that had transpired upstairs, she fell quiet, wedging herself into the crook between Jordan's arm and chest.

Chris joined them, as she feared he would. He sat across from her, stealing meaningful glances as the night progressed. No one seemed to notice. Not even Jordan. No one commented on her conversational absence. Perhaps they chalked up her silence to fatigue.

Maybe they were right. Maybe she had not yet fully recovered from life on the road after all.

She refilled her glass more times than she dared. Anything to erase the thought of being in Chris's arms—his hot, sinful breath on her neck, his lips on hers, the feel of his hair in her hungry fists.

Had they not caused enough pain that night in New York?

Jordan kissed her cheek, drawing her out of her contemptible stupor. "I'm off to the studio for a bit. Join us?"

Her mind felt like cotton. "You go. The last thing I want to see right now is a microphone." She wondered if she sounded as wasted as she felt.

Years back, Ben had converted they guest house into a recording studio. Cheryl referred to it as "my husband's mistress."

Ben asked Chris to join them, but he begged off as well. Jordan did not appear suspicious as he and Ben disappeared out the back.

Only Chris and Cheryl remained with her in the living room. She consumed another vodka cranberry as Cheryl shared humorous anecdotes related to her sons. Farin caught snatches of the conversation through her growing drunken fog...something about Christmas...neither of the boys believed in Santa Claus anymore...looking forward to school break...lazy days sailing on their father's boat...drifting...swimming...water...

"I'm gonna step out for some air." She shot up, defying her reverie and the spinning room.

"All right then, pet?" Cheryl stood and touched her shoulder. "You look pale. Shall I get Jorie?"

Farin dared not look at Chris. She could imagine his victorious grin.

"I'm fine." She teetered slightly. "I just need some air. I'll be back."

Outside, Farin darted across the lawn on wobbly legs. Past the Olympic-sized pool, the studio, and to the end of the yard. The property bumped up against Hurricane Harbor, leaving her no beach access. Instead, she raced down the wooden dock spanning the width of the property, snagging her stockings on a dead palm frond before taking a seat on the bench at the far edge, where dense landscaping obscured her whereabouts.

The moonlight-upon-water shimmered like a roomful of fans holding up lighters during a melancholy ballad. She stared at it trance-like, recollecting her triumph on the road and wondering why the success she had chased—and had finally caught—was still not enough.

She relished her body's numbness. Better numb than to confess, even to herself, the feelings Chris had aroused within her again. Jordan was safety, commitment, love. The antithesis of every blameworthy desire that had tempted her after seeing Chris tonight.

Desperate to banish the attraction, Farin cataloged Chris's faults. She found many. Arrogant. Insensitive. Swaggering. Disrespectful of family. Too tall, too lanky. And, frankly, he wore too much cologne.

That was it. He smelled. Chris Grant was just a man—a man who smelled.

***

Jordan and Ben switched off amplifiers, speakers, and engineering equipment in the studio, content with the night's progress. "I don't know, Ben. I didn't think the nightmares could get any worse, but they have. Last night, she woke up in a cold sweat, screaming. I keep thinking I should figure out some way to find him."

"Who?"

"James Wellingham. I think he could help her."

Ben plopped down into his console chair and stroked his bearded chin. "Is it really that bad?"

"I think it is."

"And you think finding this bloke will help?"

"I don't know. At least if she confronted him, she might realize he's not a threat. It was an accident. The kid was drunk."

"If she's still so upset about it after all these years, she may need professional help. Sixteen years is a long time to hang onto so much grief. Besides, the guy might not want to meet her. How keen would you be to face the family you destroyed if you killed a man?"

"You're right." Jordan fingered the platinum CD hanging off his chain. "It might not even matter, anyway. Every time I try to find information related to the accident, I'm shut down."

Ben tilted his head.

"I started with the police. There's no accident report, no arrest report, and no record of an accident on the night her father died..."

"Do you have the right date?"

"There's no record of an accident involving Kelley O'Conner at all. I called the local papers. Same result. It's like the incident was erased—or never occurred." Jordan sat beside Ben at the console. "It's bizarre."

"He was underage, right? Maybe the records are sealed."

Jordan pointed at him, brows raised. "I didn't even think about that."

There came a knock at the door, then Chris slipped inside. "Am I interrupting?"

Ben waved him in and indicated a chair. "We were just shutting down. It's late."

"That's what I came to tell you. I'm heading home."

Jordan slapped him on the back. "I'll be calling in that rain check soon. We'll take my boat. I don't trust your driving."

"Tomorrow?"

He mentally reconstructed his schedule. "*People Magazine* has me all morning but I'm free in the afternoon. I'll see what Farin has planned and get back to you."

***

Farin decided that, for the first time since her return, she would spend the night alone at her house. The move, the tour. Everything had happened so fast. Maybe she was losing her identity. Or maybe she was more worried about Marci than she realized. The call earlier had upset her. Marci had always been the strong one. But she sounded anything but strong when they spoke.

Also, she found her recent clinginess with Jordan troubling. Whether due to the several months' separation or the nightmares, she had started to fear sleeping alone. In her conscious state, she recalled little more of the nightmares than the chaos they conveyed. Only vague, far-off images. More like a feeling than a memory. They left her confused.

Many things confused her. Like her unwillingness to move in with him.

Maybe she should relent. Her repeated pleas for Jordan's understanding had caused tension in their relationship. They loved each other. He was stable and true. Why not take the leap?

Save her father, she had never lived with a man. The thought of giving up her freedom scared her. She had wrestled with self-reliance for so long. As an adult, she severed romantic connections the moment she felt herself slip into the trap of dependence. Dr. Logan had said she habitually sabotaged intimate relationships to avoid abandonment.

Soon after, she had stopped seeing him.

"Miss O'Conner," came a familiar, taunting voice from behind her.

She spun around, then scowled.

"Straying a bit far from the security of the house, aren't we?"

Farin summoned her mental list of Chris Grant's many faults. Arrogant. Insensitive. Disrespectful. Smelly. She struggled to ignore how attractive he looked in his short sleeve silk shirt and tight jeans. His musky cologne wafted in the breeze. "Like I said—I needed some air."

He sat beside her on the bench. "Better now?"

"I'm drunk," she remarked flatly.

He mimicked her tone. "I know."

They sat in silence, which unnerved her. She hated silence, especially when it was so loud. Through her alcohol haze, she felt the steady pulsing of her heart spread to her limbs and head. She beseeched herself to leave. Jordan would be worried. And Chris? He was just a smelly man—with hypnotic eyes, a sexy smile, and a confidence she envied and detested. "Say something."

"Every time we talk, it becomes a bloody row."

She resented his British accent and how it sounded so much like Jordan's. "Then what're you doing here?"

He coughed out a teasing chuckle. "You may be drunk, Farin, but you're not stupid."

She focused on the water sloshing against the dock. The alcohol gave her more courage than she would have liked. If she harbored any residual fascination with Chris, it was his fault. She had never pursued so much as a conversation with him.

Smelly man. Insensitive, smelly man.

Her nostrils flared with cologne and disgust. "You don't care about anyone but yourself, do you? You'd do this to your own brother."

"What Jordan doesn't know won't hurt him."

She mentally added to the list of Chris's faults: *speaks in clichés.*

"You promised. We both did. And maybe I'm not into you. Have you ever thought of that?"

"Yes, actually." He stifled a laugh, inched closer, and stroked the side of her face with the back of his hand. "If I believed it, I wouldn't be here."

Farin jerked sideways. The aching between her thighs sickened her. Or maybe it was that last vodka cranberry. Either way, she cursed her body's betrayal and the memory of that damnable evening in New York.

She faced him, hoping to understand his motivations. And perhaps her own. "Why are you here, anyway? You love New York. Your band's there...your life's there."

His stare skewered her. "My life moved south."

She knew her inebriated state could not absolve her. In fact, it made it all the more impossible to suppress the awful secret she had long banished to the deepest part of herself.

Her eyes fused in agony of the inevitable. She loved Jordan. The thought of betraying him made her physically ill. But for reasons she could not even assimilate in her mind, she could no longer deny the truth.

She wanted Chris.

She wanted his lips on her. She wanted his hair in her hands again. She wanted to smell his cologne mixed with sweat upon her skin.

"You should go now, Chris. Please."

He leaned in and brushed the hair off her shoulder, then kissed her neck, savoring her shiver of surprise, her soft hitch of breath. "I think not."

"Then I will." Unsteadily, Farin stood and staggered across the dock's whitewashed planks. She needed to get back to Ben's house, back to Jordan. He deserved better than this. Did she possess no free will? No strength to stave off the disastrous result such an encounter would bring? Damn her feelings, anyway. She could not—*would not*—make such an unpardonable mistake.

Chris pursued her. When he caught up, he grabbed her arm and swung her around to face him. Beads of perspiration from the humid night air had formed on her skin despite the cooling breeze and her skimpy sun dress. "I don't think so, Farin. This moment is long overdue."

Farin panted from arousal. She swallowed the bile and alcohol rising up within her as she met the intensity of his stare. She hated him, and hated herself even more for standing there, making no additional attempt to leave.

For years, her life had been an endless struggle. Now, she had the love of a good man and the success she had craved. Her life was complete. Yet, when faced with the grim choice that lay before her, she had nothing left inside her.

"We can't do this to Jordan."

"Shhh." He ran his fingers across her glistening brow.

"I love him, Chris," she barely squeaked, unsure if she said it loud enough for him to hear. Unsure if she said it out loud at all.

"I'm so hard right now." He took a fistful of her hair in his hand and pulled her head back, exposing her neck to him.

Farin shut her eyes at the contact. Her body came alive. She feared she might scream, unclear whether it would originate from the pain or pleasure of the moment.

Chris slid the straps of her dress off her shoulders, delighted as her chest heaved in anticipation of his touch. He released her and stepped back, fixing her eyes with his as he unbuttoned his shirt.

Farin watched him undress, unable to flee. A tremor shook her. She glanced down, horrified to see her own hands in motion, slipping her body free of her dress, her cream-colored chemise, her marred stockings.

Something inside her brain exploded. Her mind shut down. She could not resist Chris. She did not want to resist him.

He pulled her body to his once more. Clutching a handful of auburn ringlets, he pulled her head back again and kissed her tepid skin. He ravaged her body, kissing and nibbling savagely, down her neck, her shoulders. He paid homage to her exquisite breasts, groaning as he passed his tongue back and forth over each of her nipples in turn. Farther and farther down, he kissed and nibbled and sucked at her beauty until at last he reached the sweet destination waiting for him between her trembling thighs.

He glanced up, noting with satisfaction her parted lips, flared nostrils, and heaving chest. He grasped her hips and burrowed into the moist mound of honey waiting to be taken.

White fire seared through Farin's body. She gripped fistfuls of his hair and pulled at his head, trying uselessly to take his mouth from her. She gasped for air, nearly falling to her knees with forbidden delight as she begged him to stop. He ignored her halfhearted protests, holding her steady until he felt the sensation overcome her.

Quaking and consumed with guilty pleasure, she slid down on top of him, scraping her knees upon the wooden slats. He took her with urgent thrusts, caressing her back, her hair, her face, kneading her breasts and buttocks. His skillful hands explored her, gluttonous as he rocked her slowly, rhythmically, back and forth, up and down until an orgasmic shudder coursed through him, sending her a second time into her welcome torment.

Finally, Chris dropped his arms in satiated exhaustion. Farin sprawled panting on top of him. He gulped to catch his breath, savoring the moment for which he had waited a tortuous year and a half.

Or longer. Perhaps his whole life. He had known from the minute he had first battled his impotence that she was the one woman—the only woman—who could bring him back. But never had he expected she would evoke such desire, such pleasure. He felt alive, as if this were the first time he had ever truly felt anything at all.

He massaged her back and stroked her soft spirals, careful to conceal this zealous awakening. He wanted to drink in her scent, to draw her inside him as she had drawn him inside her. He kissed her body, damp with their comingled sweat. He listened as her breathing calmed. He touched her full, supple lips, remembering their taste.

Chris had pleased Farin tonight in a way instinct, or pride, told him no other man had ever pleased her. And for the first time in his life he, too, had known true elation. What a waste that she would soon hate herself, and him, because of it. Still, no matter what transpired from here, his life had changed tonight.

They lay together for several minutes. Her bare skin against his stirred him. But as he moved to take her again, she rose and gathered her clothes. Her body glistered in the moonlight.

He longed to reach up and shout out, "Stop! You can't leave me! Not now!" Instead, he lay still, silent, as cool as ever. He watched her dress, his manhood hardening at the sight of her moon-drenched nakedness.

Stuffing her torn stockings into her dress pocket, Farin gathered her sandals and stumbled down the dock toward the house. As she passed him, he caught sight of a tear rolling down her cheek.

The guilt has already begun.

CHAPTER 15

*F*ARIN HURRIED DOWN THE EMPTY *street, inspecting every doorway, every shadow. Her white silk nightgown wafted and curled around her tiny legs. A brass clip held her tangled mass of curls. Her eyes narrowed in a futile attempt to peer through the dense fog as she advanced on bare feet, searching and searching, checking every inch of the dark night.*

Nearing the corner of State and Cabrillo, music suffused the air. She could not place the tune.

"Daddy!" Farin yelped. "Where are you?"

… oh, and while the king was looking down
… the jester stole his thorny crown …

She trudged, fear-stricken, toward the driver's door. Afraid to look, afraid to turn back. Two feet from the door, she perceived movement. She squinted at the blurry figure floating ghostlike from her father's car to the smaller vehicle. The figure was no more solid than the mist engulfing the scene. Fluid in movement. Detached from gravity.

… now the half-time air was sweet perfume
… while sergeants played a marching tune
… we all got up to dance
… oh, but we never got the chance …

***

Farin opened one bleary eye, then the other. An instant wave of nausea coupled with a lack of equilibrium prompted her arms to shoot out and clutch the sheets on either side of her. The ceiling fan rotated at full power above her, its twirling blades aggravating the queasiness. She glanced at the clock radio, then fused her eyes and held still until the room stopped spinning.

The fog of her mind lingered. She labored to separate troubling images and disjointed snatches racing through her thoughts much like the room raced around her—some a product of her nightmare, others the residual effects of alcohol. As her focus improved, she recalled the events that led to her waking alone, in her own place, with one hell of a hangover.

Unmistakable, sated pain radiated from her core. She gasped out loud as reality beset her. Ben's house. Vodka. The dock. Chris.

Save an occasional fantasy, she had acknowledged their mutual attraction only when other thoughts so tormented her, they threatened to consume her. Mentally indulging him combatted the nightmares. They helped her escape the stress of her waking reality. At least that was the lie she sold herself.

Now, everything had changed.

As she lay there on her back, she saw herself clearly for the first time in her life. Loathsome images disgusted her with an intensity more frightening than any nightmare. She was no better than Ginny Stevens.

As the dizziness abated, she formulated a plan of action. Chris would doubtless expect to continue their dalliance now that she had succumbed. She refused to have an affair. It was a one-time thing. It ended now.

Nausea wracked her body. She bolted from her bed and dashed to the bathroom. Slumped over the porcelain toilet, she purged alcohol toxins and what little undigested food she had managed to eat last night.

How had Jordan not seen through her flimsy excuses once she had found her way back to Ben's house? Clothes wrinkled, missing stockings, tear-stained cheeks. He had expressed concern more than anything else, then displeasure over her decision to sleep it off at her own house.

She had claimed she felt ill. No lie, in the end. Her actions sickened her more than what must have been the gallon of vodka she drank.

Crouched on the cool bathroom tiles, the stench of her own vomit filling her nose, Farin wondered how she could ever face him. She could not play sick forever.

By force of will, she showered, fixed her hair and makeup, swallowed four Advils, packed a bag, and then headed out her door to her new, red Mercedes 450 SLC hardtop convertible. A congratulatory gift from Jameson for her tour's success. Beyond her security fence, a group of smiling, cheering fans beckoned her attention as camera shutters clicked madly for a shot of the celebrity flying to the safety of her vehicle.

There was only one thing to do.

***

Jordan's property sat peaceful and bright. The sun pierced through a cluster of billowy white clouds, casting intermittent shadows on the lush, green landscape. As Farin parked her Mercedes around the side of the large driveway, she spotted the *People Magazine* van. She swore under her breath.

Better not to disturb him, she decided. She shifted her car into reverse, but before she could reactivate the security gate, Jordan strolled out the front door with some cameramen. He waved when he spotted her. His brilliant smile hit her square in her emptied stomach.

"Feel better?" he asked.

She stumbled from her car, nervous and nauseous. When he kissed her, her eyes darted toward the cameraman, as if his lens would expose her crime, afraid the whole world knew her secret. The heavily-tinted aviator sunglasses she sported in an effort to disguise her sin and ease the sun's cruel assault brought zero comfort.

"I know you're busy. I think I forgot to tell you last night. I'm on my way to the airport."

Jordan's smile dissolved into a confused frown. "But...Thanksgiving's days away. Cheryl counted on your helping her with the turkey."

"I'm no cook, Jordan. Besides, it's my mother." She thought she might get sick again.

He put his arm around her waist and led her aside. "You hate your mum."

She studied him with anxious eyes. "She needs me. She's worse. Marci said so last night when she called."

He stared off into the distance a moment, then back at her. "Give me two hours. I'm going with you."

Farin collapsed into his arms and sobbed into his shoulder. "I need to do this myself, Jordan. Please don't make it any harder for me than it already is."

***

Marci leaned, arms crossed, against a temporary construction wall erected opposite the long row of passenger gates at LAX. One foot hiked up behind her, it bounced against a slab of nailed sheetrock as she awaited Farin's arrival. More notice would have been nice. Still, she refused to complain. By the sound of it, Farin had reconsidered visiting her mother. It was about time.

A massive crowd bustled around her with hurried comings and goings. Families greeted out-of-town relatives arriving for the holidays. Others waited to board flights for various destinations. No fog or smog had grounded air traffic, and most everyone looked happy despite the intermittent rain.

As Farin waded through a sea of cheerful faces, Marci covered her mouth with her hand to stifle a laugh. A large straw hat sat upon her wigged head, the brim almost completely shrouding her face. Dark, oversized sunglasses concealed her eyes. A bulky tan trench coat added an extra fifteen pounds to her sleek figure.

The ridiculous garb left her unrecognizable. Probably by design. But no costume in the world could fool Marci. She recognized, among other things, Farin's full-hipped gait and the way she carried her bag and purse over separate shoulders.

"Blonde, huh?" Marci indulged herself a bark of laughter as they embraced, but when Farin pulled her dark glasses down the bridge of her nose to reveal her soulful, swollen eyes, all whimsy evaporated. "What happened?"

Farin jerked her head left to right, sizing up their surroundings. She replaced her glasses. "Get me out of here. I'll explain on the way home."

***

"Don't expect sympathy from me, Farin. Not now. Not when I'm on the other side of a similar scenario." Marci set her jaw and sneered in disgust. "And of all people! Chris kiss-my-ass Grant! How could you?"

Farin held her head and slumped back into the familiar old couch with its bright floral print. The beach house looked different with Jordan's belongings no longer filling its space, replaced now with Marci's and Dan's things. Jordan had offered Marci the use of his Malibu place when Farin moved to Florida. Los Angeles was too expensive to live alone on a bank manager's salary.

Still, she felt Jordan's presence everywhere. "I can't face him, Marce."

"You have to go back eventually. What then?"

Farin sniffed and raked her fingers through her hair. "I don't know. I can't think about it. I feel so...guilty."

"You *should* feel guilty! And using a dying woman as your excuse?"

"I didn't know what else to do. I had to leave."

Marci shook her head in disgust, twisting he lips to the side. "You're gonna turn that lie you told to get here into the truth. Your mom's not improving. If you expect me to cover for you when Jordan calls—and we *both* know he'll call—we're going to Santa Barbara. Tomorrow."

Reluctantly, Farin agreed.

They left the next morning for their hometown. The once-familiar drive overrode Farin's emotions. Laughter. Despair. Hope. Rage. Myriad memories shifted together then moved apart and realigned as the miles vanished behind them. They transformed like the rotation of colored bits of glass inside a kaleidoscope, reflecting their mirrored patterns in a succession of symmetrical design.

Heading north up the PCH from Malibu, the seaside towns and houses dotting the coast knotted Farin's stomach. A decade had passed since she had left Santa Barbara.

"I swore I'd never come back while Mom lived," she protested under her breath.

Marci's grip on the steering wheel tightened. "It won't be the only promise you've broken this week."

Farin shifted in her seat to stare out the window.

A part of Marci wanted to apologize for coming down so hard on Farin. Another part wanted to throttle her. That she could hurt Jordan so cruelly mystified her. Sure, Farin had a tragic past. But that was no excuse.

Cypress trees bowed from years of wind and ocean air, miles of sand and sea, and the occasional pocket of dust or dirt whipping in the breeze whizzed by them as they traveled. As they neared their destination, the tension riddling Marci eased. Thanksgiving at home. The idyllic salve to heal her own wounds. It still stung that Dan had not invited her to meet his family. She questioned their future. Moreover, she questioned his commitment.

"So, what did you think of him?" she asked, breaking the silence of the last ten miles.

Farin side-eyed her. "Dan?"

Marci nodded.

She turned away again. "He seemed like he was in an awful hurry to leave."

Marci's shoulders tensed. She laser-focused on the highway. "He's not home much."

"You've been miserable the whole year you've been together. Why'd you two even move in together?"

"He has his good side."

Farin's brows arched above an eye-roll. "Is he ever around long enough to see it?"

"Thanks for the advice." Marci faced her friend intermittently. "It means so much coming from you."

"Because I want you to find someone who makes you happy?"

"Ooooh, okay. Just...go 'find' someone, huh?" She palmed her forehead. "Why didn't I think of that? Maybe I'll follow in your footsteps. Maybe I'll find the man of my dreams and then sleep with his older brother."

Farin folded her arms, scrunching her lips into a sullen pout. "Can we turn on the radio?"

She jerked the radio dial to the "on" position. "You think it's easy finding someone? Maybe if you're a star who has to disguise herself to walk through an airport, but for a branch manager at a bank, not so much."

The radio filled the silence for miles. They heard Milli Vanilli, Paula Abdul, Janet Jackson, and Jody Watley before Marci's countenance shifted. "So, how was he?" she asked at last, trading resentment for a mischievous simper. "I have to know."

No matter how badly Marci wanted to make up, Farin could not bring herself to gossip about Chris Grant's legendary sexual prowess. She had replayed their encounter on a loop the entire flight from Miami. Chris had touched more than her body. They had *connected*. It terrified her. She had responded to him as if she had wanted him as desperately as he wanted her.

Had she? Had she wanted him the whole time?

"Well?" Marci pressed. "Out with it."

She tucked her folded hands beneath her chin, wedged herself against the door, and stared at the glove compartment latch. "I don't remember much. I was really drunk."

***

Santa Barbara Cottage Hospital loomed menacingly over Farin as they pulled into the main entrance and left Marci's Chrysler LeBaron with a valet. The hospital stood on a rise among mature trees like a towering tombstone over a gargantuan grave.

They cut through the emergency room entrance. Antiseptic smells and sterile uniforms overwhelmed her with memories of the night Chase drowned. Her gait stiffened as they trod the hallway and through the ICU. They passed clusters of white-smocked nurses, doctors standing at tall counters writing in charts, blue-clad orderlies pushing gurneys, and young female volunteers with their simple candy-striped uniforms.

Beth O'Conner convalesced in the last bed at the end of the third-floor hallway. She appeared oblivious to the attendants as they slipped inside her semi-private room and crept through the long canvas curtain separating her from a recent heart attack victim.

The room was immaculate and clean, permeated with the smell of antibacterial disinfectants and bleach. A florescent light above her mother's bed illuminated the nearby space with an eerie, flickering, false-looking glow. A solitary bouquet of mixed flowers sat on an otherwise unoccupied rollaway table of adjustable height.

Farin covered her mouth at the sight of her mother, who she scarcely recognized. Once, she was the most beautiful woman Farin had known, with long, sleek, black hair and exotic brown eyes. Warm, smiling eyes in the days and years before Kelley O'Conner's accident. Before the funeral. Before the whiskey.

Now, her mother—if the emaciated creature she beheld was indeed that woman—lay in a hospital bed, a shadow of that vital lady. Time, and booze, had been unkind. Dull, silver hair lay gnarled and matted against her head from lack of washing. Gaunt-faced and cadaverous with the exception of a distended abdomen, she disappeared into her many-sizes-too-big hospital gown. Farin struggled to determine where her mother's jaundiced skin ended and the yellow garment began. Small veins covered her face, arms, and chest, etched upon her skin like a map of meandering crimson rivers.

Though Beth had been stone drunk the last time Farin had seen her, she had still carried a shadow of her striking beauty. Now, that lovely creature, however sorrowful, had disappeared.

Marci placed a gentle hand on Beth's shoulder. Farin stood behind her in open-mouthed shock. "Aunt Beth," she whispered, softly squeezing her frail, lifeless arm. "It's Marci."

Beth blinked open her eyes. "Marci?

Farin stepped back, wishing she could fade away completely.

"What are you doing here?" Beth asked, her voice weak and cracking.

Her teeth were blackened in patches. Others were chipped. Some were missing altogether. Farin caught a whiff of the foul-sweet stench of rot.

Marci smiled and gestured behind her. "I'm here to visit you, and I've brought someone with me."

An immediate scowl found Beth O'Conner's thin, dry lips. "Well, well. My long-lost daughter, the big star. You shouldn't have bothered dragging her here, Marci. She wants nothing to do with me."

Defying her gag reflex, Farin forced herself into a bedside chair of chrome and plastic. A half-full bag of clear saline hooked to an IV pole dripped into a reservoir connected to a length of tubing, delivered by needle into the rice paper-thin skin of her mother's hand. The incessant rhythmic beeps and ticks of the contraptions monitoring Beth's vital signs unnerved her.

She swallowed hard, willing away the fear she might faint. "Let's not argue, Momma."

"How long has it been?" her mother continued, mustering some of her lost strength. "Ten years? Twelve?"

"Eight." *Eight years since I realized you would never change. Eight years since you threw an empty bottle at my head and I told you I was leaving.*

"Oh...*eight*. Well then, who am I to complain, right? Why are you here, Farin? What do you want?"

"I came to make sure you were getting proper care," she said, almost sincerely. Almost the dutiful, spirited child she no longer knew. She scooted the chair closer and plucked a ball of lint off her mother's scratchy blanket.

"They treat me lousy. Better than you do, though."

Farin battled bitter images of the last sixteen years. To her dismay, she missed the mother of her youth. The O'Conner household she knew had vanished so long ago. Had it ever really existed?

She extracted a stack of magazines from her bag. "I brought these for you. I figured you might get bored in here."

Beth's hands trembled as she struggled with the weight of the magazines. She rested them atop her lap and leafed through their pages. "I suppose these all have articles about you? How great your career's going with *Lockhardt*'s company?"

She clenched her jaw. "There's *Family Circle, Red Book*—all your favorites, Momma."

Beth studied her with disapproving eyes. "Your hair's a rat's nest."

"Curly hair's in style now, Momma."

She gave her hair a defensive stroke. Such remarks usually warned of other hurtful words to come. Would her mother call her a whore in front of Marci?

"Your father would be ashamed of you," Beth spat. As the words escaped her lips, her eyes bulged with what looked like instant regret.

Farin gazed down at the spotless vinyl floor, her eyes brimming with tears. The words shot through her like shrapnel. It was a lie. Her father could have never been ashamed of her.

"Well," Beth continued, her tone contrite, "I guess you should give me a hug. It might be the last one in me."

Farin rose, then fell into her mother's arms, weeping. Beth soon joined her, briefly visiting the stranger inside as she petted her daughter's hair and hushed her sobs.

"What happened to you, Momma?"

Beth lifted her daughter's chin. "I tried, Farin. I did. You don't know what it's like having fifteen years of happiness ripped out from underneath you. He was my *life*. My *h-heart*." She swiped at the tears flowing down her face.

Marci retrieved three tissues from her purse. She handed two over before stepping out of the room.

"They took my husband," Beth continued, dabbing her eyes. "Then, they took my dignity. And now...now you. I lost you, too."

Farin sniffed. "You still had me! I miss Daddy too, you know. I think about him every day. And all the nightmares all these years about James Well—"

Beth winced at the name as if it were a physical blow. "Don't ever speak that name to me."

"You keep saying 'they,' Momma. Who's *they*?"

"It doesn't matter anymore." She adjusted her frail shoulders and jutted her chin. "I didn't know how to be strong for both of us, Farin. I still don't. At first, I drank out of grief. Then, anger. Later, it was to forget. It was the only way to get through the day, eventually. And now? I want to be with him again, wherever he is." She broke off into weak, mournful sobs.

Farin wanted to disagree. She wanted to offer hope she had never in her own life possessed. But her mother was right. Beth O'Conner had refused to go on. In many ways, they both had.

She took her mother's hand. "What do the doctors say?"

"You know doctors. They've mentioned hospice. I overheard the nurses whisper something about spring."

"What can I do?"

Beth stared past Farin at the far wall. "There's nothing to do. All that's left in the house is the desk. I couldn't bear to sell it. The bank foreclosed a long time ago. They've let me stay there because of the friendship they had with your father."

"The house? Why didn't you tell me? I can give you money! I can—"

Beth patted her hand. "It's worn, Farin. You haven't been there in so long. Please don't go back. If you want the desk, I'm sure Joseph and Carol would ship it to—where? Miami?"

Farin nodded her tear-stained face.

"Are you still dating that handsome boy? That singer? Is he good to you?"

Farin looked down at her mother's liver-spotted hand. A fresh wave of guilt welled up inside her.

"He looks a little like that Shaun Cassidy you used to have a crush on."

She softly snorted. "That's what Marci said."

Beth stared at her as if she wanted to say more but had lost her strength. "I'm glad you came."

Farin kissed her mother's hand, then stood and grabbed her purse. "I'll be here a couple of days."

She looked at her from somewhere deep and far away. "Don't come back, honey. This is as good as it gets for you and me. Remember it and let me go. I know how much your father's death impacted your life, but you need to let that go, too. You're still so young."

Farin blotted her eyes with her damp tissue.

Beth wagged a bony finger her way. "And don't let anyone wear black to my funeral."

A rebellious smile broke through Farin's tears.

"One more thing." Beth winced as she engaged the bed controls to sit up.

Farin reached out but she waved her off.

"The desk. There're some papers. You've needed to see them for a while. They may change things for you. Make sure you can handle it before you read them. Maybe have a drink...or two."

"What are they?"

Beth shook her head. "I tried to tell you before. The booze muddled things up, I guess. For what it's worth, I always loved you. I wish you a happy life. I'm sorry things turned out this way."

Farin turned to leave. When she reached the door, she looked back at her mother, surrendering herself to the little girl inside. "What if I miss you?"

Beth kissed her fingertips, then held up her hand in Farin's direction. "Goodbye, my darling. And—"

She lifted her brows.

"You're not a victim, Farin. Don't live like one."

Her mother's words pierced the deepest part of her.

***

"You sure you're okay?"

"I'm fine. It was a long flight, that's all. I don't feel like going anywhere."

"Then I'll come to you. Cheryl sent home leftovers. We could have a make-up Thanksgiving."

"I just wanna sleep, Jordan. Can we do it tomorrow?"

It was more than the soft rejection that hurt. More than missing their first real holiday together. Sometimes, it seemed Farin did not want him too close. Especially when it came to her past.

"It's not personal," Marci had assured him multiple times.

But sometimes, Jordan found that difficult to believe.

When he arrived at her place the next evening, something undefinable was absent from their embrace. She neither smiled nor volunteered details of her trip.

Nonetheless, he warmed, then served, the scrumptious turkey, mashed potatoes, stuffing, and corn leftovers alongside a fresh salad. As they dined, he shared anecdotal highlights of the dinner she had missed. Farin contributed little to the conversation.

"How is she?" he dared to ask.

Her expression was flat and unseeing. She pushed food around her plate with her fork. "She wants to die."

Lost for words to comfort her in the face of such a tragic announcement, Jordan cleared their dishes, then poured after-dinner cognacs.

"Jameson called to wish us a nice holiday. When I told him you went to see your mother, he sounded concerned."

Farin tucked her legs beneath her on the sofa. "That was sweet of him."

"Actually, it sounded more like he didn't want you to see her. It wasn't what he said. It was more the vibe of the call itself."

Farin tilted her head. "Jameson doesn't even know my mother."

With her current distractions, Jordan opted not to tell her just *how* strange the call had been. Since the day Jameson met Farin, something had seemed off. Ben and Chris saw it, too. An odd protectiveness, or preoccupation, none of them could understand.

In addition to Jameson's mysterious behavior, Jordan grew exasperated with his search for James Wellingham. Dead ends, all. Last week, he had placed ads in both the *Santa Barbara News-Press* and the

Independent. So far, no response. Not even in hopes of collecting the five-thousand-dollar reward offered in exchange for information.

He wished he could call Beth O'Conner, but Farin might not forgive his crossing an invisible boundary, illness or no illness. Thus, it appeared James Wellingham had disappeared off the face of the Earth, or had never been on it in the first place.

They sat together, cuddling and sipping their drinks.

"I'm sorry for running out on you," Farin said, emotionless.

He squeezed her closer. "You don't have to face this alone."

"I know."

"Let me be here for you."

"I'm trying."

He kissed the top of her head, inhaling the scent of her. "I want us to be closer."

"I want that, too."

"Move in with me. It's time to say yes."

She pulled away to face him, then nodded.

He turned and clasped her shoulders. "You're sure?"

She buried her face in his chest. "I love you."

Jordan gave Farin no chance to reconsider. He moved her in the next day. Though he disliked feeling compelled to tiptoe around her moods for fear she would tumble back into the pit she had fallen into, over time, she adjusted to the change.

As a Brit, Thanksgiving held no significance to Jordan. While disappointed she had missed it, he let it go. However, he fully intended to make this the best Christmas either one of them had experienced.

She agreed with minor hesitance to host a Christmas party for the family.

"We always go to Ben and Cheryl's. It's our turn. Besides, what better way to celebrate your moving in?"

"You don't throw a party because you move someone into your home," she said as they decorated their first Christmas tree together, placing a handmade star of paisley printed cloth on the tree and setting aside a coil of garland.

He dug through boxes of ornaments. "I do."

She broached no further arguments.

While she busied herself decorating and planning the menu, Jordan went Christmas shopping for her gift: a yellow gold band with a perfect marquise cut, three-karat blue diamond. He would propose Christmas Eve.

***

Chris wanted to beg off. Whatever the big announcement was, he was in no mood to party. He had had a crap day. Further, Jordan's blissful oblivion had irritated him. Did he harbor no suspicions about Farin's sudden trip to California?

The impulsive sojourn had stunned, yet somehow, satisfied him. He had intended to contact her upon her return, but Jameson had sidetracked him when he summoned him to New York.

The meeting was brief and bitter.

"I warned you not to move! I warned you to stay away from Farin! Look what you've done to the band!"

"You're not my father, old man. And don't blame Faith's problems on me!"

Without fanfare, Jameson dropped the bomb. "It's over, Chris. When your contract's up, so is Mirage's relationship with Lockhardt Sound."

"*Fine!*" Chris had seethed, though inside his stomach wrenched at being so unceremoniously discarded. At least the old man had decided against canning their last album.

Sod Lockhardt. He, too, had had a bellyful. His primary concern was Faith. He loved and respected her more than anyone in- or outside his family. He also accepted that she cared about him more than she would admit.

After the meeting, Chris tried unsuccessfully to contact his bandmates. Maybe they blamed him, too. Lockhardt had doubtless convinced them the breakup was either his fault or his idea.

After a two-day phone campaign, Faith agreed to meet Thursday morning. He arrived at her Brownstone early, so as to make his return flight to Miami in time for Jordan's party the next night. As it turned out, that fateful decision meant the difference between life and death for Faith Peterson.

He had found her passed out on the floor of her kitchen. Repeated shouts, slaps, and shoulder-jostles brought her around.

"What did you take?" he demanded.

She gazed at him through angry, unfocused eyes and shook her head.

"Tell me!"

"Leave me alone!"

"Not until you tell me what you took!"

"Everything! I took fucking *everything*!"

He dealt with the emergency room, which included the obligatory bribing of doctors, nurses, and several staff members to keep quiet. Things were touch and go at first. Chris stayed at her bedside, leaving only once, to change his flight to Friday afternoon.

When Faith came to, he insisted on rehab. Obscenities notwithstanding, she relented—but only after he threatened to call her parents.

He helped make the arrangements, then caught an afternoon flight home for Jordan's party. Better late than a no-show.

Jameson had changed. That change had affected them all. But by the time Mirage's contract ran out, Chris determined that he would have Farin, Mirage would have a new label, and Chris would start his new life.

***

Jordan waved him in with an enthusiastic smile. "You're late! Everything okay? Why the last-minute summons?"

Chris stepped inside, his eyes darting about the house in all its flickering red and green. *Together with Cliff Richard* sounded from the stereo. Neither his brother's jovial disposition nor the merry embellishments soothed him. Rarely had he beheld such a ridiculous display of Christmas cheer. Not even in their childhood home.

Fresh pine branches with tiny woven Christmas lights blanketed the fireplace mantel, giving a rustic feel to the modern house. Lighted angels rested on two shelves of the floor-to-ceiling bookcase against the living room's far wall. Garland laced through and twisted around the railing of the staircase. A twelve-foot Douglas Fir stood in the corner of the room, decorated with family ornaments collected over the years, notably the handmade construction paper cross Chase made in kindergarten two years ago, which rested in the most conspicuous place.

"He canned us," Chris spat, crossing the foyer into Father Christmas's living room.

Jordan's smile vanished. "What the—?"

Chris leaned in, adding in a whisper, "Faith went nuts. When I got to her place, she was passed out. She'd taken everything including the Flintstone's Chewables."

Jordan stood aghast.

"I had to take her to the bloody emergency room to have her stomach pumped. I checked her into rehab."

Chris glimpsed Farin disappear into the kitchen. Her hair was stacked festively on her head, with loose ringlets hanging down her neck, touching the bareness of her shoulders exposed by a strapless green hostess gown. She looked amazing.

"I'm sorry," Jordan said.

Chris waved his hand. "So, what's the big announcement?"

"Farin finally agreed to move in with me."

His day just could not get any worse. "Really? Well, that's just ducky now, isn't it?"

Jordan tucked his chin. "Problem?"

Chris shook his head. "Forget it. It's been a helluva day." He scanned the house again, searching for her, then looked back at Jordan. "I need a drink."

***

When Farin dragged herself out of bed late the next morning, she found Jordan's note, saying he had gone Christmas shopping. Sipping her morning coffee, she realized she needed to think about shopping as well. With only days left, she could think of nothing she could get him that he did not already have. She should have waited to give him the necklace.

The more her celebrity grew, the more challenging it was to move about freely. People recognized her. Whatever she bought turned fodder for the press, including price and color photos, before she got it home. How Jordan mustered the determination to brave the scrutiny this morning, she did not know.

On one hand, this was exactly where she had always wanted to be. Jameson had kept his promise. On the other hand, the air was mighty thin at such heights. Sometimes, she struggled to breathe.

As Farin rinsed her mug, a loud pounding at the front door thundered through the house. She panicked for fear Jordan had forgotten to activate the security gate. She hurried to the living room. Before she reached the keypad, Chris stormed inside.

Arms down, gait stiff, he stomped toward her as she backed away. "Why?"

She gathered together the folds of her red silk robe. "What are you talking about? What are you doing here?"

He swayed before her, nostrils flared, face flushed. "You rabbit, you return, and now you're *living* here? Why?"

"Are you drunk?"

"Tell me!"

"Why do *you* think?"

He staggered closer. Again with the cologne. And those damn brooding eyes. Visual snapshots of their dalliance on Ben's dock flashed in her mind.

"If you feel nothing for me, why the sudden change of address?"

Farin raised a defiant chin, then dropped down on the white leather sectional. "Don't flatter yourself, Chris. I barely remember that night."

Chris towered over her. "Pfft. Jordan may believe your rubbish, but I know you."

"You '*know*' me?"

"Better than you know yourself, I'd wager. You never knew what you were capable of until you lost control."

Farin scrambled to her feet and marched toward the kitchen. "Get out! You're drunk and you don't know what you're talking about."

Chris stalked after her. He caught her arm and spun her around. His gaze skewered her. "Every time I see you..."

Farin jerked free. "Jordan's all that matters to me. Doesn't that mean anything to you?"

"Not when I think of you lying breathless on top of me, it doesn't."

Her heartbeat throbbed inside her. "Please go."

"You'll never be happy living a lie."

"You're wrong. I'm happy with Jordan."

"Who are you trying to convince? Jordan? Me? Or *yourself*?"

"Jordan will be home soon. If he finds you here—"

He kissed her hard, wrapping her in his arms despite a perfunctory attempt to wriggle free.

Since before her return, Farin had known the only way to prove her love for Jordan was to sacrifice her freedom. She believed the sacrifice would end her forbidden lust for Chris. She believed whatever game he played, he had lost.

Now, everything blurred. Unable to resist his commanding desire, she surrendered herself as she had before. Every second of the encounter, she told herself to stop. Yet, she gave herself willingly, right on the cold tile floor of Jordan's kitchen.

As before, they laid together in total silence after their mutual climax.

She stared at the ceiling, aware of his body on hers, the slow stabilizing of his pulse, of him still very much inside her. "I'm not like you. This isn't enough for me."

He kissed her damp face, pushing back the spirals clinging to her cheeks and neck.

He hardened again as he moved rhythmically inside her. Her body responded accordingly.

"If Jordan were enough for you, why would you be with me?"

"I'm not 'with' you. And I...I don't know why."

"I know why," he said, taking her again.

Her climax so consumed her, she nearly fainted.

When he stood at last to gather his clothes, Farin sat up and hugged her knees, watching his naked body move as he strode around the kitchen collecting his boxers, his jeans, his shirt. She wanted to taste him. She wanted to know what he felt like in her mouth. She wondered what he wanted for Christmas. Then, she remembered that Jordan would be home soon.

"It stops now, Chris." Her eyes turned cold when he faced her. "Unlike you, I have a conscience. Maybe someday you'll understand."

He headed out, then turned back, his jawline rippling as he spoke. "People with consciences? They usually make an effort not to repeat the same mistake twice. First time, shame on me. Second time, shame on you. Don't fool yourself, Farin. I'll be back...and you'll be waiting."

She pulled her robe onto her lap and hung her head, knowing he was right.

CHAPTER 16

THE BEACH HOUSE STOOD IN stillness beneath the first rays of dawn. Marci lay awake, staring out at the pepper-colored sea as daybreak seized the shadowy waves, turning the white, foamy froth thrashing its sand a silver-gray. Dan Albright snored beside her in their California King as the light crept up from the east.

Marci loved Dan—and oh, how she hated him. No longer did she question the possibility of an affair. Calls had started coming in, the other party hanging up upon hearing her voice. And still, Dan denied her accusations with his every breath.

Studying his still, sleeping frame, she ached with emotion. He did not love her, though he claimed to every day.

She slid out of bed, wrapped her afghan around her shoulders, and padded downstairs for coffee, cherishing the remaining moments before he would rise to resume living their lie. As the coffee brewed, popping and hissing and freeing its strong aroma, Marci walked to the bay window.

The sun rose higher now. The ocean's palette transmuted to Aegean-blue under the growing light. Clouds gathered in the westward sky, promising a winter storm. Christmas approached. And as he had done for the last two years, Dan would spend the holiday in Riverside with his family, without her.

There came a knock at the door. Marci turned, startled and confused. Six thirty in the morning. No one had visitors this early. She went to the door and peeked through the peephole, deflating as she beheld the pathetic figure on the other side.

Expressionless, she opened and held the door so Farin could bring in her bags. "Did he catch you this time?"

Farin's clothes sat oversized and wrinkled upon her frame, her attire more appropriate for Florida weather than for California. Canvas shorts, simple tee, sandals. Her hair sat banked upon her head in a disheveled mass, raccoon eyes from smeared mascara, and swollen lids.

Marci led her to the kitchen, draped her afghan over a kitchen chair, and poured them each a cup of fresh brew.

Shoulders slumped in remorse, or self-pity, Farin sat down at the table and dumped three packets of artificial sweetener into her cup. "I thought once Jordan and I were living together Chris would leave me alone."

"In Jordan's *house*, too?" Marci dropped a spoon on the table so Farin could stir her coffee, then slid down with an agitated thud. "Farin Shae O'Conner, for all the relationships I've seen you walk out on, you've never been a cheater. Didn't you learn your lesson the first time? I guess not, or you wouldn't be here." As an afterthought, she shook her head and spat, "Weasel."

"Can I stay here until I get my head back on straight?"

"Will you see Dr. Logan?"

"I can't stay unless I meet your conditions? Like last time?"

"That's not what I meant." Marci propped her head on one hand. The back-and-forth of her own life exhausted her. She was none too certain she had room for Farin's. "Did you leave a note?"

Farin looked up through downcast eyes.

"Farin!"

"I can't talk to him right now. If he calls, tell him you haven't seen me."

Marci leaned back and folded her arms. "You're suggesting I lie for you?"

Farin looked down and away.

"I hate this. I hate it for your sake, and I hate it for mine. I'd hoped I might find someone who made me as happy as Jordan's tried to make you. If you don't get yourself together—and fast—you're gonna lose him."

Farin swiped beneath her eyes and nodded.

Marci sipped her coffee, unmoved by her friend's tears. She had no more advice to give. No answers. Her own love life was hanging by a thread. She could fix no one else's.

Farin spent a week in Los Angeles, holed up at the beach house. The one time she wandered out to Rodeo Drive, she noticed people watching her. They looked at her the way she had always looked at passing celebrities. Living on the other side of those stares, her world felt like a giant fishbowl, surrounded by hundreds of gawking, often unkind eyes. If the paparazzi spotted her, it would blow her anonymity.

Jordan called Marci every day, sometimes more than once, hoping for some news. Marci warded off the calls without lying—*exactly*—and gave them each loads of advice they did not want to hear. "He's not buying it, Farin. He knows you're here."

The one person Farin did call with her whereabouts was Bobby Lockhardt.

"Do you need me? I can be there tomorrow."

"I'll be fine. I figured you should know where I am in case you needed to get in touch with me."

"You realize you're too smart to do something so stupid, right? Now do you see why I don't want anything to do with this love stuff?"

She rubbed her forehead with the heel of her hand "What's wrong with me?"

"It's probably sex-related," he teased. "Most things are, right? My advice is to take two cold showers and call Jordan in the morning."

"Thanks. For everything."

"Don't get mushy, Farin. I'm perfect if you want to go out and have a good time, but sloppy true confessions aren't my bag. Besides, I'm no different from any other man you know. I'm crazy about you." He panted into the telephone.

Farin hung up with a laugh as Marci stomped in and dropped a bouquet of jonquils down on the table. "Welp, someone knows you're here."

Farin made a face as she leafed through the yellow flowers. "Why won't he just leave me alone?"

"That's his game—like not sending a card. He operates in a vacuum of silence. And I'll tell you something else." She snatched the bouquet up and shoved them at her friend. "I really hate these things."

The telephone rang and Marci answered it while Farin dumped the flowers in the trash can out back. When she returned, she found Marci sitting motionless in the living room, her face drawn and pale.

"You okay?"

"Sit down."

Farin's stomach dropped. "What happened?"

"That was my dad. The hospital called him. Your mom died."

Her body numbed. She thought she heard ringing in her ears.

"Farin, I—"

She shook her head, incredulous as Marci scooted over and draped her arms around her shoulders. Their last visit had gone so well. Farin had even considered visiting again, despite her mother's insistence she stay away. She had hoped to salvage their relationship. Had Beth needed her as much as Farin needed a mother?

Marci held her tight and sobbed.

Farin was oblivious to the tears streaming down her own face.

The next morning, they headed to Santa Barbara for the second time in a month. Farin scheduled Beth's funeral for Friday. Though Joseph and Carol Williams begged her to stay, she opted for a hotel room. She needed to be alone. She needed to think. She needed answers.

The day of her mother's death, Farin had called the hospital to see what they needed her to do. They informed her the arrangements and outstanding medical bills had been handled by an anonymous source. Peaceful Rivers Funeral Chapel transported and prepared her mother's body. After asking both the hospital and the chapel who had made these arrangements, she had come up empty-handed.

Beth O'Conner's will was simple. Her only possession, save some clothes and personal items, had been the hardwood desk, which she had told Farin to take. No other assets remained. Some unseen hand had cleared her mother's outstanding debts. Farin assumed her father's former colleagues had made these considerations. Or Joseph and Carol. Either way, naming the day for the funeral and showing up were her only tasks.

She slept until noon Friday and woke up thinking about Jordan. He would doubtless stop looking for her soon. He would probably wash his hands of her altogether. She hoped so, for his sake.

Though she yearned for him, shame prevented her from calling. Worse, she was a horrible liar. Jordan would deduce it all if they spoke.

If by some miracle Jordan gave her one more chance, she swore to herself she would remain faithful. Her desire for Chris sat like a lead weight in her belly. It no longer aroused her; it repulsed her.

Christmas was three days away. Much of California had turned to sticky mud beneath a much-needed rain. Farin hated that her mother would be buried in the cold, gloomy rain.

She hated her mother, period.

How could Beth leave her *now*, when they had finally found hope in their relationship? In all the years Farin had not needed a mother, she sure needed one now. And as usual, Beth was MIA.

Farin showered, put on her makeup, and pulled her old black dress from the closet. She had plenty of others now, but would wear this dress one last time. Sure, Beth had made her promise not to let anyone come to her funeral in black, but Farin had no intention of going to the funeral. She could not stand in the cemetery as her mother's coffin was lowered into the ground beside her father.

Farin no longer felt alone; she *was* alone.

Once ready to go, Farin stepped back and examined herself in the mirror. Black shoes, black stockings, black dress—even a black hat with a black veil. She certainly looked like she was going to a funeral.

She picked up the phone and rang the front desk. "I need a cab."

The O'Conner house crouched as a distinctive eyesore amidst the cozy neighborhood on Mason Boulevard. The dirty white paint of the bantam two-story had chipped and peeled. Its neglected yard lay overgrown, shabby with crabgrass and dandelion. As Farin passed through the rotting gate of the rotting picket fence, unshed tears brimmed her eyes. She covered her open mouth with her hand.

A For Sale sign hung from a white-wood pedestal wedged into the ground next to a large, untrimmed shade tree. Kelley O'Conner had planted it the day he had moved his young family into their new home some twenty years ago. In younger days, Farin and Marci had sold lemonade and enjoyed tea parties under that tree.

Split, sun-faded wooden stairs creaked as Farin crept toward the door. To her right, their old porch swing dangled by a single, rusted chain. She and her father would sit outside on warm nights, swinging as he read her stories of brave knights, dragons, and damsels in distress.

Farin reached for the door handle, then pulled back. Her mother had understated the situation when she described the house as "worn." It looked as though it could topple down upon her if she entered. As if no one had cared for it in the sixteen years since her father's death. With a determined intake of breath, she pushed opened the unlocked door and entered the home of her youth.

The emptiness of her surroundings left her dumbstruck. Her spiked heels echoed upon the unpolished, ill-repaired wood floor. Dust particles floated in slanting streaks of sunlight through threadbare curtains.

A shudder coursed up her spine as she spied the top step of the staircase. She could almost hear the echo of police sirens. Probably better, she decided, to spare herself the agony of going upstairs. By force of will, she moved on.

A two-thirds-full bottle of whiskey sat open on the kitchen counter. A large puddle of rust-colored blood had dried on the floor below, probably from when Joseph and Carol had found her mother the day of her hospitalization nearly three months ago.

She peeked out back through thin, faded curtains at the sad remains of her treehouse. The unforgiving sea breeze and rain from a thousand showers had degraded its exterior.

Doubling back to the den, Farin found her father's desk. It sat polished and pristine amid its musty surroundings. She sat down on the worn leather executive chair and pulled out the top left-hand drawer. Inside was a long, hinged metal box. It felt heavy and unevenly distributed in her hands as she retrieved it. Something shifted inside. Morbid curiosity swelled within her. She wondered what it could possibly contain that would have the power to "change things" for her.

Farin ran her flattened hand along the top of the rustic green metal. Was she ready to confront its contents? What could be worse than seeing her childhood home in its present condition?

"Make sure you can handle it before you read them. Maybe have a drink...or two." Of course Beth would say that.

With trembling hands, she raised the lid back on its hinges. Inside, she discovered a stack of papers. Beneath them, several Polaroids. At the bottom was a disintegrating brown paper bag.

She lifted up the wrinkled bag, peered inside, and encountered an empty tequila bottle. Her lips curled in disgust. Beth must have left the bottle inside amongst the papers during an evening of drunken, bitter memories.

Replacing the bag, Farin glimpsed a handwritten obituary and a receipt from the *Santa Barbara News-Press* dated two days after her father's death. She recognized her mother's penmanship. Liquid of some kind had spilled on its surface, smudging it so badly, she could only make out two lines. Something about Kelley O'Conner, beloved husband...survived by his loving wife, Beth, and only daughter, Farin.

She sucked in her cheeks as she slid the paper and its receipt beneath the bagged tequila bottle. What little remained of the alcohol had likely found the obituary and made the ink bleed across its page.

Yet another thing you ruined.

Leafing through the stack of papers, she searched for the published obituary, figuring her mother would have kept a copy, but found nothing. Yellowed letters and documents made up the bulk of the papers in the box—no newspapers.

She gathered the Polaroids and studied the first picture. Farin recognized the images the photographs had frozen in time. Those same images flooded her waking, and sleeping, mind. The twisted brown metal made Farin want to vomit. As she forced herself to look through more pictures, she saw the wreckage of the black Porsche that had caused the destruction.

It seemed impossible that such a compact vehicle—at least compared to a Chevy station wagon—could induce such destruction. The Porsche must have been traveling at incredible speed at impact. Farin shuddered at the thought. How had the Wellingham boy survived the crash? And why had Beth kept photographs?

She replaced the photos and picked up the first document in the stack of papers—a copy of her father's death certificate.

The tears flooding her eyes impaired her ability to read the document, though it told her nothing she did not already know.

Name: Kelley David O'Conner

Age: 37

Cause of Death...

Farin had been asleep when the police arrived sometime after midnight that mid-April evening. Flashing red and blue lights strobed against her peach-colored lace curtains. The radio dispatcher's scratchy, broken calls alarmed her. Her first thought: alien invasion.

Lights strobed her room in spiraled, soundless rhythm. She could not make sense of the series of letters, words, initials that drifted in the night air outside her window.

"...two-Adam-fourteen. What's your twenty?"

Farin wiggled out of bed and scampered to her second-story bedroom window. Wide-eyed, she parted the lace curtains and stared into the clear night sky. Red and blue radiance spun in circles, reflecting off the olive-colored leaves of their Australian willow tree's drooping branches. Not a spaceship in sight. With a disappointed half-frown, she followed the lights down to the sidewalk in front of her house. There, she spotted a police car.

At that same moment, there came a thunderous knock at the door. She had never seen a police car up close, let alone a real live policeman. Her daddy had many friends who were policemen, but she had never met one all dressed up in uniform. She rushed back to bed, threw on her robe, stepped into her slippers, and scurried to the stairway.

She plopped down on the top step and folded her arms in her lap, unable to contain her glee. What did the policeman want to talk to her daddy about? Did a monster terrorize her neighborhood?

Her daddy would be the perfect person to help capture a monster. He had killed many shadow-dwelling monsters beneath her bed. She giggled with anticipation. Her daddy was the strongest, bravest, most handsomest man in the whole world. After tonight, he would be a hero. She could hardly wait to tell Marci.

Farin watched her mother set her book down on an end table and rise from her easy chair in the living room. She gathered the folds of her silk robe and tightened its belt as she stopped at the stereo console and turned down the volume. Don McLean's *American Pie* fell to background noise as she crossed the room and opened the front door.

... bad news on the doorstep
... I couldn't take one more step
... I can't remember if I cried
... when I read about his widowed bride ...

Something in the officer's somber disposition sent her mother back two steps as he entered. The officer removed his hat and held it at his waist with both hands. Outside, a second patrolman waited to follow his partner inside. Farin only saw half her mother's face, but could see the color drain from her beautiful features. Soon, both officers were inside. The latter closed the door behind him.

Farin linked her arms around two wooden posts on the banister, peeking her small head between them. It occurred to her she had not seen her father. She pondered his absence, then figured he had gone to bed. He had missed dinner earlier and had not tucked her in. He often worked late. The stairway posts gave little comfort as she sat frozen in place, curiously unable to go wake him up to help her mother.

A series of beeps sounded from the police car outside. The dispatcher's voice clipped through the radio static, "Standby all units to copy a ten-eight-fifty-one down at the pier...fifteen minutes ago."

"Mrs. O'Conner?" the first officer asked.

Beth wrapped her arms around her body. She nodded, then unfolded one arm long enough to tuck a stray tendril of black hair into the braid which fell down her back.

"I'm Sergeant Bill Kinsey with the Santa Barbara City Police Department." He pointed over his shoulder. "This is Officer Sam Klein. I'm afraid we have some bad news for you, ma'am."

Kinsey glanced left, then, right, then back at Beth. "Is there someone we can call to be with you, ma'am? A neighbor, perhaps? A friend or relative? I apologize, ma'am. Normally, there'd be a female officer with us to talk to you. It's protocol. Unfortunately, tonight's roster's a little lean."

Beth searched Kinsey's cheerless blue eyes. She clutched her robe at her chest. "It's not Kelley."

Sergeant Kinsey's arms fell to his sides. He stared down at the hardwood floor. A beat later, he cleared his throat, set his jaw, and straightened his stance. "I'm sorry, Mrs. O'Conner. At approximately ten thirty this evening, your husband was involved in a car accident. I'm afraid he didn't survive."

In that split second, Beth O'Conner tested Sergeant Bill Kinsey's dexterity. Her eyes rolled back in her head, her arms went limp, and she fainted. Kinsey broke her fall, catching her before she hit the floor. His hat dropped from his hands, bounced once, then landed upside down.

... and them good ol' boys were drinking whiskey and rye
... singing, "This'll be the day that I die
... "this'll be the day that I die" ...

Farin's eyes bulged as her mother collapsed. "Mommy!" She bolted to her feet and jogged three steps down the staircase before locking eyes with the patrolman holding her mother in his arms.

Officer Sam Klein's hand jerked to his holster. When he spotted her, he relaxed his hand but exchanged glances with Kinsey.

Farin took another step. "Leave my mother alone!"

Officer Klein started up the stairs. One hand on his black leather belt, the other extended toward her, he took calm, slow steps. "It's okay, hon."

"*No!*" Farin shrieked. She turned and ran as if her life depended on it. Her father needed to wake up and make the bad men go away. He needed to save her mother.

Farin raced to her parents' bedroom at the far end of the hall. She stopped at the foot of their bed, blinking, her body trembling with confusion. On her mother's side, sheets and blankets lay in disarray. On her father's side, the pillow remained tucked neatly into the bedspread.

Her mind struggled to reconcile their empty room. Visions of aliens and monsters flooded her imagination. Her father swore aliens and monsters did not exist. Where could he be?

"Daddy!" Farin wailed as she jumped onto the bed and crawled from her mother's side to her father's. "Help! Mommy's in trouble! Where are you?"

The echo of the policeman's words pierced her consciousness. "...your husband was involved in a car accident...I'm afraid...didn't survive..."

"Daddy!" She jerked away the bedspread. Her father slept in this bed, *at this very moment.* She had to find him. He had to hear her.

She yanked the electric blanket from beneath her as her mournful cries continued. "Daddy, help!"

By the time Officer Klein reached the O'Conners' master bedroom, Farin had clawed every piece of bedding off the bed. He crept forward, arms out, fingers splayed. He scanned the scene, brows knitted in disbelief.

"Daddy! No!" She wailed as cruel reality overtook her. Her nails had ripped down to their nail beds, yet she continued her frantic clawing, certain that if she dug deep enough, she would find him.

"It's okay, honey." Officer Klein approached the bed with caution. He entered Farin's line of vision, hand stretched toward her, palm down.

Farin abandoned her assault on the bed and scampered in desperation to its farthest point from the policeman. "Leave me alone!"

"I'm not gonna hurt you," he said, maneuvering himself into position so she could not run. "Let me take you downstairs. Mom's gonna need you."

When sorrowful acceptance replaced Farin's horror, she dissolved into a fetal position and sobbed atop the place in the bed where her father had slept the night before.

Farin replaced her father's death certificate and slammed the box shut. It contained nothing she needed to see or had not seen before. She had lived and relived the hell of that night. Her mother had lied, again. No mysterious revelation awaited her discovery. Her life had changed long before she opened this box.

She checked her watch. Four o'clock. The funeral was probably over.

Farin flew up out of the chair and dashed to the kitchen. She seized the whiskey bottle and gulped greedily as she returned to the desk.

"Here's to you, Momma!" she cried, holding the bottle aloft.

Farin crumpled into the chair. The late afternoon sun cast a dim, dusty glow through the dirty windows of the O'Conner home. Head on her arms and sheathed in black, Farin spent the early evening sitting at her father's desk, in the house her mother had asked her never to return to, crying like she had not cried in sixteen years.

***

Though the Williamses begged her to stay through Christmas, Farin returned to Los Angeles the next morning. Before she left, she arranged to ship the desk to her home in Key Biscayne. Nothing remained in Santa Barbara for her. Besides, it was past time to figure out what to do about Jordan. She had lost her mother. She did not want to lose him, too.

Dan Albright looked surprised when Farin arrived Saturday afternoon. He lounged on the couch in wrinkled business garb, tie loose, his short, side-parted hair shaggy and in need of a trim. He regarded her with a harrumph. "Back so soon?"

Farin dropped her overnight bag in the foyer, then her purse on top of the bag. "I've been here a week. Maybe if you stuck around once in a while you wouldn't miss so much."

He grumbled into his lowball, then drained its amber contents. The ice slid forward then back, clinking into a melting cluster as he finished.

She lifted her chin at the glass. "Mind if I join you?"

"Where's Marci?"

"With her parents. She left a note in your bedroom. Guess she should have left it near the wet bar."

Dan sneered. "Marci never mentioned you were such a bitch."

"You're never with her long enough for her to tell you much of anything." Farin snatched up the glass, then freshened it as a courtesy as she poured her own. "What happened to Christmas in Riverside?"

"I got tired of the company."

She handed him his refill, then flopped down on the couch.

Dan eyed her as they sipped their cocktails. "Your album cover doesn't do you justice, you know. You're prettier in person."

She scoffed, unmoved as the stench of many previous bourbons stunk up the space.

"You still dating Jordan Grant?"

"Why, that's none of your business, Dan."

He gave her a sloppy grin, scooted closer, and kissed her hand. "When did you say Marci was coming back?"

Farin pulled away. "Even if Marci wasn't my best friend, you're not my type."

"Lighten up." He snickered. "I know women. We're all your type. Anyway, I'm a big fan of yours."

"Then remind me to leave you an autograph. Until then, stay away from me or you'll lose your happy home."

Jordan's telephone rang at half-past three, sending him straight up in his bed from a sound sleep. He fumbled for the phone and voiced a groggy, "Hello?"

Farin's sweet, silky voice met his ears. "It's me."

He sat up, palmed his sleepy eyes with his free hand, and glanced at the bedside clock. "Where are you?"

She sniffed. "My mother's dead."

Jordan collapsed back onto his pillow. "I'm so sorry, love. You're in Santa Barbara, then?"

"I'm in Malibu. I drove down today."

"Why did you leave without saying anything?"

Farin's tone morphed into one of pure disdain. She hiccoughed twice. "You know Marci's boyfriend, Dan? He's a pig. Marci's still in Santa Barbara and he had the nerve to come on to me!"

Jordan frowned and stared at his ceiling. "You sound drunk."

Her indignance melted into a giggle. "Do I?"

"What's going on, Farin? You left without a word, then you didn't call."

"I'm sorry," she slurred. "My mother left me just when she needed me."

"I'm flying out for the funeral."

"That was yesterday. They buried her right there, next to my dad. They're together again, Jordan, my mom and dad. Isn't that good news?"

His concern grew as Farin's drunken stream of consciousness continued. He wanted to bring her home. Knowing the terror of her nightmares over her father, Jordan doubted she would handle her mother's death any better.

Again, he said he would fly out. Again, she declined. As her speech garbled, his patience drained. "When are you coming home?"

"Please don't pressure me right now."

"I'm coming to get you."

"You can't. You have work and Jameson would be royally piss—"

"Screw Lockhardt. Do you *need* me?"

"I think I need another drink." Farin giggled again.

"That tears it," Jordan uttered with disgust. "Sober up and get home. I mean it, Farin."

She paused again. Jordan's stomach churned with anxiety.

Her voice broke with emotion. "I can't come back yet. I need to think."

"About *what*?" Frustrated, he raked his fingers through his hair. "Are you having second thoughts about us? I want to make you happy, Farin. I'm starting to wonder if I can."

"I love you."

"Then come home."

"I don't feel good. I think I'm gonna be sick."

"It's the alcohol," he spat impatiently. "Farin, come home! If you've things to work out, let me help you."

"A little more time," she half-whispered, half-slurred. "That's all I need."

A little more time turned into three weeks when Farin ended up sick in bed. When she had not improved by the end of the second week, she made an appointment with her former physician.

It did not take him long to come back with the diagnosis.

"Morning sickness," he beamed happily.

Farin blanched as she constructed a mental calendar of the last few weeks. "Are you sure?"

"Very. I'd say you're due around the first of September. You'll need to establish with an OB in Miami as soon as you get home."

"Thank you." Farin slid off the exam table and began dressing before the doctor could leave the room.

"What if Jordan doesn't want to be a father again so soon after Chase?" Farin asked Marci that evening as they cozied up in the living room beside a fire, to commiserate over hot chocolate she wished included a shot of Bailey's.

"What if Jordan's not the father?"

"Stop it."

"Well?" Marci tapped out a rhythm on the side of her mug with her fingernail. "And what about your career? Jameson hid Chase away from the public, remember? How can he promote your sex symbol persona when you're as big as a house?"

Farin watched tongues of flame dance in the fireplace, the wood snapping and popping as she considered Marci's words. "You're right. I was supposed to start recording weeks ago. The doctor gave me medication for the nausea. I should probably fly up and talk to him in person."

Marci set down her mug and folded her arms. "And after New York?"

She rubbed her hairline hard with the ball of her hand. Too many thoughts rattled and raced inside her. Would Jameson be angry? How would Jordan take the news? She had probably pushed them both beyond their limits by now. And what about Chris?

Only one thing was certain: the time had come to face the music.

CHAPTER 17

J AMESON DISLIKED FEAR. FEAR MADE him angry. Very angry.
He had learned of Beth O'Conner's death the moment the duty physician called the code. Since then, he had endured a nameless tension. A dread that Beth had laid waste his plans and efforts before taking her leave. It dwelt in his middle and saturated his every cell. Worse, he had not heard from Farin in over a month. Until today.

Now, she sat before him, deflated, contrite...and pregnant.

"I'm sorry, Jameson. I should've called sooner."

His blue eyes darkened to a deep aquamarine as he glared at her, trying to ascertain what she knew. His mind toyed with various scenarios—few of them pleasant. A vein jutted out of his temple. Aside from his personal interests, her now-second disappearing act had cost him money, time, and resources.

Bracing his desk, he rose from his chair, clasped his hands together behind his back, and began pacing. Pacing helped him think, and he needed to think.

"It's not that you were gone so long without a word. Or because Jordan's useless in the studio for worry. It's not that you'd agreed to start your next album at the first of the year in exchange for some time at the holidays." He paused, looked down his nose at his desk calendar, and pointed out the date with a broad finger, "Which, by my calculations, is weeks past. It's not the commitments Bobby and your publicist have had to reschedule. And it certainly isn't indifference over your loss."

He faced her with probing eyes. "I have two concerns. First, the pregnancy. Your debut record was a phenomenal success. Fans accepted your relationship with Jordan. But you're both sex symbols—*that's* the business. We discussed this the first time we met in this office. Do you remember that conversation?"

"Yes, I—"

"Did you know 'Opposites Attract' shot up from number forty-seven to number eight this month alone? *Forever Your Girl*'s been charting for months while you've been traipsing about the country, hiding out, getting pregnant."

"But we've had some great success with—"

"Meanwhile, the Blond Ambition Tour's only a couple of months off—do you see Madonna taking a break to explore the joys of motherhood? Her little contretemps with the Catholic church bolstered her sex appeal. It didn't evoke maternal visions harkening back to the nineteen-fifties."

Head down, hands in her lap, Farin fidgeted with her fingers.

"*Rolling Stone* magazine's lauding Janet Jackson's 'artistic growth' and concern for social issues. And you? What did you envision for your sophomore album, Farin? A collection of lullabies?"

As intended, his words assaulted and scolded her. "You entrusted your career to me. I delivered. But you haven't held up your end of our bargain. You've behaved recklessly. With your personal life *and* your career."

She nodded, but did not meet his eyes.

"We've moved from the eighties into the nineties by mere weeks. Each decade brings certain industry shifts. Some foreseen, some unforeseen. And while this fickle field of ours is supremely unmerciful to women, I believe we'll see a surge in successful female artists. You just turned twenty-seven. You could *own* this decade. But not with last year's accolades. How will you maintain your image while carrying a child?"

"I don't know."

Jameson studied the withering form of his musical ingénue. Her words sounded as small as she looked, slumped piteously before him. Part of him was satisfied with his verbal lashing. Another still needed to know.

She looked at him at last. "I'm sorry I let you down."

"Careers die over things like this."

She swallowed hard.

"Are you keeping it?"

Aghast, her eyes narrowed under knitted brows.

"You haven't told Jordan about it, yet, have you?"

"*It?*"

"I can take care of everything. No one would know."

Farin leaned back and crossed her legs, clutching the armrests. "I'm keeping the baby. I may not have planned this, but I'm prepared to deal with whatever happens."

"Let's hope the rest of us are." He blustered an indignant snort, then muttered a quasi-placating, "No matter. Accidents happen."

She gave him a quizzical tilt of the head.

"Here's my second concern." As he lowered himself into his chair and fixed his eyes upon hers, his confidence grew. Farin had yet to shout at, or assault, him. Perhaps Beth had gone gently into that good night without a parting shot. Better for everyone. Better for him.

"When you first came on board, I promised to be here for you. Any hour. Any reason. Yet in your time of grief, I wasn't afforded the opportunity to help you."

Farin repositioned herself in the chair with an awkward shift of her hips. "My, uh, mother and I weren't close. It's just...I had some personal problems to deal with."

"Is that all?" he blurted, chuckling with relief.

Again, she cocked her head.

"Don't underestimate Jordan's feelings. He's a sensitive lad. If you're determined to continue this pregnancy, I'm sure the news will clear any bad air between you."

The knots in his stomach slowly untangled. The silly child had no idea. Farin's erratic behavior revolved solely around her pregnancy. In the darkness of his mind, he offered Beth O'Conner a parting salute.

Thanks for drinking yourself to death quietly you stubborn old cow.

He stood at last and gestured toward the door. "Let's move on from here, shall we? Go home and straighten things out with Jordan. And be prepared. I want your record out before the delivery. No more excursions or excuses."

Farin rose from her seat and gave her stomach a tender pat. "I'll be sticking pretty close to home from now on. You're right. But please, don't mention the baby to Jordan. I haven't decided how to tell him yet."

***

Travis Duncan and Joel Andrews had worked with Standards Recording Studio for twenty-five years. A couple of aging hippies with wiry, waist-length manes, full facial hair, tie-dyed Grateful Dead T-shirts, tattered jeans, and incomparable reputations. Joel and Travis worked with, and made, music royalty, claiming responsibility for many of the framed gold and platinum albums hanging in the studio's lobby.

Today, they languished behind Studio D's eight-foot-wide console, staring in disbelief—and a little disgust—as Jordan Grant ruined yet another track. The same track they had worked on for over a week.

Wedged between them, Ben drummed his pencil on the edge of the 8-bus mixer. He wrestled over what to do. Jordan had aimed to make this his most successful record to date. He had written some of the compositions himself, freeing up Ben to ease in as producer. Even Chris had agreed to lend his talent to a few of the songs.

"He's flat," Joel complained, adjusting the mid-range frequency knob.

"He skipped the second verse," Travis spat, holding and shaking his head. "His attention span's zip, Ben. Maybe we should break for a couple of days. It's your dime, but what we're doing here's a big donut hole of nothin'. We could be working on something else and leave at the end of the day with something besides practice sessions. We're backlogged as it is."

Ben caught Chris's eye from inside the soundproof recording booth. They exchanged knowing looks.

"No-no-no," Travis snapped as Jordan went flat once more. "Hold it, hold it!"

Joel stopped the tape with an angry switch and pressed the intercom button to the recording booth. "We're gonna take ten, buddy. Long day."

Jordan removed his headset and turned to Chris. "This isn't working."

"You noticed." Chris rested his instrument on a nearby guitar stand.

Ben joined them. He gave Jordan a reassuring pat on the back.

"Sorry," Jordan told them. "My head's somewhere else. Farin called last night."

Chris's eyes darted his way.

"Finally," Ben said. "Is she okay? What did she say?"

"We got things settled. She's coming home."

Chris smirked. "Gracious of her to agree to return."

"It's this thing with her parents. We've got it pretty good, you know? We have Mum and Dad, and we have each other. She's a twenty-seven-year-old orphan."

Chris fidgeted with his guitar, battling his amusement. His younger brother's naiveté never failed to surprise him. Her mother?

Ben pursed his lips. "Like I said before—"

"I know, I know."

"It's been going on an awful long time. It's not normal. She needs help."

"I'll help her. I'll make her feel safe."

"You still haven't recovered from Chase's death. And how understanding can you be when you're still hurt she left in the first place?"

Chris looked away, his lips sucked in to hide a smile. "Perhaps couples therapy."

Ben shot him a warning glance. "She hasn't even gotten over losing her father, what—seventeen years ago? And those nightmares she has? She needs someone more qualified than any of us."

His blithe mocking transformed into an incredulous head rattle. "A bit dramatic, innit? She'll be fine. She's strong."

Jordan tapped Chris's chest with the back of his hand. "Exactly! As long as she has our family, and Marci and Bobby, we can get her through."

"And Bobby bought that house in Coral Gables to be closer to her."

The observation drew puzzled looks from both Jordan and Ben.

"Why?" Jordan asked. "Bobby runs LSI's publicity department. Isn't he needed in New York?"

Chris bobbed his shoulders. "Ask him."

The session ended there. With Farin's homecoming on his mind, Jordan's attempts to work were bootless.

Chris wished his brother good luck for Farin's return, then stayed behind to pack up his equipment when he and Ben took off. He yanked his guitar cord angrily from an amplifier and slammed the guitar into its case.

It was not supposed to happen. Not to him. Try as he might, he could not deny it. He missed her. As in, *everything* about her. And it was more than physical longing.

His feelings confused him. Since he had stopped catting around seventeen months ago, he had taken a sober look at his life. Except Farin, and in a smaller way Faith, everything in his personal life weighed in somewhere between useless and meaningless.

Farin's absence made his soul ache. It maddened him. Could it be...*love*? He had no such experience to draw upon, but feared it might be so.

Either way, Farin had a choice to make. And Chris was determined to help her along with the decision.

***

A tearful reunion notwithstanding, Farin's second homecoming felt strained with distrust and unease. The first had ended with her agreeing to move in with Jordan. This time, while pleased to have her home, he acted distant at first. It did not help matters that she immediately started back in the studio. Especially since their schedules often clashed.

This second album felt more like work than her first. The initial album had no prior success upon which she needed to build. No fame to protect. No risk of coming up short with a lesser product. No pedestal from which she could fall.

Thankfully, Bobby was nearby, ready to cheer her on. If only he would stop the nagging.

"It's been a month," he pressed one day over lunch.

"And?"

"And...?"

"How am I supposed to tell him when we're both so busy? Besides, he's only just started acting like he forgives me for leaving."

"The sooner you tell him, the sooner we can decorate the nursery."

"Wait—you're gonna help with the nursery?"

And why not? Bobby helped in so many ways. He oversaw each session. Kept Jameson abreast of her progress. In her spare time without Jordan, they shopped for odds and ends for the baby. Bobby accompanied her to the doctor to set up her regular visits. She had come to rely on him for everything.

"I'll tell him," she promised.

He gave a doubtful smirk. "As your second trimester's on the horizon."

Comments like that always drew her back to the calendar. To the due date. To the probable date of conception. To the one other person who needed to know.

Chris often invaded her thoughts. With her tight schedule, she had found it easy to avoid him. In fact, she had little time to spend with any of the family. Short phone conversations with Cheryl kept her informed of all the important family goings-on, but she rarely dropped by.

Jordan's March birthday drew near. As usual, Cheryl planned a do. Chris would surely attend. Farin could not avoid him forever. At least he posed little temptation in her present condition. To fortify her resolve, she vowed to tell Jordan about her pregnancy well before the party.

One warm night in late February, the time came.

Jordan returned home from the studio looking distant. Contemplative. He watched her with questioning eyes. A hint of what felt like suspicion, or betrayal, wove itself into the subtle worry lines etched into his brow.

"You okay?" she asked, repositioning herself on the sofa and lowering the book she was reading.

He lifted his shoulders.

"Is something wrong?"

"Is everything okay with you?"

"I'm tired, but that's about it."

"Something's different." He looked her up, then down. "I can't place what it is. A feeling, I suppose. I've had it a while."

Her stomach twisted into nervous knots. His puzzled expression ignited a spark of intimacy within her. Something beyond physical. Something she had suppressed without realizing it. Jordan cared for her. He felt in tune with her. How could she rob him of her excitement, and his own? It was selfish. They should be sharing it—all of it—together. They should have been all along.

In her heart, she was sure the baby belonged to Jordan. And Chris? Well, best not to consider that.

She marked her place and laid her book aside. "I guess I can't put it off any longer. There is something."

Jordan sat beside her and took her hand. "You're not leaving again..."

She softly shook her head. "I...I'm pregnant."

He sat motionless at first, as if the announcement had not fully registered. He blinked. Then, he blinked again. "A baby?"

"A baby."

Jordan placed his hand on her stomach. A glimmer of something between joy and mourning flashed across his features.

Relief washed over her, cleansing the strain of countless sleepless nights. She covered his hand with hers. "I didn't know how to tell you. I wasn't sure you were ready."

He stared at their hands. Soon, elation bested his sorrow. "When are we due?"

"September first. You're not angry?"

"Angry?" He drew her close and brushed her lips with his own. "I can't imagine anything I could be less angry about."

Farin settled into his arms, losing herself in their warmth.

He gave her a loving squeeze. "Does she kick yet?"

She snorted softly. "Not yet."

"Does Cheryl know? Ben?"

She shook her head against his chest.

He kissed her forehead, then tucked his head back in concern. "Should you be working such a busy schedule?"

"I need to finish before the baby comes. And did you say 'she?' What makes you so sure it'll be a girl?"

"Intuition. But seriously, Farin, don't push yourself."

She lifted her head and shot him a coy smile. "Women have been having babies for thousands of years and living to tell the tale."

He rubbed the width and breadth of her abdomen. "Kim didn't."

His response sprouted fresh regret. It seemed she could do or say nothing but cause him pain. She cupped his cheek with her hand.

"Thank you for making me a father again," he whispered, cuddling into their embrace. "I never thought you could look any more beautiful to me than you did before."

Farin shut her eyes. "I love you."

He held her tighter. "I can't wait to tell my family."

Her eyes opened and stared ahead at nothing in particular.

"It's too bad Chris is out of town. He loves kids. You've seen the way Derek and Kyle adore him."

Something told her Jordan's birthday would be one for the books.

Their news traveled fast. The next morning, Ben called her from the studio to offer his congratulations. His voice sounded flat. And knowing. "How are you feeling? Jordan's been chuffed all morning."

"The morning sickness is no fun." Farin wanted to sound enthusiastic, but had expected to find Chris at the other end of the line instead of Ben. "I'm glad I finally told him."

"We haven't had a lot of time to talk, you and I. You can tell me to mind my own business, but...I can't help wondering. There may be a problem. Am I right?"

She opened her mouth to speak, but the words would not come.

"When you left back in December, you had a reason."

Farin paused. "It's that obvious?"

"I had a feeling. Chris was a bit too calm about the whole thing."

"Does Cheryl know?" She cringed at her own words. They made her sound as shallow as she felt. "I love Jordan, Ben. Please believe me. It was stupid and short-lived with Chris, and it's over."

With a heavy sigh, his voice lowered in patience or mercy. "Chris is as reckless as Jordan is observant. You should stay clear of him or Jordan will find out. He may anyway."

"The baby." She felt a lump in her throat. "You must hate me."

"I'm not here to judge, kid. What're you going to do?"

Farin's eyes darted around the unoccupied room. "I'm going to make a future with Jordan, and stay as far away from Chris as I can."

***

The next day, Farin arrived at the studio eager to make progress despite the fact that her morning sickness had worsened. A long night of tossing and turning had left her fatigued. Before leaving the house, Jordan had mentioned that Chris was due back and planned to sit in on Jordan's afternoon session. They would be there around four. She planned to leave early.

When she broke for lunch, Bobby found her sitting in the break room. He dropped into the chair beside her. "Jordan called. He says he's running late and asked you to let Chris know."

Her lips parted. "I'd wanted to leave early."

"Are you gonna tell him about—"

"*No!* And please stop it with the 'aren't you gonna tell so-and-so' crap. I don't want to be anywhere near Chris when he finds out."

Bobby leaned back and folded his hands in his lap. He chin-pointed at the small bulge in her belly. "You won't be able to keep it from anyone, soon. It's a wonder we've managed to keep it out of the tabloids this long."

"I have you to thank for that, don't I?"

He smirked half-seriously. "I just wish you'd met me before the brothers Grant. At least my family wouldn't try to sabotage your personal life behind your back."

"I'm making this work with Jordan. And even if we had met before, it wouldn't be my personal life I was worried about. Did you hear about Mirage?"

Bobby stretched his legs under the table and crossed his ankles. "Dad's been talking about it nonstop for months. He almost didn't release their last album. Then, he remembered the profits."

"I'd heard the rumors but I didn't believe them."

"The one I worry about is Faith. She's not even out of rehab."

"Rehab? You mean it's true?"

He nodded. "If Chris hadn't been there, she'd be worm-food by now. He saved her life, if you can believe it."

She rubbed her abdomen. "You don't like Chris much, do you?"

"Never have. I used to respect him, though. He's so talented. But with everything he's put you through, I only tolerate Chris Grant when I'm forced to."

A familiar British accent, thick with sarcasm, sounded from behind them. "You, Robert? Forced? Since when has a Lockhardt ever been forced to do anything?"

Farin spun around, checking her watch. "You're early."

His right eyebrow cocked up nearly to his hairline. "Miss me?"

Bobby stood and swiped his flattened hands along his beltline to give a fresh tuck of his dress shirt. "Jordan's gonna be late. You've got plenty of time to go home and unpack from your trip."

He addressed Bobby but kept his eyes locked on Farin. "I've already been home, mate. Think I'll stick around and watch Farin's progress."

Chris hung out in the control room with Joel, Travis, and Bobby the better part of the afternoon. He watched her like a starved cat at a trout hole. His attention distracted her. It also strengthened her resolve. After slipping twice, she was all the more determined to never end up alone with him again.

Jordan arrived as Farin finished up for the day. His buoyant countenance made it obvious something profound had happened. He strode with purpose into the live room where Farin stood with Bobby at her side. When Chris joined them, Jordan kissed Farin's cheek. "Did you tell him?"

Farin shot Bobby a look of desperation. "I waited for you."

Jordan preened as he encircled her waist. "I guess you're the last to know, then."

"Know what? Last I'd heard, she'd left you."

"Well, she's back. And you're going to be an uncle again come September."

Chris's cocky grin disappeared. His features paled. "She's pregnant?" He jerked his head her way. "You're pregnant?"

Bobby smiled. "Yes, Chris! Isn't it wonderful?"

He looked back at Jordan. "How far along is she?"

Jordan beamed with pride. "Three months. I just found out two days ago. You were with Faith, so we waited to tell you. The family's thrilled. Mum's started knitting again."

"I bet," Chris muttered, stealing long, wounded glances at her.

Farin stared at Bobby, brows arched in desperation. She mouthed a soundless, *"Do something."*

"Uh, I guess we're done here." Bobby hitched his thumb toward the door. "I'm gonna head on home. Walk me out, Farin?"

They hurried off, leaving the brothers alone.

Jordan clasped his brother's shoulder. "You don't look too good, buddy. Is Faith okay?"

Chris stared at the closed door. "Better. I'm knackered, though. Long flight and all."

"Should we pick up here tomorrow? I still have other tracks to work on."

He lifted his chin, then nodded.

"You have no idea how happy I am."

Chris slapped Jordan on the back as he turned to leave. "That's great, little brother. I'll see you tomorrow...congratulations."

CHAPTER 18

THE WHITE PORSCHE SCREECHED OUT of the parking lot. Chris forced his attention away from Farin, who stood outside chatting with Bobby.

He drove Miami's streets like a madman, stopping at the first dive bar he could find. He burst inside and plopped down upon a cold, cracked vinyl barstool and demanded a shot of bourbon. Fortunately, he was one of only three patrons, the other two a couple of tie-loosened businessmen buried in conversation at a table against the far wall. Unfortunately, his anonymity was short-lived.

"Ain't you Chris Grant?" The bartender barged toward him, bright-eyed and heavy-gaited, favoring one leg as he delivered the drink.

He downed the shot and twirled his index finger. "What if I am?"

The man grabbed a full, unopened bottle and slid it in front of Chris. "I'm a big fan!"

Chris gave him a curt nod of gratitude, opened the bottle, and downed a mighty swig, wincing as the bitter liquid flooded his gut. He assessed the man warily. When he hit Miami's seedy underbelly, he had expected to encounter bums and drunks too impaired to recognize him. Instead, he found Mr. Talks-a-Lot with the missing left canine.

The barman rested his elbows atop the rugged bar and gawked at him like a tourist strolling Hollywood Boulevard. Portly and unshowered, his stringy black hair slicked back over his head, probably with its own grease. He wore a stained white T-shirt and faded, saggy jeans, and reeked of pungent, days-old perspiration. Late thirties, Chris guessed, and too old for stargazing.

"What's your name?" Chris asked, his tone rough and raspy from the liquor burning his throat.

The bartender wiped at the stained apron tied beneath his protruding belly and stuck out his hand. "Joey Stokes." He gave a hearty chuckle as he surveyed the room with unabashed pride. "I own this rathole."

Chris rose, scooted the barstool away with the back of his legs, and grabbed his bottle. "Think I'll go sit at one of those back tables, if it's all the same. I need to be alone and you, Mr. Stokes, talk too much."

"Hey!" Joey snapped with marked indignance, then softened. "I-I'm sorry, Mr. Grant. I usually don't get no bigshots like you in here. In fact, you're the first famous dude I ever met! No harm done, right?" He stuck out his hand again.

Chris wrinkled his nose at the gesture. He slumped into a seat at a table near the run-down jukebox, as far from the bar as possible.

Half a bottle later, Chris squinted at the stained-glass window by the door. Darkness had descended upon the world outside. He wanted to go home and sleep off the alcohol but figured he should not drive.

The place had filled to capacity. Intent on calling a cab, and in desperate need to relieve himself, he wove and wobbled through groups of other patrons in search of the men's room, hoping to avoid drawing any attention. Passing the bar, he stumbled and fell, only to be caught by a young man in a cheap business suit.

"Whoa-ho-ho! You all right there, pal?"

"Where's the loo?" Chris murmured, untangling himself to stand upright.

The man pointed down the hall and Chris doddered away, giving him a two-fingered salute. Upon his return, the gentleman had relocated to his table.

With a scratch of his head, he collapsed into his seat. "Did I ask you to join me?"

The young man smoothed down his tie. "You look like you might need a friend."

"I don't trust men in cheap suits."

"This suit cost me almost three hundred bucks! Who the hell do you think you are, anyway?"

Chris picked up and cradled his bottle in his arms. "I...am a crazed lunatic. Positively mad. Best run along, Mr...."

The man extended his hand. "Miles Macy. Nice to meet you, Mr. Lunatic."

The good humor disarmed him. He chuckled and shook the man's hand. "Okay, Macy. You got me. You can stay."

They talked for hours. What a relief to find someone he could unload his problems on—someone who neither mattered nor recognized him. A witty, astute young twenty-something. Sharp. Eager to participate in his negative observations about women in general. Macy was precisely the breath of fresh air Chris needed. No family. No Lockhardt. No bandmates with their constant reminders of all he had sacrificed by abandoning them for Miami.

"She's pregnant." He buried his head in his hands. "I found out today."

"And the baby could be yours?" Miles edged forward in his seat.

Chris nodded. "She just stood there, trying not to look at me. She wouldn't even look at me!" He bolted up and grabbed his chair. A moment later it flew across the shabby room.

"Hey!" Joey barked from his station behind the bar. "That's about enough of that!" Star or no star, Stokey's had standards.

"He's okay, Joey," Miles assured, helping Chris into an alternate chair as if they were lifelong friends. To Chris, he whispered, "Calm down, pal. You're gonna get us both kicked out of here."

He waved a cack-handed arm in the air. "I could buy and sell this dump faster than ol' Joey could clean the cobwebs off the ceiling."

With a slow shake of his head, Miles sat back in his seat and clicked his tongue. "This Farin chick must really be something."

Chris erupted a second time. He grabbed Miles by his shirt collar. "Don't you even speak her name."

Miles tucked his chin, startled. Joey barked another warning and they both settled back into their seats. "You really love her."

"Psh. I don't do love."

"Oh, yeah? What do you do, then? You never said."

Chris touched his bourbon bottle to the glass of wine Miles had nursed. "I'm unemployed. Here's to sodding Lockhardt and here's to my sodding brother and here's to sodding Farin."

Miles watched as Chris gulped from the neck of the bottle. "Tell me about the day you met her again?"

Chris looked up, bleary-eyed. "Who?"

"Farin."

"Screw her," he sniffed ruefully.

"Sounds like you've done a pretty good job of that already."

"Yeah, now I'm screwed, too." He harrumphed and muttered some choice expletives before taking another drink.

Chris studied his blurry drinking partner in the ensuing silence. It seemed he had done all the talking. He decided to share the conversational wealth. "You never told me what you do. With a name like Miles Macy, you sound like a bloody reporter—"

"For the *Post*," Miles beamed, indicating the bar. "I believe you know my friend, Mr. Stokes."

Shock and anger assailed him as the situation, if not his vision, cleared. Too drunk to stand again, he stabbed the air with his finger. "Print one word of this and I'll break every wiry bone in your bloody carcass!"

"Don't sweat it, Grant. Lovelorn English rock stars are a dime a dozen. It'd have to be a lot juicier for me to use it. But I'll be interested to see who the baby's father is."

"Stay out of it," Chris warned. "If any of this ends up in the papers, you'll rue the day you were born."

***

Farin raked dress after dress along the wooden closet dowel. Too soon for maternity clothes, but her regular clothes were snug. Her belly had thickened. The fullness in her breasts left them swollen and tender. Proper hydration was imperative, what with carrying the baby through the summer, so she drank plenty of fluids throughout the day. It made her feel bloated.

To help curb the resulting self-consciousness, she chose a sleeveless cotton dress with ample give in the waist. She tossed the dress on the foot of the bed, adjusted the towel wrapped around her head, and sat down to do her makeup.

Cheryl had planned tonight's ruse. Farin had tricked Jordan into thinking she made plans for an intimate celebration. On the way to the restaurant, she would claim she had left something at Ben and Cheryl's and ask to pop in to get it. Once inside, the family would jump out of their hiding places and scream, "HAPPY BIRTHDAY, JORDAN!"

She expected to have a miserable time.

Whether a byproduct of guilt or hormones, she did not want to show her face. She hated leaving the house. She hated everything.

Anymore, Farin wanted to stay home with Jordan. When alone, she often cried. Personal phone calls had ceased. More and more, Jordan and the baby became her entire world.

Her eyes teared as she applied her eyeliner. "Not now. Not tonight."

She grabbed a tissue to dab her eyes, then reached over to turn on the radio on her vanity. Michael Penn's "No Myth" blared through its compact speakers.

Preoccupied with the identity of her baby's biofather, she had withdrawn. She assured herself her motives were true. All she wanted was to spare Jordan the inevitable hurt should he ever find out. Surely, the truth would stay buried. Chris and Jordan were family. Chris would not want to hurt his own brother.

In her mind, she wrapped the entire scenario into a neat and tidy package. A momentary lapse of judgment. So short-lived, it could not even be classified an "affair." Best to forget about their indiscretion altogether.

Sometimes, she even succeeded.

At least her recording had made progress. If she continued as scheduled, she would finish by late June. Plenty of time to relax before the baby arrived.

She squinted into the vanity mirror to weed out any mascara clumps, then went into the bathroom to fix her hair. A simple banana clip would keep it off her shoulder. Nothing big or dramatic. Casual was her go-to these days.

The tension over the coming evening settled in her shoulders as she dressed. She had heard nothing from Chris since the studio. He had looked gut-punched when she and Bobby watched him skid out of the parking lot that day. An odd reaction. Vulnerable. Human. Even sad. Unlike when he learned she and Jordan had moved in together, she had not heard from him since.

After applying a finishing touch of hairspray, Farin heard the buzzer from the outside gate. It buzzed a second time as she trotted downstairs to the entryway. The third time, it annoyed her. She stabbed the button and barked an irritated, "Yes?"

"Hello, Miss St. John. My name is Miles Macy. I'd like a minute of your time."

Farin peeped through the blinds by the door and cursed. Reporters crowded around the house, circling like vultures. They had ensconced themselves at the gate every day for the past week—ever since the *Miami Post* exposed the news of her pregnancy. How they had found out, she could not imagine. Had someone from her obstetrician's office made a deal? Whatever the source, every sleazy reporter in town now lined up outside their house, desperate for a scoop.

At first, she and Jordan had been cordial. Though never stopping to talk, they wore their manufactured smiles when passing the group. They waved when stepping out to collect the morning paper. Then, the buzzing started, with constant requests for one or the other of them to come out for "a minute of your time." It made a quick transition from annoying to dangerous when one of them attempted to scale the fence.

This afternoon, it wore on Farin's last nerve.

"What do you want?" she shouted into the intercom.

The buzzer sounded confident and, curiously, amused. "A little chat. I'm not with the rest. I think you'll see me."

"Stop buzzing my house or I'll have you arrested for harassment!" She turned on bare feet and stomped into the living room.

Outside, Miles pushed the button one last time. "Ms. St. John, I'm the reporter who wrote that piece on your pregnancy. Surely you have some questions or comments for me? Or should I just go back and get the rest of the story from Chris?"

Miles did not have to wait long. As expected, the gate buzzed open, much to the envy and grumblings of his competition. She probably figured he wanted hush money, but bribes were the farthest thing from his mind. Miles coveted Pulitzers, not presidents.

Despite his youth, Miles Macy was no rookie. He intended to go as far as possible in his chosen field. Ambition was the only thing he possessed more of than tenacity.

The door swung open as he reached the top of the porch steps. "What did he say?"

Miles adjusted his suit tie and stepped inside. He extended his open hand. "Miles Macy. *Miami Post*."

Farin sneered with unmasked revulsion, but moved aside and waved him in. "Tell me everything he said, verbatim."

His eyes darted about as he helped himself to a seat in the living room, impressed with himself as much as the class-A surroundings. He unbuttoned his jacket, rested his arm along the back of the sofa, and smirked. "First, he insulted my suit. Then, he said you wouldn't look at him."

Farin knitted her brows, missing his attempted humor.

"He said when he found out you were pregnant, he tried to catch your eye but you kept turning away."

She folded her arms, shifting her girth to one hip. "I don't care about his reaction. Did he say anything else?"

Miles looked her up and down. Trendy sundress. Fresh makeup. Pinned hair. A real knockout. "Oh, yes. He said a number of interesting things."

"About what?"

"About the affair you two've been having, for starters."

Her tightened features slacked, pulling open her glossed lips. "That's a lie."

Miles crossed his legs and barked out a doubtful chuckle.

"He's a liar! It's hardly an affair!"

"Whatever it is, he's not taking your condition very well. You two may not be having an affair, but you're certainly having something. He's convinced the child is his."

"*What*?" she gasped and tucked her chin as rage gripped her in steel talons. "Why would he tell you that? Are you blackmailing him?"

Miles twisted his mouth to the side. "Of course not."

"Then why are you here? What do you want?"

"A story. So far, all I have is the blathering of a lovesick rock star during a drunken, jealous fit. Then again, he *is* Chris Grant, and you *are* the woman who captured his unobtainable heart." He uncrossed his legs and leaned forward, pointing at her middle. "I'm waiting for the good stuff, though—like finding out who that child you're carrying really belongs to."

Her indignation evaporated. Wild-eyed, she sniffed and began massaging her hairline with her fingertips. "Don't you people care how you ruin our lives?"

Nonplussed, Miles stood and buttoned his suit jacket. "I didn't ruin your life, lady, *you* did. And when the truth comes out, you can bet it'll be my byline."

She marched to the front door, jerked it open, and stepped aside. "This baby belongs to Jordan."

That evening, Farin's mind roamed far away. She tried to sound exuberant when they yelled, "Surprise!" but Miles Macy's words echoed in her head. He had hovered outside their gate, staring at her from the crowd, as she and Jordan left the house.

Until tonight, she had avoided Chris. Now, she could not wait to get him alone. How could he be so stupid?

As she browsed the buffet table setup in Ben's dining room, she listened as Cheryl praised him and all his positive changes over the past year. "We're proud of you. But isn't it time to find someone to share your life with?"

"What about Faith?" Ben suggested as he tonged Asian dumplings onto his porcelain plate. "With all you two've been through? Any sparks?"

Chris stood on the sidelines opposite her, the long dining table a barrier between them. Neither of them attempted the food. She knew her reasons and could only guess his as he downed his third bourbon. At least he could have something stronger than a glass of iced tea dripping with condensation.

"Faith's like a sister to me, like you and Farin." He shot a guarded look her way. "Besides, you heard your wife. I'm reformed now."

Liar. Farin glanced down at the servers of smoked oysters and caviar. Nausea bubbled up from her stomach.

When Chris went to the kitchen, Farin started to follow, but Jordan cozied up from behind and nuzzled her neck. "Feeling okay?"

She lifted a shoulder and smiled. "It's the food."

"What me to get you some peanut butter? That usually helps."

"I'll be okay. How about you, Mr. Thirty? Did we surprise you?"

"I had no clue. As for turning thirty, I don't know." He turned her around to him and waggled his eyebrows. "It is a milestone. Makes me feel like doing something...unexpected."

"Mysterious." She sipped her iced tea. "What did you have in mind? Rock climbing? Sky diving? A trip to the moon?"

Jordan called everyone together in the living room, saying he had an announcement. He waited for Chris to return from the kitchen, then stood in the center of the room, in full view of his family. "No big speeches or anything. I'd actually planned on doing this at the restaurant tonight." He took away Farin's glass and set it on the coffee table, then retrieved a small velvet box from his suit pocket.

Farin gasped.

Ben and Cheryl audibly sighed.

He bent down on one knee. "Farin, I love you more than anyone I've ever known. You've changed my life in every way. And now, we're having a baby."

Chris paled as he realized what was about to happen. He watched in abject horror, like someone watching a car wreck or an execution, fascinated and simultaneously sickened. He looked at Farin, then Jordan, then back.

"I can't imagine being without you...ever. And I don't want to." Jordan opened the box and took out the diamond ring he had purchased back in December. "You've made me a father again. Please make me a husband as well. Marry me."

Farin reached out her trembling left hand. She chirped a nervous giggle as Jordan slid the ring onto her finger. "This is supposed to be *your* birthday."

Ben, Cheryl, and Jordan chuckled.

He stared up at her as his laughter dissolved. "Then make my birthday wish come true. Say 'yes.' Don't make me wait like you did before moving in."

Farin tilted her head and smiled at the good-natured jab, wiping her damp eyes to avoid smearing her makeup. In one fluid movement, Cheryl lunged forward and handed her a tissue.

She palmed the tissue, threw her arms around Jordan's neck, and then stood him up to face her. "Of *course* I'll say yes. Yes!"

They embraced and kissed before his cheering family.

Only one voice remained silent.

Farin willed away that silence even as it sliced through her otherwise joyous moment like a Reaper's scythe. Their discussion about Miles Macy would have to wait.

CHAPTER 19

"A ND HE COULDN'T DO ANYTHING about it!" Bobby guffawed. His eyes twinkled amid his winking, spasming facial tic. Chris Grant being forced to witness the most significant moment in Farin's life elated him. Yet inside him grew a feeling for Farin St. John he dared not confess—to himself or anyone else. As happy as he was about Chris getting his just desserts, part of him sympathized with the man he mocked. "I wonder what he'll do."

"He's done enough." Farin steadied the ladder Bobby climbed to paint the nursery's ceiling. "He leaked my pregnancy to the papers. Apparently, Chris gave the creep who wrote the story quite an earful. He's currently stationed outside the house. You probably saw him on your way in."

Bobby propped his roller against the pan of bone-colored paint. "Dad won't be happy if he finds out. And what if it gets out about you two?"

"It won't." She gazed down at her engagement ring. "It can't."

Bobby descended the ladder, then surveyed the room. "We're gonna need that last can of paint."

"You're all speckled. I'll get it." She maneuvered the plastic tarping as if it were a mine field, avoiding globs of paint as she headed out toward the garage.

Bobby had painted huge swatches on the ceiling, then primed the walls. He had done a fine job—even if he did say so himself. Moreover, Farin's news had put him in a cheery mood.

He whistled as he repositioned the tarp, paint pan, rollers, and brushes to the last remaining wall. Whistling became singing as he hauled the ladder over and masked off the window and trim. "*So come on, Jack be nimble, Jack be quick ... Jack Flash sat on a candlestick ... 'Cause fire is the devil's only friend ... Oh, and as I watched him on the stage ... My hands were clenched in fists of rage ... No angel born in Hell ... Could break that Satan's spell ... And as the flames climbed high into the night ... To light the sacrificial rite ... I saw Satan laughing with delight ... The day the music died ... He was singin' ... Bye, bye, Miss American Pie ...*"

Farin returned hauling a freshly stirred gallon of paint. As she neared the nursery, she heard him. Chills crawled up her back. She hesitated outside the room. Finally, she took a deep breath and marched inside, swinging the paint can before her.

Bobby winked and gave her a boyish smile. He picked up a wet paintbrush and held it like a microphone. *"The courtroom was adjourned ... No-o-o verdict was returned ..."* He swayed and jazzed up his voice, dancing around the nursery with an invisible partner. *"Drove my Chevy to the levy but the levy was dry ... and them good ol' boys were drinkin' whiskey and rye ... singin' this'll be the day that I die ..."*

Farin fused her eyes shut, rattling her head with desperate shakes. "I really hate that song."

Bobby froze mid-verse, mouth open. His jaw clamped shut. He cleared his throat and straightened his shoulders. "Sorry."

Softened with regret, she moved to him and touched his arm. "No. I like it when you sing. But, please, not that song."

Bobby took the paint can. He poured a generous amount into the waiting pan, soaked his roller, climbed back up the ladder, then finished the ceiling in silence.

Farin grabbed the ladder as before. "It really looks good in here. Jordan'll love it. I couldn't have done it without you." When Bobby's wounded expression did not change, she added meekly, "Not in my condition?"

He glanced down at her growing belly, a smile coaxing the sides of his lips. "You know, it's sort of ironic. You were just named the sexiest woman in pop music."

They laughed as they discussed the file photo used on the *Entertainment Magazine* cover. Over the last three months, she had won two American Music Awards, a Grammy, and a People's Choice. Not one of the events had she attended. Fortunately, with the breaking news of the baby, she had avoided Ebony Suede-level accusations of her feeling superior or of her snubbing the industry with her absence.

"I won't be able to live up to it looking like this. Trying to shoot around me in my videos has been difficult enough."

He descended the ladder again, their bodies inches apart, and gazed at her. "You're beautiful, Farin. No one's complaining."

The seriousness of his tone made her uneasy, and not for the first time. Usually, Bobby acted like a protective, older brother. Not unlike Ben. Other times, he unnerved her. Not like the nervousness she felt around Chris, but dread. She refused to hurt his feelings by saying so, but sometimes Bobby Lockhardt frightened her.

Or maybe she felt creepy about him singing that song in her child's nursery. She did not want the poison of her tortured nights killing the joy of daylight, especially in the room her baby would occupy.

She stepped back and inhaled a whiff of fresh paint. The nursery looked refreshed and new.

Bobby swiped his nose with the back of his hand as he looked around the room. Paint smudged his hands and clothes. It smeared his face. Misted droplets dusted his hair.

Studying him as he inspected their progress, Farin admonished herself. No one had forced Bobby to help. Sure, he had quirks. Everybody did. Maybe she should stop acting like a baby and accept his unconditional friendship.

She smiled at him and he smiled back before resuming his task.

Later that afternoon at the studio, Joel Andrews interrupted their session to tell Farin she had a call holding. "I think it's Jordan," he said.

She took the call in the hallway and giggled her hello, anticipating hearty praise over her and Bobby's masterpiece.

"You can't marry him, you know."

Her cheerfulness dissolved. Her eyes darted up and down the hallway, hoping no one loitered within earshot.

"I want DNA tests."

"You sound drunk," she spat, her tone low.

"That may be, my child. And that may be my child." He chuckled at his own wit.

Her nose wrinkled in disgust.

He sounded raspy and broken, as if he had come to his end. "Don't marry him, Farin. You belong with me. Since the day we met. Remember?"

She winced at the memory.

"I didn't think it could happen to me. Not *me*! Meet me. I have to see you."

"I could kill you for talking to that reporter," she whisper-shouted into the phone, jabbing the air with her finger. "What were you thinking?"

"No worries about Macy. Please. We need to talk."

For a second, she felt compelled to oblige him. The desperation in his voice crushed her. He was always so calm and in control. Indeed, her polar opposite. "I love him, Chris. I'm marrying him and there's nothing—"

"You can't! Don't you get what I'm saying here?"

"It's this thing between us, Chris. I understand. I do. But it can't go on." Standing in the empty corridor outside Studio D, she began to panic. She and Jordan were a family now. Chris could destroy everything. "Forget me and move on."

"You really believe it's that simple." He snorted, then cleared his throat, his tone finally contained. "That may be my baby, Farin. *Our* baby. Don't tell me to forget. Can you? Can you walk down that aisle in front of God and everyone and vow to be *honest* and faithful? It'd be a lie—worse than the one you're living right now. If you think I can just stand by and watch you do this, you're bloody toys in the attic."

Farin slammed the phone into the receiver.

Throughout the session, the drive home, and dinner, his words haunted her. She paid intermittent attention to the details of Jordan's day, replying with monosyllabic answers to his questions.

Chris had not threatened to expose the truth. Had he?

"You look exhausted," Jordan observed. "I'll draw you a bath. I'll add that lavender concoction you love so much. It'll relax you."

Farin teased him with a weary grin. "You love it more than I do."

"I love the smell of your skin when you use it."

Her smile waned as she picked at the remnants of food on her plate.

"Still no appetite, then?"

She shook her head.

"Go upstairs and rest. I'll be right behind you."

As Jordan cleared and rinsed their dishes, he rebuked himself for his paranoia-level concern over Farin's non-existent complications. Memories of Kim's pregnancy had reawakened after many dormant years. Even as he anticipated the new addition to their family, the pain of losing Chase remained with him. He could not imagine losing Farin. Still, his hovering did neither of them any good.

Once upstairs, he drew a warm bath while Farin removed her makeup and banked her curls atop her head, securing them with a barrette. She gave his shoulder a thankful squeeze as she eased herself into the fragrant water.

"Did you see the nursery?"

"I did." He grabbed a porous sponge and knelt down beside the tub. "It looks great. But those fumes—"

"I know. I'm sorry." She raised a wet hand and placed it on his cheek.

The simple contact aroused him. He moved in, kissed her glistening skin, then lingered before pulling back to lather the sponge. "Sit forward a bit. I'll get your back."

Grateful sighs told him she enjoyed the pampering as he washed and massaged her body. He took exaggerated care as he ran the sponge across her beautiful, growing belly. "Let's set a date."

"You proposed yesterday."

"True."

"There's a lot to do before the baby comes."

"I called Ben today. He's going to be my best man."

"Besides, we're both tied to the studio until mid-June."

"I may ask Bobby to be a groomsman. He's been such a good friend to you. What do you think?"

She moaned her approval as he knuckled a knot in one of her hips.

"I already asked Chris."

Her body tensed.

"A June wedding would be nice." He rinsed the soap from her back.

She shot up into a sitting position. Water sloshed and splashed around her and over the rim of the tub. "*June*? We won't have time for a honeymoon if we do it then. I'll be the size of Montana!"

He kissed her wet shoulder. "Motherhood becomes you."

"We should wait until after the baby comes."

He frowned. "What?"

"It would give us more time. I-it's all happening so fast."

Her words wounded him, but he dismissed them as hormone-induced. He eased her back into the tub. "You're tired. We'll talk about it more later."

She wrapped dripping arms around his neck and pulled him into the water with her, clothes and all, as she nibbled at his neck. "I'm tired, all right. Tired of talking."

He groaned at the feel of her naked body. "I hope our daughter looks like you."

"We'll be so happy."

He kissed her damp skin. "I'm already happy. Marry me, Farin. Soon."

***

Marci was thrilled, though annoyed that Farin did not tell her about their engagement until May. "You haven't returned my calls. I've been worried sick."

Farin examined her baby bump in the full-length mirror on the bedroom closet door. "Sorry. I've been working like a dog. You wouldn't believe how fat I am."

Marci chortled. "I'm gonna be an aunt. Well, by proxy anyway. Jordan must be on cloud nine."

"He's been bugging me to set a date ever since he proposed."

"So do it already."

"I can't marry him 'til the baby comes." Softer, she added, "Chris wants a paternity test."

"To be expected. Tell me you're not still seeing that weasel."

Farin lay down on her bed and stared up at the ceiling. "We haven't talked since the day after Jordan proposed."

"Good. Forget about him."

"You're right. Ben said the same thing—Bobby, too."

"So, set a date and worry about the rest later. Jordan's gonna get suspicious if you keep putting him off."

She gave her head a cleansing shake. "Enough about me. How're things with you?"

"Work's fine. Dan's the same. We still sleep together when he's home, but we're sorta just roommates."

Farin flattened her lips. "I hate that for you."

"Yeah, me too. But for now, this is what I've got."

"You'll fly up for the wedding, though, right? You're my maid of honor."

"Maid," Marci echoed. "That's me. Yeah, I'll be there."

"I wish my dad were here to give me away."

Marci's tone saddened. "Have you thought about asking my dad?"

"Actually, I'm thinking about asking Jameson."

Marci gasped. "Shut *up!*"

"Do you think your dad'll be upset?"

"No, that's great! Honestly? I hated the idea of him giving you away before he could walk me down the aisle. Petty, I know. I'm sorry."

"Not at all. I get it."

"So go on and set the date, already. You've waited too long to be happy."

"I know. But not until I know for sure the baby's Jordan's."

***

Jordan finished recording at the end of May. An exhaustive effort he felt, in the end, would produce the album he had envisioned. Lockhardt Sound gave their stamp of approval. For Farin's sake, they pushed the release date to greenlight some time off. Overjoyed, he utilized that time researching venues, choosing a caterer, and finding a church.

He assumed Farin objected to setting a date because she had no time to plan the wedding. But each time she put him off, it dashed his hopes. He wanted to marry her now. She wanted to wait. There seemed no middle ground. Lately, they had started fighting. He probably owed her an apology for his temper, which he seemed to lose with increasing frequency.

When his frustration rose to the level of desperation, he called Cheryl, as he did whenever he needed a woman's perspective.

"There's two of her now, Jorie. Mind your mood. She's already said yes."

"*Yes* isn't *when*," he protested. "I know she's tired. Maybe she needs some help."

Despite initial warnings that Farin might not appreciate having the details of her wedding arranged without her input, Cheryl agreed to help. Together they planned every detail, including the date. Farin would not have to worry about a thing.

Now, all he needed to do was let her know.

She returned early the evening they finished confirming the plans. As he beheld her slumped shoulders and swollen feet, remorse filleted him. She greeted him at the doorway with a kiss. He pulled away despite himself, as if he had grown accustomed to the distance between them. As if going behind her back to plan her wedding was her own fault.

He fondled his record necklace.

At first, his reaction appeared to sting her. Then, hurt became surrender. She dropped her purse and keys on the entryway floor, kicked off her shoes, and beelined for the couch.

He stalked after her. "Do you ever intend to marry me?"

"There it is." She pushed out an irritated breath, lifting her left hand to wiggle her fingers. "I'm wearing it, aren't I? Do we have to do this right now? I'm beat."

Guilt threshed him like wheat. "When?"

"I don't know. I—"

"You *never* know."

"I just walked in the door!" She propped her swollen ankles atop the coffee table. "Please, Jordan. I can't do this. Not tonight. What's the rush?"

"*Rush*?" He stood before her, arms akimbo. "It's been two and a half months and you won't even discuss it."

"I do discuss it. I just don't agree."

"When, Farin?"

She looked up at him and swallowed. "After the baby's born."

"I won't wait that long."

"It's four months!"

He set his jaw.

She searched his eyes, as if unsure he meant what he said.

The hurt over repeated rejections returned. He had gone too far to back down now.

"You won't wait four months to marry me?"

"I want to marry you now, not four months from now."

"Fine," she growled at last, hefting herself off the sofa. "You've got time off. *You* make the arrangements. Whenever you decide is fine."

"Right, then." He watched her climb the stairs. "What about July first?"

She flourished her wrist as she disappeared down the hall. "July first it is."

***

At sixty-four, little surprised Jameson. Nonetheless, he nearly fell out of his chair when Farin called to request he give her away at her wedding. For two long years, he had campaigned to earn her trust. Despite Beth. Despite Ross's words of warning. The thought of making his personal Doubting Thomas eat the harsh words he had served up lately pleased him. Allowing Bobby and Farin to develop a relationship had not ended Lockhardt Sound after all.

Beth O'Conner dying with no parting word to her daughter was one of the greatest triumphs of his life. Being granted the honorable task of walking Farin down the aisle at her wedding, of giving her away to a groom, eclipsed that victory.

Jameson buzzed Ross's office with quick instructions. "It's time."

His old friend's deep and weary voice answered back, "You're sure about this?"

"I know what I'm doing!" he barked through the intercom.

From now on, Farin would be the daughter he never had.

***

Marci arrived in Miami three days early. She and Farin spent the night before the wedding together at a hotel on Bayshore Drive, near the *Miami*

Post. Jordan had suggested she and Marci take the house and offered to stay at Ben's, but Farin argued she wanted room service. He disliked the idea of her spending the night away, but did not argue. In fact, he had not argued with her since she had agreed to move forward with the wedding. Besides, Farin claimed, it was tradition.

Then again, tradition did not normally include the bride spending her pre-wedding evening filled with dread that the groom's older brother would burst through the church doors to destroy the ceremony. But such was the life of Farin O'Conner, St. John, soon-to-be Grant.

"He called my bluff," Farin grizzled as they lounged in their suite. She propped her bare feet on the coffee table to stave off the swelling. "I can't believe he planned all this."

Marci picked through the fruit basket sent up by the front desk. "At least you got to pick out your dress."

"Well, if we do have a girl, she'll need to have it taken in before her own wedding."

"You hope." Marci smirked.

"I hope he's happy." Farin rubbed her belly.

And he was. Jordan had smiled nonstop for the last month, his happiness so deep-rooted he seemed oblivious to her misery.

At least after tomorrow, it would be done. Maybe it was for the best.

The next afternoon, Farin sat alone in her dressing room at the church. Surrounded by floral arrangements sent by fans and peers, she waited for the procession to begin. Nails manicured. Hair coiffed into an elegant updo. She smelled of baby powder, iris, and mandarin, and looked like royalty, save the enormous belly bump. Now seven months into her pregnancy, she feared she had gained too much weight. Jordan disagreed, as did her obstetrician.

She hefted herself up and waddled to the full-length mirror hanging on the door. Her gown was exquisite. Circumstances be damned, she had opted for a silk, off-the-shoulder cathedral gown in stark white. Swarovski crystals were embroidered in flower-lace patterns throughout the deep scooped, bustier-style bodice and skirt, its accented train trailing ten feet behind her. A veil of English tulle with crystal edging was fastened to an ornate, beaded hairpiece, functionally detachable for the reception. A true work of art, however rushed and uncomfortable for a July ceremony in the sweltering heat of south Florida.

Cheryl had been a godsend, helping commission the ensemble. "You're an angel!" she had exclaimed, hands clasped, when they went for the final fitting.

But Farin was no angel.

Chris's words reverberated in her mind. Could she go out in front of God and everyone and make vows to Jordan with the possibility that the child she carried belonged to another?

There came a knock at the door. She set her jaw. *Show time.* "Who is it?"

"It's me, kid."

Farin gathered up her yards of fabric and let him in.

Ben paused to admire her. "You're stunning."

"I'm fat." She pouted, inspecting her soon-to-be brother-in-law's attire. She straightened his tie. "I may be bloated and ridiculous, but you're awfully handsome in that tuxedo."

"You're gorgeous," he assured, kissing her forehead. "And thank you."

"I should be floating over Herald Square on Thanksgiving Day morning."

"Don't be silly."

"The shoes and stockings are history at the reception. I don't care what Cheryl says."

He laughed, then handed over the enormous bouquet of yellow jonquils he held. "You can take that up with her. In the meantime, these just came. I'm afraid there's no card."

Farin scowled as he placed them down on her dressing table.

He gave her a brotherly embrace. "Nervous?"

She closed her eyes and held him tight, wishing she could remain in his protective arms until the ceremony ended. "This isn't right, Ben. Not like this."

He leaned away and cupped her face. "Do you love my brother?"

She nodded into his gentle hands, tears brimming her eyes.

"Then that's all there is. The answer to everything."

Another knock sounded. Jameson entered the room, full-mouth beaming, his genuine smile transforming his typically staid features. His black tuxedo gave him an air of gallant elegance. It softened him, somehow.

He gave Ben a formal nod, shook his hand, then offered Farin his arm. "It's time, my dear."

Farin glanced at Ben one last time as he disappeared to take his place beside Jordan at the altar. No turning back now.

"Well?" She inhaled through her nose, exhaled through rose-stained lips, and held her arms out for inspection. "How do I look?"

His eyes swept over her with unabashed pride. "Like a queen. You've no idea how honored I am to be escorting you down the aisle, my child."

"I'm the one who should feel honored. You've been...like a father to me." She stared soulfully into his eyes as she linked her arm in his. "I love you for it, you know."

He patted her hand. "I have something for you at the reception. I hope it makes you happy."

Beyond the door, she heard the organist begin to play. Her stomach flip-flopped. All expression vanished from her powdered face. "I can't imagine anything you'd do could make me feel otherwise." She looked past him and through the door.

Jameson pulled back. "Everything all right?"

"Of course. Please, you go ahead. I need a moment."

She closed the door when he stepped out, then walked to the mirror and primped her updo with her fingertips. She made a mental note to thank Marci for having the presence of mind to remember to buy cucumbers before they checked into their hotel. Her eyes bore no sign that she had sobbed long into the night.

Ben was right, as always. She did love Jordan. Nothing else mattered. Not today. She touched her swollen abdomen.

Glancing over her bare shoulder, she beheld the jonquils on the vanity. Before she realized what she was doing, she rushed over and cleared the table with a single sweep of her arm. The crystal vase holding the buds landed on the floor, shattering into hundreds of pieces.

Chin high and face forward, she marched in step past white roses attached to the end of wooden pews lining the long cathedral, deflecting the bitter glares Chris shot at her like a loaded gun while Jameson led her down the aisle.

At least she assumed it was Jameson who walked beside her. It could have been anyone holding her arm, keeping her from stumbling as she reached the altar, a heavy mass on uncomfortably high heels. Though aware of her body, every other part of her floated elsewhere.

Unintentionally ignoring her groom, who smiled beside her as Jameson handed her off, she fixed her eyes on the large golden crucifix suspended high upon the wall behind the priest. Hanging from the center was the crucified image of Jesus. Guilt squeezed her throat until she could not breathe.

In front of God and everyone.

She happened back into reality as the priest called her name, "...Farin St. John, take this man to be your..."

Farin hesitated. She looked at Jordan, glanced past him at Chris, then back to Jordan again. Her hesitation flickered in Jordan's suddenly troubled eyes. In haste, she faced the priest and sputtered an unconvincing, "I...I-I do."

She felt Jordan lift her veil. She felt him kiss her. The ceremony concluded. Chris had not caused a scene after all.

It was over. No longer a grieving O'Conner child, or a wholly fictitious Ms. St. John. Farin was now Mrs. Jordan Grant.

"This *is* what you want?" Jordan whispered as they strode arm-in-arm down the aisle amidst the congratulatory cheers of their guests, many of whom Farin had never met.

"More than anything in this whole world. I love you."

He kissed her hand. "You frightened me there for a minute."

"I'm sorry." She reprimanded herself for causing him discomfort. From here on out, she would make him the happiest man alive. She owed him that. She owed him more than that.

Jordan had booked the Vizcaya Museum for the reception. A breathtaking venue off Biscayne Bay, with its historic architecture, fountain, and dense, lush gardens. Tonight, the grounds swam in red and white roses both inside and outside the enormous frame tent with its billowing, crisscrossed satin tulle draping, string lights, and chandeliers. Keeping with tradition, she and Jordan arrived last and were greeted with smiles and more cheers, hugs, and kisses. Friends and family made toasts, music filled the warm breeze, dinner was served, and finally, the dancing began.

Jameson led Farin to a semi-secluded area near an enormous hedgerow when she and Jordan finished their first dance. "As I said earlier, I have something for you, my dear," he said, handing her a large manila envelope.

Eyes narrowed in curiosity, she began to open it.

He rested his hand atop hers. "Let me explain first."

The dapper, regal father figure who had ushered her down the aisle to her groom momentarily disappeared. Jameson appeared unsettled. Stammering and shifting his weight from one leg to another. She had never seen him at a loss for words. It touched her.

"You know how fond of you I've always been."

She smiled up at him through downcast eyes and nodded.

"You're special to me. Talented. Loving. Intelligent. And bloody stubborn, just like—"

Her smile faded as his voice trailed off. "Like...?"

He cleared his throat and waved her off. "I've put you in my will."

Farin's lips parted. She felt blood rush to her head as she searched his eyes.

"I've left you a good deal of company stock. Some real estate and a few other assets, as well."

The impact of his declaration hit her in waves. As a child, she had only ever wanted to be part of Lockhardt Sound. Now, it would forever be part of her. "I don't know what to say. I don't feel worthy of such a gift."

He arched a finger and touched her chin, fixing his gaze upon her. "It's what you were born to have."

Out of the corner of her eye, she saw Bobby watching them from the tent's perimeter. When he knew she had seen him, he held up his fists in a mock fighting stance, a playful reminder of his only child status. She winked, then turned back to her benefactor. "You've made me everything I am. And now this...you've made all my dreams come true."

Jameson led her to the dance floor, intoxicated with deserved praise. "The best is yet to come, my dear. Believe me."

When the band began playing "In My Life" by the Beatles, his countenance shifted. He stiffened beneath her hands.

"Is everything okay?"

"I'm grand." He twirled her under his arm, then drew her close. When he did not elaborate, she lowered her head onto his shoulder.

Several couplings away, Jordan danced with his mother. Next to them, George Grant swayed in nostalgic elegance with Cheryl in his arms.

And at the far end of the tent, Chris glowered at Farin. He had intended to speak up when the priest said to "do so now or forever hold your peace." His reticence bewildered him. He could have made it one hell of a memorable occasion.

But who cared? He would not sit around holding his peace anymore.

He waited for the song to end, then approached her from behind as the band's keyboardist played the soft vibraphone introduction to Taylor Dane's "Love Will Lead You Back."

"I believe this is my dance." The shock and disappointment on her face ripped through him.

He ignored Jameson's blustering protests, wedging himself between them. Chris felt a lump in his throat as they swayed together, his arms tight around her waist.

"Why are you doing this?" she asked, her lips thin and stiff.

"You've danced with Ben. And Bobby. You even danced with Derek. It's customary for the groomsmen to dance with the bride."

"Don't play games. Not today."

"Me? What happens when your new husband discovers the baby you're carrying is, in fact, his nephew?"

"This baby belongs to me...and to Jordan. This is *our* child."

He danced like a pro. She wondered if Lynda had taught him as a child. For a while, they fell silent, moving in time with the sad melody. As it rose in intensity, he stepped back and spun her around, then pulled her back to him. "He'll divorce you within a year."

"Stop it."

"The only reason he asked you to marry him was because of the baby."

She looked away, searching for Jordan in the crowd. "I mean it. *Stop.*"

"He still hasn't forgiven you for what happened in New York, you know. Amusing considering all that's transpired between us since."

"I said stop it!" She stepped back. "Jordan loves me!"

Amidst the happy chattering and the amplified music, her outburst went unnoticed by the guests.

"He pities you," he seethed. "Poor little orphan has no one. Bleeding heart wants to play hero. He doesn't even know who you are, Farin. But *I* do."

She scanned the grounds for her husband. She wanted to leave.

A sudden, sharp pain in her abdomen doubled her over. She winced and grasped her swollen belly.

With the second pain, she knew.

Farin kicked away her shoes and hurried away from the reception, then through the building. No one followed. No one called after her.

She climbed into her waiting limousine and demanded, "Get me out of here."

With a nod, the driver engaged the vehicle and headed for the exit.

"Where to, ma'am?"

"Just *drive*." She twisted her body around with some discomfort to look back over her shoulder, then cursed under her breath. Of course. Jordan may not have realized she left, but the press did.

"What's your name?" she snapped.

The driver glanced at her through the rearview mirror. "Charles, ma'am."

She settled into her seat. "Charles, I need you to do whatever it takes to lose those vultures behind us. Understand?"

With a sharp nod, he eyeballed his side and rearview mirrors.

Farin rummaged through her purse as they wove through main and side streets. Intermittent turns and shifts in speed caused her body to sway or pitch sideways or forward. Thankfully, the pain she had experienced at the reception had ceased.

"Any place in particular you want me to go?"

Moments later—and to her great relief—she found her passport. Her luggage and a change of clothes had been loaded into the limousine along with her purse to ensure she and Jordan could slip out during the reception to start their honeymoon.

Obviously, there would not be one.

"I don't see any more cars," Charles told her. "We've lost them."

"Are you sure?"

He made several more turns and doubled back twice to cover the same ground. "All clear. Where to, ma'am?"

She bit her bottom lip. "The airport. But pull over. I need to change."

Losing the press proved a far simpler task than talking a ticketing agent into letting a woman well into her third trimester board a plane. Charles stayed nearby until she secured a ticket, ever watchful for stray reporters or strangers taking undue interest.

"I need your first flight out of the country," she pleaded with the ticket agent of the fourth airline counter she approached.

"Destination?" he asked, impassive.

"What have you got?"

The man looked over the rim of his glasses, eyed her with casual suspicion, then consulted his computer screen. Farin squeezed the three one-hundred-dollar bills she had tucked into her palm, ready to buy the agent's silence, but he showed no sign of recognition.

"There's a flight to London leaving in twenty minutes. There are two seats available." He smirked at his own wit.

"England? Is there anything else?"

The man clacked more keys on his computer. "There's a flight for Rome leaving in about an hour."

"Italy?" The impact of her actions hit her.

"Look, lady. It's the last international flight leaving tonight. If you want someplace exotic, try back in about twelve hours."

The man's tinny voice annoyed her. She handed him her credit card and passport. "I'll take it."

The man did a double take when he read the name on the passport. He looked up at her, his mouth opening as if to speak.

She reached across the desk and pressed the money into his hands. "You never saw me. Understand?"

A grin played at the corner of his mouth. Whether for her or the money, it did not matter. He processed the transaction without objection.

CHAPTER 20

SAMANTHA DRAKE WAS SURPRISED, AND more than a little pleased, when Nancy buzzed her to sit in on Jameson's meeting. The topic? Farin Grant. Of course. It was *always* Farin Grant. Two years ago, she had arrived on the scene. A nobody. From Nowhere. Since then, Samantha had dangled helplessly on the middle rung of LSI's corporate ladder.

Now, Jameson needed her. After months of shoving her aside, placing his confidences in Ross Alexander, and leaving her to order the muddled chaos of Mirage's demise. Fielding Faith Peterson's drug-fueled tirades. Redirecting Chris Grant's demands for answers she could not provide.

Samantha now suffered from high blood pressure, insomnia, and ulcers. At the age of thirty-nine.

She marched toward the office, a self-satisfied smirk stretched across her lips. Confidence sheathed her like armor. She clutched her resignation like a sword. How convenient that the old man should bring her back into the fold hours after her decision to leave this would-be Camelot.

Nancy pushed her glasses up the bridge of her nose as Sam heavy-heeled past her. "They've already start—"

"Of course they have."

She had given him seven years. Seven years to groom her for LSI's coveted, and as yet unfilled, executive vice president position. But that was before Ms. St. John, a.k.a. Miss O'Conner, had turned Lockhardt Sound's founder into a mad—well, madder—recluse.

In fairness, she harbored no ill-will toward Ross. He was an LSI staple, though curiously not a partner. The head of Legal, *not* A&R. Until recently, his duties had never infringed upon hers. Jameson's actions made no sense from a corporate structure standpoint. And personally, it was a slap in the face.

Her Ferragamos champed the broadloom carpet as she strode by the lesser Lockhardt's office. His presence evoked a cynical snort. Another rarity. These days, he spent most his time in Florida, orbiting Farin as if she were the sun.

"Sam!" he called. "Can you—"

"Not now, Bobby."

And even if Ross's title had not changed *technically*, Samantha was no fool. Record labels ate each other whole. LSI had gorged itself on plenty of them. This refashioning of duties reeked of an impending reorganization. Maybe Jameson sought to eliminate her. Maybe she had misjudged the corporation's stability. Maybe Lockhardt Sound's reign had peaked. Bottom line: time to go.

Head high, she entered his office. "You wanted to see me?"

Jameson greeted her with an irritated wave and a sharp, if distracted, "Come in," and pointed to the unoccupied seat beside Ross. "We're discussing *Ulterior Motives*."

"The new album." The corner of her mouth twitched before she could fully suppress an unamused frown. *Farin Grant, please do me a favor and drop dead.*

As usual, Jameson paced, hands clasped behind his back, as if his ability to think was woven into the worn fibers of his office carpet. Worry lines etched into his face told her he was deeply troubled. This, she would not miss.

She crossed her legs. Her arms draped casually atop the armrests. "*Ulterior Motive*'s first single debuted at number one last week. That's three consecutive singles in a row for her, over all. The album's already been certified platinum. Not bad for a relative newbie and mother-to-be."

"I want the second single released as soon as possible but, with her gone, I can't schedule a new video."

"Still no word?" Samantha pitched her voice in feigned concern. Classic. Jameson's little pop princess was not the dutiful lamb he had doubtless anticipated. "Think she's okay?"

"How would I know?" he roared.

She lifted an indignant eyebrow and tilted her head. As she opened her mouth to speak, she felt the soft patting of Ross's hand on her stocking-sheathed knee. She glanced his way to catch the subtle shake of his head as he gave her a knowing look. "We'd have heard if there was trouble. Jameson wants to ensure *Ulterior Motives* doesn't suffer under her absence."

Bobby slunk inside the office, shoulder's bowed, hands plunged into his trouser pockets. He perched himself upon the wide window ledge.

"What kept you?" Jameson asked.

"I was returning calls."

Heeding Ross's unverbalized warning, Samantha waited a beat before continuing. "All right, Jameson. I understand your concern. How do you wish to proceed? A-and-R hasn't been as involved with Farin's career as it normally would be. You've...opted to stay...more directly involved. Either way, my department can't very well be her label liaison if she's nowhere to be found."

Her verbal acrobatics dizzied her. Why even bother?

Jameson lowered himself into his chair and glared at her. "I'd like you to develop some creative alternatives for the next video. Location, costumes, etcetera. Maybe find a look-alike, use her in some silhouette shots."

She blinked, then blinked again. She had earned her MBA at Wharton—Magna, no less—only to be bumped to the position of video consultant?

To her left, she perceived Ross begging her with silent desperation not to react. Perched on the window ledge behind and out of her line of sight, Bobby broached no objection, even though his department should handle such tasks. More blurred lines. More humiliation. Seven years. For naught.

She uncrossed her legs, stood, then smoothed down her skirt. "I'm sorry, Jameson. It just so happens that before you buzzed me in, I took a call from the West Coast. Minor Sixth Records made me an offer. I've accepted."

Behind her, Bobby gasped. "Sam, no!"

A series of angry sputters bubbled up from within the old man. "What are you talking about? I don't have time for this right now, Sam. Call them back. Stall them. Things should calm down soon and then we can discuss a raise."

"A *raise*?"

Closing his eyes, Ross shook his head and rubbed his bald chin.

"This isn't about compensation, Jameson. It's never been about money."

His stare chinked her armor like shot pellets. No matter how his response insulted her, she had overstepped some invisible boundary. He could ruin her if she went too far. Better to consider career over temper.

She willed away the tension in her shoulders. "I'm tired of New York. I need a change. My family's in LA. I realize it's a bad time for you, but there never is a good time, is there? I wanted to notify you as soon as possible. Please consider this my two weeks' notice." She placed the resignation letter on his desk and slid it his way.

Jameson stood and straightened the lapels and cuffs of his suit jacket. "You must have a lot of packing to do, so I'll not keep you. Have your desk cleared out by the end of the day. Leave Mirage's files in plain sight. Accounting can discuss your stock buyback, if you like. I'd offer you a farewell lunch, but you sprung this on me at a most inopportune time. Goodbye, Ms. Drake."

They faced each other in vacuous silence, unblinking, chins jutted.

Jameson arched his brows. "Is that all?"

"I believe so," she said.

"Wonderful. Leave your keys with Nancy on your way out." Jameson sat back down and reached for a stack of papers. "I haven't finished my meeting, Sam. So, if you'll excuse us."

He did not look up as she turned on her heel and strode away. "By the way. You didn't mention your new position."

Samantha paused and turned back, straightening her posture. "Executive VP. I hope you won't feel I'm a traitor. Please, wish me well."

"Your dream job. Impressive," he growled as she shut the door behind her.

Bobby moved to Samantha's vacated chair. He and Ross exchanged uneasy glances. This was a side of the old man neither of them had witnessed in a while. Using his middle finger, he leafed through his papers with rageful flips. Nostrils, flared. Jaw, fixed. Contemplative and deadly. Betrayal, perceived or otherwise, was a sin never left unpunished.

Ross poised his pen above his notepad. "What now?"

Jameson propped his elbow on his desk and waggled his index finger. "Get me a meeting with Ira Niederman over at Minor. I'd like to congratulate them on finding such a talented new file clerk."

He scribbled a note. "And *Ulterior Motives*?"

"Give this to someone good, Bobby. I can't have Farin's career suffering because she's not here."

Bobby leaned in. "I bet we could find her if you want to hire someone."

"We're not going to drag her back against her will, son. This is a personal matter between her and Jordan. I'd think he'd be searching for her himself."

"He's not handling things very well."

"What does that mean? Isn't he out promoting the new album?"

"I can't reach him. He won't talk to anyone, not even Bill Taft."

"You live there, now. Go over and make him talk!"

"I've tried. He won't answer the door. I've had to reschedule the entire campaign. According to Ben, he's there drinking himself blind."

"Do we know why she left?" Ross asked.

"Probably because of Chris."

Jameson gritted his teeth. "I warned that boy. I thought disbanding Mirage would discourage him. I must have underestimated his senselessness."

Bobby tucked his chin. "Is *that* what happened?"

Jameson stared at and through him.

He scooted back in his chair and gave his head an irritated scratch. "So let me get this straight. First, you cut loose the biggest money maker we have. And then, you let the best A-and-R executive in the business walk out the door to go work for a competitor? Losing Sam's bad enough. But Mirage? This could end LSI. What were you thinking?"

Lips straight-lined, Ross shot an expectant "I told you so" glance at Jameson across the desk.

"I was trying to avoid something like *this* happening! Farin's going to be bigger than Mirage ever was. And Chris is trouble, pure and simple. He's a dangerous influence to someone of Farin's emotional frailties. I won't apologize for protecting my own interests."

***

Faith side-stepped along the corridor, dragging behind her what felt like a fifty-pound bag of cement. "I didn't realize how much shit you brought. You pack like a fucking girl."

"And you swear like a longshoreman."

"Yeah? Well, you're powerless and your life's unmanageable."

"Enough with the recovery clichés, Faith. I've listened to them for three days."

"And learned nothing." She grunted under the weight of the luggage.

He wedged one of the two bags he carried under his arm and reached back to relieve her of the suitcase. She slapped his hand away and trudged on.

"I guess a stint in rehab and a month-long spa vacation doesn't change everything, does it? Stubborn old cow."

"Really wanna go there, Don Quixote?"

He looked askance at her. "Called your family yet?"

She scoffed. "Asshole."

They cleared the lobby and stepped out onto the terrace, the suitcase scuffing up and over the threshold, then dropping heavy onto the entry step. Chris stopped before descending the Brownstone's steep set of steps to the waiting limousine.

Faith watched him peer up and down the street, his drawn face mournful and ruminant. He looked miserable. And uncharacteristically worried. She wished she could say or do something to help him.

Who was she fooling? Sure, she was clean for the first time in years, but Chris had only come up to stay after the second time he had to talk her out of relapsing. She could barely help herself, let alone anyone else.

Chris Tetris'd the bags in his arms and descended the steps before she could speak. She followed down behind him, massaging her biceps.

"You sure you wanna do this?"

The bags tumbled in a heap onto the sidewalk as he reached the rear of the limousine. "Will you please stop asking me that? It's been weeks."

"You don't even know where to look. What're you gonna do? Work your way around the planet? Do you even know where to start?"

"Stop asking me that, Faith." He nodded at the driver. "This is it."

The driver began hoisting the luggage into the trunk. "Flight's on schedule. We're good on time."

Chris slapped his back and instructed him to wait while he walked Faith back to her apartment. They jogged back up the steps. Faith moved forward and opened the entry door, but he stopped short.

She released the door, letting it ease shut, then turned to him. Without her boots, her five-foot, three-inch height was anything but commanding as she peered up at him. She cupped his face. "You're an idiot, you know."

He averted his eyes. "Maybe I am. But I'll find her."

"Her husband should be the one looking, Chris, not you."

He shot her a look of disgust. "Her husband won't look. He's too busy drinking and moaning incoherently about her nightmares. How he failed her or some such rubbish. 'Oh, if she wants to come home, she will.' You know Jordan, Faith. He's an emotional marshmallow."

Faith creased her forehead. "He loves her. He doesn't want her to feel crowded."

"He's so understanding, it's nauseating. I wonder what he'd do if he knew the real story."

She jabbed a long, slender index finger in his face. "Don't you dare! He's the victim in all this. She's fucking him on one side and you're screwing him from the other."

His face turned solemn. "She belongs with me."

Faith gave a sad shake of her head. "You've chased her for years, Chris. All she's ever done is try to get away."

He sifted a handful of trembling fingers through his dark mess of hair. "She's living in a fantasy world," he snapped. "She thinks she needs a certain kind of security—and she believes Jordan's the one who can give it to her."

"What makes you think he's not? Sexual innuendos and clever comebacks don't make you the better man, you know. And between you and me, your come-ons are sorta played. So what if Farin had a reaction to you? We women love bad boys. It plays out this bullshit romance novel fantasy we all have. But Chris, that's not love. Love is closeness and feeling and caring and openness—things you and I aren't about."

He looked away, noting his driver had gotten into the cab to wait.

Faith stepped back and studied him top to toe. "Get some rest on the plane. You haven't slept more than a few hours since you got here. You look like shit."

He chewed the inside of his cheek. "I'm scared, Faith. I don't know who I am anymore."

She raised up on her tiptoes and wrapped her arms around his shoulders, sneaking a whiff of his cologne. "You're Chris Grant, womanizing lead guitarist of Mirage—that once-famous rock group that got its ass kicked right when it was in its prime. And maybe you're also Chris Grant, the guy who's starting to realize that Jordan and Farin really do belong together. That he can give her everything she needs."

"No." He pulled away and jogged back down the steps. "I'll find her and make her understand. I'm not giving up."

CHAPTER 21

FARIN SPENT HER FIRST THREE weeks in Rome holed up in a tiny, one-room apartment she had sublet from an elderly widower who owned a small, rundown café in a financially devastated area of the city. She had met Anthony Gianatasio at the airport coffee shop shortly after her arrival. He had come to the airport to purchase tickets for his first American vacation, one he and his wife had dreamed of for twenty years before she died of ovarian cancer eight months ago.

She had eschewed the man at first, rebuffing his offer for company while she finished her tea. When she declined, he sat at an empty table near hers, instructing the server to bring him a coffee and the bill for both tables.

He embarked upon a one-way conversation in impressively accomplished English, speaking aloud, often with his hands. "I need some advice, you see. I've never been to America. If only someone could tell me, should I go to Hollywood or New York City? What do I know of such things?" He looked up, clasped his hands, and sighed. "Ah, Maria. We should not have waited so long."

Inexplicably, the balding Italian with the kind eyes won her over. Anthony spoke woefully of Maria. Of the last year of her life. That night, Farin agreed to accompany him to dinner. He took her to a restaurant near his café. To Farin's relief, no one recognized her. But everyone recognized Anthony, and obviously loved him.

Two days later, she accepted the offer to stay in his apartment above his café. If she stayed in a hotel, she risked her anonymity. Anthony needed an apartment-sitter anyway, so the arrangement benefitted them both. She spent the first night on his couch after refusing to take his bed from him.

"How did you know I needed help?" she asked as she helped him pack.

He cupped her chin with a big, work-worn hand. "Your sad, beautiful eyes. They remind me of her." He pointed to her belly. "Besides, how can someone who carries such joy be so unhappy?"

When Anthony left for America, Farin was on her own.

She lay low, emerging only in the mornings to share coffee, milk, and pastries with café employees. It worked well until the morning the manager's teenage daughter happened to come in for a visit. She recognized Farin almost immediately, then scampered away to share the excitement with her friends.

Though Anthony would not return for another week, Farin knew she had to move on. She left a thank you note and five thousand American dollars on the nightstand beside Maria's photograph. She wished she could have said goodbye, maybe listen to his American adventures, but she had grown accustomed to running out on people without a word.

Bags in hand, she went to the train station without a destination in mind. She was no tourist. Europe's history and grandeur were lost to her. She needed someplace secluded, where she could think without disruption. Or detection.

She spent the next week in a roach-infested dive in Milan, where she indulged no fashion excursions and toured no Italian cathedrals or ancient ruins. Whatever food or incidentals she needed, she collected after dark. She became a phantom—a pregnant phantom—whose eyes abhorred the light of day.

Farin brooded, wondering how Jordan felt, what he thought, and what he did. She longed to call, but dreaded questions for which she had no answer—number one being why she had abandoned him on their wedding night; and number two, why she refused to come home.

Eventually, she asked herself that question. What had she accomplished hiding in a Milanian slum? Did it expunge her guilt? Erase the affair? Jordan probably knew everything anyway. Miles Macy had surely outed her by now.

Farin's major concern centered on the baby. Prior to the wedding, its movements had slowed. Since arriving in Milan, it had barely moved at all. Once, she nearly made a doctor's appointment, then reconsidered. The baby was fine. It had to be.

Once she delivered, she would return to America. She would know the truth. If Chris had indeed fathered her child, she would return to California and raise it alone. If Jordan was the father, she would beg for forgiveness and another chance.

Her self-imposed isolation soon depressed her. She had arrived a fugitive and incarcerated herself with invisible chains. Again, it was time to move on.

Back at the train station, she consulted a map of Europe. She considered Spain and Ireland before glimpsing France. She had dreamed of visiting Paris since her childhood. Her father had loved the City of Lights.

Her father. If only he could see what a mess she had made.

Worse, perhaps he could.

In Paris, her first order of business was scheduling a doctor's appointment. The language barrier proved frustrating as she sought the most qualified obstetrician in the city. The effort challenged her patience and her anonymity. Finally, the Concierge found her an office with a bilingual receptionist. Their earliest availability was five days later.

Defying her paranoia, she had taken a room at the Ritz. She had tired of sharing her room with various species of vermin throughout Europe's less-advantaged neighborhoods. She wanted her own shower. As a precautionary measure, she registered under her maiden name.

Room service and clean sheets lifted her spirits. Housekeeping brought fresh linen and toiletries each morning. Until recently, Farin had taken such luxuries for granted.

She familiarized herself with her surroundings while awaiting her appointment. Mindful to maintain a balance of rest and activity, her increasing girth challenged her attempts to explore the Louvre, the Eiffel Tower, and Notre-Dame Cathedral. She limited her excursions to a three-mile radius from the hotel, mostly along the Seine, and always in disguise.

Lately, her feet and hands throbbed with edema. She consumed gallons of water. The stares of people she encountered confused her. Were they glimpses of recognition? Or pity for the pregnant tourist waddling down the streets, dining alone in city cafés?

At least she had a nice view during lonely hours sitting with elevated feet. Her Coco Chanel suite overlooked Vendôme Square.

Remorse over numerous bad choices took up residency in her conscience. She yearned to be the wife Jordan deserved. He had looked so happy as they exchanged their vows. And almost immediately, she had broken every one of them.

She missed Miami. Living in isolation took its toll. She withered from the lack of basic human interaction—even the adoration of her fans. Jameson was probably furious. Something had to give.

The morning of her doctor's appointment, she rose early, showered, then ordered breakfast and a copy of the *New York Times*—a real luxury—

from room service. When it arrived, she nestled into a plush fabric chair, stuffed a pillow behind her to support her back, and caught up on the news from the States. As she finished her last strawberry, there came a knock at the door.

"Perfect timing," she called out to the maid as she waddled to the door, supporting her lower back with her right hand. "I was just leav—"

Chris stood perched against the door jamb, arms crossed. He towered over her, sleek and dark, his hair damp from a recent shower, his cologne strong and musky. His eyes bored into hers.

In an instant, she was equally caged, caught, guilty, and grateful to see a familiar face. When the shock subsided, she tried to slam the door on him, but Chris shouldered his way inside.

"Hold on a minute! It wasn't exactly easy tracking you down!"

"What are you doing here? How did you—"

"I'm not even sure you're worth what I paid to find you, but what's done is done."

A lump formed in her throat. Jordan had not come for her, but Chris had.

Farin backed away as he closed the door behind him, and sulked back to her chair. "What do you want?"

He moved past her to the table. "Breakfast any good? I'm famished. Think I'll call downstairs and have something brought up."

"No, you won't! You can't stay."

Chris lifted the receiver and dialed room service. "This is Ms. O'Conner's room. Please send up some coffee, poached eggs, and sourdough toast. For one. And bill the Chopin Suite. That's right. Cheers." Replacing the receiver, he wrinkled his nose at the phone. "Bloody frog."

She lifted her brows expectantly.

He sat opposite her, scrutinizing her at length. His heart ached with every bitter rejection. "I'm here to talk."

"That's why I left in the first place, so I wouldn't have to hear you talk anymore." She lowered her eyes. "Does Jordan know I'm here?"

"I doubt it."

"Does anyone?"

"Not unless you've told someone. My motives for coming are selfish, I assure you. Yes, I was worried, but the real reason I'm here is to try to work this out." He rose and walked toward her with outstretched hands.

"Don't." She jerked her head to the side and slapped him away. "Isn't ruining my life enough?"

His arms dropped to his sides. "I never meant for that to happen."

"Then, go. Leave me alone."

"Hear me out."

"It's over."

"Farin, I love you."

Her eyes darted up and fixed upon his. Studying him, she realized he meant it. Or, believed he did. He was a broken shell of the man she had run from the last two years.

Anger swelled within her. How dare he let his heart go to her. She could not decide which of the two of them she hated more. "You don't love me or anybody else, Chris. You're incapable of love. And I belong to Jordan."

He moved closer as if to protest, but Farin pushed him away.

"Don't say that." His voice broke. "You're right. I've never loved anyone in my life before. But I love you. I need you. And you need me, too."

"We have to forget what happened." She buried her head in her hands, frustrated at Chris's presence, weary from her time abroad, exhausted with her pregnancy. "As soon as I have this baby—Jordan's baby—I'm flying home. I'll make it right. I have to, and I will."

He paused and clenched his jaw. "Too bad you didn't realize that before it was too late."

"What do you mean?"

He sauntered to the window and parted the sheers with his hand. "He's done. He waited two weeks. When you didn't return, he annulled the marriage."

She blanched, her voice a mere whisper. "You're not serious."

He lifted a shoulder. "Afraid so. He said he couldn't wait forever."

"But the papers. I check them every day. And—"

"And every day you see nothing, right?"

She nodded.

"You think Jameson would let a scandal like this get out?"

"What...what did he say?"

Chris scoffed. "Nothing to me."

Annulled. The word churned in her stomach. She realized she had not acted like a wife for more than an hour after their vows, but *annulled*? Her mind dizzied with tentative plans. She had to get home. She decided to book a flight the moment she left the doctor's office.

Enraged, she shot out of her seat and marched toward the door, unwilling to share her grief with its creator. As she passed the sofa there came a sudden, stabbing pain in her abdomen. It sent her to her knees, gasping for air.

Chris rushed to her side. "What is it?"

Her face paled as her eyes rolled back in agony.

"Farin, what's wrong?"

She winced and doubled over. "Get an ambulance."

***

Chris trod the *Pitié-Salpêtrière Hospital* waiting area while nurses settled Farin into a room. She had passed out on the way to the hospital, nearly scaring him to death. He recalled following a similar ambulance to a similar hospital not so long ago.

He berated himself for the lie. Why had he told her Jordan annulled their marriage?

"*Monsieur* Grant," a young nurse came to get him at last. "You may go in now."

Chris glanced up and breathed, "*Merci.*"

"*D'accord.*"

He hurried to Farin's side. She lay in the bed, dressed in a yellow, sweat-soaked hospital gown. An IV pumped fluid into her arm. He stroked her hair. "How do you feel?"

She trembled. "They can't find a heartbeat."

A second nurse pushed past him, holding what looked like a large belt with a beeper attached. "*Excusez-moi, Monsieur.*"

"What is that thing?" he demanded, aghast as the nurse attached the apparatus around Farin's abdomen.

"The fetal monitor," she answered in her best English, pronouncing each "th" sound as a "z." "It...er...monitors the *bébé* heartbeat."

"Anything?" Farin's voice broke with panic. "Can't you hear anything?"

Another nurse entered the room, tapping tiny air bubbles out of a syringe as she approached Farin's bedside. "This takes the pain away, *Madame* Grant. The *docteur* is on the way."

Farin shuddered as the needle injected medication into her IV. "Is he good? What's his name?"

"*Il s'appelle Docteur Lardan. C'est un bon docteur. L'un des meilleurs.*"

The medication numbed her thoughts but did little for the pain.

"*Je suis tellement désolé, Madame,*" she added. "Your husband must go to wait outside while the *docteur,* he looks at you."

"He's *not* my husband," Farin snapped in Chris's direction.

Evening came before Chris heard anything. He tried to ascertain the status of the baby but got nowhere. When the weary physician finally emerged, he knew the worst had happened. He had seen that same expression on the face of another doctor the day Chase died.

"*Bon soir, Monsieur* Grant," the doctor greeted. "*Je m'appelle Docteur Lardan.* Sit, *s'il te plait.*"

"I've been sitting all bloody day! What's happening?"

"*Madame* Grant, she rests. It was *très difficile* for her."

"And the baby?"

The doctor released a deep sigh. "So sorry, *Monsieur. La petite fille…*she did not live."

By mere chance, Chris flopped bonelessly back into the chair he had just risen from when his knees buckled.

"*Madame* Grant, she has the petite hip bone." Lardan struggled with his broken English as he tried to explain, using his hands to illustrate. "The cord wraps around *le bébé* neck until…*elle est morte.* The baby, she was not living long before today."

Chris grasped the sides of his face. He threw back his head against the unbearable news. "It was a girl?"

"*Oui,*" the doctor whispered faintly.

A daughter. Or, a niece. "Does Farin know?"

"*Oui, Monsieur,*" he nodded. "She will wake after a few hours more. You may see her then."

Chris slumped forward, resting his elbows on his knees. Memories of Chase, of the day he had met Farin, looped in his mind. He had encouraged Chase's dreams of swimming in the water like the older Grant males. Though he had never uttered his thoughts to another soul, he blamed himself for his nephew's fate.

He covered his face with his hands and rubbed his temples to banish the images.

Dr. Lardan tarried beside Chris, momentarily dropping his professional demeanor. He rested his hand on Chris's shoulder and gently squeezed. "*Monsieur* Grant, *j'apologie. C'est la vie, non?*"

Chris drifted in and out of sleep the entire night, his head bobbing up and down, occasionally hitting the bed as he sat and held Farin's hand. Dried, diluted mascara streaks across her face told him she had cried herself to sleep.

"My baby's dead," she whimpered as she woke and saw him beside her.

He scooted closer and squeezed her hand.

She smacked and licked at her dry lips through the haze of potent medication infused through her IV. "How can I tell Jordan?"

Chris looked down and bit his cheek. "Don't worry about that now."

"How could he annul our marriage?"

He swallowed hard.

"*Ah, Madame. Bonjour,*" Dr. Lardan greeted, entering the room. "Feeling better this morning?"

She struggled to reposition herself. "It hurts."

Again, the doctor spoke with animated hand gestures to support his broken English. "You have *les agrafes.* The, uh...staples from the...surgery...the, the...*la césarienne, non*?"

"When can I leave?"

Dr. Lardan paged through her chart. "After another day or two, I think. I must run the further tests...*aussi*, I'm afraid there will have to be the autopsy."

Farin sucked her pursed lips. "M-may I see her first?"

Chris fused his eyes and turned his head.

"*Bien sûr,*" Dr. Lardan answered softly. "*Aussi,* a name for the record?"

Heartsick, Farin nodded. A name. She and Jordan had never settled on one, though they had discussed it at length. It felt wrong to do it without him. Even worse that she would be the only one of the two of them to ever see her.

"Will there be a blood test?" Chris asked.

"*Mais oui, certainement,*" the doctor replied, his aspect decidedly puzzled. "*Pourquoi?* Is there the *problème*?"

"No problem." Farin jerked her hand from his.

"*Madame* Grant, you must not fly, you know, for several days. If you fly, you can...you can hurt inside *toujours, éternellement,*" he moved his hand in a circular motion in front of his stomach, "how you say, forever. *D'accord*?"

When Dr. Lardan left, Chris stared after him. "We need to know, Farin."

"Marci was wrong. You're not a weasel, you're a heartless pig! What was I thinking?"

"Maybe that's something you'll consider. Like I said, I want to give this a shot." He placed his hand near hers on her bed. "I love you."

Those words again. "Well, *I* don't love *you*. Jordan's the only man I'll ever love."

He stared at the floor. "So...my coming all this way doesn't matter to you."

Farin turned away. She wanted to lie. To punish him for loving her. But, were she honest, she would admit that waking to find him holding her hand had comforted her.

"I can't stop how I feel, Farin."

Her tone weakened with sorrow. "Can't you be my friend, Chris? Like Ben? Or Bobby? I really need a friend right now."

He longed to comfort her. But where his proclamation of love had missed its target, Farin's arrow of insensitivity found its mark. He had never once professed love to a woman—not even to get her into bed. And while this meant everything to him, it meant nothing to her.

He stood and cleared his throat as he hiked the belt loops of his jeans. "I'm not your friend, Farin. I was inside you. I felt every part of you. And if you don't remember it the same way, fine. I'll sort it. But don't insult me by asking me to move backwards."

***

Marci's desk phone had rung all morning. The recent promotion had not made her job any easier. In fact, she was busier than ever.

"There's an international call for you on two," her secretary buzzed in. "I couldn't get a name."

She thanked her and picked up the phone. "This is Miss Williams."

"Marci?"

"Farin!" She threw herself back in her chair. "Are you okay?"

Farin wept. "I wanna come home."

"You're scaring me. Where are you?"

"In the hospital. The baby...she...I...I had a girl."

Marci choked back joyful tears. "I can't believe you ran off like that. You shouldn't be alone. What did you name her? She's early, isn't she? When did she arrive?" *Aunt Marci*, she thought wistfully.

"Two days ago. There were...complications."

Marci's smile drowned in a sea of disbelief. "Oh, Farin. No."

"I...I lost her, Marce."

"Tell me where you are."

"They're saying I probably won't be able to have any more children," she sobbed.

Marci lowered her head onto the tips of her fingers. "Does Jordan know?"

A pause filled the line, interrupted by mournful, intermittent sniffs.

"You have to tell him, Farin."

"As soon as I'm released, I'm going back to Miami. That's why I called. Could you and Dan put up with me for a couple of days while I look for a place? I'm moving back to LA."

"Wh—? What about Jordan?"

"It's over. Don't make me explain right now."

Marci did not press the issue, though shock upon shock left her confused. She had spoken with Jordan several times over the weeks. He had never hinted that the relationship had ended. If anything, he was desperate for her return. "Of course you can stay. You don't even have to ask."

"I should be there in about a week. I can't fly yet."

Marci bit a nail as she thought aloud. "Do you mind if I call Jordan and tell him about the baby? He really should know."

***

The call caught Jordan tidying up the front room. He had embarked on a weeks-long drinking binge the night Farin walked out on their wedding reception. Jameson, Bobby, and Chris had made a scene yelling at each other until Ben got between them. Jordan had no memory of how he got back home that night. Or most nights since.

The time had come to clean up his life—and his home. He would no longer fight a losing battle. His life had been suspended since the night she left, the worst part of which had been time spent sitting by the telephone, afraid she might call if he dared to leave.

But no more. He would not jump every time the phone rang. His love for Farin would no longer destroy his sanity and monopolize his thoughts. He had an answering machine. If she wanted to call, or come home, she would do it.

Despite this newfound resolve, the warble of the ringing telephone made his heart leap. He willed himself to continue his task as the answering machine kicked in.

"Jordan, it's Marci. Look, Farin called about five minutes ago—"

He dashed to the machine and snatched up the receiver. "Where is she?"

"Somewhere overseas, I think. Maybe Europe?"

"*Europe*? What did she say?"

She exhaled through her nose. "I hate having to tell you this."

"Tell me what?"

Jordan heard the cry in her voice. His body quaked. He set a bag of spent liquor bottles down beside him.

"She lost the baby, Jordan."

His body numbed with flashes of Kim in one emergency room and Chase in another. It could not be. Not again. Quietly, he asked, "Is my wife okay?"

"It was pretty rough, I guess. They're saying she probably can't have any more children."

"Was it a girl?"

"Y-yes. I'm so sorry."

The numbness subsided as pain paralyzed him. "Is Farin coming home?"

"As soon as they release her."

He sank to the floor and surveyed his newly uncluttered surroundings. "I've done everything, Marci—everything I can to make it work. I love her, but I don't know if I can hold on any longer."

"She loves you. You know she does. It's just...she runs away when she feels overwhelmed. It's not you. We all know she's troubled. She'd never hurt you on purpose. Believe me."

"I don't know what to believe anymore." Anger over the past seven weeks battled his grief and Marci's pleas for mercy on Farin's behalf. "Did you know we've been together for over two years and we've never even spent Christmas together? If she loves me so much, why is that? Why did she make a fool out of me on my wedding day? Why wasn't I invited to be with her when our child was born? You'd sodding think she'd need me right now. I sure need her. I've been mad with worry. And now... now...*this*?"

"Don't give up, Jordan. *Please*. Love her through this thing."

"Loving her isn't the problem. I'll love her until the day I die," he said with no hint of emotion, as if stating a simple fact. "But I won't spend another Christmas alone. I'll never go through this again."

CHAPTER 22

DARK CLOUDS UNDULATED ACROSS THE Florida peninsula the day Farin returned, weeping as if the sky itself mourned for her and her lost child. As if it understood her. As if it shared her grief.

She had ignored Dr. Lardan's advice to wait two weeks before traveling.

Her cab dropped her in front of Jordan's house. It did not feel like home. Not her home. Maybe, it never really had. She felt alone and discarded as she dragged damp luggage up the front steps. Surprisingly, her gate code and key still worked.

Inside, the sight of scattered—even shattered—liquor bottles throughout the living room startled her. She checked her watch, which still registered Central European Time. Calculating the difference, she figured Jordan was still asleep.

It took time to clear the debris from in the living room, dining room, and kitchen. She worked in silence, pausing often to rest. The hospital had removed the staples days ago, but the inner sutures still felt tender and painful. They pulled at her abdomen, impinging free movement.

She would not pack until she saw Jordan. Then again, he might have already sent her things back to her place.

The phone rang through the tomb-like silence, causing her to start. She winced in pain, then considered answering. But this was no longer her home. The ringing stopped abruptly, stealing the decision from her.

Minutes later, she heard the familiar padding of drowsy feet descend the stairway. When Jordan saw her seated in the living room, he stopped and rubbed sleep-filled eyes.

"Hi," she whispered softly.

He walked toward her, then stopped again. For a fleeting moment, he looked happy to see her. She could not tell for sure.

"Marci said you'd be coming home soon."

"I guess I'll get my things...if they're still here."

Weeks of hurt and longing had rendered Jordan incapable of feeling surprised. She had come home, all right. To pack. "Where to this time?"

"California."

He nodded softly and set his jaw. "Where was our daughter born?"

She glanced down at her fidgeting fingers. "Paris."

"Were you there the whole time?"

"It doesn't matter. We both did what we felt was best."

He raised his hands to his hips. "What did *I* do?"

"I know about the annulment, Jordan. I get it."

"What annulment?"

They exchanged puzzled glances.

"I heard you waited two weeks, then had our marriage annulled."

"There's no bloody annulment." He stepped toward her, frustrated and confused as he pointed at the phone. "I've waited for a call for almost two months. You think I'd annul our marriage after only two weeks? Seriously, *two weeks*?"

Farin struggled to connect the dots. Then, everything became clear. Chris. It seemed his cruelness knew no depth.

She flew into his arms, defying the pain, afraid to let go. Afraid she had heard him wrong. Afraid to be physically separated from Jordan another second.

Jordan held her as if letting her go would destroy him. "I wanted to follow you. I should have. But I didn't want you to run any farther. What happened? Why did you leave?"

They held each other tighter. He had a million questions—not the least of which, who had told her he had ended their marriage—but they could wait. Everyone she ever knew had deserted her in one way or another. He would not be one of them.

Farin sobbed into his shoulder. "Melody. Her name was Melody."

The words shattered what little strength Jordan thought he had. The idea of her losing their child alone, in a foreign city, made him feel he had somehow failed her, though it was she who had left.

But none of that mattered now. She was home where she belonged. She needed to heal. They both did. Now, they could do it together.

***

Chris slid an empty bourbon bottle down the groove-worn bar. "Bottle's dry."

Joey Stokes scratched his balding head. "Don't you think you've had enough?"

He grinned through his drunken haze. "Precisely why I'm here. I've had enough. Of everything. Now get me another drink."

Joey came out from behind the bar and tried to roust him off the stool. "Why don't you go home and sleep it off?"

Chris pushed free. "Because bourbon's better than sleep."

Joey returned to his station. When Chris laid his head atop his folded arms, he poured half a fresh bottle of bourbon into the spent one and added water to the fill line before setting it before him.

They had formed a sort of loose companionship over the last few months, and Joey knew something besides booze ate at Chris's insides. He had come in every night that week and drank until he could not stand.

Reporters and paparazzi swarmed his run-down establishment. The stories they penned about the drunken rock star were less than flattering. Stokey's had exploded in popularity, becoming Miami's number one dive bar. Profits boomed, but Joey felt rotten they did so at the expense of his pal.

Chris sloshed a sloppy pour into his shot glass. As he tossed back his head and gulped, the diluted brown liquid spilled down either side of his mouth. He ran the back of his hand across his mouth. "You ever love someone?"

Joey watched as Chris attempted another pour from bottle to glass.

"You know, I thought she'd change her mind when I came for her."

For his part, Joey could not condemn her the way Chris did. He had never confessed it to his friend, but he thought Farin was the most beautiful woman in the world. "I hear she's doing great." He busied himself drying freshly washed glasses with a damp bar towel as he extolled her latest video. "So sexy and all. Too bad she's hidden in the shadows most the time."

"That's not even her." Chris regarded him coldly. "They had to improvise. She was...out of town when they filmed it. But yes. She's doing quite well. She has a bright bloody future ahead of her."

The pain and sarcasm in his friend's voice saddened him. "I sure felt bad when she lost her baby."

Chris shut his eyes against the still-fresh wound. The hospital in Paris had refused to give him the paternity test results. Probably all he needed to know. Had he been the father, they surely would have told him. She would have been his niece. The first girl in their family. Melody Rose Grant.

"Is Farin better now?"

He shrugged. "Haven't seen her. I heard her bitch-from-hell friend's flying in soon for a visit. We don't get on well."

"I wish I knew what to say, buddy. You've been hittin' it pretty hard lately. What happened?"

Another drink disappeared. "Farin happened."

***

Farin's limousine parked curbside at Miami International near Baggage Claim. The chauffeur disappeared inside to greet Marci at the arrival gate with a hand-lettered sign bearing her name.

She dug her compact out of her purse to touch-up her makeup, irritated at the dark circles that had formed beneath her eyes. She dabbed on additional concealer, then added more powder. It would have to do.

A quick rake of her fingers through her curls and a touch of lip stain later, she tossed the compact back in her purse and grabbed the cell phone Bobby had insisted she start carrying. Somehow, it was always ringing. And always Bobby.

"I'm at the airport. Can this wait?"

"Just confirming tomorrow. I'll pick you up at six."

"Bring coffee."

"I always bring coffee, Farin. You don't have to remind me every time."

"You know what? What if I just drive myself and meet you there?"

A strained breath filled the line. "You're not driving yourself."

Though thrilled with her career's upward trajectory, Farin found herself resenting its consequences. *Ulterior Motives* had catapulted her so far into the stratosphere of fame, her every move drew crowds.

A brutal schedule accompanied her return and her increased celebrity. The attention, acclaim, and responsibilities dizzied her. And wherever she went, fans and paparazzi swarmed her, begging for autographs, photographs, or a quick word as she disappeared into a restaurant or hotel.

"I'm trying to keep you safe."

"You and Jameson are trying to keep me controlled, you mean."

"I'm not having this conversation again, Farin. I stand between you and Dad plenty. Besides, you brought this on yourself."

She bit the inside of her cheek. "Fine. What about the questions?"

"All vetted."

"Hope they know I'll walk if they pull any stunts. I won't have a repeat of last week."

"You won't. And they know."

Certain questions were now deemed verboten in the universe that was

Farin Grant. Interviewers had to submit each one for pre-approval. Her team put them to careful scrutiny, ready to put the kibosh on any inquiries about her trip to Europe, Melody's death, or her brother-in-law. She had not even fully recuperated from her surgery yet. About this, Bobby did not seem to care. Jameson certainly did not. Everybody wanted a piece of the star.

Farin held the cell phone to her ear as she peeked out the window at the airport doors. It's mirrored reflection in the afternoon light made it impossible to see inside.

She leaned back into the seat. "I'm tired, Bobby. Are you sure I can't get any more time while Marci's here?"

"I did the best I could. See you tomorrow."

His dismissive tone left her less than reassured.

As she awaited her driver's return with her friend, she indulged in precious seconds of calm. She rested her head back, shut her eyes, and tried to practice her breathing. The sparkle of her synthetic smile had faded weeks ago. Routine had dulled her feigned edginess. But usually, she waxed happy. Usually, she gave more than she had to give. Only she and Jordan knew her duties had kept her so busy, they had not yet consummated their marriage.

Nevertheless, the *Ulterior Motives* publicity campaign raced forward at full speed, and so did Farin Grant.

"Great car!" Marci giggled as she climbed inside the limousine and hugged Farin. "I thought you were picking me up alone."

"This is the only way I can get around anymore. It's ridiculous, I know."

"Ah." She sighed as she settled in. "Poor Farin, the superstar. Did Jameson agree to some time off while I'm here?"

With a nod and a dismissive wave, Farin gestured their readiness to take off. As her driver pulled away from the curb, she scrunched her mouth into a disappointed frown and sank back into her seat. "He's punishing me with a full schedule. I got three days off just before you leave. And since you're leaving the day after Halloween, I thought we'd do a party."

With narrowed eyes and a suspicious smirk, Marci dropped back, laid her purse beside her, and crossed her arms. "Spill it."

"What?"

"Farin, you don't willingly plan, throw, or attend parties. Something's up."

As their eyes locked, Farin realized how much she missed having someone around who knew her cues. Someone around whom she could be herself.

"Start at the beginning," Marci prodded.

Farin dropped her head onto the back of the leather seat. "You want business or personal?"

"Start with business. You look like crap."

"Okay, business it is. Jameson's decided I need to work until I pass out as penance for running off, and in order to grieve Melody's loss. And I guess it's working because, right now, I don't even have the energy to cry."

Marci reached across and squeezed Farin's hand.

"Bobby's acting weird. But not normal-weird with that stupid facial tic and all. On tour, we were really close. He was fun. Kept me going. Now, he's got this dark vibe about him. And honestly? It's starting to creep me out. Why? I don't know."

Marci nodded as she listened. She noticed their driver steal occasional glances in the rearview mirror. When Farin noticed as well, she engaged the privacy window.

"So, you're busy and Bobby's strange. Got it. It's probably 'cause you took off and didn't tell him. He doesn't know you like I do. If he did, he'd expect it."

Farin rolled her head along the back seat and smiled at the unsubtle jab. "I knew you'd understand."

Marci gave an unrepentant shrug. "So, that's business. What about the fam."

At this, her aspect shifted. She rubbed her hairline as her features tightened. "Well, if Bobby's changed, Jordan's gone from day to night. At first, he was caring and understanding. We grieved Melody together, as a couple. But after a few days, things changed. He's distant. Like, pulling away. We don't talk—about anything. I'd thought it was our schedules. Then, I thought it was the restrictions on our...well—"

"Your sex life."

"Yeah. You know, while I healed. But Marce, he sleeps in the downstairs guest room."

"*Seriously?*"

Farin nodded. "And whatever he's got, it's contagious. Ben and Cheryl haven't said a word to me in two weeks."

"What about Chris? Have you seen him?"

She shook her head. "Not since Paris."

"And what about...you know?"

Farin stared out the window and watched as they passed businesses, other cars, and foot traffic along their way. She had known the question would come sooner or later.

"Well? Did the results come back or not?"

"Looks like I ran for nothing. Melody was Jordan's after all."

Farin could not remember lying to Marci before that moment.

They rode in silence toward I-95. Marci ruminated on the similarities and differences of their situations. She had not shared the circumstances that had fostered her decision to use some accrued vacation. As usual, Farin outpaced the crises in her own life.

"So, you're an outcast trying to push your way back into everybody's good graces. Okay. All caught up. I can't tell you how good it is to get away."

Marci's vacation passed without a thought of Dan Albright, the bank, or the escalating dissatisfaction with her life. At first, she tagged along with Farin's whirlwind business commitments. She got to know Bobby better and experienced firsthand the lifestyle lived by those she had admired in her magazines. Recording. Photo sessions. Guest appearances. Interviews. Radio shows. Conference calls to discuss *Ulterior Motives'* campaign, progress on the third album, plans for future videos, and even another tour. Peeking behind the grand façade, it took no time for Marci's perception to shift.

Being a celebrity was hard work.

Five days into her trip, she begged off and decided to hang out with Ben and Cheryl. Maybe she would uncover why the Grants had started giving Farin the cold shoulder, a fact she had witnessed with painful clarity the moment Jordan carried her bags to a guest room—one he did not already occupy.

Fortunately, the reception she received from Farin's brother- and sister-in-law did not hint at any guilt by association. In fact, Ben's family welcomed her visits. She swam with the boys, helped Cheryl cook, and even played around in the studio with Ben. If nothing else, her vacation yielded one discovery: Marci Williams was no singer.

Subsequent visits found her nowhere near the studio.

"I'm sure Jordan's told you already, but Farin wants to throw a

Halloween party the night before I leave." She accepted a glass of iced tea and joined her hosts at their kitchen table.

The air-conditioned room chilled an extra degree or two as Cheryl's eyes darted toward her husband, then off into the middle distance.

Ben cleared his throat. "He didn't mention it."

"I thought it'd be fun. Maybe the boys can give me tips on a costume."

"We could have it here," Cheryl suggested with a perfunctory smile.

"I think Farin wants to try to cheer her place up a bit. It's been sort of dreary over there lately."

Ben lowered his head. "Things okay?"

"I'd say no." She took a sip of her tea.

"Well, it's no wonder, is it?" Cheryl stood to busy herself in the kitchen. She wiped down a clean countertop, then visually inventoried the refrigerator. "Ben, can you start the grill, please? Marci? Would you join us?"

Marci looked on as Ben excused himself to start the grill.

Farin heard Jordan at the door as she and Marci decorated the house for their nautically-themed party that night. She greeted him with a hopeful smile and a hug. "Happy Halloween!"

He offered a prosaic embrace, patted her back, then headed to the kitchen to sort a stack of mail that lay on the table.

She followed behind. "How was your day?"

"Busy." He sorted the envelopes as if the task demanded his full attention.

"Anything interesting?"

"Nope. Usual stuff."

"We've just about finished with the decorations. Wanna see?"

"I'll look later." He discarded some ads into the trash and turned to leave.

"Jordan?"

He stopped to study her, then trotted upstairs. "I have to get ready."

He did not resurface until everyone had arrived. Then, he buried himself in conversation with Ben, staying clear of Farin as best he could.

Ben squared his shoulders and adjusted the sash of his uniform costume. "I see we're both royalty tonight. Between you and me, I think Cheryl's getting a kick out of wearing that Grace Kelly wedding dress. Our own wedding wasn't nearly as grand."

"How I let my nephew talk me into being a fairytale prince is beyond me." Jordan smiled. "What are you two letting him watch, anyway?"

Ben chuckled. "He'll watch anything with boats and water. Besides, I think he likes redheads. And you had to be Prince Eric if Farin was going to be Ariel."

Jordan's smile evaporated. Ben pretended not to notice.

Marci appeared before them. She struggled with a tray of hors d'oeuvres. "You two have nothing to complain about. At least you can sit down."

Ben laughed. He relieved her of the tray and laid it on the coffee table. "I can't believe you agreed to it."

"I didn't know what a 'nautical figurehead' was until after I'd promised. Now, this 'headrail' I'm attached to—see how much I've learned?—prevents me from doing anything except, I guess, warding off sea spirits."

"Admit it. He flattered you into it."

She softened. "How can you resist a ten-year-old who says you remind him of one of Neptune's Wooden Angels?"

Jordan grinned. "He could have had you dress up as a wench."

Marci conceded his point with a bark of laughter, then excused herself upon hearing Farin call from the kitchen. As she left, she called over her shoulder, "How did you and Cheryl avoid this whole oceanic theme, anyway?"

"Simple." Ben winked. "We said no."

In stolen moments throughout the evening, Prince Rainier and Grace Kelly behaved like newlyweds in their nuptial attire, flirting playfully in hushed tones. Marci volunteered for any job that would not require her to stoop, bend, or sit. She kept a lively stream of music playing on the CD player, refilled drinks, and posed for pictures with swabbie Kyle and first mate Derek when they returned from trick-or-treating with Captain Weasel, who left shortly after returning the boys to their parents. Between tasks, she leaned—against kitchen counters, the dining room table, doorways...

Meanwhile, Prince Eric barely moved from his place on the sofa and limited his interactions with Ariel to mostly grunts or gestures.

Ben and Cheryl took the boys home but returned after corralling them to bed. Without the children, tension replaced the earlier gaiety of the evening. The group of five sat together as if all their words were spent.

Marci ached for Farin. Her friend had tried so hard to make it a festive evening. She looked radiant in her costume, with aquamarine accents and body glitter. An ethereal, voiceless mermaid, wanting only to be part of Prince Eric's world. A tragic yet apropos footnote to every bad event of Farin's life.

When she retreated to the kitchen, Marci joined her.

Farin sulked over a tray of vegetables. "I don't know what else to do."

"Give it more time. They're feeling Melody's loss. It'll get better. You didn't really think a party would undo everything, did you?"

"She was *my* baby. And Jordan's. Don't they think we're miserable too?"

Marci picked up the vegetable tray and headed out. "C'mon. Just keep smiling and being cheerful. The night can't last forever."

But Marci was wrong.

Farin lingered in the kitchen as long as she could without appearing rude, then rejoined the others. She returned to hear Jordan offer to drop Marci at the airport the next day. "I've got an appointment downtown at eight thirty anyway."

When the telephone rang, Farin excused herself and answered from the kitchen. Wrong number, but a welcome pretense under which she could remove herself from the unkind eyes of her surrogate family.

What had happened to the laughter of the Grants? The warmth? It seemed she would have been better received if she had dressed up as Hester Prynne, with a big fat "A" across her chest.

The doorbell rang, but she stayed put. She felt miserable. Since Bobby had declined her invitation to join them that evening, she was not expecting anyone. It was probably another reporter, anyway.

Seconds later, Farin heard a succession of doors slam throughout the house. When the kitchen door flew open, it startled her. Before her stood an exceedingly drunken pirate. His silk poet shirt hung loosely, only half-tucked into his scallywag breeches. He staggered as he drew near, his breath saturated with rum.

"Well, if it isn't Ms. O'Conner."

"That's *Mrs.* Jordan Grant." She prayed no one could hear them from the living room. Oh, how she would enjoy giving him a piece of her mind. "I'd hoped you wouldn't come back tonight."

"I bet! Sorry I didn't drop by earlier to welcome you home. I've had a lot on my mind lately. I'm sure you understand." Chris wove and pitched forward as she backed away. Looking down, he pointed to the floor beside her. "Remember that? Remember how you begged me to take you again right there on the floor?"

"*You!*" she seethed with a furious hiss. "You stalk me all the way to Paris—telling me how much you love me—then swear Jordan annulled our marriage? Did you think I wouldn't find out the truth? How can you even show your face after what you've done?"

Jordan rushed through the door, followed closely by the others. "What in bloody hell is going on in here?"

Chris whirled around, curled his lips into a curious grin, then passed out cold.

Cheryl glared down at him, visibly appalled. "He's completely pissed!"

Farin glanced at Cheryl, then Ben, and then Marci, wondering if things could possibly be as bad as they seemed.

Jordan remained calm, but Farin detected a hint of anger behind his mask. He looked at her with blaming eyes that bore straight through her. "What was he yelling about?"

Marci adjusted herself uncomfortably and added, "He looks awful."

Ben and Jordan scooped up their brother and relocated him to one of the spare rooms upstairs. Shortly thereafter, they decided to call it a night. Ben kissed Farin's cheek and gave her hand a squeeze on his way out. At least one member of the family had rallied to her side. She could tell he understood. She hated that he had to.

When Jordan walked Ben outside, Cheryl lingered behind with Farin and Marci long enough to say her peace. "I can't pretend I don't know what's going on," she huffed. "It's a miracle Jorie hasn't caught on by noo. Really, Farin, we should all try to be happy with one man. Especially one who treats a woman as well as Jorie's treated you."

With that, she left.

Once the family departed and Marci went to bed, it took every ounce of strength Jordan could muster to resist Farin's charms. She found him in the den, watching *The Razor's Edge* on television and nursing a stiff drink. She stood before him, bathed in silk, her wet lips enticing.

She obscured his view of the TV as she disrobed. He watched impassively, though he felt himself stir. He wanted her—almost enough to give in.

"You're in my way."

"I want to be in your way."

He had agonized over their situation for so long, desperate to wake up one morning in his makeshift master suite and realize the past had been an illusion. He needed to believe Farin had never left him. More than that, he needed to believe her running out had not caused Melody's death.

Farin straddled his lap, then bent down to kiss his neck. "Let's go upstairs. I want us to be together tonight."

It took everything Jordan could muster not to wrap his arms around her smooth body and take her right there in the den. Resentment won in the end. "You go on ahead. I'll be up later."

Her lips parted as if she would object. Then, she stood and slipped her white silk robe over its matching negligee. "Wake me when you come up?"

Jordan looked at her, flat-faced. "Of course."

She leaned against the doorframe as she left. "I love you."

His eyes fixed on the television.

***

Farin rose early the next morning determined to send Marci off with a hot breakfast. The hum of water pipes told her at least one other person had not slept well last night.

She wished Marci would stay. They had spent so little time together during her vacation. Coupled with Jordan's disinterest and Bobby's continued resentment, she felt virtually abandoned.

Jordan was the first to join her. She did a double take when she saw he wore a business suit. "Morning."

He grunted from behind the paper.

She bit her lower lip. "You didn't come to bed last night."

He lowered the paper, accepting the cup of tea she offered with a nod.

"Good morning," Marci greeted as she entered the kitchen. She grabbed a mug from the cupboard.

Jordan's smile was a thin disguise against his mood as he greeted her and checked his watch. "You almost ready? We should probably leave soon. Don't want to be late."

"I'm all packed," she chirped happily, stirring sugar into her mug. "All I need is one cup of coffee to get me going."

"I'll load the car while you two say goodbye, then." He stood up to find his keys.

Farin hovered over the toaster as it ejected two pieces of browned rye. "We need to talk."

Again, he ignored her.

Chris stumbled in from the hallway and collided with his brother. Jordan propelled him into the kitchen with a contemptuous grin. Chris rubbed his eyelids, collapsing into the first chair he bumped into.

Jordan gave a humorless chuckle. "He lives. Feeling better?"

Chris winced at his brother's voice, his hands shooting up to cup his ears. Squinting, he grumbled, "The last few months have been crap."

A flicker of something too quick to identify raced across Jordan's features. He slapped Chris hard on the back. "Buck up, now. Can't keep the ladies waiting."

Farin watched Jordan, mystified.

Marci spoke loud enough to inflict further discomfort. "Good morning, Chris. You look like death." She finished her coffee, then sniffed the air. "And you smell even worse."

Farin hurried after Jordan as he grabbed Marci's bags to load into the car. "Wait, please."

He stopped and looked through her.

Quietly, she repeated, "We need to talk."

"Not now, Farin." He stomped out the door, slamming it behind him.

Farin exchanged hugs and tearful goodbyes with Marci, waving furiously at the car as Jordan pulled out of the driveway and drove through the usual crowd of reporters and fans. A distinct hollowness filled her as she returned to the kitchen to confront the mess she had made in her attempt to start the morning off right. Defeated, she flopped down into the seat farthest from Chris, who had slowly regained the color in his face.

"Want some breakfast?" She pouted, waving a hand at the frying pan.

Chris walked over to stand behind her, then bent down to kiss her cheek. "Your life's falling apart, but your main concern is scrambling a few eggs. I'm not sure which one of us is more pathetic. You, for courting an impossible dream, or me for sticking around to pick up the pieces."

She folded her arms across her chest. "If my life is falling apart, I have you to thank for it. But don't be so smug. I'll fix things."

"Your intentions may be well and good, but I've seen that look on his face before—with Ginny. He's through."

"Like the annulment, right?" She sat straighter in her chair and glared at him. "Stop trying to confuse me, Chris!"

He moved in and placed a gentle kiss on her lips.

She pushed him away.

He studied her as he sucked his teeth. "I suppose that's my cue to go."

***

Farin wandered the house and grounds the rest of the day and into the night. Jordan never returned. Somehow, she believed he was okay. Maybe he was giving her a dose of her own medicine. She deserved as much. Still, she worried. The look on his face when he left had warned her of momentous trouble had she cared to acknowledge it.

When he finally returned the next morning, he looked terrible. She looked worse.

She greeted him at the door. "Where were you? I was worried. You've never just not come home before."

"You have," he pitted harshly. He beelined into the living room and sat down, dropping the manila envelope he carried on the coffee table. "You want to talk? Let's talk."

His icy tone stifled Farin. She moved to join him on the sofa.

Jordan stared straight ahead as she sat down. "When you left me this time, I couldn't see straight. I couldn't work."

"I'm sor—"

"Quiet!" His voice rose with his temper as he faced her. "I'm not finished."

Farin shrank back in her seat.

"I drank. A lot. I drank so I didn't have to worry about you. Or miss you. Or wonder if you'd ever come back. All I wanted was for my *wife* to come home. And where were you? You were delivering our child—a daughter I'd never see—in bloody France! *France,* Farin!"

Guilt rattled her to her core. She had deserved his angry words for so long. But at least now, they could begin the healing they so badly needed.

"Then, you finally came home...only to say you're leaving again. I guess you decided to stick around awhile this time. I appreciate that. Yet, no matter how many times I ask, you refuse to tell me why you left in the first place." He looked askance at her, awaiting an explanation.

His stare knotted her insides. "There was just so much going on inside my head with the baby and the wedding happening so soon. I needed space, I needed—"

"You needed *out,* plain and simple!" He surged to his feet, towering over her as he pointed an accusing finger and spat harsh words. "When you came back, I was happy you were home and sick to death about Melody all at the same time. I've lost two children now, Farin! I can't tell you what kind of hell I've been living in!"

He dropped back onto the sofa, crushed at the impact of his own words. He thought about Chase and the little girl he would never even see. However unfair, he could not ignore a series of constant images in his head.

In his mind's eye, he saw Kim bring Chase into his life at the cost of her own while he watched outside the delivery room. He saw Farin hovering over his boy, trying to breathe life back into his tiny body while he stood by powerless to help. He saw Farin flee their reception, carrying Melody inside her, with him unable to stop her from leaving.

She had forced his helplessness upon him, rejecting him time and again.

These images entwined until they became essentially the same moment. And in the end, they defied banishment. They mocked his attempts to ignore them. In fact, they became high on his list of priorities. Though he tried to separate his present life with Farin from the storm raging inside him, he now realized she was forever and irreversibly tied to it.

Still, he had made a vow to God, in front of everyone he knew in his life. He had accepted the responsibilities of his manhood, that of husband and father. In his heart, his honor, his integrity, his devotion, his truthfulness—what those who knew him best described as his "quiet nobility"—everything within him challenged him to make it right.

And so, he had tried. He would remain faithful to her above all others, despite their circumstances. In the days and years to come, they could rebuild trust.

Then, two nights ago, he knew it would never happen. A new set of images had presented themselves—images more painful than he could fathom. She had left him utterly unmanned.

He loved her—and *oh*, how he hated her. Sitting there, in his enormous home, with his stunning and talented wife beside him, Jordan realized the depth of failure his successful life had been all the way to this very day.

He thought he might vomit.

Farin lowered her head, shutting her eyes in anguish as hot, wet drops slid down Jordan's face. She tried to speak but words failed her. What might she say to comfort him? The baby for whom he grieved had not belonged to him. What lie might ease his pain, now? What could she offer him but more lies?

She glanced up and saw his bloodshot eyes fixed upon her. Hoping to spare him further pain, she scooted over and wrapped her arms around his shoulders. "I'm sorry," she whispered, the words so small they evaporated the moment she uttered them.

Jordan removed her hands from him in deliberate fashion and put them at her sides. He sniffed and cleared his throat. "Then, I started thinking. That was the third time you'd left me, and the second time you'd run out without a word. I can't live my life wondering when you'll 'need space' again, or thinking I might return home one Christmas day to find you gone for weeks or months without a backward glance."

Her eyes widened as she began to suspect where their conversation might lead. She rattled her head. "You don't have to wonder, Jordan. I'd give anything to redo the last year, but I can't. I can only try to make it up, somehow. I'll never leave you again. *Never*."

His face turned to stone. "You're right. You won't."

She froze as all expression left his features. His eyes, which used to look at her with such unashamed love, now regarded her with less concern than a python shows its rodent prey.

"There was a time when, if you'd assured me, I'd have believed you. But you've left me thrice. There're things you still won't tell me. Other things you hide altogether. If you can hurt me so remorselessly, I figure this relationship has been less than mutual. I can't trust you. I *don't* trust you. And if there's no trust between us, what's left?"

Her forehead creased. She stared at his sedate features. "What are you saying?"

He lifted his chin toward the manila envelope he had cast aside. The label in the center bore the name and address of John Knowles, Esq. "I went to my lawyer's office yesterday after dropping Marci off. Our marriage is over."

The proclamation was a blunt instrument. It struck her, rendering her immobile.

Jordan rose and walked out of the room without looking back.

When Farin regained her composure, she scurried upstairs. She found him packing an overnight bag.

"Don't do this. *Please*! If you'd give it a little more thought—"

"*Thought*?" he bellowed, temporarily halting his packing. His stomach felt hollow. His throat squeezed and strangled him. His pulse throbbed in his ears and the tip of his nose. "I've been thinking nonstop since the night of our wedding when I was here *all by myself!*"

Farin collapsed onto the bed, sobbing. "This can't be happening. Please don't do this...*please!*"

He shut his suitcase with an angry snap and prepared to leave. He checked his wallet and keys, glanced at his watch, then grabbed his bag and headed for the stairs, pausing momentarily to look back at his wife curled up on the bed in a tiny ball, weeping as if her world had ended.

He searched his feelings and decided he felt no pity, no remorse...but also, no satisfaction.

"One more thing," he spat in the direction of the pitiful, huddled form on the bed. "I heard your conversation with Chris last night."

Farin's crying abruptly ceased. She looked at him in disbelief.

He nodded. "I guess I should have figured it out before. Perhaps I did but couldn't admit it had happened to me twice. I don't know how long it's been going on, and I don't want to. What's done is done. I'll be at Ben's. Call when you've moved your stuff out of my house—and be quick about it."

He stormed from the room at last, feeling a kind of hatred he had never known, and knowing he was right to get out. He loved her more than she could imagine, but she had destroyed their bond. And she had broken his heart.

CHAPTER 23

BOBBY FOUGHT TO UNDERSTAND FARIN through her wracking sobs.

"I-I...can you come over?"

"Where are you? What happened?"

"Jordan. He...he *left*."

"Did he find out—?"

"I can't breathe. I n-need you, Bobby. *Please*."

"I'm on my way."

I need you. The three words he thought he might never hear from her. Or anyone else. From the moment he received the disconsolate call, Bobby stuck to Farin's side like a mealybug on an African violet.

A couple of days after Jordan left, reporters witnessed Bobby supervising two men as they moved cardboard boxes and suitcases out of Jordan's house and into a small moving van. The rumors started immediately.

Jameson intervened, ensuring neither Jordan's nor Farin's publicists responded to requests for comments. The only official word on the Grant separation came from LSI's Vice President of Publicity, Bobby Lockhardt, who stood beside a broken, forlorn Farin Grant during an impromptu press conference outside the chain-link fence surrounding Standards Recording Studio.

"Mrs. Grant has temporarily relocated to a private residence while she works on her next album."

Reporters clamored for details, shouting over one another as cameramen positioned their equipment for optimal shots, capturing images of the visibly shattered pop princess for their next issue or telecast.

"Is your marriage in trouble, Farin?"

"Farin! Why move out? Are there creative differences?"

"Is he abusive, Farin?"

"Farin, is he having an affair? Are *you*?"

With a wave of his hand and a condescending head shake, Bobby rejected their accusations, labeling them ridiculous, as he positioned himself between Farin and the reporters who pressed ever closer.

"You're manufacturing a problem that doesn't exist. Farin and Jordan are both creative people. Their unique artistic expressions simply demand an impermanent increase in their individual space. Trust me. The newlyweds are doing fine—maybe too much so, if you catch my drift! This provisory change made sense for both of them."

Reporters who followed the Grants every hour of every day knew better. Miles Macy knew better. But despite valiant efforts, the media could not infiltrate the sanctuary of silence into which Jordan and Farin Grant had escaped. Undeterred, the famous couple could not so much as sneeze without it showing up on the front page of at least one gossip magazine or tabloid.

"You've done well keeping the details of their relationship under wraps," Jameson told Bobby during their weekly conference call. "I'd had my misgivings at first about you being down there, but it appears it may have been a fortuitous move."

Bobby cradled his home phone between his shoulder and his ear as he cleaned up his sandwich fixings. He would have liked to have had lunch with Farin, but her appetite had dwindled to practically nothing since the move. "Paparazzi's camped out at both their places," he explained, wiping down his countertop.

"Have you talked to Jordan?"

Bobby tossed dirty paper towels into the trash, surveyed the kitchen, then leaned against the counter. "He's pretty angry. Says he doesn't care what the press—or you—think. But he's agreed not to talk to anyone. The last thing he wants is another Ginny Stevens fiasco. He's more concerned about his privacy. He did tell me to tell you, though, not to expect him to change his mind."

"And Farin?"

"Not so good. I'm heading back over there now."

"I hear she's rescheduled some personal appearances. Probably best to keep her out of the public eye. I trust you're still getting her into the studio."

"She was there this morning for the first time since the split."

"So, she lost about a week. She can make it up. It'll do her good to work."

"She, uh...she left after about an hour."

The silence on the line conveyed his father's displeasure.

"You know her, Dad. She doesn't handle crises well. Let's be glad she hasn't taken off again."

He listened as his father ticked off Farin's accomplishments for the umpteenth time, as if the fresh reminder might inspire him to make a deeper commitment to her career. *Ulterior Motives*—seven-times platinum. Five consecutive singles—all in the top ten. Chart records—breaking. Discussion of a world tour. He knew. He knew all too well.

"...and her fan mail's clogging the LSI mailroom. At this rate, she may outdo Jordan's success. I *cannot* and *will not* have her lying in bed, feeling sorry for herself! Understood?"

"I'll do my best. But I've gotta tell you, Dad, she's worn out."

"Have her over for Thanksgiving. I'll come down and chat with her."

Bobby's head dropped, causing the phone to slip off his shoulder, testing his response time. "You're coming?"

"You do still celebrate the holiday, yes?"

Neither of Bobby's parents had shown interest in traditional American holidays. As a boy, he used to sneak out of his mother's house and down to Stearns Wharf each Fourth of July to catch the fireworks. Once or twice, his friend next door had invited him for Thanksgiving. Only as an adult had he participated fully in such festivities—though he did so alone.

Maybe this year would start a new tradition.

***

"—and if you'd pick up the phone instead of screening your bloody calls, tell me you're all right, I'd stop pestering you!"

Farin rolled over on her side and snatched the handset off the phone base on her nightstand. "Leave me alone, Chris!"

"Don't hang up!" he said. "I'll call back if you do."

She exhaled an exasperated breath and lay flat on her bed, staring up at the smooth white ceiling. Her eyes were swollen from days of crying. Now, nothing remained. No tears. No fight.

"Tell me you're all right."

"If I say it, will you leave me alone?"

"Is it the truth?"

She frowned and rubbed the palm of her free hand along her hairline. "My eyes are dry. Does that make me okay?"

He paused. "I'm sorry about the other night."

"Is that it? Can I go now?"

"Do you need anything?"

"Gee, Chris. What could I *possibly* need? Haven't you heard? The world's my oyster."

More silence ensued. "Will you call me if you do?"

"I wouldn't hold my breath."

"I worry about you being alone."

She scoffed as she let her arm drop next to her. "Who said I'm alone?"

"Is someone with you?"

In one continuous movement, she rolled out of bed and went to her window. She side-swiped the curtains and looked down at the crowd standing at the edge of her driveway. "Let's see. About two dozen reporters are camped outside my house. And Bobby's on his way over to try to convince me to go back to the studio."

"You're working, then. That's good."

"You sound like Jameson."

A cynical burst of laughter came over the line. "Old habits and what-not."

She backed away from the window and sat on the edge of her down-cloaked bed. She noted a dust bunny atop her dresser. It felt like a lifetime ago that she and Marci used to clean their apartment together.

Her voice softened. "Have you talked to Jordan?"

"Uh, no. Ben called, though. Told me what happened. Made sure I knew it was my fault and that I'd best make other plans for the holidays."

"What are you gonna do?"

"Faith invited me up for a visit. You?"

"I'm...I'm staying here."

"Why don't you come to New York with me? Stay at Faith's? It might do you some good to get away."

"We're not friends, Chris. Remember? You said it yourself."

"You're not going to make this easy, are you?"

"Not on your life."

***

Bobby watched Farin nap beside him. When the pilot announced their ETA, relief washed over him. Relief that his father finally believed he had not exaggerated his concerns. That Farin would finally get the help she needed. Mostly, he was relieved that either stress or exhaustion had finally wrestled her to sleep.

By his count, she had been up for three days prior to boarding LSI's corporate plane for their New York-bound flight.

"I quite enjoyed the turkey," Jameson told him, breaking the silence that had filled the vessel for most of their flight. "The yams I could do without."

He smiled and took in the city lights through a cabin window. "I'm not much for yams, either. But it was your first time, so I ordered everything."

Jameson uttered a guttural "humph." Bobby guessed it represented approval—a rare occurrence coming from his old man.

He glanced down at Farin as the *Citation III* began its descent. Her mouth had slacked open. Unkempt curls framed her face. As he beheld her beauty, he congratulated himself. What had Jordan or Chris ever done to help her? Only he knew what a wreck she had become in such a short time, and only he acted when it began to take its toll.

Though he did not know the details, he knew Farin battled insomnia. Nightmares plagued what little sleep she stole between studio sessions. Sessions which had yielded less than promising results thus far. She could not sustain the pressure of creating a better, bolder product for her next album. Not in her current state.

The brutality of his father's accusing tone startled him.

"Something you want to tell me, Robert?"

His shoulders slumped in resignation. He turned to stare out the window.

"Need I remind you, son, that—"

"Believe me...I *know*."

Jameson cleared his throat. "Childs is meeting us at the office in an hour."

He nodded.

"Any chance she'll reconsider the Christmas benefit? She's here, anyway. Perhaps she should stay the month. Get her out of Miami for a while."

Farin yawned and stretched her arms. "I can't," she muttered groggily. "I need to get back. You promised, Jameson. You said if I agreed to see your doctor, you'd get me right back home."

Bobby looked at his father and shrugged.

Jameson's face transformed into that of her genial benefactor. "You're right, my dear. I did. And I'll keep my word. I guess I'd rather hoped you'd change your mind once you put some distance between you and your circumstances."

Bobby added, "If you don't want to do the concert, maybe you could stay anyway. Dad and I are going to London for Christmas. You could come with us."

She curled into an upright fetal position and burrowed into the luxurious leather seat. "I can't go. What if Jordan wants me to come home? Besides, I need to get back into the studio."

The pilot announced their final descent and instructed them to prepare for landing.

"Farin, you went from not wanting to go to the studio to practically living there. You made Joel and Travis set up a cot for you in the back room—not that you're sleeping."

She buckled her seatbelt, then pulled up her hair and secured it into a bun atop her head. "Why commute when I'm there so much anyway? All I have to go home to is a bunch of leeches with cameras and microphones."

Bobby frowned and turned away.

"Hear, hear," Jameson encouraged. "If only more of my artists had your discipline. Pay no mind to Bobby. Childs will fix what ails you. You'll be back to work in no time."

Dr. Lionel Childs was a monstrous, bespectacled older man with thin silver hair and a thick stomach. His voice sounded like gravel. Authoritative, like Jameson's. He met them at LSI's corporate office, commandeering a small conference room on the executive floor for his makeshift examination room.

Jameson made quick introductions, then disappeared into his office with Bobby in tow. Childs offered Farin a terse nod and a forceful handshake. "Have a seat. This won't take long."

She lowered herself onto one of the two upholstered black cherry reception chairs and scooted up to the table. Childs remained standing. He propped one foot onto the second chair and rested his elbow on his knee, leaning in and leveling his eyes upon her.

"Sorry Jameson called you in on a holiday."

Childs ignored the pleasantries. "Before we get to what brought you up this evening, I'd like to get some family history..."

She answered questions about her parents, confessed she knew little of her grandparents on either side, and confirmed she was an only child. No cancer or heart disease to her knowledge. Only her mother's alcoholism. When asked about any history of mental illness, she denied any family or personal history of depression, omitting the fact that, since the break-up, her life felt increasingly meaningless. With only a fading memory of her father, Farin could not face life without Jordan. If their situation did not improve soon, she might have to do something drastic. The pain was unbearable.

Childs retrieved a pen from his shirt pocket and sat down to scribble notes on a notepad. "So based on what you've given me, and the information Jameson relayed through Bobby, it sounds like stress. The recording, the obligations...mix that in with the separation. You've got a lot on your plate, young lady. Nothing too alarming. We can get you back on track—if you'll forgive the pun."

Farin cut eyes at him, comforted by the hint of warmth in his otherwise frigid disposition.

He reached inside his suit pocket again, this time retrieving his prescription pad. "I'm prescribing something to help take the edge off."

She accepted the script with a frown. "But I'm in Florida and you're in New York. Won't I have trouble getting it filled?"

He chuckled. "I'm licensed in every state Jameson works or has interest in. There'll be no trouble getting you what you need."

"Thank you, Dr. Childs. I'm glad I came to see you."

He pressed a flat, peach-colored tablet into her hand.

"What's this?"

"Valium. We'll start you off on five milligrams, I think. You can let me know if it's too strong...or if you need a bit of a bump. Go ahead and take that now. I have a few more to send home with you. They should tide you over until you can fill your prescription."

Farin studied the pill. It had what looked like a heart-shaped hole in its middle. Appropriate. Maybe it would help mend hers.

Childs handed her the white paper cup of water he had procured from the cooler near Nancy Chambers's desk. "Here you go. Unless you have anything else, I'll be on my way. Have to rest up. I promised my daughter I'd go shopping with her and her husband tomorrow. And Jameson told me you're headed right back. Have a safe flight."

She placed the pill on her tongue, then chased it back with the water.

Ten minutes into the return flight, an unexpected and nearly euphoric sense of calm settled upon her as if from nowhere. Different than any buzz she had experienced with alcohol. Relaxed, level. Like she was suddenly the person she always wanted to be, as if she had slithered, snake-like, out of her old skin.

This is how normal people feel all the time. And now, I'm normal, too.

***

Chris sped into the Standards Recording Studios parking lot, none too happy as he stomped the brake pedal and skidded his Porsche into the first available space. He resented the summons, particularly now as he and the rest of his band could do nothing but watch Mirage die its slow death.

Reporters begged for comment as the electronic gate closed. He saluted them with his middle finger, jerked open the glass door, and went inside.

Bobby met him at the front desk. "Thanks for coming."

"Does Jameson know about this?"

"I'll talk to him."

"So, the answer's no."

"When he hears the finished product, he won't care. Trust me."

A doubtful scoff escaped his lips. "*Trust* and *Lockhardt* used in the same sentence."

"Really, Chris? This? Now?" Bobby drew his hands up to his waist.

"Why not now? Is there a better time?"

"You know I had nothing to do with ending Mirage's contract."

He raised his hands, palms up. "Of course. Daddy never did let you rise to the level you'd hoped, did he?"

The arrow hit its target. Bobby dipped his head and set his jaw.

Chin high, Chris waited for his nemesis to launch a countershot. When it did not come, he was neither surprised nor repentant.

Bobby cleared his throat. "I'm not here to fight with you. If you don't want the gig, I understand. It's a pretty tall order for someone like you. And if you're asking me what you'll get out of it, I'll be honest. Nothing but my gratitude. Maybe scale. We'll have to see how things shake out."

Chris sucked his teeth as he considered the request. His pride urged him to tell Bobby where to stick his "scale." Then again, he still had some good ideas. Artistically, he had grown since leaving New York. He had been writing a lot lately. Maybe he had something to offer. Experience counted.

"You realize she's not talking to me."

"She'll talk. She'll have plenty to say. I'm just hoping she'll listen. She sure won't listen to the rest of us."

"Really? A challenge!" He grinned despite himself and extended his arm with a flourish. "By all means, lead on."

They found Farin in Studio D, perched in the sound booth, arms crossed. Joel reclined in an office chair, tapping the eraser end of a pencil against its arm, his jaw clenched in frustration. Travis sat with his elbows propped on the console, head in his hands, gripping handfuls of his long, gray, wiry hair. He swore under his breath.

When Joel spotted Chris, he bolted up and grabbed his arm, leading him back out into the hallway. "She's gonna ruin this album."

"What's going on?"

"It's those pills!"

"What pills?"

With an incredulous rattle of his head, Joel scoffed and unloaded the frustration of the last two weeks. "*Two weeks* and she's already popping them like candy from a PEZ dispenser, man! She teeters from being calm and sweet and *completely ineffective* to bitchy and uncooperative! She's Michael Jackson one minute and Diana-freakin'-Ross the next! Yesterday, we finally had to tell her she couldn't sleep here anymore because—"

"She's *sleeping* here?" Chris's eyes widened in disbelief.

"Oh yeah! *Yeah*! Not that she's slept much. But she can't go home. Oh, no! 'Gotta keep working! Let's *all* work, all the time!' Jameson's breathing down our necks to send him what we've got. And we've got *nada*, brother. Nothing!"

"Whoa-whoa-whoa." Chris held up his hands before him. "I need a second to think."

Joel dropped his head backward as he heard banging on the door. "We don't have a second to think, man. 'Ms. Ross' is ready to ruin another take."

The door flew open, nearly hitting both men as it swung past them. "Joel! Where are you? I want to lay something down before you break for lunch—and *no*, don't ask me again. I don't want a sandwich! I'll grab something later. *Joel*?"

Joel ground his teeth. "Behind you, Farin."

She spun around, mouth open, ready to continue her verbal assault, but stopped when she saw Chris. Her shoulders slumped but her eyelids narrowed to slits. "What are *you* doing here? I thought you were in New York with Faith."

He met her outrage with an indulgent smirk. "Change of plans. Thought I'd come down and catch the show. Looks like I'm right on time."

She turned on her heel and stomped back to the sound booth.

Chris slapped Joel on the back, then followed. "You heard the lady, mate. Let's lay something down before lunch."

***

On Christmas Day, Farin stayed in bed well past noon. She tried to sleep but could not—even after doubling the dose of medication Dr. Childs had prescribed. Next time she spoke with him, she would let him know she needed that bump he had mentioned.

The phone had rung two hours before. She had let the machine take it. A less than enthusiastic Marci had left a less than cheerful greeting.

"Farin, it's me. Get out of bed. Take my call. I miss you. It's Christmas. My mom and dad were disappointed you changed your mind about coming out for the week. I know you say you need to work, but this is the season for *family*. And we're your family. Is anyone even in the studio today? If so, I hope it's not that weasel. If you're trying to get Jordan back, working with Chris isn't the way to do it. Call me back. I love you. Bye."

The last thing Farin needed was a lecture. In fact, she had reconsidered flying out for the holidays, at least in part, because she did not want to listen to the same incessant "I told you so" speeches Marci had been famous for the entire time she had known her.

Employing her cotton-brain logic, she added to her reasons for avoiding California. She did not want to endure Marci and Dan arguing. Most of all, she could not confront the pain of staying at the beach house again. Her life in Miami was small. She liked it that way. With any luck, she would soon feel nothing at all.

Besides, Jordan might change his mind.

He had not answered the few times she called him. If he would agree to talk things out, she knew their marriage would rebound. Recent rumors surrounding an impending divorce had sent her off an emotional cliff. She had seen the envelope the day he kicked her out. The fact that she had not seen any papers left her clinging to a fraying strand of hope.

With little else to occupy her mind and no reason to leave her bed, she grabbed the television remote. Her head felt fuzzy as she cycled through the stations. Most of the day's programming targeted happier people with big, smiling families.

In passing, it occurred to her that, at a time of growing counterculture, Christmas Day remained clean, untouched by the cynicism of an unbelieving world. Normally, that sentiment might comfort her.

Her eyes misted over, which angered her. She turned off the set and flung the remote across the room. It did not hit anything breakable, but the force caused the back compartment to pop off. The batteries bounced out.

She considered praying. Maybe God would forgive her, show her mercy for the affair and for letting everyone believe Melody belonged to Jordan. Maybe God would end her suffering and bring her husband back to her.

She fused shut her tear-brimmed eyes, brought her hands together, laced her fingers, and bowed her head, but could think of nothing to say. In that moment, she felt the full force of her self-imposed isolation.

I can't even talk to God.

When she opened her eyes, the room tilted left. Her arms automatically shot out to either side of her, her hands clutching her sheets. She lay still until the sensation passed, then sat up and found the phone handset buried in the folds of her rumpled blankets.

The numbers on the keypad moved in and out, occasionally overlapping as she dialed Bobby's number. The answering machine picked up.

Her voice was a raspy whisper. "It's me. Happy Merry Christmas. Are you supposed to come over today? I thought—anyway, call me back when I get the message. Maybe I'll stop by later."

Disappointed and lonely, she deliberated whether to call Chris.

She had agreed to have him over a couple of times. He often reminded her of his undying love but had cooled his steamy pursuit after coming to her aid at the studio. She had begun to trust him a little, against her own instincts, the advice of everyone she knew, and the advice of everyone who knew him. At least Joel and Travis no longer looked at her with unmasked fury when she entered a room.

But no. Better not to initiate anything.

She cradled the phone atop her chest as she lay there, releasing an audible breath through thick lips. Then, as if pulled by an unseen force, she rolled her head left. In the corner of her room stood her father's desk.

Her eyelids grew heavy. As she drifted off, she mumbled, "I wish you were here, Daddy. I didn't get a tree."

She awoke at dusk and forced herself up for a shower. The water did little to clear her head but worked miracles on tense muscles. When she finished dressing and drying her hair, she decided on a drive in her beloved blue Celica.

Limousines being her primary form of transportation anymore, she missed sitting behind the wheel. Taking the Celica instead of the powerful and luxurious candy-apple red Mercedes Jameson had given her so long ago might protect her anonymity.

She grabbed her keys and purse, then peeked out the front window. A handful of paparazzi lurked at her gate. She wrinkled her nose. "Here goes nothing." Briefly, she considered her blonde wig but then decided against it.

She crept out to her car and slipped inside without a sound. When her garage door engaged and she pulled out onto the driveway, the small crowd erupted into a cacophony of yowls and camera flashes illuminating the night.

"Mrs. Grant! Farin!"

"Rumor has it Jordan's filed for divorce!" shouted one enthusiastic young man as he rushed her door. "Care to comment?"

The "d" word enraged her. She bit her lip and forged ahead, hoping no one was foolish enough to stand in front of her car. She would not stop. Not today.

Shouts and questions continued until she thought she might go deaf from the echo of ugly accusations. Before pulling onto the road, she rethought her position. She stopped the car, rolled down the window, and stuck her head out.

"Don't you people have families? Don't you bloodsuckers have anything better to do on Christmas Day than watch my house like the bunch of leeches you are?"

She gripped the worn steering wheel and stomped the accelerator. Her lips curled in disgust as she considered the irony of her circumstances. She rubbed her scalp with the palm of her hand, then reached inside her purse. She grabbed her prescription bottle and popped a pill into her mouth, swallowing it dry.

From the heights of fame, it took every effort to catch her breath from its peak. Touring was easier. Fans knew their boundaries. But once transported back from that timeless, magical place, she felt inconsolably removed. Her life did not belong to her anymore. She belonged to the world.

The Valium slayed her inhibitions, giving her enough courage to drive past Jordan's house. His lights were out. The grounds appeared quiet, so she made a U-turn, took a right off Matheson, then continued down Harbor Drive.

Past the roundabout at Westwood, she spied the Jaguar parked in Ben's driveway. Drawn curtains filtered the light within the house, reflecting it onto the street. It cast a dim but powerful beacon of illumination, like a lighthouse directing an aimless vessel.

Farin imagined Derek and Kyle's smiling faces as they bounded through the house, making immediate use of their gifts. Cheryl would have doubtless prepared a feast yet still donned her most exquisite holiday gown. Ben would carve and serve the ham, standing proudly and contentedly before his family at a candlelit dining table Cheryl had decorated for this festive day—and regardless of Chris's banishment, they would find laughter. Perhaps Ben would take Jordan and head out to the studio. Even if Jordan struggled through the day, even if he missed her, or Chase, he had his family. And they had him.

She shuddered. The sensation of an icy drizzle trickled down Farin's spine, mocking the warm December evening.

Why had she turned down the Central Park gig? She could be on stage right now, surrounded and adored—even if not for who she really was. No one loved her for who she was. Why would they?

Her mother's final words haunted her.

You're not a victim. Don't live like one.

She drove on, maneuvering her Celica through downtown Miami and then Coral Gables. Certain Bobby had told her to come by when they spoke earlier, she grew frustrated searching for his house. How could she forget the way? She had visited so many times.

As she strained to read the mailbox numbers whipping by her in the dark, she perceived a passing blur in front of her car. Before she could swerve or brake, she felt a thump beneath her tires. She heard a woeful yelp and then, silence.

Farin mashed the brake pedal squarely to the floorboard, locking up all four tires. The seatbelt cut painfully into her chest and hips. The front of the car dipped forward. The rear rose in response.

In an instant, she was ten years old again.

Her mother had driven her to school the Monday morning after her father's funeral. Farin still believed her daddy would be home when she returned from school that afternoon, even though she had seen him in the coffin and seen the coffin buried. It must have escaped her mother's mind that their usual route took them by the Santa Barbara police station and the impound lot beside it. Perhaps it had not occurred to her what vehicles might still be there.

They had been doing fifty in a thirty-five when her mother locked up the brakes in front of the police station. When she used both feet to slam on the brakes, the abandoned clutch had only let the motor run a few more seconds.

Farin's head popped the dashboard before her seatbelt snatched her back into position. Her mother whimpered pitifully, like a wounded animal. Behind them, commuters parked their fists and palms on their horns as traffic stacked up in front of the station. Her mother made no move to restart the car.

Farin rubbed her forehead with her small fingers, then looked at her mother, who covered her face in her hands and emitted heaving sobs. She looked through her side window and saw the wreckage of the brown station wagon.

The front of the station wagon had folded up almost to the rear. Through what remained of the driver's side window in the wreckage, Farin saw dried blood covering the seat and dash. Shards of glass covered the hood.

Her head itched, so she rubbed it again, this time with her right palm. Policemen started walking in their direction. The honking behind them turned into angry yells as drivers stepped out of their vehicles.

Seconds later, Farin noticed the bright red blood covering her hands. She had cut her forehead at the hairline on the glove box latch at impact. Frightened, she began to wail. When she held her hands up to show her mother, her mother had become hysterical.

Farin exited her car and forced herself to view the poor creature she had run down. It was a small, hairy dog—a Lhasa Apso, she guessed. She scratched her head, then meandered down the street of upscale homes in search of its owner.

An older gentleman at the first house on the corner recognized the description of the animal and said it belonged to a young couple who had just moved down from Rhode Island. Their name was Woods. Farin thanked him for directions and continued on. When she reached her destination, she wobbled up the brick steps and rang the doorbell. A petite young blonde answered the door with a smile.

Farin sniffed. "Hello, Mrs. Woods. I was just talking to one of your neighbors. I'm sorry but I think I just ran over your dog."

Merry Christmas.

The woman called for her husband. Mr. Woods accompanied Farin to the scene, stopping on his way out to grab a blanket.

He made small talk as they walked. Farin struggled to follow the conversation as the Valium battled with the adrenaline surge resulting from the accident. She did notice he was a handsome man and thought what a lovely couple he and his wife made.

When they got to the scene, Mr. Woods crouched down and gently stroked the motionless animal's wavy white fur. "That's him, all right." He draped the blanket over his pet's body.

"I'm sorry. I didn't see him until it was too late." Tears filled her red-rimmed eyes.

Head cocked, he squinted through his wire frame glasses. "Forgive me if this sounds rude. But...aren't you Farin Grant?"

She thought it a miracle anyone could recognize her without her heavy makeup. She nodded, rubbed her hairline, then looked at her hand. Her vision blurred.

"Did you hurt yourself stopping so suddenly? I didn't even think to ask."

"I'm fine," she murmured. "I'm sorry about your glass."

Mr. Woods regarded her quizzically. "Glass?"

"Dog."

He approached her, arm extended. "Did you hit your head back there?"

Farin looked around, disoriented. "I'm fine. My mother took me in for stitches. I just...I'm late for dinner." She gazed down at the blanket and sniffed. "What have I done?"

Mr. Woods explained that Winston—his name was Winston—was old, mostly deaf, and going blind. "He must've slipped out when I emptied the trash. He probably didn't even see your lights."

All at once, she could not remember turning her lights on. Maybe that was why she had such trouble finding Bobby's place.

She stumbled toward her car. Mr. Woods followed.

"Hey, maybe I should call a doctor or something, huh? You don't look so good."

She tunneled inside through the open window and snagged her purse. "I'll make this right."

He shook his head. "You don't need to do anything. Please. If you won't let me call a doctor, at least come inside until your nerves settle."

"I couldn't. But thank you." No matter how lonely she felt, she was in no mood to share the holiday with the owners of the pooch she had just murdered.

She pulled several one-hundred-dollar bills from her wallet. "Here. Take this. Give Winston a decent burial. Everybody deserves a decent burial."

Mr. Woods stood in the middle of the street, dumbstruck.

She waved her cash-filled hand at him. "Take it. Bury him in one of those nice pet cemeteries. I'll send a bill if this isn't enough. *Please.*"

"Frankly, at this point, I'm more concerned about you getting in that car of yours. You shouldn't be driving."

Farin sobbed as she climbed—then fell—into the driver's seat. She dropped the money in the street and started the engine. "I'm sorry." In the confines of her Celica, she whispered, "I destroy everything I touch."

She drove away, leaving a confused Albert Woods standing in the middle of the road with Winston's lifeless body and twelve one-hundred-dollar bills at his feet.

CHAPTER 24

*F*ARIN STARED AT THE REMAINS *of the brown station wagon, her eyes nearly even with its crumpled roof. It looked as if an immense fist had squeezed it, picked it up, and smashed it down again like a spent soda can. Thousands of beads and shards of glass lay over the wrinkled hood and on the road at her feet, a field of cold sapphires refracting the paved road below them.*

    ... did you write the book of love
    ... and do you have faith in God above
    ... if the Bible tells you so ...

She stood in the center of the deserted intersection. In each direction, the roads vanished into murky fog. No headlights came into view. Above her head, traffic lights changed from green to yellow to red. Thick blood spilled over the folds and grooves in the tortured metal before her, dripping soundlessly onto the fog-covered blacktop, transforming the tiny glass crystals into a field of rubies. Music from the car radio filled the misty night air.

    ... do you believe in rock'n'roll
    ... can music save your mortal soul
    ... and can you teach me how to dance real slow ...

Farin's nightmares worsened. Whether the Valium helped or hurt, she could not decide. But as time went by, she had to double her intake to get the same effect. An obliging Dr. Childs increased her dosage.

***

No sooner had Bobby deplaned from his transatlantic flight than he received Farin's call, informing him she intended to quit Standards. She refused to return to the studio and threatened to send LSI's car away if he did not come right over. He vowed to be there within the hour. Truth told, he had missed her during his trip to London.

When he arrived, he found Farin's driver, Charles Russell, languishing inside the LSI limousine. Bobby knocked on the window with the knuckle of his middle finger.

"How's it going?" he asked as the driver lowered the automatic window.

"Fine, sir."

Bobby grinned. "How's it *really* going?"

The man cleared his throat and dipped his chin. "Some days, she's ready when I get here. Some days, she tells me, 'Go,' so I go. Some days, I wait."

He nodded and reached inside the car to shake the man's hand. "You have a family, Charles?"

"Not in Miami, sir."

"No girlfriend?"

Charles shrugged uncomfortably. His dark skin masked any visible blush such a personal question might evoke.

With a casual nod, Bobby scanned the lush tropical landscaping lining the streets of Farin's neighborhood, then peered back at the driver. "You work a lot, don't you?"

The man chortled. "That I do...that I do."

"Does LSI pay you well?"

Charles shifted in his seat. The smile left his face. "I can't complain, sir."

"Or you won't." Bobby pulled out his money clip and peeled off several bills. "He never pays people what they're worth. And he underappreciates the loyalty you've shown our friend here." He jerked his chin toward Farin's house and saw her standing at the window, glaring at him.

Charles peeked up at Farin from under the visor.

"Here." He shook the driver's hand again, palming over the bills. "Take a couple weeks. Visit your family. I'll cover it with the boss. In fact, you'll return to a nice pay increase."

Charles gave Bobby a curt nod and pocketed a thick stack of bills. "Thank you, Mr. Lockhardt. But what about Mrs. Grant?"

Bobby slapped Charles on the shoulder, then headed up the walkway. "She'll be fine."

Farin waved at Charles as she tugged at Bobby's arm and drew him inside, slamming the door behind him. "How was your trip?"

He opened his mouth to speak, but she cut him off. "I'm *done!*"

"Done?"

"You heard me. *Done.*"

She trod her living room, stomped, flailed her arms, and screeched—all hallmarks of the new, hyper-emotional, though physically unsteady, American pop princess. "It's missing something. And *no one*—not Joel, not Travis...not even Chris—can tell me what it is."

He probably should have stopped to change out of his suit before heading over. Who knew how long it would take to settle her down?

"*Chris.* I don't know why we're using him. I mean—yes, I know. He's made the album what it is. That SOB has more talent in his little finger than—"

"Wait-wait." Bobby held up his hands and wrinkled his forehead, trying to catch up. "Isn't he the only one you listen to these days? Before Christmas, you said Chris had the sound you're looking for and we needed to listen to him."

She flopped onto her sofa, jaw set, and glared at him.

"What changed in the last three weeks?"

She grabbed her purse and waved at Bobby to fetch her water bottle from the fireplace mantle.

He obliged, then tossed his suit jacket over the back of the couch and sat beside her. "You haven't been sleeping. I'd bet you haven't been eating, either."

She snapped, "I'm fine."

"It's those pills."

"Don't start with me, Bobby. I've already got Chris breathing down my neck. And in answer to your question, *he's* changed. They've all changed. Joel, Travis...*everyone*. I need to finish this album, start the campaign, and get out on the road. By the time I get back, Jordan should be ready to talk. But I can't get the album done because no one will tell me what's *missing!*"

He loosened his tie and draped his arm around her. She bristled at first, then relaxed into him. Soon, he heard a faint sniff. Her body began to shudder against him. He rubbed the middle of her back.

"I want to go home. He hasn't sent the divorce papers. I keep thinking he might change his mind. Every day, I wait for him to burst in and say he wants me back. Why won't anyone tell me what's missing?"

"Does this have anything to do with the fact he just changed studios?"

She buried her face in his chest and wept louder.

"Travis sent me what we have so far. I listened on the flight back. It's great. Even Dad liked it—and he's not one to pass out compliments. But if there *is* something missing, and we fix it, you're still in no shape to start a publicity campaign. We've been cancelling your personal appearances for months."

She clung to him like ivy to a garden trellis. This foreign yet visceral connection both moved and excited him. How long had it been since someone held or comforted her? Surely it could not compare to his years of longing for such intimacy.

Ten weeks had passed since she had called, begging to see him. Before that morning, he would have never envisioned she might one day return his undeclared feelings. Realistically, he could ill afford romantic entanglements—especially with someone who had more troubles than he. They were friends, after all. He had spent so long resenting her for leaving without confiding in him. He had questioned what he had believed was their growing friendship. But now, she lay in his arms, holding him, wanting him to hold her. Dare he...*kiss* her?

His heart raced at the nearness of their bodies. Yet as strong as he felt the urge to kiss her, he felt an equal, near-debilitating fear of rejection. What if he had misread her signals?

It took little time to settle his internal debate.

He lifted his arm from her back to her shoulder. Timid fingers drew her hair from her face. "Do you need anything?" he asked tenderly, bringing up his free hand to touch her face.

Farin sniffed and righted herself on the sofa. Eyes upturned, she blinked several times, her fingertips swiping away tiny pools of moisture. She stood on unsteady legs and grabbed a tissue box off the coffee table. "Sorry. I shouldn't have broken down like that."

Bobby's face fell. Their moment faded like the outro of a melancholy tune. "No apologies. I'm always here for you."

***

Farin's existence became a still-frame photograph in a moving pictures world. Her image blurred, disproportionately small. While those around her came into vivid focus, she evanesced. Tethered to that November morning when Jordan left her, life advanced—but she receded.

Bobby convinced her to stick with Standards, arguing the album's near completion. And Chris again brokered peace between her and her engineers.

In late January, they surprised her with cake and champagne for her birthday. Chris, Bobby, Joel, Travis, and the studio's staff sang a harmonic

"Happy Birthday." Twenty-eight candles glowed atop an enormous lemon chiffon sheet cake with buttercream frosting. To her, they resembled a klieg light at a movie premiere, but she smiled and thanked them for the thoughtful gesture. When prompted to make her wish, she closed her eyes and wished her husband would bring her home.

Employees and clients flowed in and out of the lounge, wishing Farin well and grabbing a celebratory slice during breaks from other projects. The sound of idle conversation mixed with intermittent cork-popping lent a gaiety to the studio that both refreshed and unnerved her. She had not interacted with anyone outside her shrinking circle since late October.

"Can I take you to dinner tonight?" Bobby asked around a bite of the sugary concoction. "Seafood? Maybe a steak?"

She scrunched her nose as she rested her head on one hand. "I don't feel like going out. Thanks, though."

"You're positively skeletal anymore," Chris observed as he joined them. In his right hand, he held an oversized hunk of cake that spilled over a small paper plate. With his left, he spun a plastic chair around and straddled it. He Frisbeed the plate onto the table, causing crumbs and a loose glob of buttercream to spill onto the table's surface. "Now, help me eat this."

"I already had some."

"You're lying."

She leaned back and folded her arms. "Prove it."

He waggled his eyebrows and produced a plastic fork. When she rejected the utensil, he grinned and rose from his chair. "Open your mouth."

She drew her head back and knitted her brow.

"You haven't had a bite." He crept toward her like a prowling cat, a frolicsome spark in his eyes. "Show me those pearly whites. I'll bet they're pristine!"

She giggled at the absurdity of the request and scooted her chair back across the linoleum floor, increasing the space between them as Bobby looked on, unamused.

"Come on, Farin. Open up."

"You wouldn't dare."

"Wouldn't I?" He doubled back to the table and stabbed the massive slice of cake, then returned with an overloaded forkful.

She set down her champagne and raised her hands as if warding off an impending blow. A hint of playfulness flickered behind her warning. "Stop it, Chris. Sit down."

Bobby looked around, uncomfortable. "Maybe you should sit down, Chris. We don't want to make a mess."

"Bugger off, Lockhardt." Chris remained singularly focused on his prey. "We'll have to force-feed this little bird, I fear."

Before Farin could react, he dropped to one knee behind the chair and wrapped his free arm around her, pinning her chest and pinching her nose. He positioned the forkful of cake, trailing the messy bite along the length of her lips. "Come on, little bird. Open wide! Time for some num-nums."

She struggled perfunctorily, stomping her feet and using both hands to pry his arms away. She parted her lips and spoke through clinched teeth. "You mess up my hair and I'll hurt you."

Several employees, including its two top engineers, surrounded them, laughing and egging Chris on.

Travis nudged his partner. "I haven't seen her smile in weeks."

Joel nodded. "That's because all she's done is complain."

The duo looked at each other and grinned. They dropped back from the rest of their colleagues, each grabbing a side of the cardboard cake pad upon which the remainder of the dessert rested. Slowly, they crept forward, hushing anyone who noticed them.

"Come now," Chris teased, enjoying her struggle. "Don't want to be rude. Everyone pitched in. Wanted to get our star a bit of a treat."

She shook her head. At this point, it was the principle of the matter.

The studio receptionist peeked into the lounge as Joel and Travis reached the wrestlers. "Farin? You have a call."

Jordan?

As Farin gasped, Chris slid the fork into her mouth. She broke free with a sudden burst of energy. Simultaneously, Joel and Travis upended the cake pad and its contents onto the top of her head. The spectators roared.

She tittered good-naturedly as she scooped handfuls of cake from her eyes, face, and hair, flinging them to the floor. "Tell him I'm coming. I'll pick up in here."

A distorted glimpse of her lemon chiffon and buttercream-covered image via the reflective metal surface of the paper towel dispenser above the sink made her laugh. She needed to get home and shower. Surely Jordan was calling to wish her a happy birthday. Perhaps ask her to dinner.

She picked up the lounge phone with sticky fingers. "Hello?"

"Happy birthday!" Marci cheered.

***

During the forty-minute drive to Standards, Ben coaxed his ten-year-old into conversation. "Given any thought to your brother's invitation?"

"I don't like the drums. Besides, Derek already plays drums."

"Didn't he say he'd rather play guitar now?"

Kyle shrugged, preoccupied with his newly completed model ship. He inspected its hull for any loose pieces. "He wants to be Uncle Chris."

Ben smirked at his youngest's keen observation, though the thought brought him no pleasure. "I think he's looking for someone to practice with at this point."

"He's got Peter. They're always messing around with guitars and junk."

"You don't want to join their band?"

"No way!"

"I guess you escaped the family legacy."

"Not all the way. I'm the one who gave 'em their name."

"What name?"

Kyle straightened in his seat. "Rebel Sea."

"That's grand!" Ben gave his youngest a proud side-eye. "So...fancy taking the boat out tomorrow after school? I can have her ready."

"It's bad luck to set sail on a Friday, Dad."

"You're right, I forgot. Saturday, then. We'll make a day of it."

Kyle agreed. For the remainder of the trip, they enjoyed a comfortable silence, bobbing their heads to the radio, occasionally singing along.

They pulled into Standards at three. Ben had become distracted by then, pondering the similarities between the basic rhythm tracks of Madonna's "Justify My Love" and Suzanne Vega's "Tom's Diner." The latter, while slower and less musically complex, sounded remarkably similar to the former, however shrouded behind the more dance-oriented tempo. He wondered if Kravitz or Betts had heard Vega's song before composing theirs.

Kyle recognized the white Porsche backed into a space near the front. He bounded out of his father's car, nearly dropping the fiberglass and resin vessel. "Uncle Chris is here!"

Ben filled his lungs, then exhaled heavily. He exited his vehicle, shading his eyes with his hand as he scanned the lot. Farin's limousine was nowhere in sight.

Chris exited the front door as they approached.

Kyle rushed forward. "Uncle Chris!"

Chris caught the lad full force. "What are you doing here? Making a record?" He tickled his nephew until he dropped to his knees, squealing for mercy.

Ben offered his brother a curt nod. "Chris."

"Ben," Chris mimicked.

Kyle held up his model ship. "See what I got for Christmas?"

Chris inspected the fragile craft with exaggerated wonder. "*Impressive*! Did you put this together from a kit?"

"Uh-huh!"

"By yourself?"

"Mom put newspapers on the kitchen table and made sure I didn't get paint all over the place, but I glued and painted it."

"Brilliant!" Chris handed it back with great care. "Did you get the gifts I sent you and your brother?"

"Yeah. Thanks!" Kyle's expression lost some of its zeal. "Why didn't you come over?"

Ben folded his arms and scowled at his brother.

"Sorry, mate. Mirage had its last video shoot over Christmas. But I'm glad you're here now." He mussed the boy's hair, then regarded his older sibling. "Didn't Jordan switch over to Tympanum at the first of the year?"

Ben nodded. "I'm picking up the last of the masters."

"Courier service, are we?" Eyes sparkling, Chris shot his brother a satisfied grin.

Ben ignored the barb. "She here?"

"She is."

"I didn't see her car."

"It's coming. She's wrapping up for the day. Hoping for a visit?" He tsk-tsk'd. "Ah, Ben. Always the go-between."

Ben's nostrils flared above pinched lips. "Leaving, then?"

He lifted and jangled his keys with his thumb and index finger.

"Don't let us keep you."

Chris bear-hugged his nephew, promised to stop by soon, but declined the invitation to join them for their Saturday excursion.

The perky brunette behind the reception desk greeted them as they entered the establishment. "Hey Ben, hey Kyle. How're you doing today?"

Kyle waved and took a seat in the lobby. Ben rested an arm on the counter. "We're good, Trish, how are you? Have a nice holiday?"

"Christmas morning, my husband and I laid out on the beach. Pure bliss."

"Sounds perfect."

"You here for those tapes?"

He nodded. "Trevor said they'd be with you."

She stuck out her thumb. "Small box there on the side. Heavy, though. Let me get a hand truck."

Ben hoisted the box onto the counter. "It's not too bad. I can—"

"Aunt Farin!" Kyle sprang from his seat and rushed toward the hallway, crashing into Farin as he had with Chris minutes before.

Farin wrapped her arms around the boy. "Hi, sweetie. What are you doing here?" She entered the lobby and spotted Ben at the front desk. Her stomach flipped at the unexpected encounter.

"Dad picked me up from school. He's picking up Uncle Jordan's tapes, so I came with."

She walked him to his father, her arm draped around his shoulder.

He wriggled free, scampered over to his abandoned seat to reclaim his property, then hurried back to her side. "Like it? I made it from the kit I got for Christmas!"

Farin knelt down. She surveyed the sails, ropes, and ornamentations in detail. She teetered but shot her hand out onto the hardwood floor for balance. "It's lovely, Kyle. You did a wonderful job."

"I brought it for you."

Ben peered at his son with a sad shake of his head.

Farin noted the reaction. She stood and hugged Kyle with her free hand. "Thank you. But you should keep this, honey. You did such a nice job. Don't you collect these? It's bigger than your others, right? You must've spent a lot of time on this."

He gazed up at her with green, saucer-like eyes. "But I put it together for you."

"You did?"

"Derek and I, well...we missed you at Christmas. We thought you could take this home to remember us."

A catch in Farin's throat prevented an immediate response. She glanced at Ben.

"We should get going, son."

Kyle wrapped his small arms around her waist. "*Please* keep it!"

Farin looked at Ben again. He nodded. She knelt down a second time.

"Okay. Thank you for the lovely gift. But I don't need anything to remind me of you and Derek. I think about you every day."

A quick-thinking Trish interjected the melancholy moment. "Ben, would it be okay if I took Kyle into the lounge and got him a juice or something?"

He nodded again, thankful for the diversion.

"C'mon, Kyle," she said over her shoulder, smiling as he followed her to the lounge. "You can tell me all about the ship you're gonna put together for *me* next year!"

Farin sulked toward her brother-in-law, crestfallen over his obvious disappointment in seeing her.

He slipped his hands into his trouser pockets. "How's it going, kid?"

She smiled weakly. "Okay. How're Cheryl and the boys?"

"Good. The boys talk about you a lot."

"I miss them."

His stare went through her. "You look tired."

She closed her eyes—*not him, too.* "It's just the pressure with the album."

"Think maybe you should see a doctor?"

"I *did* see a doctor. He says I'm fine."

"The recording going okay?"

"We're making it work."

"I hear Chris is helping out."

She nodded. "Jameson wasn't happy about it at first, but I guess he's warmed to the idea. It's a different sound this time around. Travis said he doesn't know if Chris is turning into a pop musician or if I'm becoming a rocker."

"Your third album. It's good to branch out. Where'd you get the material?"

"Chris, mostly."

"Really?"

"He's been writing a lot. Trying to get me to write."

"You're both stretching your legs, then. Good for you."

She looked down at her fidgeting fingers. "Has Jordan said *anything* about me?"

His hesitation answered her question. Her heart ached inside her chest.

"There's no hope for us, is there? That's why Jordan left Standards. You know LSI wasn't happy about the move. They own this place."

Ben patted her arm. "In fairness, Tympanum's a lot closer."

Farin tossed back long, untidy hair that had once shimmered fiery red, but now lay in dull, lifeless strings. She shifted her weight from left to right.

When her car pulled up, she thumb-pointed at the door. "I should go. Tell Kyle I said goodbye?"

"Of course."

She secured the model ship tenderly under one arm and swung the strap of her purse over her shoulder with the other.

"Wait." Ben hugged her small frame, mindful of the fragile cargo. "You take care of yourself."

She shouldered through the lobby door.

Charles held the ship while Farin settled into the back seat, then hustled back behind the wheel. "Straight home, ma'am?"

She procured her prescription bottle from her bag.

Part of her wanted to hole away and mourn the death of everything she had ever cared about. Ben could not even offer her false hope.

Another part of her feared going home. Though Jordan had made no definitive moves, they could not exist in their current state forever. For all she knew, the papers had arrived and were waiting for her at the house.

The idea lay in her stomach like a sixteen-pound shot put. "I don't want to go home tonight, Charles. Not yet."

"Yes, ma'am. Where to, then?"

Farin strained to recall the name. "Take me to Stokey's."

CHAPTER 25

JOEY STOKES STOOD BEHIND HIS bar drying highball glasses with dingy, threadbare rags when the door creaked open. In walked one of the most beautiful women he had ever seen. On the skinny side. A bit worn out. But gorgeous. Her fine clothing told him she belonged nowhere near North Miami. As the pneumatic door closer hissed shut behind her, he glimpsed a black limousine drive off toward the back parking lot.

The bar crawled with suited businessmen who had escaped their offices early that Thursday afternoon to let off a little steam before heading home to wives and children. Seated amongst the more regular bums and barflies, they looked incongruous within the confines of the filthy dive. But Joey embraced the diverse clientele frequenting his recently-popular watering hole. In a few hours, groupies would filter in, hoping for an encounter with Stokey's most famous regular.

An aging jukebox competed with benign chatter, laughter, and the occasional drunken debate. "High Enough" by the Damn Yankees played through dusty, overworked speakers suspended in each corner of the ceiling.

The woman struck Joey as uncomfortable as she scoured the crowd. Her eyes darted back and forth like an erratic goldfish in an undersized bowl. She bypassed the few unoccupied tables before finally climbing up on a cracked vinyl bar stool.

Joey dropped the rag, wiped his hands on his stained white apron, and greeted her with a smile. "What's your poison?"

Face downward, she avoided eye contact. She combed her red curls forward with her fingers to conceal her features. "Is Chris Grant here?"

The request turned Joey's expression flat. This was no lady, no matter how expensive her clothes looked. Just another broad hoping to get a little action from his buddy. "He ain't here. Now, order a drink or take your sweet ass somewheres else. Got it?"

She flinched as if physically assaulted by his words. "I'm sorry. I need to see him. I'm a…friend…of his."

"They all are, lady. Whaddya have?"

The woman hesitated, then ordered a Jack Daniels on the rocks. Joey kept a suspicious eye on her as he went about his business, serving patrons and stocking inventory.

Three or four drinks later, the waterworks started. It began with a few gloomy sniffs. But as the afternoon crowd trickled out, leaving only a couple of stragglers at the bar, her weeping intensified. "She Talks to Angels" by the Black Crowes played in the background.

Though miffed at first, Joey regretted the harsh treatment. She seemed harmless enough, if unstable. Plus, she smelled good. He sidled up before her and handed her a cocktail napkin. "Calm down, sweetie. I'm sorry, okay? You gotta understand. Most girls come in here, they're lookin' for one thing, you know? I can't pay the mortgage on this heap with people comin' in to stare and not drink."

"I understand."

Joey freshened her drink. He stretched his arm and placed a thick, calloused hand on her sylphlike shoulder. "Listen, where did you say you knew Chris from?"

She glanced around, then pitched her voice low. "I'm his sister-in-law."

He peered closer, then drew back, eyes bulging. "*Farin*?"

"You know me?"

"Of course! I mean—I know *of* you. And not just by your records, neither! Chris talks about you all the time!"

Farin dabbed her eyes with the scratchy cocktail napkin. "He does?"

"That's how we met—sort of. You in some kind of trouble or somethin'?"

She folded the spent cloth several times, then wrapped it absently around a delicate finger.

He wiped his hands on his apron, then extended an open palm. "I'm Joey."

She shook his hand. "I really need to see Chris. Will he be in?"

Joey rubbed the dark stubble carpeting his fleshy cheeks. "Hard to say. Why not go to his place or something?"

The sides of her mouth stretched to either side. "Reporters."

Joey excused himself and trotted over to the jukebox. He fed it a few quarters and pushed some buttons. When he returned, he became not only friendly, but jovial as he leaned in on hairy forearms, all smiles. "Wait for it..." A moment later, "Down Deep in Love" came blasting out of the speakers. "Ya like it? I got all your songs on that ol' juke!"

Before long, the tears resumed. And no matter how he tried, Joey could not make them stop. "N-n-no! Don't cry, Farin—Mrs. Grant—Farin. He may show up!"

"I should go." She slid halfway off the barstool onto one foot and stumbled.

Joey dove over the bar before she fell, grabbed her arm, and held on while she righted herself. He congratulated himself for having decided to water down her drinks. He thought he had seen her pop something into her mouth an hour ago. What, he did not know, but he had seen plenty in his day. Either way, she did not need alcohol at its full strength.

And where *was* Chris, anyway? As much as he sulked over her, Joey doubted his buddy was unaware of Farin's disposition. Or location.

Then, he was rescued. Chris barreled in from the back door and dashed to Farin's side. She dissolved into his arms and wailed, unfettered, against his chest.

"I called your driver. What are you doing?"

"Something has to go right. Tell me the album's going to be okay."

"It's fine. What happened?" He stroked her curls, hushing her like a child.

"I-I-I murdered Winston on Christmas! I killed him!"

Chris frowned. "What? Who did you kill? What happened?" He traded a wide-eyed glance with Joey, then stared out into the middle distance, confused as Farin skipped from one random topic to the next like an inexpertly thrown stone skidding lopsided across the surface of a lake.

"He looked like such a nice little dog."

"A *dog*?"

She nodded against his chest. "Winston."

"On Christmas."

"Mm-hmm. And everywhere I go, someone's watching or f-following me or asking for an autograph...and I-I missed my Celica!"

Chris glared at the barkeep. "How many has she had?"

Joey raised innocent hands. "A couple?"

"How many's *a couple*?"

Joey hung his head. He counted on his fingers. "Six, I guess. Maybe seven. But I watered 'em down."

"Did she take anything? Any pills?"

A flicker of recognition registered on Joey's chubby face. He snapped, then shook his index finger. "That's what that was!"

He clenched his jaw and winced. "*Bugger.*"

"Come home with me, Chris. Send Charles away. I want to ride in a normal car without killing anybody's pet."

He scowled at Joey. "Remind me to leave you my cell phone number next time I come in."

Chris half-carried, half-dragged a barely conscious Farin to his car. He dismissed her driver, then maneuvered her into the passenger seat of his vehicle. When he pulled the safety belt across her torso, her head rolled to the side. Before he could buckle the strap, she lunged sideways out the car door and vomited onto the asphalt, missing his black leather boots by inches. He sprung back, holding the passenger door open until she finished.

When Farin came to, she found herself in the back parking lot of Stokey's, reclined in Chris's passenger seat. A damp, musty-smelling bar rag covered her forehead. As she adjusted the seat control upright, it dropped onto her lap. She sent it to the floorboard with a distasteful flick of her wrist. Beside her in the driver's seat, Chris rummaged through her purse.

"What are you doing?"

"Being the bloody hero," he spat bitterly.

She grabbed for her bag, but he jerked it away.

"Give me my purse."

He held up and rattled the bottle of Valium. "Is this all you have on you?"

She swiped at him, trying to snatch the bottle.

He extended his arm beyond her grasp. "Is that a yes?"

She huffed back into the bucket seat.

Chris discarded the bag onto the floorboard atop the rag, pocketed the prescription bottle, and started his engine. "Buckle up."

She grabbed the rag, flung it into the compact back seat area, then secured her safety belt. Her stomach felt strained and hollow. "Where are we going?"

He slammed the car into gear and peeled out of the parking lot. "I haven't decided yet."

Chris jumped on the freeway at Ives Dairy Road, then motored north on I-95, driving directionless as he contemplated the best course of action. With her fully coherent now, there appeared no need for a doctor.

Farin lounged beside him as if resigned to whatever fate awaited her. She turned on the Blaupunkt radio.

He switched it off with an angry snap.

They reached Boca Raton before he loosened his death grip on the leather steering wheel. "Ready to talk?"

"About what?"

"When I left the studio earlier, you were fine."

The signature Porsche emblem sat embossed in the grain leather of the dashboard in front of her. She wondered fleetingly if Chris had always driven a Porsche. Marci had always been a Chrysler girl.

"I don't know whether to take you home, or to hospital, or what. Was this an accident? Or do I have another Faith Peterson fiasco on my hands?"

Numbness enveloped her, penetrating deeper than the pills and booze. She was on the cusp of something inevitable. What, she did not know. Chris wanted an explanation she could not even give herself.

"My dad died." The answer meant nothing—and everything.

He mentally inventoried what little he could remember hearing about her past. "You were what, ten? Almost twenty years ago? The most I can remember from twenty years ago was starting with LSI. I sure as hell can't remember being ten."

They exited near Delray Beach, then doubled back, heading southbound on I-95.

"We should stop for a bite on the way home. You need to eat."

"Is this your idea of a date? Kidnapping me and driving me halfway to Orlando?"

"You asked me to take you home, remember?"

She gestured out the window at their darkened surroundings. "Does this look like home?"

"Well, it's no date. We've kicked that bloody beast to death."

She plucked her purse off the floorboard and searched its contents.

"You won't find what you want in there."

She dropped the bag and frowned. When she eased back into her seat, she smiled seductively and angled toward him. "You can keep the bottle. But maybe give me one? I'm sober. It's all out of my system."

"I know it is. It nearly ended up on my shoes."

She inched closer, touched his arm, and let it linger. "I'm sorry."

He furrowed his brow. "What're you doing?"

"Apologizing."

He adjusted himself in his seat. "Whatever this is, Farin, it won't work."

"No?" She slid her hand down, splayed her fingers atop his right thigh, and gently squeezed.

Her touch ignited him, dividing his attention between the road ahead and the mounting discomfort caused by the constriction of unyielding leather pants. He clicked his tongue, chuckling as he clutched the wheel. "You keep this up and we'll be making a detour."

She giggled softly into his ear. "Yeah?"

"Don't say you haven't been warned."

The gear shift prevented her from drawing any closer. She slipped her left hand behind his neck and played with his hair.

A less experienced man might have taken the bait. "Interesting...you'll flirt with me, but you won't eat with me. You'll fuck me, but you won't date me."

Frustrated for lack of results, she scooted back to her side of the compact vehicle. "I have a prescription for those, Chris. They're mine." Her shoulders slunk as she peered out the passenger's window, certain she would find a manila envelope waiting for her upon her return home.

"Come now. You give up too easily." He extracted the pill bottle from his pocket and jiggled them at her. "Perhaps we can come to an agreement."

She recoiled, aghast at the insinuation.

He chortled, splitting his attention between her and the road.

"What?"

"What a hypocrite! You can tease but I can't call it what it is?"

She nestled into the seat. "Keep 'em. I'll just get a refill tomorrow."

"But you'll sober up tonight."

"You think I have a problem."

"I *know* you have a problem."

"Why? Because I'm having trouble coping with the life *you* created for me?"

He thrust the plastic bottle back into his pocket. "For the love of Edgar! At some point, you have to let go, Farin. Of your dad, Jordan...even that bloody little dog you ran over."

"Have you ever lost someone you love? Have you ever even loved anyone besides yourself? Well, *I* have! I loved my father, but he's gone. And Jordan? I know I've done awful things, but I won't walk away!"

"*He* walked, not you!"

She swallowed the ballooning feeling in her throat. "Take me home."

"*Gladly.*"

They traveled in silence most of the way back to Key Biscayne. A feeling of dread overcame her as they reached the Rickenbacker Causeway. She shuddered as they neared Virginia Key.

"You cold?"

She shook her head. "Please give me back my pills. I won't sleep tonight."

"We could still come to an agreement."

With a downturned mouth, she spat, "Pig."

"Move in with me."

She spun around to face him. "*What*?"

Without warning, Chris locked up his brakes, skidding to a stop as they crested the William Powell Bridge. Northbound traffic swerved and screeched to a stop behind them.

He fixed his dark eyes upon her. "Move in with me."

Farin looked around in shock and embarrassment.

"I can give you what you need—help you through this thing with Jordan. I-I love you. And I'd never walk."

Horns sounded from the cars behind them, urging them on.

Her eyes softened at the sincerity of his words. She knew, one day, he would hate her for hearing them. "But I don't love you."

"I know." He swallowed hard, his voice a faint crack. "But I still have the pills."

***

Marci took out her frustration on her typewriter, punching the keys as she typed. Somehow, her anger improved her accuracy. She required few corrections.

> *Dear Mr. Wentz,*
> *Per our conversation yesterday, I'm writing to confirm*
> *the dates of my vacation. They are as follows...*

When she finished the memo, she signed and sealed it inside an envelope and had her assistant walk it up to the executive offices. Task completed, she turned her attention to the next—and more painful—item on her agenda.

She grabbed the receiver from its cradle and dialed Jordan's number from memory. She had intended to call Ben for the information, but had left his number on the kitchen counter this morning.

He answered on the third ring.

"Hi Jordan, it's Marci."

He did not sound unhappy to hear from her, though she inarguably represented the more negative aspects of his life—aspects he might prefer to avoid.

"I'm sorry I haven't called lately. I thought you might need time."

"I appreciate it. I trust all's well with you? I've been meaning to call and coordinate the best time to have some maintenance done on the house. I want to have the roof inspected and have the plumbing and electrical systems checked. Sea air and all."

She grabbed a pen and scribbled a note in her day planner. "Absolutely. I could arrange all that from here if it would save you some time."

"That'd be great. I'll have my people call you directly, then."

"Is it okay to ask how you've been?"

"Of course." His tone was neutral, neither happy nor sad. "It's been...an adjustment not having her here. I miss her. But I'll be honest, Marci. I don't miss the roller coaster."

She rocked gently in her chair. "I understand, believe me. Of course, with this recent development, I guess we both realize her physical absence doesn't exempt us completely."

The line went silent. Marci feared she had touched a nerve. She berated herself for leaving Ben's number at the house. "Sorry. That was insensitive."

"No, not at all. Ben told me he saw her last week. Said she lost a lot of weight and what-not. I'm sorry about that. The move to Tympanum made sense. I realize that hurt her."

Marci sat forward and pinched her temples with her free hand. "So, you haven't heard."

"Heard what?"

She swore under her breath. "Well, Jordan, it appears I'm once again the bearer of your bad news."

"What happened?"

"I called to get Chris's number. I want to try to talk some sense into her."

"Why would you need my brother's number to reach Farin?"

"Because she's obviously lost her mind."

***

Farin received a copy of the divorce papers two days later—Valentine's Day—ready for her signature. Jordan sent them to her attention, at the address and in care of Mr. Chris Grant.

***

Megastar. Libertine. Black sheep. Knight-errant.

Like so many other aspects of Chris's life, the most impressive parts of him lay hidden beneath a dedicated affectation. And while his Key Biscayne property could not claim the sizable acreage surrounding Jordan's home—with its mature landscaping, walking paths, and straight-line architecture—it was, in the purest sense, an extension of himself.

In front, a horseshoe driveway seamlessly bordered a brick terrace. An enormous grand stairway divided a white-stained cement veranda running the length of the front of the house. Green wrought iron bistro chairs and tea tables were concealed by skillful landscapers who maintained a virtual Eden, its gardens obscured from Harbor Drive traffic by tropical foliage overgrowing the iron fence encasing three sides of the estate. Corinthian pillars supported a second story balcony above their cornice, framing the second floor with a rail of wrought iron, imitating vines.

Arched, floor-to-ceiling windows dotted the façade, spaced evenly at intervals above the architrave. Though constructed of steel-reinforced concrete, the bulk of the home had incongruously Midwestern-style stucco. The entire structure, a mélange of styles both ancient and contemporary, sat as a singularly unique construction in the village of Key Biscayne.

Chris had commissioned the interior as an homage to a more genteel 17th century with beautiful, if uncomfortable, Louis XIV furnishings and classic works of art. Collectible first editions overfilled his library. A multizone in-home stereo system—one of his few concessions to modern living—pumped longhaired symphonies and operas throughout the house, the volume and selections made according to his whim.

The house personified the truest part of him...and soon became Farin's haven from the real world.

***

Before her, a black Porsche intertwined with what remained of a brown Chevrolet station wagon. The Porsche had slammed into the driver's side of the vehicle like a brick slamming into a block of clay. As Farin approached the twisted metal beneath the traffic lights, tiny beads of glass crunched beneath her likewise tiny feet. Intersecting roads vanished on all sides into the murky Santa Barbara fog. Music from the radio drifted to her ear on the dense salt air.

... but February made me shiver
... with every paper I'd deliver
... bad news on the doorstep
... I couldn't take one more step
... I can't remember if I cried ...

"Daddy?" she called. She walked up and stood beside the wreckage. The hood of the station wagon wrapped around the smaller car, embracing it, kissing it with twisted metal, and gifting it with jewels of shattered glass. The windshield and windows had burst. Blood covered the dashboard. Steam rose from the hood before her. Everything had been shattered inside and out.

***

As part of their negotiated cohabitation, Chris gave Farin all the space she needed, and she needed plenty. He consigned the entire south wing—the side with the optimal view of Biscayne Bay—to her to do with as she pleased, with the assurance he would not disturb her.

Upon the arrival of her divorce papers, she withdrew to her room for weeks.

He kept his distance as promised, limiting their interactions to quiet, twice-per-day knocks at her door, when he would swap out mostly-untouched meal trays for fresh ones. Though concerned, he consoled himself with the knowledge he controlled her Valium intake—another part of their negotiated cohabitation.

Their *modus vivendi* worked, even if it did leave both parties frustrated...and confuse those privy to their unorthodox circumstances.

Bobby voiced the primary complaint. "I want to talk to her. It's been three days. What have you done to her?"

"I promised to leave her alone." Chris delighted in his role as gatekeeper, if for no other reason than to shut down the Lockhardts' efforts to push him around.

Two days later, the Key Biscayne PD showed up at his gate, explaining they had received a call about a possible kidnapping. Chris buzzed them in, led them upstairs to Farin's room, and knocked. "The constabulary needs to see you. Apparently, LSI thinks I have you tied up."

He left the officers waiting at her door, wishing he did. Perhaps someday.

On day eleven, Chris reneged on their deal. He did so for two reasons. First, he had not heard a peep from her in several hours. When he brought her dinner, he found her breakfast tray untouched, save the Valium. Second, a thunderstorm raged outside that night—an odd and early weather phenomenon about which local meteorologists seemed ecstatic. Through the door, he heard what sounded like water.

He knocked, then waited. No answer. "If you don't open the door, I'm going to let myself in." When she failed to respond, he made good on his threat.

Her room hosted two sets of glass windows, one on either side of her sitting area, each as expensive as they were gigantic. Both were open. The wind whipped viciously through the room. Rain splattered into puddles on the hardwood floors, saturating oriental rugs.

Farin stood on the balcony, soaked to the skin, shivering, and heavily sedated. She jutted her chin against the gale as if daring it to pick her up and carry her away. Her wet hair whipped and curled at the ends, dancing like a child in a playground. A drenched white silk nightgown clung to her body. The wind forced the fabric to cling to her curves.

He raised his arms against the squall. "What are you doing? Come inside!"

"Go away! You promised!"

"You'll catch your death out there!" He stepped forward, hoping to help her back inside.

She edged closer to the balcony wall, nearly losing her balance as her bare feet slipped. "I'll be fine! I'm *always* fine!"

"Dying of pneumonia was *not* part of our arrangement!"

"Leave, Chris! Or *I will*!"

Futile attempts to talk her inside, coupled with her screams to let her be, made for an endless night. The storm subsided near dawn and Farin returned to her bed where she lay crying for three days straight.

On March first, she met him in the kitchen, disheveled but coherent. He sat reading the morning paper over tea and toast. When he saw her, he froze mid-bite.

She padded softly to him, crawled onto his lap, and wrapped her arms around his neck.

He wiped his hands on his jeans and embraced her, afraid to speak for fear one of them might be dreaming.

"I'm ready."

Ready?

"I need to get better."

He drew her closer. When she pulled away, he searched those brown eyes he loved so much, perceiving a faint spark of life for the first time in months.

"Will you take me to the studio? I think I know how to fix what's wrong."

"You do?"

"Maybe it's not a matter of addition. Maybe it's a matter of subtraction." She kissed his cheek, then stood and headed upstairs for a shower.

He watched her leave, then looked down. In his hand, he found the morning allotment of Valium he had dispensed with her breakfast an hour before.

That was the good news.

Over the next month, Chris watched Farin's transformation from immobility to nobility. She finished the album, her appetite improved, and she began showing her face in public. Her determination so energized him, he called Faith in New York and suggested they accept some of the interview requests they had avoided while mourning Mirage's end. "No use fading slowly into the limelight, love. That's not us, is it?"

She agreed to call the others. "Todd probably won't talk to you."

"No?"

"Lance says he's been buying posters of you and using them as target practice for some new hobby. Darts, knives, bullets—I don't know exactly what, but he's still pissed. Anyway, how're things in the Orange Juice State? Maintaining your tan?"

"No fun in the sun here, I'm afraid. We've been slogging away for months."

"I hear the old man caved and agreed to credit you on Farin's album. Congrats. You're now a bubblegum producer."

"While I'd agree I have been a bit orally fixated in my life, I assure you this record will be Farin's transition piece."

"Trying to turn Debbie Gibson into Joan Jett?"

"Maybe I can hook her up with your leather guy, eh? Get her a new wardrobe?"

"Screw that. I'm starting my own line. She can buy it from me."

He chuckled. "Let me know if Todd can't tear himself away from target practice. Otherwise, I vote we do *Headbanger's Ball*. We can meet you in New York next week."

"We? You're bringing *her*?"

"Problem?"

"Keeping her leash a little short, aren't you?"

"I'm merely exposing her to what she's missed living with a homebody like Jordan."

"She's getting that from *you*?"

"She's had enough of the reality of this business. Time to start enjoying the fantasy."

"Ah, your favorite."

"Indeed."

"Well, good luck with that."

"I've got something better than luck. I've got her."

That was the better news.

At Farin's request, her publicist coordinated her schedule with Mirage's. She accompanied Chris to his personal appearances. He reciprocated. From Miami to New York to LA, they became a notorious and heavily sought-after power couple. Resigned to the disintegration of her marriage and the reality she need not feel trapped by her fame, she blossomed before his eyes. She enjoyed the fuss her fans made over her. And under his tutelage, she learned to control the press like a sorceress mastering the elements.

Once outside the limelight, however, Farin struggled to maintain the fervor she exhibited to the world. She continued to abuse her prescription despite his rationing. At night, she would retreat to her room with little more than a simple goodnight, leaving Chris emotionally and physically frustrated by the one hurdle over which it appeared he could not jump.

The news of Conor Clapton's death near the end of March set her back further, so much so Chris decided it unwise to fly to England for the funeral. He would not risk leaving her alone.

Farin protested the decision over breakfast the morning after they received the news. "You can't not go."

"I've sent Eric and Lory my condolences."

She picked at the multigrain bagel on her plate. "Please don't stay for me."

He folded his copy of the *Post* and set it aside. "We both have commitments in Cincinnati next week."

She looked far away as she forced down a few small bites of cantaloupe and finished her tea. He considered telling her he had sent roses to Melody's grave in Paris but figured it would bring her as little comfort as it had brought him when he sent the same to Chase's grave in Los Angeles. How similar the circumstances, Chase and Conor. Had he been honest with himself, he would have admitted Farin was not his only reason for skipping the funeral.

"I feel so bad for them," she whispered.

He cleared his throat and nodded. "Tragic."

"Such a beautiful little boy. I don't even know how something like that happens."

"I guess the building janitor opened the window for some air. Conor and the nanny were playing hide and seek. He must not have realized the window was open."

She swiped at her eyes. "Someone once told me 'accidents happen.' What a hollow thing to say. I hope no one says that to Lory."

He scooted to her side and dared to rest his arm on the back of her chair. She did not pull away, which he took as progress. "Want to take the boat out today? The sunshine would do us both some good. We're getting better, remember? And it's the first full day we've had at home in a while."

Slowly, the corner of her lips rose. "And the last one we'll have for a long time. Yeah. I guess it'd be good."

He cleared their dishes while she perused the paper, stealing glances at her as he cleaned. Her morning look was his favorite—wrinkled night clothes beneath a cotton robe. Wild curls pinned effortlessly atop her head. The luster had returned to her hair and skin. She was breathtaking.

"*What*?"

"What's wrong?" He rinsed foamy soap from his hands and grabbed a nearby dish towel.

The newspaper crinkled inside her fist. "Did you know about this?"

"About what?"

She tossed the paper across the table. He flipped a seat around and straddled it, then unfolded the creased paper. "What am I looking for?"

"You can't miss it."

He scanned the Entertainment section. "The Sony deal with Michael

Jackson?"

"Further down. Macy's article."

He read the piece with interest, unsure if the information would sabotage his efforts.

"Did you know?"

"I'm not my brother's keeper, Farin. I haven't spoken to him since October."

"Do you know this new girl?"

He dropped the paper on the table and laughed despite himself. "I only got involved with pop music because it's you. I'm certainly not into country."

"Jameson never mentioned signing some little country singer." She slid the paper back from across the table and studied the picture of Jordan alongside the young blonde.

"If it makes you feel any better, I'm sure it's for publicity."

"Or revenge."

"You're not the only one plugging a project, Farin. The article said the girl's promoting her debut record and Jordan's just finished his. Now go on and get ready."

She folded her arms. Extending one hand, she made a beckoning palm gesture.

He lifted his shoulders. "What?"

She raised an expectant brow. "I finished my breakfast."

His eyes held hers as he fished the plastic bottle out of his unbuttoned jeans. "How about half this morning?"

She shook her head. "Fork it over."

He placed a Valium on the counter and procured a glass of juice. When he turned from the fridge, she stood before him. He stopped abruptly, almost spilling the juice.

She stared up at him with carnal eyes as she placed the pill on her tongue, took the glass from his hands, and downed its contents. "Thank you."

Her sudden nearness aroused him. His nostrils flared as their eyes remained locked on each other. His heart hammered beneath his chest.

"I'm ready."

Ready?

"I want to get better."

Three years of patience had finally paid off. From that day on, he woke beside his little damsel in distress every morning. She was finally right where she belonged.

That was the best news.

CHAPTER 26

FORESEEN CIRCUMSTANCES FORCED MARCI TO postpone her originally-scheduled trip by three weeks. She had suspected for some time, and felt oddly relieved when the truth surfaced.

For two and a half years, she had allowed herself to be Dan Albright's doormat. In that time, she had endured insults and betrayals, bore the humiliation of his abandonments, and defended him to friends and family who pressed for an answer to the question she could not bring herself to ask. Three Halloweens, three Thanksgivings, three Christmases—they had not spent one of them together. Would he ever fully commit?

Now, she had her answer, and was determined to keep it to herself during her vacation—if one could call it that.

The seven-hour flight was long but uneventful. She had purchased several tabloid magazines at the LAX terminal that morning. Reading through them seemed to cut the travel time. They jettisoned her far from the afternoon she had discovered her accountant boyfriend balancing another woman's books—in *her* bed. Moreover, they prepared her for what she might look forward to in Miami.

Somehow, Chris had bamboozled Farin into his home. Marci knew little else, since Farin had dodged her calls for months. And although it was not the first time Farin had forgotten to call her on her birthday, it hurt nonetheless. Judging by the picture on the cover of *Sun*, her friend was in bad shape. She looked anorexic. Reports labeled her suicidal. Knowing Farin as she did, Marci did not doubt this claim for a minute.

In diametric opposition to the gaunt and harrowed accounts of Farin's decline, the rags portrayed a smiling Jordan in the company of LSI's newest artist and tabloid sweetheart, Megan Price. Young. Blonde. Beautiful. A shy Midwestern country and western singer who embodied the naiveté of the recently arrived. Her debut record had captured Nashville's heart. And, apparently, Jordan's as well.

Marci had never seen him look healthier. Or happier.

After collecting her luggage and rental car, she headed for Chris's place. A part of her felt guilty for not calling ahead. Then again, Farin had mastered the art of the drop-in.

She buzzed the gate, hoping she had not arrived while Farin was off promoting her new album. When Chris answered, she barked into the call box. "It's Marci. Can you buzz me in?"

A moment later, the gate opened.

She parked and unloaded her things, miffed but unsurprised at the lack of chivalry he exhibited when he did not assist her. As she rolled and hefted her luggage across the terrace, the front door opened. He met her at the base of the steps, shirtless and barefoot. The top button of his jeans was unbuttoned.

"To what do we owe this completely uninvited—er, rather, unexpected visit?"

They exchanged hard looks. "I'm here to see Farin. Is she handy? Or do you have her drugged and tied up somewhere so she can't escape?"

"No worries. The local authorities already covered that one."

She tilted her head and frowned, then followed him into the entrance hall. Winded, she set her luggage down and stole glances at his mansion. It creeped her out a little.

Chris stood at the base of the staircase and called upstairs. "You'll never guess who's coming to dinner."

Marci looked up to see Farin at the top of the steps, her eyes wide with surprise. She wobbled downstairs to greet her. When they embraced, Marci felt nothing but skin and bones.

"Why didn't you tell me you were coming? I'd have sent a car for you!"

She pulled back and inspected the emaciated creature before her, noting the haze in her eyes. "I had to see you. Are you okay? You look...*awful*. Are you eating?"

Farin waved her off. "I was down about twenty pounds, but I've gained five back."

"So," Chris cut in, "how long did you say you were staying?"

Farin shushed him, hooked her arm around Marci's, and walked her into the living room. She called back over her shoulder for him to be a dear and take Marci's things up to a spare room. "I'm so happy you're here!" She hugged her again before taking a seat. "How long can you stay?"

"A week, unless you've got somewhere else to be."

"Perfect! Chris and I just finished a stretch away from home. We're here for, I think, the next month or so. And oh! Mirage is playing a benefit concert next Saturday. You can keep me company."

"I didn't bring anything formal. Should I go shopping?"

"Think trendy, not formal. It's for some arts foundation Chris supports. Quite the to-do, but not formal-formal. Trust me. It'll be a blast!"

He joined them in the living room and sat beside Farin. She wrapped a reed-like leg around his, hooking her foot under his calf. He took her arm onto his lap and held her hand.

Marci grimaced, cursing her inability to manufacture a poker face. The victorious grin etched across Chris's smug features nauseated her.

Farin peeked at Chris's watch, then looked up at him. He nodded and stood up. "What can I get you to drink, Marci? Farin made a pitcher of sun tea earlier. Fancy a glass?"

"That'd be decent of you. Thanks."

Farin smiled as he retreated to the kitchen. "I know you hate following me around to my commitments. I only have a few this week, so we should have a lot more time together this time than we did..."

Marci grew concerned as Farin's words vaporized. Her expression grew troubled, as if the words had snuck up on her. "You okay?"

Farin rattled her head. "I'm fine."

"We need to talk. Alone."

As if on cue, Chris returned with the drinks. Farin scooted to the edge of the sofa and fidgeted, impatient for him to sit down. When he did, she grabbed her glass and huddled into him. Marci saw him slip something into her hand. Farin popped her hand against her mouth and took a drink of her iced tea, flipping her head back to swallow.

"What is that?"

Farin shook her head. "Something to relax me. It's nothing."

Marci glared at Chris. He stared back, impenitent.

Unlike her last visit, Marci had little time to fill while awaiting Farin's return from an interview or photo shoot. She spent most her free time poolside, intermittently swimming and absorbing the healing rays of the sun to the soothing, if annoyingly repetitive, chamber music Chris refused to switch off—or down—while he and Farin were out.

She considered arranging a visit with Cheryl but thought better of it. A restless vibe had settled on the Key. Though preposterous, it felt as if calling from Chris's place might cross some undrawn line of loyalty—to or from whom, she did not know.

The one person Marci did call was Bobby, who she agreed to meet for lunch at Wolfie's that Thursday at two. They both decided it best to keep their meeting between themselves.

When she entered the deli that afternoon, he waved her over to the booth he had obtained. They hugged as if they were not almost complete strangers. He pecked her cheek and she pretended not to realize how strange it was to see him outside Farin's presence.

She slid into the booth and set her purse aside. "It's good to see you."

He draped his napkin across his waist. "Thanks for meeting me."

Marci had seen him only two or three times before and could not recall noticing his slight facial spasm. In fact, the most memorable thing about him had been his social awkwardness—something he had not shaken. She picked up and perused a menu so as not to stare. "What's good?"

"I like the pastrami. But I think the corned beef's their specialty."

"Corned beef sounds terrific."

When they had placed their order, Marci folded her hands on the table. "So, what's going on with Farin?"

Bobby fidgeted with his tie, first loosening, then tightening it. "I haven't really talked to her lately."

"I thought you two were close."

There was a desperation-laced sadness to his tone. "It's been hard for her since Jordan...I-I tried to help."

Marci reached across the table and laid her hand on his arm. "She's not an easy one to help."

"Tell me about it."

"How did she end up with *Chris*?"

"Because I failed."

She leaned back, utterly lost. "I've spent the last five days with them. It's *weird*. It's like she's become *physically* dependent on him. Whatever she's on, he's controlling it."

Bobby stretched both arms across the table and played with the tips of his fingers. Marci sensed his frustration, though she could not discern if it had to do with Farin's predicament or a resentment toward Chris.

"She clings to him like an addict to her supplier. And worse—he's feeding this dependency as if nothing about it is the slightest bit...*wrong!*"

"Have you talked to her?"

"I can't get her alone! They're either at his stupid house—have you *seen* the inside of mad scientist Dr. Franken-Chris's castle?—or they're out dancing. She pretends everything's great, but I've got a bad feeling."

"When are you going back to California?"

"Sunday."

"Mirage has a gig Saturday night. The band'll need to get there early to pull a sound check. Try her then."

Marci nodded, more determined than ever.

The minute Chris left Saturday afternoon, Marci beckoned Farin to her room, feigning the need for help with her wardrobe.

Farin raked hangers across the closet dowel searching for something hip and exciting. "If we can't find something here, you can borrow something of mine. But I don't own anything pink."

Marci pulled gently at her arm. "Can we sit down and talk a minute? I'm worried about you. What have you been taking?"

Farin followed Marci over to sit on the edge of the bed. "A doctor prescribed some Valium, that's all. They help me relax. I've been edgy lately."

"What about Jordan? Why did I have to learn about your divorce in the *National Enquirer*? And what the *hell* are you doing with Chris? Isn't he the one who got you into this mess?"

Farin's expression filled with patronizing patience. "I know how you feel about Chris. But he's been good to me. I don't take half the pills I used to."

"*Half* the pills? What about Jordan? The stories in the papers say—"

"*Stop* with the papers, will you?" She clutched her head with both her hands as the last remnant of a cosmetic smile melted away. "If it hadn't been for them, Jordan would've never gone through with this divorce!"

The bitterness in her tone pained Marci. "Something bad's happening to you. If your father could see you like this, it'd crush him."

Farin slapped Marci across the face. They both shot up off the bed, staring at one another in disbelief. Marci rubbed her jaw as red welts in the shape of Farin's palm appeared on her cheek. Her eyes watered from the sudden, stinging pain.

Farin gasped, eyes wild with regret. "I'm sorry." Her hands trembled, one clutching her stomach, the other rubbing her hairline.

Marci stabbed her index finger at the floor, her voice quivering with frustration. "I came down here because I care! And because my life isn't exactly perfect right now either—not that you've asked one question about that my entire trip. I love you, Farin. That's the only reason I'm not gonna walk out of this house right now and never look back."

Briefly, it looked as if the fog had cleared. Marci almost glimpsed the real Farin break free from whatever spell she was under.

Her eyes darted about the room in what looked like paranoia. "Don't make me admit the hell this business forces me into every day. When you leave your office at night, you get to go home. Your job is your job, not your life. But for me, my life *is* my job. I can't separate it—ever."

A chill ran the length of Marci's back.

"If I don't start forgetting my past, it's gonna swallow me whole. Chris is trying to teach me to take things less seriously. So don't remind me who I am, Marci. Or who I was, or who I'm supposed to be. Don't make me say how much I miss...J-Jordan. I'm begging you. Be my friend. Let it go."

Bewitched by the raw honesty in her friend's tone, Marci realized for possibly the first time the gravity of the situation. Farin had turned herself inside out and built a wall around the exposed innards, daring anyone to breach its stronghold. The only question was, how long it would take before that wall came crashing down around her.

***

The boy-gets-girl-but-loses-her-to-his-older-brother story had paid off for everyone—though at the expense of a few broken hearts.

Several record labels pursued Chris, courting Mirage's past success despite Jameson's clear interference.

Farin managed to avoid a nervous breakdown as long as her publicity stayed positive and her prescription held out.

Jordan's nice guy image was blown full-scale. Tabloids claimed the Royal Family considered a Knighthood for the resident alien.

Megan Price morphed from struggling young country singer to overnight sensation after appearing beside the forsaken pop idol.

And Lockhardt Sound? It held contracts with all four notables and enjoyed a tidy profit to boot. In a stunning reversal of position, Jameson decided the only thing sweeter would be to convince Mirage to sign another contract.

Jameson called a meeting at the LSI offices in New York City but discovered too much muddy water had passed beneath the bridge. The only member of the band willing to entertain the idea turned out to be lead singer Todd Dalton. Lance Turner was in talks with another band. Bass player and group mastermind Elliot Lawrence had commitments for several motion picture projects and announced plans to relocate to

California.

Faith Peterson cursed Jameson and his company from the minute she stormed in for the meeting until he finally had security physically remove her from his office kicking, screaming, and spitting the entire way.

Chris did not even bother to show up. He left word he would be available by telephone should things get interesting.

Jameson did not wallow in disappointment for long. The break-up would ensure him a respectable profit. He would win either way—and of course, winning was the most important thing.

***

Despite a weakened art market and sluggish economy, the Benefit for the Arts Endowment Fund sold out the day the one-thousand-dollars per plate VIP tickets became available. Held at the Miami Arena, the event drew artists, dealers, local politicians, and art aficionados throughout Dade County and beyond.

Outside the arena, klieg lights pierced the night sky. A swell of fans screamed and catcalled from behind a human barrier of police and security. Their camera flashes resembled strobe lights as event headliners and celebrities arrived in limousines and paraded up the front steps. Gigantic images of the band were projected against the arena's exterior walls.

Inside, coordinators and curators dressed the wrap-around concourse with works donated for a silent auction and select pieces sent over to preview the highly anticipated Post-Impressionism Exhibit opening at the Fine Arts Center come fall.

Three hundred banquet tables dotted the arena floor, set apart from the general public by barriers and a team of security personnel. Long buffet tables bordered either side of the floor, teeming with culinary delights including fresh seafood and hand-carved meats. A large dance floor had been constructed at the foot of the stage.

Farin played her celebrity role to the hilt, decked out in a leather jacket, paisley vest, and a burgundy-colored beret with matching leather flats. She had finally mastered the role her fame demanded. Her false smile, as exquisite as the paintings on display, never left her face.

The press stalked her like a lovelorn teenager pining for a first date. Or, in her case, a quotable comment for their next edition—the more scandalous, the better. They moved with her, a single unit undulating across the arena floor.

"How does it feel to have another hit on your hands?"

"Like I did my job!" she simpered as she strode toward the two tables reserved for Mirage and their guests.

"Rumor has it you're looking at another tour! Are the dates finalized yet?"

She drew her head in and to the side. "Come now, John, you asked me that question last week."

"Are you worried Jordan's new single jumped ahead of yours this week?"

"It's not about competition, it's about a good product. Besides, didn't you just congratulate me on my newest hit?"

Marci watched them bait her friend, impressed with Farin's ability to draw them in with a few bats of her eyelashes while simultaneously rebuffing their inquiries. Even more impressive was her ability to feign indifference at their more injurious attempts to goad her.

"When's the divorce gonna be final?"

She shook her head and tittered. "What *is* it with you and dates tonight, John?"

"Have you signed the papers yet?"

"You're camped outside our house every day. Have you seen any outgoing mail?"

"What do you think about Jordan's new girlfriend?

They reached the table en masse.

Farin spun on her heels. "Enough for tonight. Tell you what. I'll grant two interviews. One for the highest bidder at the auction, and one for the person who takes home the most pieces."

Farin and Marci ordered drinks, then made a pass through the buffet.

"Is Bobby coming tonight? I thought he was your shadow."

Unmoved, Farin obtained a plate and a set of silverware rolled up in a cloth napkin. "He doesn't come around much anymore, outside business. He's mad because I'm living with Chris."

"I can see it."

"What?"

"Chris isn't the most popular guy, Farin. Don't act so shocked."

She opened her mouth to speak, then pressed her lips together and shrugged. "Let's eat. The doors open at five. I don't want to be stuffing my face with fans pouring into their seats."

Marci glanced over her shoulder at their table. "Where is everyone?

We have two big tables and we're the only ones there."

"Chris never eats before a show. I don't know about the others."

When they finished their meal, Marci declined Farin's request to accompany her backstage. Instead, she strolled the concourse, perusing exhibits and people-watching while the buffet tables were cleared and stowed. She admired sculptures, rare artifacts, and even placed a bid on a Stephen Althouse print, noting with some amusement that reporters had placed jaw-dropping bids on a number of items.

The house lights dimmed at eight. The capacity crowd roared with delight as Mirage took the stage. Farin cheered with the throng, whistling through her fingers. Chris sent his sexiest smile down at her and winked. When the music started, she raised her arms, snapped to the beat of Lance Turner's drums, and swayed to the hypnotic lull of Chris's guitar.

They played two forty-five-minute sets of heart-pumping, sexually-charged rock'n'roll replete with exuberant stage movements and plenty of pelvic thrusts. As Marci watched them perform, she mused over Farin's steamy account of her first encounter with Chris. The way he worked his instrument, she could almost see the attraction. The show left her spent, emotionally raw, and surprisingly lonely.

When the house lights went up, she clutched her chest, turned to Farin, and did a wide-eyed shake of her head. "Wow."

Farin patted her back. "I know."

Piped-in music played through arena speakers as the crowd slowly filtered out. Those who had submitted bids for the auction and fans hoping for a glimpse of the band moved closer to the floor. VIP guests mingled and ordered drinks. Before long, Marci spied a group of reporters lined up near the stage, awaiting the auction results.

A voice from behind them startled her. "Hello, you two."

Farin whipped around, then glowered at the man standing behind her. "I should've known I wouldn't be able to escape you for even one night."

"I do my best." With a grin and a slight bow, he helped himself to a seat at their large and, thus far, mostly unoccupied table. He withdrew a pad of paper and a pen from his suit pocket, then turned to Marci. "We haven't been introduced. Miles Macy, *Miami Post*. Are you a friend of the bride or the groom?"

She accepted the reporter's outstretched hand. "Farin's. I'm Marci."

"Is that Marci with an *ie* or a *y*? Any last name?"

"It's Marci with a *g*," Farin spat, "as in, go *f*—"

"You're in my spot." Chris arrived amid the cheers and whistles of arena stragglers. His dark locks lay damp along his forehead and collar line. Fans whooped and called his name. Leather jacket draped across his arm, he towered over Macy, chest out, and lifted his chin. "Time to go."

Unruffled, Miles scooted his chair back to leave. He leaned in sideways to Farin. "I came over to let you know your husband of record just walked in. If my sources are correct, and they always are, you haven't signed the papers yet." He stood and plunged his hands into his pockets, rocking back on his heels. "What-say you, Grant? Gonna make an honest—well, somewhat honest—woman out of her once this whole thing's behind you?"

"Still wearing those cheap suits, eh Macy?" Chris parked himself in a folding chair as Miles retreated. He grinned and waved up at the small crowd.

Farin surveyed their immediate surroundings, then turned to him with downcast eyes. She raised a cupped hand his way.

Chris laid his hand atop of hers. "Sorry, love. You've been drinking. You'll be fine. Don't worry."

Marci spied the exchange, mesmerized. She had long recognized Farin's need for someone she could not manipulate. Chris undeniably fit the bill—not that she enjoyed the revelation.

Farin gasped. "He's at the bar."

Marci saw him, too. "Are you gonna talk to him? Looks like he's alone."

Chris craned his neck and scanned the room. "Ben said he was bringing Megan."

Farin jerked her head and stared at him, open-mouthed. "You knew he'd be here and didn't tell me?"

He touched her chin. "I wanted you here tonight. If you knew, you'd have scampered off to the beach to brood. It was for your own good."

Reporters dogged Jordan to his table and stayed long enough for his usual, "No comment." Only Miles Macy lingered, talking and pointing in Farin's direction. Jordan looked up briefly, then returned to the company of his drink.

"*Say something,*" Marci urged. "You've already seen each other."

"Can't you leave it?" Chris barked.

Farin cleared her throat. "We're all alone at this huge table. Where is everyone?"

"Elliot's on his way," he replied, eyes narrowed in Marci's direction.

"Todd's backstage with a saucy brunette he met on his flight down, so that's a no for him. A rather rotund older gentleman captured Faith's attention earlier, so I'd wager we won't see her. Don't know about Lance. He's not the artsy type."

Farin grabbed Chris's arm. "Let's dance. You mind, Marce?"

Marci flourished a wave. "Have fun."

Farin affixed her manufactured smile and marched onto the dance floor. Public visage intact, she even managed a whimsical laugh as Chris twirled and dipped her to Will to Power's cover of "I'm Not in Love."

Marci watched them on the floor. Though she had not monitored her friend's alcohol intake, she recognized the effects. Uncoordinated, flirtatious, carefree. As she watched, her mind roamed backwards, to Dan. Probably out of habit. She peeked down at her watch and calculated the time difference, wondering how he was spending his night.

"Excuse me," a voice called from the next table. "Are you Marci?"

She recognized Mirage's bassist. "Yes."

He leaned forward and reached across the table. "I'm Elliot."

She moved in to shake his hand. "Sorry. My mind was somewhere else. I didn't hear anyone come over. How'd you know my name?"

"Chris mentioned he had a house guest."

"I bet he did."

His chin-to-cheek smile was contagious, triggering a roguish glint behind impossibly blue eyes.

Marci glanced down at her hand, embarrassed to realize he still held it in his. He followed her gaze, then released his grip with an apology. When he rose to switch tables, edging past her to take a seat, she detected an intoxicating mixture of spice and sweat.

"He was wrong about you."

"Chris?"

"Yes."

"How so?"

He sprawled out, nearly prone, in the folding chair and crossed his ankles. "You have beautiful hair. Not a snake in sight."

A soft giggle bubbled up from somewhere inside her.

Elliot flagged down a server and ordered a beer. "And could you refresh the drinks all around?" He dug his wallet out of his back pocket and tossed it onto the table as the gentleman headed out. "If I fall asleep before he gets back, kick me. And please, don't let me forget to tip him."

"Anyone who can fall asleep in these chairs must need the rest."

"Can't sleep yet. I need to find out if I won the auction."

"You bid on something?"

He yawned, rubbing the dark stubble along his jawline. "There's this brilliant Stephen Althouse print."

"You didn't!"

"I didn't?"

She clutched her chest. "*I did!*"

When the server returned with their drinks, Elliot groaned, forced himself upright, and felt his back pocket. She inclined her head toward his wallet as a reminder. He winked and fished out a few bills, then handed them over.

Marci glanced at Farin and Chris, then spotted Jordan at the far end of the room, watching them dance. He sat alone.

Elliot took a long drink of his beer. "Not much to be done about that, I'm afraid."

"I feel like I should go over and talk to him."

"I'd hate to see Chris boot you out of his guest room."

"I don't care. Besides, I'm going back to LA tomorrow anyway."

"You live in LA? I'm buying a place in Studio City next week."

"I'm in Malibu."

"You're kidding."

For the remainder of the evening, the media spied gluttonously as Farin and Jordan avoided each other. If one went to the dance floor, the other ordered a drink. If one mingled on the left side of the room, the other wandered casually to the right.

Marci watched their little tête-à-tête with a sorrowed heart. Out of the corner of her eye, she saw Chris grudgingly hand Farin a pill despite her alcohol consumption. Maybe he was not as strong as she thought.

To make matters worse, neither she nor Elliot won the Stephen Althouse print.

***

Farin knew certain things. She knew her successful career would not save her marriage. She knew Chris cared for her more than she did about him. And she knew he was irritated when she moved back to the south wing of the house.

Before the benefit that night, five months had passed since she had laid eyes on Jordan. Could Chris not understand the impact of seeing him again? Apparently not. But no matter. The one good thing about his obsession over her was his ability to rebound.

A glimpse in the mirror prompted a change of wardrobe. Something simple. More casual. She settled on a gold sun dress, an orange Blossom hat, and matching chunky wedges, then headed downstairs for lunch.

Perhaps Chris had stopped pouting. She hoped so. If he insisted she eat three times a day, he should at least try to act pleasant while she choked something down. Besides, the thought of calling a car to run a few errands was such a production.

He greeted her with a cool sneer. "And what might the queen be able to stomach today?"

"Still upset, I see. It's been four days—"

"—five."

"Okay, *five*. Five days. Is this a permanent thing?"

"You tell me."

"Guess I'll have to call for a car after all."

He leaned against the counter, arms crossed. "Where are you going?"

"I told you last night. I have some errands."

"What errands?"

She huffed and tossed back her head. "Joel called and said he'd found the bracelet I thought I'd lost. I need some things from the store. The bank. Maybe a little shopping. Errands. Why?"

He went to the fridge, yanked open the door, and stared sightlessly at its contents. "What do you want for lunch?"

"I'm not hungry."

Without protest, he snatched a chocolate nutrition drink off a shelf and propelled the door shut. "Here." He slammed the container down before her.

She dropped her hat and purse onto the table, then flounced into a chair. Reaching for the unappetizing beverage, she noticed a stack of tabloids. "What are these?"

"I thought I'd better show you before someone else did. I know how you are about your press."

She extracted a copy of *Sun* from the stack and studied the cover. Two obviously spliced photographs, one of her and one of Jordan, took up the majority of the front page. Above it, the bold headline: "Farin's Torment: 'If I can't have his love, I'll take his money!'"

Wild-eyed, she flipped through the pages and scanned the article. "Where did they get this? It says I'm suing him for half of everything!"

"Ah, yes. Let's overreact. After all, everyone knows these publications are *treasured* for their honesty." He plopped down opposite her at the table.

"What if he thinks it's true?"

A puff of air escaped his lips. "Jordan doesn't read this tripe. The only people who do are either at his beach house or my table. Now drink your lunch."

She sucked in her cheeks, snatched up the drink, and visually swept the table. "Where is it?"

"What?"

"You know what. My pill. Where is it?"

"After you put something on your stomach."

Her face tightened into a dark mask of annoyance. "Who are you, my mother?"

"Don't bark at me because a story in some rag offended you."

"Don't tell me how I feel."

"No worries there, love. Your feelings at any given moment are a complete mystery to the lot of us."

She leaned in on folded arms. "Which part bothers you more, Chris? Your inability to read my mind or your fear that, if you did, you'd find another man?"

The cutting remark sent him back in his chair. To her surprise, he did not respond with his typical British pomp. In fact, he did not respond at all.

Their eyes locked. His expression confirmed her poison arrow had hit its mark. Normally, she would regret the wound. But not today. Today, it galvanized her. His momentary weakness made her want to unleash her full fury upon him. Or maybe it was the irritation that he had refused to dole out her morning dose of temporary tranquility.

When he spoke at last, his sincerity disarmed her. "We've been living together for two months. In that time, our conversations have largely revolved around you, your problems, and your failed marriage. I know you don't feel the same way I feel about you...yet. But I'd think you'd see by now I'm doing my best to help you."

She swallowed, unsure how to respond.

"It's time to sign the papers. Let that be one of your 'errands' for the day."

She bristled, waving her hands head-to-waist as if for inspection. "I put on a sun dress today. A bright one at that. I'm going out instead of holing up here, away from the world. If you can't see the progress there, I don't know what to tell you. You need to stop trying to manipulate and control my feelings. We both know your end game here."

"End game?"

"Yes. End game." She slid her chair back, clutched her hat and bag, and stood. "Jordan and I are still married. If you find that so hard to deal with, maybe I should move out."

Chris set his jaw and rapid-tapped his foot on the floor. He looked at her, then away.

She turned and stomped toward the door, abandoning her nutrition shake on the table.

"So that's *it*?" he called after her.

She did not look back. "It is for now!"

CHAPTER 27

O NLY AFTER HER DRAMATIC EXIT did Farin realize she had neglected to arrange transportation. Returning inside to use the phone might weaken her position, and she had left her cell phone upstairs. She rummaged through her bag, peeking up periodically to make sure Chris was not staring at her from a window. When she found her keys, she headed to the garage.

Her first stop was the pharmacy, where she bullied the pharmacist into filling her prescription out of queue. No reason for Chris to pick up the medication. In fact, maybe the time had come to start taking her life into her own hands.

When she climbed back into her car, she realized she had not been followed. Not one car, van, motorcycle, or camera in sight. The exhilaration of the temporary illusion of privacy emboldened her.

She opened the prescription bottle and poured half its contents into her hand. Holding the small pile felt thrilling and oddly rebellious.

The little blue tablets with the heart-shaped hole in the center understood her. In fact, they might be the only things that did. Chris did not. Jordan did not. Bobby did not. Even Marci did not. But they did. And now, there was no one around to tell her how many she could take or how often they could dull her pain.

She swallowed one of the little gems with the bottled water she had purchased inside. Then, she swallowed another—just to spite her lover. She returned the rest to their plastic container, which she tossed in her purse before heading for the studio.

The warm, humid day told her to expect an afternoon thunderstorm. She engaged the air conditioner and flipped on the stereo. An all too rare sense of contentment settled upon her as she sang along with Robert Palmer's "You're Amazing." She grooved with the music, motored through the Key, across the Rickenbacker Causeway, and headed north on I-95.

By the time she pulled into the Standards parking lot, she enjoyed the beginning of a nice buzz. She decided to blow off the bank and the market. Thunderstorm or no, it was a great day for a drive down the Keys.

The radio stopped mid-beat when she killed the engine, but the music lingered in her mind like the trail of smoke from an extinguished matchstick. She exited her car, humming and bopping to "Impulsive" by Wilson Phillips.

"Hi, Farin."

She stifled a scream as she spun around. Jordan's sudden appearance set her heart thundering in her chest, obliterating her sedated high. She blinked, afraid she might be hallucinating.

He touched her shoulder. "Are you okay? I didn't mean to startle you."

"I..." But the words died in her throat. She noticed his keyring hooked around his ring finger where his wedding ring should be.

He stepped back and buried his hands in his pockets. His eyes avoided hers, as if he was disappointed, or repulsed, at the sight of her.

"What are you doing here, Jordan?"

"I'd called earlier to see if you were about. Joel said you'd be stopping by."

She squinted from beneath her hat. "Why didn't you call the house?"

He shook his head. "We've had about enough drama, haven't we?"

She drew her bag up in front of her like a safety blanket, clutching its soft leather in the vicinity of her prescription bottle inside. "I guess you're right."

"Anyway, I was cleaning up the other day and came across some of your books. There were some pictures. I divided them up. Hope you don't mind."

She shook her head.

He gestured over his shoulder with his thumb. "I have them here in a box. Thought I'd leave them for you if I missed you. It's rather warm. Care to get in and go through them? That is, if you're free."

She defied her hopeful heart and loathed its racing beat. Jordan had made his decision. The only thing its cursed thumping could accomplish was the depletion of the Valium's effect.

Easing into his passenger's seat, memories of happier times flooded her system until she felt their undertow might drown her. She fused her eyes and swallowed the pain, wishing she could chase it down with another pill.

Jordan grabbed the smaller of two boxes from his back seat, then hopped in front. He started the car to engaged the air conditioner.

Farin watched him rifle through the contents of the box, desperate to reach out and touch him. But she did not dare. Did Megan touch him now?

"Most are from around here," he said. "Some in Malibu."

"Such a long time ago."

He said nothing.

"What about the one of us at that restaurant in New York? Remember? Gosh, what was the name of that place?"

"Le Cirque."

"Le Cirque. That's right. It was beautiful."

"*You* were beau—" He cleared his throat and held up the picture. "It's here."

"What about that one Cheryl took of us at the beach house?"

His voice dropped to a nostalgic whisper as their eyes met. "I kept that one."

"Can I get a copy?"

The disappointment blanketing his face earlier transformed to one of painful regret.

"Did you have plans today?"

"None. Why?"

"Maybe we could go somewhere, get a drink. Maybe have a chat."

She willed herself not to appear too eager. Inside, her dulling nerves fired as if she had run a marathon. "I'd love to."

"Fancy any place in particular?"

"I was thinking earlier about driving down to the Keys."

He bobbed his head. "Sounds good."

"Can you give me a minute while I run inside?"

His soft green eyes searched hers. "I'll wait."

Farin rushed inside, fetched her bracelet from Trish, then dashed to the ladies' room. She removed her hat, fluffed her hair, freshened her makeup, and swallowed two Valium to make up for the two that had failed her earlier.

They headed for the Overseas Highway. Not long into their journey, the presaged thunderstorm hit. She peered out the passenger's window. Dark clouds churned, rumbling like an empty stomach. It dawned on her she had not eaten all day.

"You always did love your storms," Jordan observed with a gentle tug at the corner of his mouth. His tone warmed with nostalgia.

"I do," she said, rapt as peals of thunder sounded in the distance.

When the sky began to weep, Jordan engaged the wipers. "The sunset'll be brilliant tonight. All these clouds?"

"Like the rain's clearing our path. Making things clean. Fresh." The words no sooner left her mouth than she realized how ridiculous they sounded.

Chest out and smiling, he drove on. His left wrist draped over the top of the steering wheel; his right arm rested on the middle console. "You should turn on some music."

She dialed the radio to WWFT, the new Spanish Tropical station, figuring the neutrality would serve them well. She did not want to chance hearing her—or Jordan's—recent single. Not today. She had lied to the reporters that night at the benefit. Everything was about competition, even if you loved that competition. Especially when they had replaced you.

The image of Megan Price stole into her thoughts. Were they cheating? On Megan? On Chris? Technically, they were still married. Could any one of the four of them complain?

She stared down at his arm, battling the urge to take his hand.

It would not do to dwell on matters beyond her control, she decided. She concentrated, instead, on the waters of Florida Bay and the authentic tackiness of aged beachside establishments bordering either side of the two-lane highway. The meds began kicking in again. She welcomed the suppression of her mind. This time, she would not let anything, or anyone, kill her buzz.

They overshot Key Largo by twenty minutes and pulled into Lorelei's on Islamorada.

Jordan eyed the establishment as they parked. "I'd heard of this place and always wanted to go. Tell me you're hungry. We'll have dinner."

A lazy, accepting grin was all she could muster. She dared not hope. He had offered nothing but a boxful of memories. Those were the past, and he had yet to discuss a future—his, hers, or theirs.

Patrons recognized them the moment they arrived. Some gawked and pointed. Some leaned in to whisper to their dining companions. A couple of teenagers let out muffled squeals before their parents could hush them.

Jordan and Farin smiled, nodding politely as he pulled out a seat for her at a table near the edge of the open-air cabana, out of the rain but perfectly positioned for the restaurant's nightly sunset celebrations.

They ordered sea breezes, then signed autographs as they waited for their drinks.

"Ginny hated people coming up to us when we'd go out," Jordan told her, flashing his famous, wide smile as he returned a signed napkin and a pen to a breathless young fan.

Farin donned her professional mask, beaming with glazed eyes as they posed for a picture with another couple. "It's okay," she said when they left. "We can't do what we do and expect complete privacy. I like interacting with fans. They're a lot better than reporters."

The novelty of their presence soon abated, passing with the storm. A stream of diners arrived as the setting sun broke through clouds, filling Lorelei's beachside tables to capacity. Together, they all enjoyed a sunset as exquisite as Jordan had predicted on the drive down. Orange and yellow hues fled the bruised semidarkness. They drank, danced, and made lively banter while awaiting their meal.

Jordan ordered the Alaskan Snow Crab platter; Farin, the New York strip. They shared both, laughing as they ate over less troubled moments in their life together. And somehow, they put their past behind them, if only for a while, if only for that moment.

When Oleta Adams's "Get Here" played over the restaurant speakers, Jordan stood and led Farin back onto the dance floor. He encircled her waist and drew her close. She wrapped her thin arms around his neck. They swayed together to the sad piano, a single body gliding ghost-like across the floor. She buried her face into the nape of his neck. He rested his head atop hers.

Farin felt blunted and euphoric—or maybe it was the alcohol, the music, the laughter, the feel of Jordan's hands on her body. Sound and motion decelerated, dreamlike, as he moved her around the dance floor. And what a welcome change from her nightmares. Public fascination sated, the crowd of diners left them alone, safe inside their bubble.

"I've wanted to talk ever since I saw you last weekend," he confided as they finished their meal and the last of several drinks. "I'm worried about you. You don't look good."

A flash of recollection wove in, then out, of her mind. Jordan had looked concerned back at the studio. But their night had gone so well, she could not bear it to end on a negative note. She reached across the table to finger the chain of his gold record necklace with delicate fingers. "Wanna know a secret?"

He leaned forward, folding his elbows atop the table. "Tell me."

"All these months, I believed as long as you wore this necklace, everything would work out. Even if you don't wear your wedding ring."

He repositioned himself and sat back, severing their connection. "I see you and Chris are getting on well."

She stared off at the bar. "It's not the same."

At last, they returned to the car. Jordan held his hand at the middle of Farin's back as they walked. She faltered but hoped he did not notice.

"You okay?" he asked, buckling his seat.

She flipped down the visor to check her face. "I might've had a little too much to drink."

"Better not chance it. I'll drive you back to Chris's. You can get your car tomorrow."

The complication of returning to Chris's in Jordan's car did not bear immediate consideration. She would burn that bridge when she reached it.

Driving back to Miami, an audible silence enveloped them. Tension filled the air, as if any sudden noise or movement would sever the evening's enchantment. Farin nestled into the familiar comfort of his leather seat and stared out at the night, hypnotized by the rippling glow of lights reflecting on the water.

Too soon, they reached the village of Key Biscayne.

Her stomach flipped when Jordan bypassed Chris's place, continuing down Harbor and then turning right onto Matheson. He turned into his driveway amid an immediate hail of bulb-flashes as the paparazzi sprung to life.

"What are we doing?"

"Come in. I'll get that picture you wanted."

He unlocked the front door and dropped his keys on the entry table.

Farin stood inside as if glued in place. Despite her self-admonitions, she found herself welcoming back the hope she had banished earlier.

"Have a seat." He poured them each a brandy, then jogged upstairs to get her picture.

She scanned the premises as she ventured forward, amazed so little had changed. The furniture configuration had not been altered. The same prints peppered the wall. Her plants, now taller and fuller, remained exactly where she had placed them. Yet, despite the preserved state, an air of loneliness hung in the room. There was something intangible and unsettling about a house once occupied by a couple, now divided.

At least she had not discovered any hint of Megan Price.

Jordan returned and sat beside her on the sofa. The absence of strangers left them sipping uneasily at their nightcaps.

When he turned to her, his face strained with unanswered questions. "I need to know why you left me on our wedding night."

She searched his sad eyes, too ashamed to tell him the truth and too numb to lie. "A couple of reasons, I guess. Does it make any difference anymore?"

He shook his head. "C'mon, Farin."

She pinched the bridge of her nose and tried to clear the thickening fog of her brain. "People were inside my head, Jordan. People telling me you were marrying me because of the baby. That you felt sorry for me. I figured, if it was true, I'd be doing us both a favor by leaving."

"*Who*? What 'people' would say such a thing? Was it Chris?"

Part of her believed coming clean would save their marriage. But she had believed that lie before, the night he walked out. In reality, the truth could only make things worse.

Before her sozzled faculties could register what was happening, they were in each other's arms. Jordan kissed and caressed her body as he guided her down from the sofa.

They made love slowly, tenderly. Like hearing a treasured, long-forgotten tune, she recalled each movement as a melody, every moan the beat of a drum, and every touch a string section of heightened sensation. Alcohol and Valium blended, sending her consciousness ever upward, until she did not exist outside the music. They had become one and the same.

Laying together in the afterglow, she fantasized about their future. Soon, they would retire to their bed. In the morning, she would call Chris to break the news of their reconciliation. Jordan would arrange for the return of her belongings. She would be home at last.

Rolling over to cuddle into his chest, she found him sitting up. She reached for him. "Let's not go upstairs yet. I want to lay here in your arms a little while longer."

He stared ahead with blank eyes, skinning on his shirt and fastening its buttons. "I'm sorry."

"Sorry for what?" She smiled lazily and rose to kiss him, her naked body flushed with sweat.

He pulled away.

"What's the matter?"

He gathered her clothes and handed them to her.

Farin's eyes bulged in panicked confusion as she covered her body, as if she should feel ashamed. "What's wrong?"

He faced her, regret lining his brow. "Maybe it was the alcohol, I don't know. I must have lost my head somewhere in all the memories. This doesn't change my mind."

"*Lost your head?*" She rose on unsteady legs and hurled her clothes at the sofa. "But Jordan, this only proves—"

He slipped on his socks, then his shoes. "I left my wallet upstairs. I'll go get it and drive you home."

Farin shivered as she dressed, tangled up in anger, humiliation, and the inability to focus through her haze. She wobbled to the entryway and retrieved her purse with trembling hands, then staggered back to the living room to fetch her brandy. A muffled, far-off echo of a voice shouted through the thick insulation of benzos protecting her thoughts from reaching her brain. Beth O'Conner's voice taunted her. *You're not a victim.*

She retrieved the prescription bottle from her purse. "Shut up, Momma! You weren't here then. I don't need you now."

When she bent down to sit on the sofa, she missed the edge and landed with a thud onto the floor. It took three attempts to uncap the bottle before she finally managed to open it. She poured the pills into her cupped hand, staring at them longingly, as if they were old friends.

Two half-empty glasses of brandy sat before her on the table. She picked up the one without lipstick stains and sloshed its amber contents into the other. Then, she chased down the handful of pills with the entire glass.

The sound of Jordan's footsteps descending the staircase brought her to her feet. She met him at the base of the steps, pitching forward slightly. She shook her finger at him. "Did you stop loving me?"

He stopped before her and raised his hands to his waist. The pity in his stare told her she did not want to know the answer.

"I need to ask you something, Farin. And I want you to know I'm not trying to hurt you."

She jutted her chin at him. Inside, she begged her stomach to hurry up and digest its contents. Maybe she should have chewed up her little gems before swallowing.

"It's about the papers."

"What about them?" she slurred, chin quivering.

"Have you had a chance to send them to your lawyer?"

"What's the rush?"

He slouched and stared at the floor. "We should probably move things along."

"Why? Are things with *Megan Price* getting serious?"

When he did not answer, she filled in the blanks. She swallowed the lump in her throat and realized her mouth was dry, so she teetered to the wet bar and poured herself another brandy.

***

Jordan's mind raced as he drove Farin home. He castigated himself for his behavior. Ben had underplayed Farin's mental and emotional instability. How could he allow himself to act so recklessly?

The possibility his actions might have been born of some sick attempt at revenge riddled him with guilt. He did not want to believe himself capable of such cruelty.

But he, too, had believed they reconnected tonight. Only after their lovemaking, as they lay together, did painful reality seize him. She had been with Chris while she was with him. When she left their home, she went to him. They lived together now. His own brother had heard his wife's sighs of pleasure, had touched her downy skin, and had undoubtedly lost himself inside her just as he had done so many times.

Jordan tried to reconcile his conflict. Once upon a time, he had promised he would forgive Farin anything—and he could. But forget about all that had transpired? It was too soon. Those wounds had yet to heal.

Sometimes, there was no going back.

***

Chris stood waiting on the porch when they drove up. He looked astonished and wounded at the sight of Jordan's car. Normally, Farin would have fallen apart by now. But not this time. The last brandy had tipped the scales. She welcomed the comfort of an endless sleep.

"I'll walk up with you and explain," Jordan said.

He grabbed the box from his back seat and headed up the front steps, Farin beside him. Jordan stopped to confront Chris, but Farin stumbled past them both and disappeared inside.

Jordan set the box on the steps. He held open his hands. "Don't be angry. We had a couple drinks. I gave back some of her things."

"And then you took her home for a courtesy fuck, right? What? A little something out of the Vicomte de Valmont's playbook? Don't you realize how buggered up she is? Every time she so much as hears your bloody name, I spend a week bringing her back to reality! Now, you made it clear you were through a long time ago. That's fine with me, but don't think you can come around and wax nostalgic every time your dick gets hard!"

Chris braced himself for a reply. Jordan set his jaw, uncut hatred etched across his face. But when he said nothing, Chris mistook the silence for submission. Emboldened, he pressed on.

"She's with *me* now," he hissed viciously, "where she should have been all along!" His eyes seared as he backed his brother down the front steps. His insides twisted with a fear he had never known—fear of losing Farin forever.

Then suddenly, Jordan stopped backing away. He grabbed Chris by the front of his shirt. Chris stood open-mouthed, soundless at the unexpected turn of tide.

Through grit teeth, Jordan growled, "I could kill you for what you've done to us—what you did behind my back! I'd have never done something like that to my own brother! How do you live with yourself? *Huh*? How do you sleep at night?"

Chris was dumbstruck, stunned as Jordan stood up to his bullying. All their lives, he had asserted his will on his younger brother without the slightest recrimination.

Jordan's fists shook the fabric of Chris's shirt before releasing it, pushing against his chest. He stepped back and Chris stared at him, wide-eyed.

"Let's settle things once and for all, shall we? She's all yours for as long as you can hold onto her." In an incongruously conversational tone, sounding somehow dissonant after the harsh words that had filled the evening stillness, he added, "You're right about one thing. I am through. With *both* of you."

Hot tears of frustration lined Chris's eyes as he watched his brother speed away. In that second, something told him their lives had changed. And it was a signpost on the road of life Chris did not see coming until it whizzed by him at blinding speed.

As for Farin, Jordan was right. Chris knew he could not hold onto her much longer. He had made a devil's deal to convince her to move in with him in the first place. In the end, all he had gained was her body—and for the first time in his life, it was not enough.

He tarried outside, pacing the veranda for long minutes as he collected himself. Once he crossed his threshold, the second half of this wretched night would doubtless commence. With few options, he considered how best to proceed. She would ridicule any attempt to pretend nothing had happened. Confrontation would drive her away.

In the end, he made the hard choice to continue his present course: deny the pain.

He surmised Jordan had treated her with the same contempt he had just unleashed upon him. Any wrong step and she would break into a thousand pieces. Gluing her back together would take weeks. For both their sakes, he needed to project his ability to understand. If not, he might not hold onto her another day.

He blew out a huge, open-mouthed breath, then stepped inside. Closing his eyes and inclining his head, he listened for any sign of her. When he heard nothing, he figured she had gone to bed. Instinct told him to follow, make sure she was okay. But he had learned his lesson. She would surface in her own time. Hours. Days. Weeks. Who knew?

He proceeded to the dining room and cleared the dinner he had prepared them—a sort of peace offering after their earlier disagreement. He cleaned up the kitchen, sealing the untouched rice in a container but tossing the no longer fresh salmon and a wilted salad. Once finished, he set the alarm and headed upstairs.

Halfway up the steps, Farin lay face down in a puddle of vomit.

He dashed to her side, shouted her name, and turned her over, using his fingers to clear her airway. Flashbacks of Faith's attempted suicide assailed him.

All attempts to resuscitate Farin proved futile. When he touched her neck to feel for a pulse, every ounce of blood in his body turned cold.

***

Jordan's telephone rang three times before he picked up. His voice was thin and raspy. "Who is this?"

"Did I wake you?"

The acrimonious tone sent him upright. He switched on his bedside lamp and rubbed his eyes. "It's three thirty in the bloody morning. We've said all there is to say."

"It's Farin," he said, as if he were about to announce the end of the world. "I figured you'd rather hear it from me than the morning news. I haven't called Ben yet. After you left, I found her on the stairway."

Jordan's eyes flew open. "Where are you?"

"Mercy Hospital. You'd better get down here."

A wave of nausea rendered him speechless.

"How many did you let her take, Jordan?"

He slammed the telephone down in his brother's ear.

CHAPTER 28

CHERYL LEANED AGAINST THE BEDROOM doorframe, arms folded across her chest. She watched her husband prepare for their daily pilgrimage to Mercy Hospital. He dressed conservatively as he did in all circumstances—even to spend hours occupying semi-comfortable wood and cloth reception chairs, waiting for Farin to wake up.

Ben tucked his shirt into his slacks, fastened his belt, straightened his collar, and shook his full brown mane into place. He noticed Cheryl in the bureau mirror. She smiled as she approached from behind and wrapped her arms around his waist. He checked his watch. "You're not dressed, love. I told Jordan we'd meet him in the cafeteria at eight."

She squeezed him gently. "I'm not going with you today."

He twisted around to face her. "Why?"

"The boys need some mum time, I think. Besides, fourteen days? It's too much. I'm not heartless, but after yesterday..."

"We have to think of Jordan. And Chris as well."

Her body stiffened. "It's bad enough with the press camped about, making a spectacle of us as we come and go, but watching you and that security guard fighting to separate them? It broke my heart. I cannae do it anymore. What are we to tell our boys?" She pressed into and held him tight.

He rubbed the middle of her back. "It's okay. I'll go."

"I'm afraid our family will never be the same."

"They love each other, even if neither one of them would admit it right now. This business we're in doesn't help. It's never bothered Chris—maybe because he's suited for it. Jordan adapted fairly well, though it takes its toll on him. But Farin...it's destroyed her."

Cheryl peered up at him with admiring eyes. "You really care about her."

"She's a mixed-up kid. I can't fault her for it. Hopefully, she'll realize what she's done to herself and finally get some help."

"My husband, the optimist." She moved to her nightstand and grabbed a tissue, then dabbed her eyes.

"Did you call Marci back last night?"

"Aye. She keeps insisting she wants to fly out. But what's the point? Until something changes, what can any of us do?"

***

"What do you mean I can't see her?" Bobby demanded of the nurse outside Farin's room. "I was here yesterday!"

The plain-faced forty-something was unmoved. "Doctor's orders, Mr. Lockhardt. We've had some trouble with her family. Dr. Clark's suspended all visitation."

Bobby planted his hands on the nursing station counter. "I'm no threat to her."

The nurse pinched her lips closed. She had rounds, and this man had become a nuisance. They all had—all these puffed-up celebrity types running around the hospital, thinking they owned everyone and everything they saw.

In the twenty years she had worked for Mercy General, she had never been involved in a case with so many parties, with such varied agendas. The media camped out in the parking lot day and night. Concerned fans jammed their switchboard. The family had created a disturbing atmosphere within the hospital's normally calm interior.

Uncompromising, she met his baby blues. His left eye spasmed under her stare. "We'll let you know if there's any change."

Bobby leaned in, his breath hot on her face. She noted the smell of coffee and peppermint breath freshener. "You have ten minutes to let me see her. Otherwise, I'll go over your head."

"I don't make the rules, Mr. Lockhardt."

He turned and stomped down the hallway, stabbing the air with his finger as he retreated. "Ten minutes! I'll be in the cafeteria!"

Downstairs, Bobby waded through milling visitors and hospital staff in their scrubs, procuring coffee and breakfast foods. He spotted Ben at a table in the far corner of the cafeteria's dining area. A morose Chris slouched beside him. One look at the bruise covering his swollen cheek and right eye pieced the puzzle together. His breathing looked strained and shallow.

"Nice shiner," Bobby said, joining them. "Jordan look any better?"

"Bugger off." Chris shifted uncomfortably in his seat. A flicker of pain skittered across his features. "Any word?"

"Not yet. I wish you two had taken it somewhere else. It would've saved me some trouble."

Chris glowered at his younger brother's arrival.

Bobby snickered, disgusted as he beheld Jordan's split, swollen lip. "Quite the pair. But did either of you consider what this could do to Farin?"

Long minutes passed. Jordan and Chris avoided eye contact. Bobby divided his attention between them, debating with himself who had received the worst of the encounter.

Dr. Clark emerged at last. He bypassed the usual pleasantries and took a seat. "I understand Mr. Lockhardt's responsible for this meeting. Let me make it clear then, sir. I won't have my staff threatened. As it is, I'd planned on updating everyone after morning rounds. Bottom line, her status hasn't changed. Her vitals are stronger, but she remains unresponsive. All we can do at this point is wait."

Ben sat sandwiched between his feuding siblings, offering little to the conversation as Dr. Clark updated them. His wife's absence distracted him as much as his brother's behavior yesterday had left him agitated. The spectacle was unacceptable. Worse, undignified. No wonder Cheryl had begged off.

Mercy Hospital had become their second home over the last couple of weeks. Each day, they sacrificed their privacy to perform this macabre dance before a media machine hell-bent on devouring them whole. The hospital had constructed a security station to ensure visitor-only access to parking. Another security team redirected fans gathering to organize vigils on hospital grounds. Three days ago, a reporter had disguised himself as a doctor and approached them for comments. Administration had the man arrested. Jordan had called Ross Alexander, informing him he intended to press charges. The hospital had started double-checking badges and identification for everyone entering the facility.

An occasional interruption notwithstanding, it had been the four of them. Intermittently, Bobby Lockhardt. Cheryl had joined them each day while the boys were at school. She made food runs, worked with faculty to redistribute the steady arrival of flowers from Farin's fans to hospice patients, and even managed to keep Jordan and Chris from bickering.

Until yesterday, Jordan and Chris had contented themselves by staring at one another, communicating silent threats and wordless ultimatums. They arrived at the hospital earlier every day, as if participating in some bizarre competition. When visiting hours ended, neither wanted to leave before the other. Yesterday afternoon, things exploded.

It began in the fourth floor waiting area beside the staircase adjacent to the elevators, near a set of vending machines. Ben sat rereading the same dog-eared six-month-old issue of *Woman's Day* for the third time. He had become an expert on why women needed proper life insurance.

Chris had risen, presumably to get a soft drink. Jordan had stalked after him. Chris fed the machine its tribute, scarcely taking his eyes off his younger brother.

Jordan had asked, "What are you looking at?" or words to that effect.

With that, the games were afoot.

Chris punched Jordan in the mouth, bloodying his lip. Jordan grabbed Chris by the front of his shirt and flung him into the soda machine. Chris hit full force, the crash echoing through the stairwell and into the waiting room before he fell to his knees. Jordan kicked him—twice.

At that moment, Ben realized the scene he witnessed actually happened. He tossed aside his magazine and dashed over.

Jordan tried to kick Chris in the face. Chris jerked sideways and grabbed Jordan's foot, upending him. Jordan sprawled backward onto the hard vinyl floor, banging his head and left elbow with astounding force. Chris surged on top of him. They grappled, frothing obscenities.

Ben arrived in short order but had no idea where to start. Cheryl stood outside the waiting room, her eyes enormous. Out of his peripheral vision, Ben caught sight of a security guard on the run.

Jordan shot his left hand out. He reached inside the vending machine tray to grab the soda can. He used it to bludgeon Chris in the face, hitting him squarely on the ridge of his right cheekbone, then the ridge of his right eye. When Chris staggered backward, Jordan struck him again, this time in the ribs. The can ruptured at the force of the blow, spewing soda all over them.

"What's the craic!" Cheryl screamed, regressing into her less Americanized Scottish dialect, something she did only under extreme stress. "Patch aht, ya gits!"

The security guard tackled Chris, pinning him to the elevator doors. Ben put Jordan in a full nelson but struggled to contain him. His little brother squirmed against him, lunging toward Chris with great force. For a moment, Ben worried he might break free.

Face flushed, eyes blazing, and bleeding from the mouth, Jordan spat, "I'll kill you!"

Ben willed away the memory, banishing it to the darkest part of his mind. One by one, he looked askance at his brothers. Chris had suffered contused ribs. His bruised cheek and blackened eye distorted his features. Jordan's swollen lip had required stitches, though he had refused the staff's initial attempts to help him.

The foot of pride, he thought, recalling a Dylan tune.

Bobby stabbed the heavy laminate table with his index finger. "I want to see her."

"I realize you all care about Farin, but none of you seem to understand the gravity of the situation. She *overdosed*." Dr. Clark steepled his fingers and glared at the three men in turn. "Based on the information you've supplied, I'd say it was intentional. Farin's been headed in this direction for some time now. I'll talk to her personally if—*when* she comes to. I'd imagine we're looking at extended psychiatric treatment."

"*What*?" Bobby bolted to his feet.

Chris winced and shifted uncomfortably in his chair.

Dr. Clark regarded him, nonplussed. "Farin appears to have been in a deep state of depression for years." He looked at Jordan. "The nightmares. You say she's had them for some time."

Jordan's words bubbled through his swollen lips. "Ever since her father died."

"I spoke to her friend in California and dug a little further. Apparently, Farin's maternal family has a history of depressive illness and alcoholism. Without proper treatment, there could be a next time. And next time, she might not be so lucky."

Ben asked, "What can we do to help?"

The doctor scratched his jaw, averting his eyes from any one person as he answered diplomatically. "I understand some of you have, shall we say, escalating personal conflicts. The pressure of these conflicts, coupled with her depression and career demands, have magnified the problem. I'd urge you to resolve your differences."

"When can I take her home?" Chris asked, a sharp edge to his tone. He skidded his chair back slowly, in case his brother attacked him again. In a way, he almost hoped for it.

Jordan sneered at him.

Ben looked up at the ceiling and shook his head.

"Best case scenario, she wakes up with no long-term neurological deficits. But she hasn't even regained consciousness. It won't be any time soon. After her physical recovery, I'll be transferring her to U of M Psych."

"The hell you will!" Bobby exclaimed, drawing the attention of nearby diners away from their hot meals and drinks. "Never, and I mean *never*, will I allow that! Do you realize who she is?"

The doctor continued, unfazed. "There are laws governing the treatment of persons deemed to be a danger to themselves. No one is above that law. Furthermore, *sir*, I don't relish the idea of seeing her back here again, or worse, dead because we didn't do everything in our power to help her."

"So, what are we looking at?" Chris pressed, his voice strained as he fought to breathe through the pain in his chest. "Days? Weeks?"

Jordan slumped in his seat. He stared at the doctor, then each of his brothers, as Chris demanded the earliest possible release date and Bobby raised all the objections he did not. His battered body ached. His conscience tortured him. More than anyone seated around this table, he bore the blame for his wife's condition.

Bobby's frustration manifested itself in angry, intermittent waves of his hands. "Farin doesn't need a shrink! All she needs is for Fric and Frac here to stop riding her like a seesaw!" He paused and rubbed the back of his neck. Calmer, he said, "You're not going to lock her up in some nut house because she's experiencing a bad divorce. She's a valuable LSI commodity. Our corporate property from her voice to her face to her thoughts."

She was also his best friend. And he had fallen desperately in love with her.

"Spoken like a true Lockhardt," Chris wheezed.

Under normal circumstances, Bobby would have let the remark slide. But these were not normal circumstances. "Spare me the moral imperatives, Grant. At least my sole motivation isn't in my pants."

"Not unless you check with Daddy first," Chris countered, unmoved.

Bobby resisted the urge to leap across the table and finish the job Jordan had started. Instead, he addressed Dr. Clark. "Thanks for your time. You'll be hearing from my attorney."

Twenty-four hours later, Lockhardt Sound's executive team descended upon Miami, escorting one Lionel Childs, M.D. to Mercy Hospital.

The septuagenarian physician had worked exclusively for Jameson Lockhardt since the day LSI had filed its articles of incorporation in Delaware in 1973. He treated the administrative staff, management, many of its artists, and had seen Bobby since before he started college.

For all his advanced years, he stood tall, not stooped, with broad shoulders and a hefty paunch to his belly. His nose sat large on his clean-shaven face. His voice boomed when he spoke. Slicked back silver hair and beady, wide-set black eyes accented his mafioso-like appearance. He looked like a thug, save his credentials and white lab coat. Keen-minded and energetic, he was more than capable of handling Farin—and anyone who tried to stand in his way.

The moment their highly polished Italian loafers hit the hospital floor, Bobby took charge. Head high, he marched their small group through security and to the Guest Services Desk. "We have a ten o'clock appointment with Ms. Leifson in Administration."

The volunteer smiled cordially, made a call, then gave them directions. "She said to let you know Dr. Clark will be in attendance."

He harrumphed, stepped aside, and extended his arm to the others. "This way, gentlemen."

When they reached the elevator, Jameson lifted a hand. "We'll take it from here, son. You go check on Farin. We'll meet you there shortly."

Bobby glanced first at Ross, then at Dr. Childs, and then finally back at his father. "But Dad..."

Jameson stepped away from the others, motioning him aside. His voice dropped to near inaudible levels. "Don't overplay your hand, son. This is *your* win. No one involved will question another word you say. They'll see you have the full power of LSI at your disposal. Take that. Be happy with it."

Bobby accompanied his wounded pride to the fourth floor, chose a seat farthest from the Grant brothers, and waited. He watched chart-toting nurses weave in and out of patient rooms while cafeteria staff collected empty breakfast trays and slid them onto a mobile, multi-shelf cart. A candy striper straightened magazine racks and picked up abandoned napkins and Styrofoam cups. Everyone had a job. Everyone but him.

He peered down the hall at Farin's closed door, his emotions ranging from fear to fury. Except for work matters, she had not called him once since moving in with Chris. To her credit, she had spared him certain humiliation that day at her place, pretending not to notice his advances. He supposed that made her a better friend to him than he had been to her.

And anyway, what could he have done if Farin *had* returned his feelings? Her internal battle between devotion to Jordan and attraction to

Chris was insignificant compared to the primary issue separating them. Even if she did feel for him as he did for her, nothing could come of it. His lot had been cast decades ago.

A scuffle at the nursing station caught his attention. He looked over in time to catch Dr. Clark's unmasked agitation. The physician rummaged angrily through a stack of charts. A nearby nurse reached over to assist him, but he jerked away and snapped, "Just make the change!"

With timid movements, she located the desired chart and handed it to him. He flung it open and scribbled notes while the nurse crept to the white board hanging on the wall beyond their station. A list of patient names and the names of their attending physicians had been marked in dry erase pen. Next to Farin's name, the nurse erased Dr. Clark's name and replaced it with Dr. Childs's.

Clark slapped the file shut and stomped down the hallway, chin raised as he returned his pen to his lab coat pocket. He ignored the three men striding opposite him toward the waiting room.

Dr. Childs introduced himself to the shift nurses as Jameson and Ross approached Bobby. They acknowledged Ben, Chris, and Jordan with a curt nod, then Jameson huddled with his son.

Ross balanced his briefcase on top of a chair back. He opened it briefly to arrange some documents. When Chris stood up and moved toward the nursing staff, he followed.

Bobby asked his father, "What happened?"

Jameson maintained his poker face. "You asked for assistance. You got it."

"But how..."

"I'm afraid we need to head back to New York straightaway. Care to accompany us for lunch before we take off?"

"Is Childs staying?"

Jameson nodded once. "Is that a yes for lunch?"

"When can I see Farin?"

"Whenever you wish. You'll find the visitation list permanently amended."

From behind him, Bobby heard Chris shout, "What's *that* supposed to mean?"

Several nurses, Dr. Childs, and Ross attempted to quiet him, reminding him there were other patients on the floor trying to rest.

Bobby glanced back at his father. A diabolical grin lifted his upper lip above his elongated canines. Behind him, the elevator dinged its arrival.

Chris stalked to reach Jameson before the doors closed. Ben moved to intercept him, determined to deescalate an already combustible situation. Fortunately, Chris's injuries prohibited meaningful protest.

Arms stiff at his sides, he shouted past Ben to the old man. "You can't keep me from seeing her!"

Ross inserted himself between Chris and Ben until the elder stepped back. "Sit this one out, Chris. I'll have them update you on any changes."

He inhaled a shallow, painful breath. "You can't do this!"

Ross spoke low and candidly. "You know Jameson almost as well as I do. You never should have crossed him. You can't say you weren't warned."

***

Consciousness returned in waves. At first, Farin's entire body felt numb, her lids so heavy she could not lift them. Eventually, she pried them open. She blinked several times, as if it were a learned thing. Through strained focus, she found herself squinting into a set of fluorescent lights. Ceiling lights.

Smells came next. Scents of alcohol, antiseptic, and sanitized linens. She lay immobile in a hospital bed, her mind as deadened as her body, attempting to reason or recollect anything beyond her name.

A thin, stiff, scratchy cotton blanket covered her body, filling her nostrils with the pungent stink of bleach. She tried to lift her hands to remove the vile fabric from beneath her chin but could not move her arms. When she endeavored to raise her knee up to pull the offending cover down by hooking her toes into it, she found her legs likewise immobile. A cry for help choked out, a squeaky, strangled whisper against her burning throat. Panic seized her.

Then, she heard voices. Female voices.

"Can you believe Childs just waltzed in and took over?"

"Hmph! You should've been here when the brothers were fighting!"

Farin's hollow stomach flipped.

Once she could focus, she scanned her surroundings. A cubicle curtain partially surrounded her bed. A wide ledge ran the length of the large, shaded window, teeming with flower bouquets and unopened cards. She spotted the top of a metal clipboard hanging off the footboard of her bed. To her left, an IV pole suspended a saline bag. It dripped into clear tubing that disappeared beneath her blanket. Beyond the pole, she saw a panel of lights on the wall. A clip fastened a call button to the railing of the bed, but she could not move her arms to reach it.

Her memory strained with disjointed images. The Keys. Jordan. Dancing. Making love on the living room carpet.

The pills.

Farin squirmed until the blanket slid to the floor. The sight of restraints binding her arms and legs paralyzed her with fear. She struggled against them, then noticed the right arm restraint had been improperly fastened. Several grunting, tugging minutes later, her wrist pulled free. Once liberated, the rest was simple.

Slowly, she edged her legs off the side of the bed. They dangled lifelessly as she lunged forward to grab hold of the IV pole, which she employed to support her atrophied leg muscles as she dragged herself to the door. Her mind scurried from one unclear thought to another. How long had she been unconscious? Was Dr. Childs in Florida or was she in New York? Who was fighting?

"Mrs. Grant!" exclaimed the nurse who arrived to find Farin propped helplessly against the wall. "Let me help you!"

Too weak to fight, she tried to speak as the nurse situated her back into bed. Her voice croaked out, "Please...husband. Where...?"

The nurse studied her watch as she checked her pulse, then dragged the flimsy blankets back over her body and tucked them in on both sides. "Mercy Hospital. Now lie down and rest while I get your doctor. Try not to talk. You were intubated, so your throat's probably still sore."

The nurse scurried out of the room. Farin heard her conversation. "I don't know how she got out of those restraints!"

"Childs checked out about ten minutes ago," came another voice. "Page Dr. Clark. He's familiar with her case and he's on call tonight."

Farin grew more frightened every minute. *Intubated*? Had they damaged her larynx? Had they ended her career?

The only telephone in the room hung on the wall by the door.

Before she could sit up again, the door opened.

A smiling, bespectacled, dark-haired man entered the room. "I'm Dr. Clark."

"Why...here?" Farin's ragged voice trembled.

Dr. Clark bent down and flashed a penlight in each of her eyes. "Your brother-in-law brought you in two weeks ago. You'd taken an impressive quantity of depressants."

"*Weeks*?" Her eyes flashed in panic.

He checked her pulse, listened to her chest, and squeezed, thumped, and prodded around the area of her bowels and kidneys.

Farin endured the examination passively and with marked humiliation.

He took her hand and gently pressed the tips of her fingers. "Looks like you're in pretty good shape. Can you drink some water for me?"

She nodded.

Dr. Clark retrieved a glass of room temperature water and held it to her lips. She sucked greedily at the tepid liquid until he pulled the cup away. "Take it slow. If you drink too much, it could be painful."

The water soothed its way down her grateful throat. She looked up at the doctor with pleading eyes. "...sing again?"

He rested a tender hand on hers. "We'll run some tests tomorrow. For now, rest and try to limit your speech."

"...husband."

"I'm afraid visiting hours are over. What's the last thing you remember?"

A hint of condescension in Dr. Clark's voice unnerved her. "...blackout?"

"You were comatose." He withdrew a syringe from his lab coat pocket.

Her eyes widened. "Coma? What...doing?"

"It's a sedative to help you relax. You can speak with Dr. Childs in the morning after you've rested."

"Just woke...!" She inched away.

He shot the medication into her IV.

"What...doing?" She slurred as her mind slipped into the warm folds of sleep. "Don't...! Why...?"

Dr. Clark dispassionately secured the restraints. "They're for your own good. We don't want you to hurt yourself."

Farin struggled until sleep claimed her. "Must...dreaming," she mumbled aloud. "Jordan..."

Dr. Childs stood over her when she woke the next morning. Fearful at the realization that the night before had been real, the sight of someone familiar relieved her.

The restraints were gone.

Without judgment or condescension, Dr. Childs explained the last two weeks of her life.

"Where's Jordan?" She rubbed her throat, relieved she could verbalize an entire sentence.

He patted her arm. "Your family's been notified about your status. I know you're anxious to see everyone, but I'd like to run some tests today and hold off the celebrations 'til tomorrow. Don't worry—the world won't stop turning before then."

The next morning Farin woke to find Chris seated beside her, holding her hand. It was hauntingly reminiscent of another morning in another hospital on another continent.

He offered a broken smile through puffy eyes. "Don't ever scare me like that again."

She lifted his hand to her cheek. "It was an accident."

He squeezed gently. "I should've taken better care of you. I'll do better from now on."

Farin brushed his wavy hair away from his face to inspect the fading signs of his black eye. "I heard something about a fight. It was you, wasn't it? And Jordan. Is he here?"

His jaw tensed. "I haven't seen him in a couple of days."

She studied the dozens of bouquets filling her room. A bouquet of yellow jonquils sat prominently upon the window ledge. She smiled weakly. "How come you never include a card?"

"Do I need to?" He gave her a lopsided grin.

"I guess not."

He looked down at the floor. "You know, those bloody things are only in season during the spring. I nearly had to buy a greenhouse and hire my own personal staff to ensure I had a supply when I needed them."

Farin's expression turned serious. "Really?"

He lifted his eyes to hers. They stared silently at one another for several moments. When he looked away, he checked his watch. "When Bobby brought in his mighty entourage, I was ousted from the guest list. In order to keep things friendly, I have to go." He kissed her hand. "I'll check in on you soon."

Bobby visited later that afternoon, bearing an assortment of tropical flowers. She smiled when he entered the room, which he took as a good sign. He squeezed the flowers into the last bit of empty space along the window ledge, then greeted Farin with a hug. The feel of her frail arms around his neck brought his senses to life. He fought the urge to kiss her cheek, settling instead for a passing whiff of fresh soap from an earlier shower.

"I could kill you for scaring me like this," he scolded, sitting beside her.

She straightened the bedding around her. "Tell me you're not still angry. I've missed you."

"You're my best friend, Farin. How could I stay angry at you?"

Her half-smile wounded him. He consoled himself, chalking up the tepid reaction to her weakened state rather than another rejection.

"Have you seen Jordan?"

"Not for days."

"I heard he'd been here the whole time I was out. Why wouldn't he come see me if he'd waited here so long?"

He took her hand in his. "Dr. Childs says you need to rest."

She looked down at her fidgeting fingers. "I was so scared."

"Why did you do it?"

"My head was full. I couldn't get out. I didn't know what I was doing."

"Dr. Clark said you're upset about your father dying. You never told me about that."

She cocked her head, a hint of a smile teasing her lips. "You and I have a strict no-family policy, remember? Why would Dr. Clark bring that up?"

Bobby shrugged. "We were groping for answers. But don't worry. You'll be out of here soon. And you'll never get rid of me again."

Days passed. Dr. Childs arranged for physical therapy twice a day to help Farin walk and regain her strength. He ordered endless tests to identify any long-term deficits. Each result, good news. Yet even as her physical strength increased, her spirit wilted like the flowers on her window ledge. Each day, she ate less. Soon, she refused food altogether. And still, no word from Jordan.

Her interactions were few. Marci called daily. Each call included the offer to fly out. Each offer was met with refusal. Chris snuck in whenever he could. She enjoyed his company and the forbidden nature of his visits. But Valium withdrawals made her irritable. She suffered cruelly, and made it her business to ensure others suffered with her.

The one glimmer of hope came when Ben visited. But when he entered her room, her heart sank. She recognized the polite disappointment blanketing his face—the same look Jordan wore the day they met at

Standards. Only his firm embrace assured her their bond had not become another in the long list of casualties resulting from her broken marriage.

She confronted him before he could grab a chair. "I know you've talked to Jordan. Why hasn't he come to see me?"

He kissed her cheek, then sat down, shaking his head as if he either did not know, or thought it foolish of her to ask.

"Jordan's carrying a lot of guilt, kid. He thinks this is all his fault because of what happened earlier that evening."

"He told you?"

Ben nodded.

She replayed the events in her mind. Her fingers pulled at the corner of the thin blanket that failed to warm her.

"He still loves you. It's obvious. I guess he figures this is the least painful way out. He's been drinking a lot."

She leaned back in her bed and stared at the ceiling. "How could I have explained the real reason I left those times? Wouldn't it have been worse to tell him the truth? I care about Chris. He saved my life. But Jordan..."

He patted her hand. "He doesn't want this divorce any more than you do, but he took his stand. Now, he feels it's best to stick by it. Not because he doesn't care, but because he cares too much."

"If we both feel the same way but we can't be together, what's the use? Sometimes I wish Chris hadn't found me when he did."

"Stop it!" Ben demanded.

She jumped at the sharp, pitiless tone of his voice.

He erupted from his seat, one hand on his narrow hip as he stalked to the end of the room, rubbing his bearded jawline with the other. When he doubled back, he scooted the chair closer and sat heavy in his seat, elbows on his knees, fingers steepled. He leveled his eyes upon her. "It's been a tough road for you. Fair enough. But you're not the first. You won't be the last."

Farin looked away, pouting like a scolded toddler on a time out.

"Dr. Clark thinks this started when your father died. To be honest, I've suspected as much for years. You need to concentrate on living instead of finding excuses to die. Stop living in the past. If we can't do that, then what's the point? We'd all be better off taking a bottle of pills."

Her misting eyes infuriated her.

"It's a sad day when someone as beautiful and talented and successful as you thinks life isn't worth having. I wish I could change Jordan's mind.

But right now, kid, I'd settle for changing yours."

Farin spent the evening inside the echoes of Ben's wisdom. They played tag with her mother's parting words—and Farin was "it."

He was right. They both were. A choice lay before her that only she could make.

When her dinner came, she refused to eat.

The next morning, Farin awoke with a start. When she looked down, she discovered a shabby, unshaven Jordan at the foot of her bed. She stared at him, speechless. His hair was tousled and uncombed. His red eyes gazed at and through her. A gash in his bottom lip appeared nearly healed.

"Morning," he whispered hoarsely.

"You're here."

He shuffled to the chair by her bed.

"You talked to Ben."

"My brother's a wise man," he said, his voice barely audible.

They sat in silence. As she beheld the crumpled remnants of the man beside her, she confronted the worst of herself. She had driven him to this low point and could only offer further pain. She did not deserve his love, but found it impossible to let him go.

"I'd give anything to take back the things I've done." Her words fell to the ground, as useless as they were sincere.

"I can't compete with this attraction between you two. I'm not even sure I understand it."

"I don't love him."

Jordan took her hand and studied its familiar tender lines. Weeks of forced hydration at the hands of Mercy Hospital and countless bags of IV-infused saline had revived the soft glow of her skin. Despite her stubborn refusal of adequate sustenance, her thin frame looked healthier than it had the last time he had seen her.

He scooted closer and took her other hand. Then slowly, he crawled into the hospital bed beside her and wrapped her in his arms. Sleep had evaded him for days. In truth, it had toyed with him for months. He longed to go home. And despite their problems, it was only home when Farin shared it with him.

Weariness slayed his pride. He buried his face beside hers.

"I love you, Jordan."

With the balance of his strength, he lifted his head. "I love you, too."

"I don't want a divorce."

He thought a moment, then propped his head onto his hand. "Marriage is based on love and trust. If you trust me, you'll never need to run away. I'd forget this whole thing if you'd promise—*promise*—you'll never leave again."

She nodded eagerly at his words. "I promise. I love you. I *need* you."

"I'm here. And I need you, too."

"I want to be your wife."

"You are my wife."

The door flew open. Chris burst inside, shattering their intimate reunion. His pained expression told them he had heard everything.

He seethed as he beheld the cuddling couple. "Run out of booze? Or are you here to finish her off?"

Jordan rose to face him. "I love her, Chris."

"*Love* her? How convenient to show up every time your conscience threatens your good guy image. She gets pregnant, you marry her. She overdoses, you're back. Quite the hero, aren't we?"

Before Jordan could respond, Chris's focus shifted bitterly to the one thing he had ever cared enough about to fight for. "And then there's Sleeping Beauty, here. Always the victim. Always lost. The consummate damsel in distress, drifting from crisis to crisis. You had everything, Farin. And I'm the one who gave it to you. *Me!* Why wasn't I ever enough?"

The battle had alerted hospital staff. Dr. Childs entered, followed closely by two security guards who forcibly removed Chris from the room.

When he was gone, Dr. Childs sedated Farin. Jordan stayed long enough to calm her down.

On the way home, Jordan executed two errands. First, he contacted Megan Price—a courtesy more than anything else. Their reported romance had never amounted to more than a convenience for either of them. As a new artist, she had gained a fair amount of publicity by showing up on his arm to the various functions they had attended. Meanwhile, Jordan had managed to fulfill public commitments by using Megan as a willing buffer between him and an intrusive media.

"I'm glad you two are trying again," she told him.

"Thanks for understanding, Megan."

"Of course. Besides...the press should eat this up, dontcha think?"

He chuckled softly.

"Seriously, though. Thanks for calling and telling me. I wish you both a lifetime of happiness. You deserve it."

Second, he stopped by John Knowles's office and announced he had reconsidered the divorce. He and Farin had both made mistakes, but the time had come to start again.

CHAPTER 29

T O THE RELIEF OF MERCY Hospital staff, Dr. Childs discharged Farin two weeks later. He did so on two conditions: she had to promise to eat regularly, and she had to find ways to manage her stress without further pharmacological assistance.

A heavier than usual paparazzi presence greeted them with a hail of shouts and camera flashes as they pulled onto Matheson, then disappeared behind the security gate. In an effort to preempt resentment from their village neighbors, Jordan called their publicists and released a brief statement.

"Farin Grant is home from her unfortunate accident. Jordan joins her in thanking their fans for their gifts, prayers, and kind thoughts. They ask everyone to respect their privacy as she recovers."

Jordan had performed miracles to turn the clock back. Not only had he reclaimed her possessions from Chris's house, he retrieved everything from her own place. To punctuate this commitment, he listed her house with a rental agency.

The affair, Melody's death, the overdose—he banished their toxic influence like a priest exorcizing demonic specters. Their journey might yet include unforeseen twists and turns, but they worked with great deliberation to face ever forward.

"Nine months," Jordan insisted.

Jameson's sardonic chortle over the line confirmed he had overshot the mark.

"Six," Jordan conceded.

"Weeks?"

"Months!"

"No deal. Childs said she's fine."

"He said she's *better*. Not the same."

"Is she eating?"

"Yes."

"And her stress level?"

"Better—but not six-weeks-out better. Five."

When he heard the old man exhale a heavy breath, he figured he had narrowed it down to a reasonable window. "So, it's five, then?"

"How long have you been with LSI?"

"Let me think." With a wink and a voiceless "thank you" to his wife, he accepted a glass of iced tea and mounted a kitchen barstool, preparing for a protracted negotiation. "I believe that would be slightly over seven years. You signed me on my twenty-fourth birthday."

"And in that time, have you known an LSI artist to abandon their career for nine, or six, or even five months?"

He bobbed his head, protruding his lower lip as if Jameson had made the most reasonable argument possible. "Good point. Then again, in those seven-plus years, I've never known you to put another LSI artist in your will."

The conversational pause meant one of two things: he had either won the argument or overstepped a boundary.

"Jameson, it's Farin."

Jordan spun around on the stool. He eyeballed the room, only to find she had disappeared. As if reading his thoughts, she said, "Bedroom extension."

"How are you feeling, my dear?"

"Better. But Jordan's right. I need more time."

"And you said it yourself," Jordan added. "Sales are up."

Jameson grumbled. "The novelty of this most recent kerfuffle will soon lose its luster. Good news doesn't sustain a temporary sales spike. Hard work and continued visibility trump sickness."

"Two months," Jordan suggested.

"Our final offer," Farin said.

"On two conditions. First, you both double your commitments upon your return until the end of the year. Full bore. Performances. Interviews. Photo sessions. Videos. Parties. Radio. TV. *All* of it. Second, you start another album."

"That's it?" Jordan checked his watch and realized he was late for an appointment. "Fine by me. Farin?"

"Wait," Jameson said. "There's more. What would you two think about recording a duet? We could release it as a single, with a cut from each of your new albums included. Three-single cassettes and CDs."

"Perfect. Sounds great. Love to." He slipped off the stool and kissed into the receiver. "Gotta run. I love you. Be home soon." A wordless fluster on the New York side of the line made him chuckle. "Sorry."

Farin giggled as Jordan hung up the kitchen extension.

Jameson cleared his throat. "I take it we have a deal then, Farin?"

"You heard my husband. But today doesn't count as day one. Time off is time off. No business."

"Well, then. If this counts as a business day, then one more thing…"

"Hey! My negotiating partner had to leave!"

"You fill him in, then give me your answer in two months."

"Okay, shoot."

"I've been talking to your people."

Farin blew out a breath into the receiver. "You want another tour."

"More than a tour. A *world* tour."

A familiar discomfort rose up inside her. "I don't know if I can be away for a year, Jameson."

"What if Jordan were with you?"

"Really?"

"Husband and wife. World tour, nineteen-ninety-two to nineteen-ninety-three. Don't get overwhelmed. Talk it over with Jordan. We'll discuss it further in two months."

"You're gonna turn us into Peaches and Herb."

Jameson barked out a laugh. "It works."

"Okay. We'll give it some thought. Does…Bobby know about this?"

"Not yet. Actually, he's flying up today. He's due in any minute."

Farin paused. "Can I ask you a question?"

"What is it?"

"I know it's probably none of my business. Is he okay?"

"As far as I know. Why?"

"He came to the hospital a few times. At first, things were great. But the last few times I saw him, he seemed…troubled."

An alarm sounded in Jameson's psyche, transforming him back into the self-preservationist he had perfected over a lifetime. "Troubled?"

"Distant. Like he can't concentrate. The twitching's getting pretty bad. I don't mean to overstep."

"His twitching, yes. Has he told you?"

"I never asked. I know he doesn't drink, and sometimes his eyes get glassy and far off. I'd assumed it was diabetes or something. But I'm getting worried."

Jameson feigned a cheerful tone. "You're the one just out of the hospital! Alas, I'm afraid you're spot-on about the diabetes. It bothers him to discuss, so I wouldn't bring it up. Really, though, he manages quite well."

"It's our secret," she promised.

"I'm glad we understand each other."

***

Jameson waited impatiently for Bobby's arrival. Seated behind his colossal desk, he drummed his fingers while systematically purging his mind. Ross had warned him. Clearly, he had misjudged the relationship between Farin and his son. He could not—and would not—allow either of them to learn the truth.

When Bobby arrived, he propped his elbows atop his desk and pressed his fingertips together in isometric fashion. With what amounted to a contained snarl, he said, "It's about time."

Plunking down in his usual chair, Bobby consulted his watch. "I'm right on time. In fact, I'm early. What's up?"

"Have you been taking your medication?"

"You know I do. Why?"

"Farin says you've been acting peculiar and asked if you're feeling okay."

Bobby's face paled. "Peculiar how?"

"She said you're distant. Like something's troubling you. She thinks you have diabetes."

"What?" Bobby snickered as if the idea were absurd.

"Similar symptoms, I suppose. It appears I've overestimated your ability to manage her. The stress has become too much."

Bobby deflated beneath the humiliating rebuke, once again a young man entering Columbia. A troubled teen Dr. Childs rescued by way of syringes and drugs that rendered him impotent—his life stolen before he could live it. The doc had painted a bleak portrait of the consequences of noncompliance.

The only son of a puissant entertainment mogul who would one day inherit his father's renowned record label, Bobby had much to learn. Initially, he had struggled with the concepts of wealth and the surgical application of power. Over the course of his father's tutelage, however, he had accepted his limitations, his fate, and his nature.

For years now, he had enjoyed his life, such as it was. He had wrestled his lamentable existence into submission. Then, he discovered what he had long considered forbidden—someone he could love. Even if she did not return his feelings right now, he knew she could never love him if he was less than a man.

And no man would endure the barrage of insults his father hurled at him.

"You'll move back to New York at once. Sell the Coral Gables place."

"No."

Jameson lifted an indignant brow. "No?"

"No. I need to be in Florida, close to Farin. You agreed."

"I'll give you a promotion. How does Executive Vice President sound?"

Bobby eased back and planted an elbow on the armrest, propping his head atop two fingers. "You're so concerned about my stress level you want to put me over *six* departments?"

"You'll be home. Close to Childs. And with no loss of face."

A sudden loathing for his father filled his insides. "What's the goal here, Dad? To keep me locked up in one of your offices like Quasimodo inside Notre Dame? Look at me! I'm *normal!*"

Jameson stood, held his hands behind him, and paced. "We need to ensure you stay that way."

Bobby stared blankly past him, out the floor-to-ceiling window. "I went to college, like you wanted. I joined LSI, like you wanted. You've led me around for years—and for what? I'll be thirty-five in three weeks and I haven't had a girlfriend since my senior year of high school. Most men want their sons to get married, give them grandchildren. But you? You're afraid it might run in the family. On Mom's side, of course."

Jameson hastened to his desk, wagging an angry finger at his son. "None of this would have happened if—"

"Don't you talk about my mother! Not after what you did to her!"

Jameson averted his eyes and dropped into his chair.

Bobby watched with marked satisfaction as his father shrank in his seat. "Don't think I haven't heard the stories about Farin and Mirage. You shattered Mirage. And you bought out Farin's contract from Warner."

"Who told you that?"

He sucked his teeth. "That's what I thought. I'd bet it's part of some cover-up. It usually is. Really, Father, your mendacity's exceeded only by your machinations. How dare you tell Farin I have diabetes!"

"That was *her* diagnosis, Robert. I merely humored her to save your skin."

"*My* skin? Farin's probably the one person who'd understand. Maybe

I'll tell her myself."

Jameson leapt up and leaned upon his flattened palms. His eyes narrowed with untamed fury. "Tell her and I'll leave you a pauper in the street. You'll no longer be my son. And you'll never have LSI."

"Did I hit a nerve?" Bobby searched his father's eyes, intrigued to see equal parts fear and rage staring back at him. "Exactly who is Farin Grant to you?"

Jameson's upper lip twitched up beneath his flared nostrils. "The brightest star in the world. And given your misplaced desire to bare your soul to her, I've decided to put her with someone more qualified—and more discreet."

Bobby shot up to his feet. "I won't move back to New York, I'm *not* leaving Coral Gables, and you're *not* replacing me. I love her!"

Jameson took his seat, guffawing and clutching his middle. "Love? What do you know about love?"

"Only that it's the opposite of everything you're about."

"She's married. Recently reunited with her husband. Still recovering from attempted *suicide*. Your feelings are pointless and senseless."

"I know they are. They always are. They always will be as long as this medication controls my life."

"Be thankful you have something controlling you. I'd hate to see what would happen if you stopped taking that medication. Childs warned you."

Bobby fixed his gaze across Sixth Avenue at the building facing theirs. "I'm thinking about risking it. I need a normal life."

***

Intermittent showers foiled Jordan's plan to begin their two-month hiatus sea camping, forcing him to delay their pelagic excursion by a week. They spent most of the time at the house, watching movies, walking the grounds between storms, and visiting Ben and Cheryl's. The night before their planned departure, Ben and Cheryl sent the boys to stay with friends and had them over for a couples evening.

"You'll write the song, then," Jordan confirmed as he and Ben settled in the living room and enjoyed a post-dinner brandy while Cheryl and Farin cleared and cleaned dishes.

Ben rotated the snifter in his hand, then sipped the Hine. "A duet sounds brilliant. But if Lockhardt's having you two tour together, why not do an entire album?"

"That'd be a tall order. We're each doing a new album by then."

Ben bobbed his shoulders. "Let's say I write several options and you two record them. When you're finished, we send them to Lockhardt to choose which one he wants."

He grinned. "And he'll want them all."

"If I do my job, he will."

Jordan relaxed into the sofa, resting his arm along the back as if preparing Farin's place beside him.

Ben lifted his glass. "It's good to see you happy again. How's her therapy coming along?"

"She's doing well. Gaining her strength back. We'll find a counselor after our holiday."

"Why wait?"

"I didn't tell you?"

Ben cocked his head.

"We're flying out to visit Mum and Dad next month."

"Are you?" Cheryl cheered as she and Farin grabbed their drinks and joined their husbands. "How lovely!"

Farin snuggled in next to Jordan. "I finally get to see your childhood home."

"Good ol' Chapel Lane." Ben gave a mischievous smile and winked at his brother.

"To Bledlow." Jordan laughed, lifting his brandy snifter.

In unison, the brothers broke into a spontaneous sing-song. "*They who live and do abide...Shall see Bledlow Church fall into the Lyde!*"

Farin watched them, completely lost, as they laughed.

"It's a medieval nursery rhyme," Jordan explained with a playful squeeze of her shoulder.

Animated, Ben scooted to the edge of his seat. "When Jordan was young, he used to crawl in bed with Mum and Dad quite often. He was afraid our house would be snatched up by ghosts of the dead and flung into the river."

Cheryl smacked the back of his head. "Don't embarrass your brother."

"What? It wasn't me filling his head with such tosh."

Farin squinted in confusion. "Why would ghosts want your house?"

Jordan gave his brother a sheepish grin. He uncurled his index finger from around his snifter, pointing it his way. "Go on."

"Our house used to be a chapel."

"A chapel?"

"Yep. Built mid-eighteen-hundreds. Dad liked the space, so he bought and converted it."

"Aye," Cheryl interjected, combing her husband's hair with gentle fingers. "As a gift to Lynda when she was pregnant with Benjamin here."

"On windy nights, Chris would try to convince me the souls of the people whose funerals had taken place in the church—now, our home— were angry because a family of heathen entertainers had overtaken it."

"Jordan went to church every Sunday from the age of six to pray for God's forgiveness."

"And note, the house still stands."

Farin cuddled into his arms. "I can't wait to see it."

Ben motioned for their empty glasses, then went for refills. "I guess that's the one good thing about Chris's disappearance. He won't be around to tell any ghost stories."

An abrupt silence fell upon them. Clearly, he had spoken out of turn.

***

It rained nearly every day of their three-week stay in the pretty village of Bledlow, giving them precious little time to relive Jordan's childhood memories, explore the green countryside with its network of footpaths and bridleways, or wander the chalk soil at the foot of the escarpment of the Chiltern Hills. They spent most their time inside, content to visit with George and Lynda, who were overjoyed to have their youngest son and daughter-in-law to themselves.

During the day, Lynda tutored Farin with various crafting projects, fussing over her as she pricked her finger while working on a needlepoint pattern or struggled with the most basic knitting instruction. Farin found herself sitting in a mess of yarn, helpless despite her mother-in-law's attempts to teach her how to cast on.

"Oh dear." Lynda rested two fingers on her chin. "Perhaps we'll start with a larger pair of knitting needles, then."

George suited himself and his son up in raincoats, then slipped out to the garage to tinker with his latest automobile obsession. He lay back on his mechanic's creeper and slid under the vehicle, enthusiastically calling for Jordan to hand him a wrench or various other tools.

"Squeeze on down here, lad! Look at the shambles that knobhead stuck me with!"

In the evenings, they reminisced over the boys' childhood. Lynda and George grew misty-eyed as they filed through family photos chronicling their lives together.

"Have you heard anything of Chris, Jorie? Anything at all?"

"Sorry, Mum. Not a word."

"Ben didn't say why he wandered off. Should we ring the authorities? Report him missing?"

George patted her knee. "Calm down, love."

"It's been weeks, George."

"You know our boy."

Out of the corner of her eye, Farin saw Jordan hang his head. When he caught her staring, the sides of his lips curved into a weak half-smile. "No worries, Mum. He has to be back soon anyway to start practice. He won't miss Mirage's last gig. You'll see—he'll turn up."

Later that night, Farin sat at the bedroom vanity, applying face cream and lotion, when Jordan emerged from the shower. She watched him through the mirror as he dressed. When he looked at her, she turned away.

He sat on the edge of the bed. "Say it."

Her voice came out strained and guarded. "Nothing."

"It's something. Let's have it."

She twisted around on the padded bench. "Your mother's so worried. And it's all my fault. We should tell her the truth."

"My mother's sixty-five years old, Farin. She won't feel better—about any of us—if we tell her our problems."

"How is it she doesn't know anyway? The tabloids were vicious over the three of us during our separation."

"My parents agreed years ago they'd be better off avoiding the rags. This wouldn't be the first shock to their system. Trust me. They'd rather not know."

When she turned back around without another word, he glanced down at his wedding band. "You're worried about him, too."

"It's not that."

"Then what is it?"

She gazed at him through the mirror. "I would have liked to have found out he was missing before Ben blurted out the big secret."

"It wasn't a secret."

"Then why not tell me?"

"Because you and I need to concentrate on mending our own lives."

"How can we when you won't be honest with me?"

Jordan's patience strained at the irony of her words. "Chris is none of your business now, love. None of mine either, for that matter. Not anymore."

"It's not that simple."

"Isn't it?"

She whirled around again, shaking her head in frustration. "I know it's hard to hear. Especially after what I've put you through. But Jordan, he saved my life. In spite of everything else, you must realize that."

"Let's not argue. He's out of our lives."

Jordan retreated to the bathroom to dress and comb out his wet hair. A part of him wondered if Farin would ever truly belong to him. Maybe Ben was right. Maybe she should have started counseling before taking this trip.

He thought about his long-abandoned quest to find James Wellingham. Despite her improving health and outward well-being, something with Farin still felt off. A part of her still found it impossible to let go of the past—any past. Now more than ever, he believed meeting this Mr. Wellingham would banish the nightmares and restore her soul.

As he catalogued his myriad failed attempts—calling the Santa Barbara PD, the library, the local paper—he contemplated other options. Maybe he had given up too soon.

When he returned to their bedroom, the lights were extinguished, save the bedside table lamp. Farin lay in bed, facing the wall. He climbed in beside her and spooned.

"I still care what happens to him," she said. "And so do you."

"What about all those things he said to you in the hospital?"

"He was hurt."

Jordan rolled over on his back. He jerked the blankets from his body. "And now you're defending him?"

"He helped me out when you left."

"Of course he did, Farin. He loves you. He's always loved you."

Aghast, she rolled over and beheld the pain in his eyes.

"What? You think it wasn't obvious? Ever since that first day in Malibu. The barbecue. The day Chase..." He shut his eyes and looked away. "Ever since that day, he's loved you. He loved you before I did."

Farin lay dumbstruck as Jordan's face twisted with bitterness and misery—over Chase, over the affair, over the fact the truth had finally been revealed.

The big secret she had tried so hard to hide all these years had never been a secret at all. "Why didn't you say anything?"

"You think it was easy? I thought if I made an issue of it, it'd make things worse. I guess the joke's on me, isn't it?"

She cupped his troubled face with her hand. "I didn't mean to upset you. I'm sorry. Chris looked so hurt that day. It's my fault. I haven't talked to him since. Not even to apologize."

Jordan stroked her arm with his fingertips. "Be my wife, Farin. I don't want him coming between us ever again."

***

The morning they left for Heathrow Airport, George took a last-minute call in his study. When he returned, his expression had relaxed. For three weeks, he had been absorbed in thought, anxious perhaps, despite the joy of having his youngest temporarily back in the nest. Now, his coarse face broke into a wide smile that illuminated the room. "Ben sends his love and wishes you two a safe trip home."

Lynda wrung her hands, frail yet hopeful as she approached her husband. "Is there any other news from Miami?"

George took his wife in his arms and drew her close. "That there is. Ben wanted to let us know Chris is home now and he's fine. He's fine."

Jordan turned instinctively to gauge Farin's reaction. He caught the fall of her chest as relief washed over her. When she glimpsed him looking at her, she glanced down to inspect their luggage tags.

He wondered if Chris would ever leave her thoughts...or her heart.

CHAPTER 30

"OUR FIRST GUEST STARTED CHARTING singles almost before the ink dried on her recording contract. Record mogul Jameson Lockhardt signed her three years ago without so much as hearing her audition—arguably the result of her whirlwind romance with pop idol, Jordan Grant. Since then, she's released three studio albums, which have sold over forty-five million copies worldwide and produced a string of Top Forty hits. Married now and living in Miami, the couple works hard to protect the private, and often chaotic, details of their romance, marriage, and recent divorce rumors. Here for the first time to sing her latest smash hit, 'Misread,' please welcome *Farin Grant!*"

When the scuttlebutt had reached the American media circuit that the industry's most infamous celebrity couple would embark upon an extensive publicity tour, Jordan's and Farin's publicists kicked into high gear, arranging and coordinating a four-month schedule of appearances from New York to LA. By the time they stepped into the probing lights of their public, talk and musical variety shows breathlessly awaited their shot at the hottest male and female commodities gracing the day's charts.

One caveat in the plan: only solo appearances. Jameson argued—and won—that fight, dangling the bait of his proposed world tour the following year as incentive.

Uncoupling them made sense, if only to those pulling their strings. It sustained competition within the circuit of hopefuls clamoring to be the first to secure a future interview. It provided ample opportunity for either love bird to make mistakes the media might capitalize upon by stoking the fires of potentially unresolved issues. And it doubled the foreseen interrogation over various scandals plaguing their lives the last two years.

Jordan joined the Club MTV Tour for a six-week commitment at the end of July, while Farin headed for the West Coast where she began recording new material at Sound City Studios in Van Nuys while making the local talk show rounds. She taped her first appearance on the *Tonight Show with Johnny Carson*. The following week, they booked her on the recently reformatted Maureen McDaniel show, *Mo!*

Despite her successful performance, a tarnished image shadowed Farin offstage amid the cheers of her fans. The previous day's Carson taping had gone well. Johnny had treated her graciously, his biting wit disarming yet encouraging her to relax as he softballed questions about her recent album.

Mo McDaniel's audience, however, was a wholly different animal. They cared nothing about chart positions or an upcoming tour. *Mo!*'s ravenous fans hungered for a feast of tasty gossip, and the sinister gleam in Mo McDaniel's slitted hazel eyes assured Farin she would be their main course.

"Welcome to the show!" Mo ignored Farin's outstretched hand and went in for an awkward embrace, as if the two were old friends.

Farin smiled, waved, and nodded self-effacing thank-yous at the audience, then squiggled comfortably into one of two upholstered armchairs. Beside her, she found the glass of water she had requested before the show. She took a careful sip as the crowd quieted.

"Nice to see you! You're looking gorgeous!"

"Thanks, Mo. It's great to be here!"

Mo sat on the edge of her seat, boney arms folded on her lap, her hands clutching a stack of five by seven cards. "We've been trying to get you on the show for some time."

"I'm glad I finally made it."

"You know, your husband's been on a number of times."

The corners of her mouth lifted. She cut eyes at her host. "We've discussed it."

"Have you?" Mo cocked her head in mock confusion.

"Absolutely. He warned me about you."

"*Warned* you?"

The audience erupted in laughter. Mo rested a skeletal hand on her hip and glanced open-mouthed into the crowd, then back to Farin. "Don't tell me he holds a grudge. He seems so sweet! Does he hold grudges at home, too?"

The audience oohed and ahhed, gleeful as they watched the cheeky quip catch Farin off guard.

"I—"

Mo waved her finely manicured fingers in the air, then shuffled through her cards. "No-no-no, let's not start there. It took us so long to book you, I'd hate to have you walk out before we've even started."

Farin swallowed and shifted awkwardly, straightening the hem of her dress as she willed herself to maintain an airy vibe. Stealing a glance past Mo to the small crowd back stage, she realized how much she missed Bobby.

"So, you're just out of the hospital. You look...vibrant. Happy! I guess love will do that to a girl, am I right?"

"That you are, Mo!"

"And you've recovered fully from your recent hospital stay?"

"I'm much better, yes. Thanks. I'm excited to get out and promote *Dreamcatcher*. I love performing and meeting my fans."

Mo rested her head on her hand. She leaned in close to study her guest. "That's good. Real good. After all, you gave your fans quite a scare when they heard the news—what was it again that put you there?"

"I, uh...I'd been working like crazy, trying to finish the album. It got the better of me, I guess. I was exhausted."

"So, exhaustion, eh?"

"That's right. But we both know you've already confirmed this with my publicist, don't we?"

The audience roared and applauded.

"You know I have." Mo leaned back, cool as wintermint mouthwash. She wrinkled her nose and grinned. "Now, correct me if I'm wrong, but...weren't you and Jordan estranged during the recording of *Dreamcatcher*?"

The studio fell silent until only a random hush or whisper could be heard.

Farin tucked a copper lock of hair behind her ear and cleared her throat. "You certainly do your homework."

"And you were living with his brother, Chris, right?"

The moment she returned to her hotel room, Farin kicked her heels into the closet and called Jordan. She let loose when it went to voicemail. "You were right. I hate that woman. Call me back when you can. Love you."

She drowned the grimy residue of Mo's interrogation in a hot bath, ordered room service, and chatted with Marci until it arrived.

"You can't possibly want to be alone. Come stay with me!"

"Schedule's too hectic. We wouldn't have a minute to catch up. Besides, the hotel's only twenty minutes from the studio. So, spill it."

"What do you mean?"

"Psh. Don't be coy. How's Elliot? And don't lie. I know you're seeing him."

A soft giggle filled the line. Farin pulled the phone away from her ear and frowned at the receiver, unclear if she had ever heard her friend emit such a sound.

"It's new. It's quiet. That's all you get."

"Taken him home to meet the folks yet?"

"Maybe."

"*Really?*"

"How long are you in California?"

"A couple more days. Jordan and I are recording as we go to try to finish as close to the new year as possible. Tour preparations are already underway. Besides, recording's a lot easier than subjecting myself to people like Mo McDaniel. Johnny was nice, though."

"You're on tonight. Gonna catch the show?"

Farin would have preferred to have traveled in quadrants instead of overlapping treks across the States. She and Jordan calculated approximately seven cross-country flights where they may have actually passed each other in the air.

He called her from Seattle near the end of September. "Check out Nirvana's new record *Nevermind*. It's brilliant!"

"Isn't it? Butch sampled a bit for me when I was in LA. You get Ben's new song?"

"Already laying down vocals. I'm using London Bridge Studios."

"I've got Oprah tomorrow. Finishing up at Chicago Recording Company. If you finish your part, send the track there. I'll work on mine before heading to Nashville."

"I'm going to Nashville! Maybe we can sneak a date."

She gasped. "Dinner Friday?"

"Bollocks! I'm not there until the week after!"

"Use Quad Studios while you're there. I'll leave the duet track with them and you can take a listen. Clean it up or add to it if you need to. Or just send the master back to Ben."

"I miss you. You doing all right?"

"I miss you, too. Only two more months, though. And hey—I forgot to tell you. Bobby's flying up."

"Good. I feel better knowing you'll have a friendly face nearby."

Bobby's presence revived Farin's spirit over the remaining weeks away. She had missed spending time with him—quirks and all. And unlike their last few encounters, he seemed more or less like his old self. Whatever his recent struggles, he appeared to have sorted them out. And just in time to come to her rescue.

"You're doing too well," he told her one mid-October night as they left for dinner.

She suppressed a grin as she applied her lipstick. "What do you mean?"

"Dad's loving the album's progress. And 'Misread' is in the top five."

"What's wrong with that?"

"You keep this pace up and he'll push to keep you out on the road."

She snatched up her purse and they stepped out into the hallway. "No chance. Come Thanksgiving, I'm home."

"In time for Mirage's big finale. You going?"

The smile ran away from her face.

Bobby pressed the elevator button, then folded his hands in front of him. "Who knows? Maybe it'll be good for you and Jordan to be there."

"Jordan's not going. He'll be in California. Wanna be my date?"

"Sure! But I thought you were both finished before Thanksgiving."

She bobbed her shoulders as the elevator dinged. "He says he has business there. Maybe something to do with the beach house."

***

Mirage's farewell concert marked the final battle in an epic war with Lockhardt Sound. LSI arranged for a pay-per-view cable event, broadcast live from the Miami Arena. Fans around the world would feel as if they had participated in ushering in the end of an era. Unfortunately, the production usurped the otherwise increased profits of live performance to which the band might otherwise be entitled.

LSI planned to release copies of the live concert video and soundtrack, ensuring a tidy and prolonged profit for the label that had burned their career to the ground. This move handed Jameson Lockhardt veto power over much of the last performance from one of rock history's most iconic bands.

Contractually, there was nothing they could do about it.

Farin and Marci bypassed the Green Room and sat atop a cluster of tour cases in the marshalling area backstage before the event, dangling their feet off the sides like schoolgirls as they watched roadies finish assembling equipment.

Farin stretched and rubbed her middle. "Cheryl outdid herself. That was the first real Thanksgiving I've had in ages."

"I think I'm still digesting."

"I'm glad you guys flew out early."

"We figured it was the perfect time to come out of the closet."

"I don't know who you thought you were fooling anyway."

Marci flinched as a passing runner thrust a magnum of Cristal and two glasses at her. "What's this?"

The young man blushed as he delivered his message. "Elliot says he loves you and he'll see you after the show." He jogged off before she could thank him.

She handed the glasses to Farin and popped the cork. "Did Jordan catch his flight out okay?"

Farin held the glasses in place while Marci poured. "He couldn't wait to leave."

"He seemed fine at dinner."

"I think he doesn't want to see Chris."

"They'll be okay." She set the bottle down between them on the case and held up her glass. "To happy endings."

Farin toasted her, then gulped down the entire glassful, defying the gassy carbonation. A moment later, she unsuccessfully attempted to stifle a belch. Her eyes darted wildly about the area. Once satisfied no one heard her, she poured herself another fluteful. "We're gonna need another bottle."

Marci covered her mouth with her free hand before laughing and spitting out her drink. "Take it easy! I'm not chaperoning tonight."

"I don't need you to chaperone." She pointed toward the backstage door. "My bodyguard just walked in."

Bobby crossed the floor, decidedly somber in his black jeans, black T-shirt, and black blazer. When he got closer, Farin noted a tremble in his weak smile.

She scanned his features. "You okay?"

"Fine. Why?"

She hopped down and felt his forehead. "You're sweating."

"It's seventy-eight degrees outside and I'm in a sportscoat. What are you doing out here? We have a suite."

Farin scrunched her face. "We wanted some privacy."

Bobby surveyed the large expanse of concrete and foot traffic, then looked back at her doubtfully. "You certainly have that here, don't you? Anyway, what are we drinking?" When they held up their flutes, he made a face. "I think we can do better than that. Be right back."

Farin climbed back atop the case beside Marci, plopped down, and drank a second glass. She extracted her compact from her purse, inspected her makeup, and added some lip stain. "When are you and Elliot flying back to LA?"

"Tomorrow morning. He's in the middle of a project for Columbia. When are you two headed out on tour?"

She snapped the compact closed and tossed it into her handbag. "Six months. Jordan still has a couple of tracks left on his album. He got so caught up finishing the duets, he fell behind."

Marci eyed her knowingly. "So, you beat him to the finish line."

Farin lifted a third glass of champagne to her lips. "That's all I'm sayin'."

Marci patted her knee.

They waited for Bobby in contemplative silence, watching roadies, runners, and security scurry about the area.

Marci upended the last of the champagne evenly into their glasses. "The papers all say what a wonderful comeback you've made. How you and Jordan are happier than ever. I'd say it's true."

"They finally got something right. I *am* happy."

Marci jutted her chin, exaggerating her satisfaction. "Told you they had to get those stories from somewhere."

She waved when she saw Ben and Cheryl headed toward the Green Room. "But there's one thing nobody knows yet."

"What?"

Farin leaned in and whispered, "Jordan and I are thinking about having another baby after the tour."

Marci's eyes lit up. "I thought you couldn't!"

"We're getting a second opinion. With the things they can do these days, all it takes is money to have a baby—and that's one thing we aren't short of."

Bobby returned with a bottle of Jack Daniels and three red Solo cups.

Farin studied him, stunned by the realization he intended to join them. He held the sides of the cups together with his fingers, sloshing a generous pour into each. He handed one to Marci, then Farin.

"To Mirage." He downed the liquor in a single gulp.

"You sure you're okay?" Farin tossed the liquor back, then rattled her head at its burning bitterness.

He poured another cupful and set the bottle down beside the spent magnum. "Other than an irritating lack of sleep last night, yes."

"Why couldn't you sleep?"

He downed the second shot, then consulted his watch. "We should head out. The show's starting soon."

They entered the second of two luxury boxes LSI had reserved for friends and family. Bobby brushed Farin's shoulder as he took his seat. An involuntary shiver ran up and down her spine.

She admonished herself as she recollected her conversation with Jameson. No wonder Bobby shied away from personal relationships. His condition made him refuse to share himself with a woman for fear of rejection. What a shame. No doubt he craved human contact.

When the lights went up and the band took the stage, Farin elbowed Bobby and passed him her cup for a refill. She wished Jordan were there.

The thrill of watching a live show had worn off. It tormented and confused her to see Chris on stage, singing and playing his guitar. He looked content with his bandmates as he pranced around, infusing the audience with a steady dose of sound and raw sexuality.

A film crew scampered back and forth across the front of the stage, capturing the best angles of the group. The heavy emotion generated by the crowd created a vibe of bittersweet sadness throughout the arena. Mirage's eighteen-year reign ended in the space of a few hours. The atmosphere was that of a funeral and a celebration combined.

As she peeked down to survey the crowd, she sensed Bobby's stare. She turned and studied him quietly, worrying over his health, wondering if she dare say anything about his alcohol intake. They exchanged warm smiles, then she returned her attention to the show.

Three encores and one tearful goodbye later, Chris stepped up to his microphone amid the roar of the crowd. He beckoned a woman to join him from offstage. Her beaming smile and the casual wave of her hand set off a collective frenzy throughout the arena. Brunette. Nearly as tall as Chris. All legs and no chest. Thin and beautiful in every clichéd manner of description. Comfortable on stage. She looked vaguely familiar. This was no backstage groupie. Then, in one crashing moment, Farin recognized her as international super model Julie Swanson.

Chris waited for the cheers and whistles sent up for Julie to subside. They looked at one another, all smiles, as Chris embraced her and then turned back to his microphone.

He peered up at the VIP suite as if searching for Farin, as if hoping to witness her reaction to their intimate gestures. His voice echoed as he took Julie's hand in his. "Thank you! I suppose it's only appropriate to end our last show with a happy announcement."

Marci grabbed Farin's wrist. Their eyes deadlocked into that wordless communication they had shared since childhood. Inside that space, Farin realized Marci knew. She knew and had not warned her. As Marci's brows arched with regret, Farin had never felt so betrayed.

Chris flashed his wide, radiant smile for the press and his many admirers. "Last month, this lovely lady and I were married. I'd like you all to give a big round of applause to my wife, Julie Swanson."

Julie poked her head in. "That's Julie Swanson *Grant*," she said, playfully correcting her new husband as she approached the microphone.

The crowd cheered and guffawed as Chris kissed his wife under the beam of the spotlights. Each band member offered a heartfelt farewell. Then, with a final wave, they turned to leave. The delirious crowd whooped, screamed, and shouted as the group exited the stage.

Farin stood open-mouthed as Bobby spotted reporters stampeding toward their suite. He raised his left arm like a crossing guard halting oncoming traffic and linked Farin's with his right as he ushered her out to the car with Marci close behind.

"We need to get over to Forge." He glanced back at Farin. "Unless you wanna go home."

"I've gotta be there," Marci said, apologetically. When Farin clutched her arm, she nodded at Bobby. "She'll be okay."

Cup in hand, Farin stared forward as they motored toward South Beach. She nudged Bobby periodically for a refill. When they arrived, she could not decide if she was grateful or irritated that they were the first to arrive. Once inside, they beelined to their reserved VIP section and hunkered down.

Bobby addressed the gregarious server who came for their drink order. "Jack—bring a bottle."

Marci scanned the room for any sign of Elliot.

Farin sat statue-like and the circular, red velvet sofa for twelve as the server returned with their order. Bathed in neon, Forge pulsed with strobing light synchronized to the cacophonous beat of nightclub music.

She knew she had no place reacting to the unexpected news. Chris deserved happiness. Besides, she tended to forget how wonderful Jordan was when he was not around.

Marci gazed at her with soft eyes. "You okay?"

She accepted her glass with trembling fingers, then tossed back her head to down its contents. She thrust the empty glass at Bobby. "Keep 'em coming. I refuse to be sober tonight."

Elliot arrived first. He kissed Marci amidst a hail of flashbulbs, then sat down, pushing his dark, damp hair into place. "I can't believe the tosser did that."

"You should slow down," Bobby warned Farin. "You'll make yourself sick."

"I'm already sick," she hollered above the driving dance music and mingling patrons as Ben and Cheryl arrived.

Ben kissed her cheek. "Sorry, kid. I should've called you earlier."

She studied him, so poised, so handsome with his wife on his arm. Her brows knit together as she glanced at Marci, then back to him. "You knew, too," she said, accusing more than asking for confirmation.

Guilt shrouded his features.

Farin tossed back another drink.

By the time Julie slunk up behind Ben and Cheryl, Farin's nose and fingertips were numb. Reporters engulfed the small group huddled together on the sofa. Camera flashes exploded throughout the room. Julie and Cheryl appeared surprisingly comfortable with one another. Julie charmed the media with air kisses. She positioned herself between Ben and Cheryl, awaiting an introduction.

Ben cleared his throat into his fist. "I don't believe you've met my other sister-in-law."

"No." Julie flashed the smile that had graced the cover of every major magazine in the world. "But I've heard *so much* about her."

Farin defied her hazy mind. She crossed her arms and tucked her head. "Oh yeah? Whose version did you hear?"

Chris appeared from nowhere and wrapped his arms around Julie's thin waist. He snuggled into her amidst an eruption of flashbulbs so constant, they appeared permanently lit. Julie tittered and shooed off the media. "Enough work tonight. Have fun now."

Farin locked eyes with Chris. Fixing her gaze, he leaned down and kissed Julie's neck.

Bobby scooted closer. He put an arm around Farin's shoulder. She tensed at the protective gesture.

Cynicism saturated Chris's laugh. "Going after married women, are we? I'm afraid that one isn't much of a challenge."

Marci opened her mouth to speak, but Elliot put a hand on her knee.

Cheryl squeezed her husband's arm, then turned to Julie. "I should get home and check on the boys. What-say you and I head back and let Chris have some time alone with his band?"

Julie addressed her husband with a tight smile. "Baby, you okay?"

"Never better. You go on home. I'll be there shortly." He drew her in and kissed her before she headed out with Cheryl.

"That was uncalled for," Bobby said.

Chris's cheerful façade dissolved the moment Julie was out of earshot. "I don't need any tips on how to treat my wife. And I don't remember inviting you here tonight."

"I represent LSI and Farin's with me."

"And where, pray tell, is my baby brother?"

"Don't start a scene, weasel," Marci warned. She turned to Farin. "Let's get out of here."

"I'm not here to make trouble." Her head was fuzzy. For the first time in months, she wished she had a Valium. "I'm sorry, Chris. I realize how hard it was for you. Let's not make this any worse than it is."

Chris dropped onto the sofa, draping both arms along its back, and glared at her.

Forge's patrons grew curious over the crowd of reporters surrounding the VIP area, their cameras flashing savagely as microphones plunged into the group. Several couples stopped dancing and wandered closer. Others stared their way.

Her voice quaked. "I never meant to hurt you."

"Isn't hurting people what you do best?"

Ben turned to his brother, wagging his finger. "Not here."

"Look!" Farin rose on wobbly legs. She teetered, arms flailing as she side-stepped past Bobby, inching toward the open space in the sofa where Chris sat. "I said I'm sorry. What more do you want?"

He jerked to his feet, coming to within inches of her face. "I wish I'd never met you. You're the reason we're here tonight, you know. Did your precious Jameson tell you he canned us over you?"

Farin's eyes bulged in astonishment. "*What*?"

Elliot stood, stepped over and past Marci and Bobby, then grabbed Chris's arm. "Leave her be, mate."

Chris shook him off. He turned back with a scowl and shouted over the din of the club. "You've caused nothing but disaster for everyone. Look at us. Look at what happened to Faith! And I won't even mention what happened to my nephew!"

"I said not here!" Ben bolted up and clasped Chris's shoulder. He pulled him back, but Chris shrugged him off as well.

Chris inched closer, his dark eyes piercing Farin's with sheer hatred.

Drunk and confused, she swayed in place, aghast at Chris's unspeakable accusations as the press closed in on them.

"If you had any class, you wouldn't have come tonight!" he hissed.

In a flash, her hurt became rage. Fists clenched at her sides, she slit her eyes at him. "If you weren't such an insufferable grandstander, you'd save it for a less public place!"

"Bitch!"

Elliot stepped forward, interposing himself between Chris and Farin. "I'm not joking, mate. Leave it!"

Brows high, Ben called past his brother to Farin. "Walk away, kid."

The crowd buzzed excitedly as more flash bulbs drowned the club's neon in near-daylight. The pounding beat of dance music permeated the air as spectators encircled them.

Farin's jaw slacked, her forehead creased in disbelief. Marci reached for her hand but she jerked it away, pitching forward. "What did you call me?"

"Enough!" Bobby stalked up from behind. With Chris distracted by Elliot, Bobby spun him around and threw a vicious right hook. It landed squarely on his jaw, instantly dropping him to the floor.

A hush fell over the room. The music ceased. Camera flashes lit the scene, popping like corn kernels.

Heedless of the sudden silence, Farin screamed, "A *bitch*? You're the one who chased *me* all these years! Does wifey know you were impotent because you only wanted me? Having any trouble getting it up with her, or do you have to pretend she's me to make it work?"

Ben threw his hands in the air, then flopped back down on the sofa.

Marci dropped her head onto her hands.

Chris scampered to his feet. He glared at Bobby as the man flexed his hand and stood at Farin's side. Blood filled his mouth from a split inside his lip, the membrane tearing against his lower teeth. He rubbed his jaw and glowered at Farin. In the silence, he spit words and blood. "I hate you."

"Good! We finally feel the same way about each other!"

Bobby grabbed Farin's purse and her arm. He dragged her through the crowd to their waiting limousine. As the car sped off, he shed his blazer and tossed it aside. "That was pleasant. I'm sure Dad'll be thrilled with tomorrow's headlines."

Farin stared out the window. The lights of Miami Beach whizzed and whirled by in a blur.

Bobby grabbed the bottle of Jack Daniels he had procured at the arena and handed it to her. "Anyone else you want to completely eviscerate before the evening's over?"

She took a hearty swig, then handed it back. "I can't believe you hit him."

He draped his arm sloppily around her shoulders as they weaved in and out of traffic. He finished the whiskey off. "Forget Jordan and Chris. Run away with me."

She laughed good-naturedly until she registered the seriousness of his expression. "You must be tired. You said you didn't sleep last night."

He shrugged, then faced the window, liquor bottle cradled in his arms.

"We're drunk," she explained, mostly to herself. "We all do and say things we shouldn't when we're drunk."

"Then it's the perfect time to tell you I'm in love with you."

She blanched. "You can't be."

He leaned over and pressed his lips to hers. "I know."

By the time they reached Coral Gables, Farin vaguely remembered stumbling into the limousine. She had a far-off memory of feeling unsteady at the concert, anger at Chris's triumphal moment, people staring and pointing at Forge, and Bobby's protective arm around her waist as he led her out into the night. She remembered laughing, and then he had kissed her. She could swear she remembered him kissing her.

"What are we doing here?" she slurred.

He stumbled out of the car and staggered up his walkway. A moment later, his left arm shot out, bracing him against the house as his body heaved into the hedgerow beside his front door.

She snatched up the blazer, then faced her driver with blurry eyes.

"Wait here while I get him settled."

The driver nodded and killed the engine.

She went to Bobby, gagging slightly as she stood beside him, patting his back. A quick search of his blazer pockets produced a set of house keys. She fumbled through them, attempting to discern which one might unlock the door. Her own drunken state left her uncoordinated and clumsy. "You okay? You're gonna need to punch in your alarm code."

When his retching subsided, he stumbled backward, then righted himself. He grabbed the keys and opened the door, guiding her inside with a certain amount of roughness.

Given his earlier disclosure, she felt out of place in his home. She felt along the wall to avoid falling. "I can't find a light switch."

He flipped on the entry light and threw his arm around her shoulder. His knees buckled beneath him. "Help me to my room."

As they climbed the stairs, the steps swayed beneath her feet. Portraits along the wall seemed to mock her with sarcastic sneers. She glanced at him. Even his face had adopted a sinister grin. His expression made her flesh crawl.

Unable to sort her thoughts, she continued on to his room. Muted leers, muzzled communication and, she was almost certain, guarded advances replaced the laughter of the ride over.

She deposited him onto his bed, then teetered backward.

When he rose and began to undress, she spun around, uneasy with his immodesty. She attributed it to the alcohol. "I should get home."

Then, everything went dark.

She drifted in and out for she knew not how long. Years of nightmares came to her, crashing down like a skyscraper imploding into its own footprint. The accident, her father's car shattered and twisted around the mysterious black Porsche, and him bent lifelessly over the steering wheel. A young man approaching the car, laughing at the destruction, at the life he had taken. That laughing face transformed into not James Wellingham, but Bobby Lockhardt.

An abrupt thud forced her back to reality. She slit her eyes, disoriented as she realized her horizontal orientation. In that instant, the second of her two shoes struck the wall, leaving a deep gash in the plaster. Her handbag flew by next, its overturned contents spilling and crashing to the floor. She perceived a draft and looked down at her body.

In the time it took to realize she lay undressed atop Bobby's bed, she felt tugged roughly to its center. He straddled her at the waist, trapping her forearms beneath his knees, his feet hooked around and pinning her upper thighs. One sweaty hand pressed down on her chest while the other reached toward the nightstand.

"What...?" she asked groggily as she began to suspect, through her drunken fog, that what she felt was not a product of her imagination. "What are you doing?"

He said nothing. Animalistic and intent, his face glowed in the moonlight seeping in through sheer curtains. He snatched his bedside phone off the nightstand, then lifted his palm off her chest long enough to jerk its cord free. He flung the device across the room with incredible force, then yanked the remaining cord from the phone jack, folding its length in half.

His eyes leered with grim determination as he gnawed through the polyvinyl casing. He twisted the exposed wires until they severed. Holding one length between his teeth, he wrapped the other around her wrist, lacing her securely to the headboard.

"You're hurting me!" she shrieked, sobering as the bond pinched her wrist. She struggled against him. "*Stop!*"

The sound of her voice appeared to startle him. He glanced down, observing her with incomprehension. Then, he slapped the side of her face with tremendous force, the sound like thunder in the quiet room, and tied her other wrist. The pain in her jaw and eye socket so shocked her, she did not anticipate the second blow, fist closed, until it struck. She gasped for breath, grimacing in anguish.

With lightning-quick movements, he thrust his knee up hard between her legs, forcing them apart, and grabbed a fistful of her hair. She screamed and struggled against the thin bonds and Bobby's sudden burst of power as he poised himself to enter her.

"I love you!" he howled. "Can't you see? *I love you!*"

Farin wailed in agony. She begged him repeatedly to stop.

She was dry. When he penetrated her, he ripped and tore her insides. He backed off momentarily to spit in his hands, then rubbed the saliva along his member for lubrication.

Again and again he thrust into her, pounding his body against her despite her pleas. Her body tensed, her abdomen ached and, as he came down upon her, she thought she felt something rupture. Unable to move, she was reduced to a few helpless whimpers.

Passionless pummeling replaced his initial outbursts. The only audible sounds were the creaking mattress springs and his own tormented grunting. A torturous eternity passed. Then, one final shudder. Release. Sleep.

Bobby collapsed on top of her.

Farin listened as his breathing steadily slowed. She waited for some time before attempting to move, terrified of what he might do if she woke him. She turned and watched the digital alarm clock atop his nightstand with her right eye, its red display telling her it was now past midnight.

For twelve minutes, she lay there, afraid to move, afraid to stay, afraid he would wake up, and afraid she would never leave his house alive.

When he stirred at last, she held her breath and prayed. He mumbled indecipherably. Then, he moved from atop her, rolled onto his side, and began to snore.

The phone cord had cut into her wrists. She hoped the pain did not indicate a fracture. Her face stung from his blows. Her left eye had swollen shut. The muscles in her thighs and calves ached from straining against his assault. Her insides felt as if they had exploded.

A keen awareness replaced her previous intoxication. She wracked her brain for some way to extricate herself from the restraints binding her to Bobby's bed. She squinted her right eye until she could focus on her bloodied left wrist, then her right. Moonlight and moist, matted blood reflected off the tubing of the cords. Finally, she noticed one of them had loosened during her struggle.

Her recent experience with extricating herself from improperly secured restraints came in handy. She wriggled free of her bondage and dragged her shaking body from the bed.

Battered, bruised, and bleeding from her wrists and between her legs, she skinned on her torn slip, gathered her remaining clothes, and scooped together the contents of her purse as quickly and quietly as possible. She crept from the room, then stumbled downstairs. A sense of relief found her as she peered out the front door's sidelight and saw the LSI limousine parked along the circular driveway.

Her driver stared in astonishment as she bounded into the car and shut the door. "Are you all right?"

She sobbed and shook her head.

He started the vehicle and reached for its phone. "The police can meet us at the hospital."

"No, Charles," Farin heard herself say. "I can't go there."

He stopped dialing and looked through the rearview mirror. "Mrs. Grant, you need a doctor—and a cop."

"Get me home. *Please*."

Without further prompting, he replaced the phone, shifted the car into gear, and focused his attention on the road.

As they sped away, the impact of her life, of this moment, of everything she knew, intersected. She did not know this beast who had taken her so viciously. Her heart broke as she sobbed for herself, for Jordan, for Chris, and even for Bobby. What had he done? What had Bobby turned into? And what could she possibly do now?

Instinct told her Charles was right. She should go to the hospital. But they would call the police, and she could not let that happen.

Hundreds of people had witnessed Bobby defending her honor and their rapid departure. Given her public image, and the affair with Chris, who would believe her? The shame of her past actions overwhelmed and nauseated her never more vividly than at that moment.

Even if she did notify the authorities, press charges, and withstand the certain public scrutiny, she did not think for one minute Jordan would believe she had not willingly betrayed him again. She could lose him forever.

Farin considered her career and the potential scandal. Bobby had not only changed his life forever, tonight. He had changed everything.

Her voice pierced the stillness in the car. "Charles, no one can know about tonight. Understand?"

"If Mr. Lockhardt finds out I knew and didn't tell him, I'll lose my job," he protested. Then, more sympathetically, he added, "Please let me take you to the hospital."

"I'll handle Jameson," she promised, projecting more confidence than she felt. "You won't lose your job."

"I'm sorry, Mrs. Grant. That sounded mighty cold, didn't it?"

"I think it's time you started calling me Farin."

Her thoughts jumped frantically between Chris's spiteful words and Bobby's violent assault. Nothing made sense.

She needed to talk to Jameson. He would tell her what to do.

CHAPTER 31

THE CAR PULLED INTO THE driveway at one in the morning. Charles hopped out of the driver's seat and hastened to help Farin exit the vehicle. She leaned on him as he led her to the door, then inside.

"I don't know what to do," he confessed. "I can't leave you so bad off."

She winced with each forced step, hobbling across the entryway. When she looked down, she noticed drops of blood pooling into a tiny puddle on the tile. Behind her, a trail of droplets disappeared out the front door.

"Please, Mrs. Grant, let me take you to the hospital."

"No, Charles. What I need you to do is help me upstairs."

She sent him to the kitchen for a roll of paper towels. When he returned, he unwound several perforated sheets, which he mashed together into a dense wad and handed to her. She held them between her legs to prevent getting blood on the carpet as he helped her upstairs and into the master bathroom.

At her request, he eased her onto the tile floor.

"I've got it from here. Thank you."

"Mrs. Grant—"

"Farin." She grimaced.

"When's Mr. Grant coming back?"

"A week and a half."

His eyes bulged.

"I'm fine. I promise."

"But young Mr. Lockhardt—what if he comes 'round looking for you?"

She raised her hand. It hurt to talk, to think. "Go now. I'll be fine."

Charles scribbled his home number on a Walgreens receipt he found in his jacket pocket. "You need *anything*, you call me."

She lifted her chin, indicating the marble counter. "I promise. Please, just go."

He laid the receipt on the countertop with some hesitation, then turned back as if to make a final plea. She shut her eyes in agony and shook her head. Finally, he walked out the door.

For the next hour, she huddled motionless on the master bathroom floor, disbelieving what had transpired, unable to force herself up and into the shower. Only the pain, her swollen face, and the blood trickling onto the blood-soaked wad of paper towels convinced her she had not imagined the entire incident.

Her body throbbed in protest when she attempted to stand. She beheld her torn and bloodied clothes piddling in a heap near the door and lifted her slip gingerly over her head, then lobbed it toward the pile, breathing as shallow as possible. The paper towel splatted to the floor, dropping from the weight of its volume. Unsure she could bend over, she snagged the bath towel she had discarded the previous morning with her big toe, slid it beneath her, and collapsed on top of it.

She inspected the ripped skin on her wrists, contemplating how best to talk to the father of the monster who had brutalized her.

LSI means everything to me. And you've been like a father. I know I would have probably disappointed my real dad with the way I've lived my life. I feel like a whore. I can't bear to tell the police or anyone but you. Please, Jameson, tell me what to do.

As she shivered nude, bruised, and bleeding on the cold tile, an even more horrifying thought occurred to her: what if Jameson did not believe her?

Through sheer will, she forced herself up at last. She needed to feel clean again. She needed to wash away the stench of Bobby's sweat and semen.

As she passed the mirror, she caught the image of her battered face and body out of her right eye. The sight nauseated her.

She fell to the toilet and vomited.

In a spark of clarity, she realized she had spent her life convincing herself she was fate's victim. That her life was predestined for suffering. Every day for the last eighteen years, she had sought confirmation of that belief—and had found it. Now, she realized all the choices had belonged to her.

As she rose from the toilet and flushed the bile and alcohol she had purged from her system, her mother's words finally rang true. *Her* choices. *Her* decisions. *Her* life. A victim?

No more.

***

Jordan boarded the Miami-bound plane a defeated man. Nearly two weeks of his life—two weeks away from Farin—only to return empty-handed. He had flown to Santa Barbara for any hints, facts, rumors, or clues that might lead him to James Wellingham. The moment he had decided to take Farin back, he had pledged to end her nightmares once and for all. He had failed.

He still believed that somewhere out there, James Wellingham agonized over that fateful night. The man had never looked at the world from the inside of a jail cell as a result of his crime. But some prisons went beyond stone, brick, and steel encasements. Could anyone ever truly be free knowing they had cut short the life of another?

Whatever the case, despite Jordan's efforts to prove otherwise, James Wellingham might as well have never existed at all.

***

Farin grabbed her compact and examined her left eye, nervous as Charles drove her to the airport. "You sure you can't tell?"

"Even without the makeup, you can barely notice."

She snapped the case shut, then folded her hands on her lap and stared out the window as they passed towering palm trees and buildings aged with faded, peeling paint.

He glanced at her periodically through the rearview mirror. "I called and checked. Flight's on time."

She thanked him, then pulled up the sleeves of her thin cotton shirt to inspect the only remaining physical evidence of the assault. Thin stripes of pink flesh healed nicely beneath a cluster of trendy bracelets. If vigilant in maintaining her disguise, Jordan need never know.

Charles had been a benison in the days following the assault. Though she had initially resisted his unannounced visits, he had proven himself an invaluable resource. He had cleaned up the blood in the entry way before leaving that night. For days, he helped ice the swelling, adding a warm compress on day two, and pumped her full of fresh papaya to absorb the bromelain and flush out the trapped blood and fluid in her damaged tissue. Daily exposure to sunlight broke down the bilirubin that caused the bruises to yellow. Before long, the visible signs of her hellish ordeal began to fade.

The memory, however, remained.

"Thanks for all your help," she told him as he turned into the airport.

"No need to thank me none, Mrs. Grant."

She had thus far lacked the requisite courage to talk to Jameson. For three years, he had treated her not unlike a daughter—but in truth, she was little more than a glorified employee. Surely, Jameson's loyalty would not lie with her. Bobby was his blood.

Blood. She shivered as she waited for Jordan's plane to land.

Charles handled Jordan's luggage while he and Farin reunited. They rocked back and forth, locked in an embrace. He inhaled the fresh scent of citrus in her curls.

"I tried to call for days. The answering machine didn't even pick up. Where have you been?"

She avoided his eyes. Her thoughts ping-ponged between her waking nightmare, Chris's shocking announcement, and his stunning new wife.

"It's okay. Ben told me about the concert. I'm sorry. I should've gone with you."

They rode home in silence, cuddled together in the back of the limousine.

Jordan realized he had returned just in time. That old familiar dragon of distance—the distance that rendered Farin incapable of sharing her problems with him—would rise up if he did not slay it. He would not knuckle under the hold Chris had on her. Not this time. Not ever again.

When they arrived home, they went upstairs to unpack Jordan's things. He attempted to lift her spirits with happier news. "Looks like Marci won't be needing the beach house any longer."

"Why not?"

"She and Elliot eloped last weekend. She tried to tell you herself but said she couldn't get through. They flew to New Zealand for their honeymoon."

A misty smile brushed her face, one of happiness for her friend and regret over having missed the ceremony. "I miss LA."

"I have their new address. I'll go get your address book so you can write it in." He left her to unpack while he went downstairs to the study.

Standing before the last surviving remnant of his wife's childhood rekindled his frustration. He reflected bitterly on his wasted trip as he slid open her roll-top desk and searched. Statements and correspondence littered its surface, but he found no phone book.

A perfunctory search of the top and bottom right-hand drawers netted nothing but office supplies and hanging file folders. As he opened the top left-hand drawer, he encountered a steel document box with a hinged lid and recessed lift-up handle. He withdrew it carefully, examined its exterior, then jiggled it. From the sound and weight distribution, he guessed something awkward and sizeable lay inside. Alas, it was locked.

He carried the receptacle back to the bedroom and handed it over. "Unless it's inside here, I couldn't find it."

Farin paled at the sight of the box. Nostrils flared, she regarded the box with the same horror she felt waking from one of her nightmares— nightmares that had recently adopted Bobby Lockhardt's cold, heartless face in place of the hazy, unclear image she had always had of James Wellingham.

He stepped toward her. "Are you okay?"

Her hand shot out in front of her, stopping his advance. "Those are my mother's personal papers. She wanted me to go through them after she died, but I could never bring myself to do it. In fact, I almost threw them in the fire one night."

He eyed the box with a zealous gleam. "I could go through them with you."

Panic beset her as if an autonomic reaction. She opened her mouth to protest but willed a less fragile response. In the privacy of her mind, she quoted her new mantra: *I am not a victim.*

"Not yet. I don't think I want to know any more than I do."

Later, Jordan made sure Farin was asleep before he crept back to the den and reacquired the metal box. Three years of trying to solve the mystery behind Kelley O'Conner's fatal car accident. Maybe he had never needed to look any further than his own front door.

He picked the box's lock with a paperclip, then lifted the lid. Papers, pictures, and a curious brown paper bag filled him with anticipation. His pulse raced as he logged a cursory inventory of the contents, certain now the answers he needed had been in this desk the whole time.

He studied the police report intently, then read the obituary notice, which he knew for certain had never made it to print. He peeped inside the paper bag, filed through photos—each discovery a vital clue missing from the Santa Barbara records.

Then, he saw the letter.

Obviously written years ago, Farin's mother had scribbled it on lined binder paper, so stained and yellowed with age it nearly broke in two as he opened it.

An attack of conscience gave him pause. Farin had insisted she did not want to confront this sadness. Nonetheless, he justified his actions. She would never be whole until she made peace with her past.

Someone had to help her. This time, it would not be Chris.

Scanning the pages, his eyes bulged in disbelief. Heartfelt apologies and confessed secrets of Farin's lifetime intersected with Beth O'Conner's pleas for her daughter's understanding. He collapsed into the black leather desk chair as Farin's mother answered every question.

It was not possible.

***

Farin wandered down to the beach shortly after noon. The sun soothed her skin even as the sand scorched her bare feet. An eerie feeling had haunted her all morning, like a premonition she could neither fully identify nor dismiss. Jordan's unexpected announcement over breakfast of a last-minute trip to New York had left her unsettled. He had claimed it was a business matter. Somehow, she knew it was more.

An inviting patch of shade under an obliging palm tree caught her eye. She settled in to watch the watercraft dotting the bay, reflecting upon their boating excursion back in June. Christmas had snuck up on her. They had not discussed purchasing a tree, but maybe that was for the best.

She thought about Marci and Elliot's New Zealand honeymoon, realizing she and Jordan had never taken one themselves. Maybe this year, their first real Christmas together, they could scurry off to an exotic location. Somewhere without the pressure of work, or family, or tragedy. On days like today, she longed to climbed aboard one of the boats out on the bay, sailing away from it all—adrift forever.

Only recently had she evaluated the undercurrent of grief she had long based her existence on. Every decision she had ever made revolved around her search for someone to heal her, someone to replace her father's love, someone to stop the pain. Not once had she looked within herself for the peace, or the strength, she lacked.

Over the past few months, she had experienced a mounting discomfort in her psyche. A truth that bubbled up inside her no matter how she fought it. Now, she understood. No one could help her. She had to help herself.

No amount of wealth, fame, love, or forgiveness could bring her something one could not acquire externally. No amount of running could free her from herself. Her mother's parting words were an inheritance more valuable than all the riches in the world.

I am not a victim.

The sea breeze stirred her auburn ringlets. Gulls cawed and swooped to the shore. Sun worshippers laughed and socialized aboard their crafts. Their gaiety eased the tension of Jordan's absence as her fingers drew lazy circles in the perfect sand.

"Nothing like a warm December."

She held her hand up against the sun. "What are you doing down here?"

Ben sat down close beside her, removed his sunglasses, and squinted out at the bay. The familiar scent of his woody cologne commingled with the salty air. "I came to see if Jordan was about. No one answered the door, so I took a chance you'd be here."

He turned his bearded face toward the water and eyed the boats coming and going. Farin studied him with lighthearted whimsy, imagining him the captain of a merchant marine vessel on a long haul from Europe.

She scooted closer. "It's just me, today. Jordan's in New York."

"Meeting with Jameson?"

"What else? I don't know, Ben. Sometimes, I wonder how Jordan and Chris do it. All the pressure to be...whoever it is we're supposed to be."

"You okay?"

She shrugged. An uneasiness she could not express crept into her mind.

"Looks like you need a shoulder. I happen to have two free." He positioned a strong, broad shoulder her way as if in offering.

She rested her head atop it. "I'm always leaning on someone, aren't I?"

"I don't mind."

"I've made so many mistakes—personally and professionally. The more I think about it, the more they seem like one and the same. You were right, you know? What you told me in the hospital?"

He peered out at the water. A motorboat sped by, its passengers whooping and waving in jollity, or perhaps fleeting recognition. They waved back and smiled.

"People have protected me my whole life. But instead of making me stronger, it made me weak. The affair—weakness of character. The suicide attempt—weakness of spirit. Even physical weakness..." Her voice trailed off as Bobby's attack flickered in her mind.

"You're twenty-eight, Farin. You're not supposed to have your life figured out, yet. Hell, who does?"

Her lips curved into a gentle smile. "You."

He chuckled. "Not me, I'm afraid. Maybe my wife."

"I've put Jordan through hell. I've torn your family apart."

"It'll all work out."

"Now that Chris is married, you'd think Jordan and I would be fine. But something's wrong. I feel it."

"Jordan hasn't said anything. Maybe there's still something between you and Chris that's keeping you and Jordan apart."

She pondered the suggestion. "It's not them, it's me. It's always been me."

He gave her arm a loving squeeze.

"I know I'm screwed up, Ben. Do you think I'll ever get better? Maybe I should have seen someone like Dr. Clark wanted me to."

Ben raised his knees and burrowed his bare feet in the sand. Her words relieved him. He had all but given up hope someone would find the courage to get her the help she needed.

"I need to come clean with Jordan. If I don't, we'll never be whole. *I'll* never be whole. Do you think he and Chris will ever forgive each other? Or have I messed it up for everyone?"

"We're family, Farin. Everyone's gonna be fine."

"Chris hates me."

"No, I don't."

Ben spun around, mystified. "What are you doing here?"

Gusts of wind toyed with the ends of Chris's wavy hair. Farin turned to see him, disheveled and visibly shattered, as he towered over them.

He rubbed his three-day growth of whiskers. "It's gone on long enough."

"You have a wife now," Ben snapped, squinting up at him. "Time to let go."

"I know what I'm doing. Farin and I need to talk...*alone*."

Ben rose and faced his younger sibling. Guilt over his protracted silence eroded his conscience like sea against the shoreline. He should have interfered years ago—before the affair, before all their problems raged out of control.

"This family extends beyond the three of us, Chris. We've all got wives...responsibilities. And right now, my responsibility is to make sure you don't hurt her, or their marriage, anymore."

Chris hung his head, numb to his brother's reproach. "She'll be okay."

Farin stood and touched Ben's shoulder. For the first time since the day they met, she did not doubt her ability to handle a personal confrontation with Chris. "He's right, Ben. We need to settle this thing once and for all."

Ben gauged her resolve, then turned to his brother. "You cock anything else up, I'll make the thrashing Jordan gave you look like a tickling match. Are we clear?"

He nodded.

As Ben trudged down the wide expanse of sand, they strolled farther down the beach until they found a private spot in an armlet among a cluster of palms.

Chris leaned back, propping himself up on his elbows as he stretched and crossed his legs at his ankles. Somewhere along the path that led him to her, his overconfidence and innuendo-saturated façade had melted away. His eyes darted back and forth, as if striving to recall a poorly rehearsed speech.

"I don't love Julie. You probably know that already."

Farin hugged her knees. "Don't tell me these things."

"I thought I did, and then I thought I could, but I don't."

She tucked her face into her arms.

"We can't go on like this, Farin—*I* can't. Every time my heart beats, you're there. Like you're in my bloody soul. It's completely mental, but it's true."

She clamped her eyes shut. "You've gotta leave me alone."

"After everything we've been through, you must feel it, too."

To say she did not have a special place inside her that belonged solely to him would only hurt him further. Moreover, it would be a lie. She was tired of lying.

She stood and brushed the sand from her shorts. "I can't love two men, Chris. And I can't stay here with you any longer. It's time we both got on with our lives."

"I'm right, aren't I?"

She headed back to the house, determined to unyoke herself from the conflicting emotions he evoked within her. Whatever the truth, she belonged with Jordan.

The greater the distance between them, the clearer it became. If she could leave Chris now, she could be the wife Jordan deserved. She could face her reflection in the mirror without feeling disgusted by the image looking back.

I am not a victim.

As she reached her front door, she realized he had followed her home.

"What are you so afraid of?" he challenged, marching through the front door before she could slam it shut.

Tears brimmed her eyes as the inevitability of the moment seized her. She locked her arms around him, knowing it was goodbye.

He held her close. "Say you love me, too. We can make this work."

"We consume everyone and everything around us, Chris—including each other. And it's still never enough."

He pulled back and searched her eyes. "We could run away."

She lowered herself into Jordan's recliner and rubbed her hairline with her fingertips. "I'm through running. I can't do it anymore."

"Farin, please. Think about this."

"I'm content for the first time in my life, Chris. I have you to thank for a lot of that—and I *do* thank you. But let's wish each other well and move on, okay? Can't we do that?"

He collapsed to his knees before her, grabbing the arms of the chair. His pleading eyes bored into hers. "Whether you leave with me now or you never see me again, we're bound together. You've fought it for years now, but it *always* comes back to us. It always will. Don't you see?"

"I'm sorry," she whispered.

She remained seated as he rose to his feet, head low, shoulder-slumped, and defeated as he trudged out the front door.

Now more than ever, she knew she and Jordan needed a fresh start. In her mind, she rehearsed her confession. The only way to salvage their marriage was to tell him everything she could bear to say and beg him to move away from Miami. No more secrets, no more lies, and no more temptation.

***

Nancy buzzed Jameson's office. "Mr. Lockhardt, Jordan Grant's here. He insists on seeing you right away."

Jameson cocked his head, curious over the unexpected visit of his most popular male star. "Send him back and reschedule my next appointment."

"Yes, sir."

"And hold my calls."

"Understood."

He leaned back in his chair and folded his hands in his lap, all smiles as his office door opened. "Jordan, my boy! What a coincidence! Ross and I just wrapped up a meeting concerning the tour. I have great news—"

"We need to talk." Jordan marched across the office and dropped a copy of Beth's letter on his desk.

He glanced down at the paper, then back at Jordan. "Is Farin okay?"

"No! She actually believes you're a trustworthy person who cares about her." Jordan indicated the letter with a terse nod. "I found this in Farin's desk last night."

With exaggerated calm, Jameson lifted the paper and read. He remained poised as his worst fears materialized before his eyes. Beth O'Conner had left her only daughter a legacy of truth after all. It was there in black and white—each word an incriminating nail in his coffin, each letter exposing the truth. "Has Farin seen this?"

"Not yet."

The subtle threat registered on Jameson's face.

Jordan glared into his steely blue eyes. "I didn't know how to tell her you've been manipulating her since the day of my son's funeral."

An impassive expression cloaked his features. He abandoned the letter, reclined into his chair, and tented his fingers across his chest. "I've ensured her a successful life. As you know, I've put her in my will."

Jordan eyed him with disgust. "You think you can keep her in the dark forever?"

"Yes, actually. After Beth died, it became fairly simple—until now."

"What about Bobby? Does he know who she is to him?" Jordan reeled at the thought of the twisted connection between his wife and the Lockhardts.

He motioned to a chair. "Let me explain."

Jordan raised his hands to his waist.

"Have it your way," he said. He glanced up at the ceiling, as if to collect his thoughts, then released a heavy breath. "My son is ill. Dr. Childs has treated his psychosis for over fifteen years now. The impact of this letter could throw him into a state of shock—or worse."

Jordan slumped into one of the two high back chairs, the implications tumbling onto his lap. "You gave her away at our *wedding*."

"I wanted to protect them. Both of them. The truth can only complicate things."

"Who are you to make that decision?"

"Farin has fame, wealth, a career, and *you*. What more could she need?"

"A father!"

He snickered at Jordan's naiveté. "Rubbish. Her future's secure. She's at the top of her career. She's done quite well for herself."

"You know nothing about her problems."

"Oh yes, her *problems*. Turns out, we have another one, though I hesitate to bring it up." He fixed his eyes on Jordan's and added calmly, "Bobby fancies himself in love with her."

Jordan's expression flattened. "You put them together and now you're pulling both their strings. How could you play such a sadistic game?"

The arrow hit its mark, filling Jameson with a rush of self-satisfaction. "I've spent a fortune keeping this quiet, Jordan. I have no problem spending more."

"You wouldn't want to damage the precious Lockhardt name."

"Your concern's touching, but this is getting us nowhere." He stood and trod the worn path along his rug, pacing like a caged lion. "Farin's happy with the way things are for her. The best thing you can do is forget you ever saw Beth's letter. Give me the original. I'll destroy it."

"You must be mad!"

He paused to face the city skyline. "Then sell it to me and I'll do what's best for everyone."

Jordan stood, stabbing the air as he railed at Jameson's back. "My brother was right about you. But you're wrong about Farin. She's *not* happy. She wants her father. I'm sure she'd want some kind of an explanation. I know she deserves one. You've no idea how she struggles every day. And every night, she wakes up screaming. Do you know about her nightmares?"

"I know everything there is to know," Jameson shot back ominously. "I assure you, it'll only get worse if you take this thing further. Everyone you know and trust will suffer the fallout."

"I'm more concerned about my wife than anyone else."

"Then go home and start making her happy. Forget about the past. Think about the damage this could do to her. In her present state of mind? I'd hate to have another incident like we had last spring."

Jameson turned back and watched Jordan absorb his warning, satisfied the man's sense of good would prevent further complications. "I'm sure you'll see in time this was the only reasonable way to handle the situation."

***

Farin had just climbed the stairs for bed when the front door opened. She raced down the steps and into Jordan's arms, stomach churning. Their bodies collided.

"I thought you'd spend the night in New York."

He held her silently at the foot of the stairs, his breath warm against her neck. She felt the fleeting shiver of his body when he pulled away, taking her hand and leading her to the living room. "Let's talk."

The words were eerily reminiscent of the night he left her. She envisioned all manner of scenarios to explain his somber disposition.

Battling her knee-jerk reaction, she cautioned herself to remain calm. She squared her shoulders, then sat down on the sofa, pulling together the folds of her robe.

I am not a victim.

"I've been thinking," she said, peering up at him.

"You have?"

She nodded. "I want our marriage to work. I'm ready. I'll tell you what you need to know."

Mouth shut, he gave her a weak but patient smile as he settled into the sofa. His full concentration rested upon her, bidding she continue. Yet something in his eyes started her heart thumping. He looked troubled. Or sad.

It was now or never.

"You were right. About Chris and me. Something's there. It's been there from the start."

Timid at first, she gauged his reaction. He sat sideways, foot hooked beneath his knee, his elbow wedged into the couch back, head propped against his hand. No hint of judgment in his features.

Emboldened, she confessed things he might not want to know, yet needed desperately to understand.

"I never sought him out, but I never really discourage him, either. I'm as much to blame as he is."

"Our reception. Was he the reason you left?"

She glanced down at her fingers, amazed at their steadiness. "He said you'd only married me because I was pregnant."

"How could you believe such nonsense? Don't you know I love you?"

"Yes. But you were in such a rush..." She hesitated, careful not to take the conversational thread too far. "Anyway, he tracked me down in Paris. He was there the day I lost Melody."

Jordan's lips curled inward. His sad expression filled her with fresh remorse.

Eventually, all her words were spent. She searched his eyes. Only two secrets remained. Melody's true paternity would only deliver a death blow to the family. But the incident with Bobby? She deferred the revelation. For that, she would await Jameson's guidance. She trusted his judgment. He would do the right thing.

"I'm through running," she said at last, scooting closer, covering his hand with hers. "All those times I left, it was to get away from Chris, not you. But I do want to go away once more...*with* you. We could move back to California. Please, Jordan. You need time to forgive him. And me."

Despite intermittent shocks to his system—the gift of the sapphire, for one—her confession chased away years of doubt and suspicion. The details blurred. They no longer mattered. She finally trusted him. Now, she could be his forever.

"You look so hopeful." He met her gaze, dreading the task before him. "Is that a yes?"

With outstretched arms, he drew her in. "We'll go wherever you want. If it's California, we can leave tomorrow as far as I'm concerned."

Farin burrowed into his chest.

He stroked her hair. "But tonight, I have a confession of my own."

She craned her neck upward. "What is it?"

"That box of your mother's. I went through it last night. You were asleep."

Her body turned to stone inside his embrace. She scooted away. "You did...*what*?"

As Jordan tried to explain, Farin's mind clicked shut. Her husband's mournful features disappeared into the fog of her nightmares. His voice garbled, evaporating into ether. She perceived only the still-painful memories of policemen on her doorstep and in her parents' room. The family station wagon at the impound lot. The haunting visions chased away the echoes of her mother's final words.

Something in Jordan's solemn disposition warned her, like her mother had years before, that her life was about to change. Forever.

She leapt from the sofa. "I told you I wasn't ready yet."

"I wanted to help you with your nightmares. I'd been searching for information on this James Wellingham. I thought maybe you'd find peace if you met him and saw for yourself he's no threat to you. That's why I flew to California, and to New York today."

She glared at him, fists balled at her sides. "Did it ever occur to you I might not want to meet him? That box was personal!"

"What's personal to you is personal to me. And anyway, I found out."

Farin covered her ears. She paced the room, head shaking. "Don't tell me! I hate him!"

Jordan reached into his blazer pocket and produced an envelope. "This is from your mother. It explains everything."

Farin lunged forward, slapping the envelope from his hand. "No!"

Jordan rose, retrieved Beth's letter, then followed behind her. "This is all about you," he said, waving the document at her. "About your life. Don't you care that you've been manipulated all along?"

"What are you talking about?" She stopped abruptly.

"There is no James Wellingham."

Farin fell quiet. Her arms dropped to her side. "What do you mean?"

Jordan clasped her shoulders, fixing her eyes with his. "Bobby Lockhardt killed your father."

CHAPTER 32

I AM NOT A VICTIM.

As the airplane lifted off, Farin's mind struggled to stay afloat in a rip current of truth. Bobby Lockhardt. James Wellingham. Her mother's cryptic words on her deathbed. How "they" had killed her husband, stripped her of her dignity, and then "they" had taken her only daughter.

A bubbly flight attendant approached her the minute the requisite chimes indicated the crew could unfasten their safety belts. "Can I get you anything to drink, Mrs. Grant?"

She shook her head, irritated that she had neglected to grab her disguise out of Jordan's trunk when he reluctantly dropped her off at the airport. "I'm okay. Thanks."

Eighteen years of lies organized themselves chronologically in her mind. The three-hour flight between Miami and New York passed slowly. She smoldered in her seat, unable to decide who she hated most—Jameson, Bobby, or herself.

After Jordan's shocking announcement, she had attempted to read her mother's letter. Though she could not bring herself to finish the entire thing, she had read enough to know what she needed to do.

Jameson had spied on them since the morning after the accident, offering financial assistance to the young widow and her pathetic child. He had made repeated attempts to buy her silence, even as he had bought the newspaper, police department, witnesses, and everyone else involved.

Over a decade later, he had bought out Farin's contract. He had bought her a house in Key Biscayne. A red Mercedes. He had showered her with wealth, ensured a prosperous career, and folded her into his legacy. She had cozied up into the pages of his will, beside the man whose actions necessitated the subterfuge. No doubt they had congratulated themselves on their victory over the naïve, pitiable O'Conner orphan. They had robbed her of her parents, her youth, her self-respect, and her name. Jameson had found her price and bought her trust.

But not her mother. Beth O'Conner had refused to be bought.

Guilt pummeled Farin over her treatment of her mother. Beth had been the good and honorable person her father had loved after all. Farin had hated her until the end, her feelings of betrayal and abandonment the foundations of the unassailable walls she had constructed between them. The Lockhardts had watched from a distance, the unseen architects of her misery.

It was she—not her mother—who had accepted their payoff.

"I'm going with you," Jordan had insisted earlier.

"I need to do this myself," she had argued as she waited on hold to purchase her ticket.

"I thought we were past this."

"We are. But this is different."

"Different how?"

"I didn't want to know, Jordan. You told me anyway. This is the way I'm handling it."

"My visit alarmed him, Farin. He's probably waiting for you."

"*Good.*"

With a clarity honed by chaotic fury, she recalled her father's funeral. She recognized now the identity of the man who had told her "accidents happen." The benevolent manner with which he had treated her for the last three and a half years, which had baffled those who knew him best, had not developed from some paternal connection he felt toward her. The ruse had begun the moment Bobby's Porsche cut through her father's station wagon.

The face in her nightmares was *real*.

Her stomach flipped as the horrific realization struck her. Which one of them had raped her? Was it Bobby Lockhardt, her manager, friend, and longtime companion? Or was it James Wellingham, the demon of her sleeping mind, the man who ripped her father from her life with bloody hands?

"Excuse me, Mrs. Grant."

Farin started. The flight attendant crouched in the aisle beside her. She looked at and through her, unable to fully disengage from her thoughts.

The woman handed her a bottle of water, concern etched into her creased brow. "Are you sure you're okay?"

She rubbed her hairline. "I'm fine. A little tired."

The attendant stood and opened an overhead bin. She pulled out a small pillow and undersized blanket. "Here. Maybe you can get some rest. We're about halfway to New York."

She thanked her, then tried to find a comfortable position—more to appease the concern of the crew than anything else. Sleep had evaded her in the hours before her flight. Rest would not find her now. Not on this flight. Not until she confronted the Lockhardts once and for all.

Jordan's revelation had detonated like a hydrogen bomb, igniting a fire in Farin's psyche. His words had exploded inside her, incinerating everything in their wake. While little remained salvageable among the devastation, in the space of time it took her to plan her northward trek, she found strength she never knew she possessed.

Intent now on avenging the memory of the casualties the Lockhardts had left in their path of destruction, Farin vowed to exact justice in the name of Kelley and Beth O'Conner. The one flaw in Jameson's strategy had been to underestimate the love burning like an eternal flame within her heart, a smoldering ember from the ash and ruin.

The Lockhardts knew nothing about love. They knew only control and revenge. Now, Farin had the control, and vengeance would be hers.

I am not a victim.

She blasted through LSI's corporate offices, her face tear-streaked and makeup-smeared, paralyzing Nancy Chambers with a deadly stare. The receptionist's hand froze above her phone.

"Don't," she warned, pointing as she marched past.

When she burst into the expansive cathedral-like confines of Jameson's office, she found LSI's hierarchy seated within, sipping lowballs of dark liquor, awaiting her arrival.

Her face contorted with the pain and hatred of two decades. "*You!*"

A brief, if well-hidden, hint of rage flickered across Jameson's face at the realization that Jordan had not kept his mouth shut. Curiously, Farin had not shattered like the delicate porcelain doll he knew her to be.

Rising to his feet, he waded in the tide of her fury, arms extended, palms up. "We can talk this out."

"You can't manipulate me. Not this time. Not anymore!"

He studied her stiff features. She teetered and trembled before him. Her hoarse voice ripped through his office, tearing raggedly through the thick air. Instinctively, he stood to assist her to a chair, fearing she might collapse if she did not sit down.

"Don't touch me!" Farin stepped back, slapping viciously at his hands. "All these years! Why didn't you *tell me*? And your...*will!*" She snatched a manila folder from her bag, struggled to rip it to shreds, then tossed the pieces in his face. "You thought you could buy me. *And you did!* I trusted you with *everything*! I even thought you might be able to replace him! I'm sure you and your son have shared a barrel of laughs over this whole thing, haven't you? *Haven't you?!*"

Ross sat mute, convinced that in her blind rage she might not even realize he was there. How many times had he warned Jameson about the inevitability of this moment?

He remained virtually invisible as she offloaded eighteen years of suffering and betrayal. How awful it must feel to have one's world fold in on itself. He wished he could console her. Instead, he remained impassive. He knew where his loyalty belonged. His hands were bound with guilty ties.

"Enough!" Jameson ordered. He stomped around his desk and wrangled her into a chair. "You're hysterical!"

She scrambled back to her feet, her voice deadly. "You bet I am! And it's not over yet. I wanted to see you first to tell you where to file my contract, but when I get home, I'm going to have a nice little sit-down with Bobby...or is it James? Tell me, Jameson, did you know your son's a rapist as well as a murderer?"

I am not a victim.

Ross's face twisted in disgust. He visualized Farin's detailed account of Bobby's assault. When she lifted her shirt sleeves to exhibit the marks on her wrists, his features paled. He made out the fading bruises on the left side of her face. Against his will, he substituted his beloved Josephine for this fragmented young woman. The grisly image sickened him.

He envisioned Bobby being called to the stand. The ruthless cross-examination. Then, his mind jerked back to his uncomfortable seat on the 18th-century sofa, set against the far wall of Jameson's office. The depth of his weakness overcame him. In reality, he could never help Farin find the justice she deserved.

The tale unfolded to its revolting conclusion. Ross sat dumbstruck. With growing astonishment, he noted Jameson's tranquil disposition. In that instant, he knew things would come to a disastrous conclusion. Ross had witnessed Jameson's fearsome dispassion before.

If Farin brought suit against Bobby, her fame would ensure a win in the only court that mattered—the court of public opinion. Not only would Jameson never let that happen, he would enlist Ross to help prevent it.

The LSI building pitched beneath his feet like a sinking ship.

Jameson addressed Farin matter-of-factly. "I've always had your best interest at heart. I was pleased to find you at Jordan's that day. I'd lost track of you after your graduation. Since then, I've endeavored to make it up to you."

"Make it up to me?" she spat, incredulous. She stepped forward, pounding his desk with her fist as she raged. "Can you bring my father back? Bobby never spent one night in jail and I've lived in hell most my life! No wonder my mother was such a lush! She had to sit by and watch you get away with it. Can you bring her back? Can you bring back my mother so I can apologize?"

Jameson lowered himself into his chair. He reclined, folding his hands in his lap.

Farin glared expectantly at him.

He flourished a wrist in her direction. "Do get on with it, child. Is there an end to this rant? When do we get over it and onto the next phase?"

The more he dismissed her, the more her frustration mounted. "Are you the one who paid for the hospital and funeral arrangements?"

"Yes. Next question."

"Why did you do this to me? To my family?" Hot tears streamed down her cheeks. She covered her face with her hands, faltering as she sobbed.

Ross looked at Jameson with pleading eyes. Jameson nodded. Ross moved his paperwork from his lap and helped Farin back to her seat.

Jameson continued. "It was an *accident*. Nothing more. If either of us could change things, don't you think we would? Perhaps it will console you to know Bobby never forgave himself for what happened. It drove him mad in the end. Childs started treating him years ago. He's ill—and not from diabetes. Believe me. He suffers, too."

Farin glowered into Jameson's soulless eyes. Her face contorted into a mask of unbridled determination. "He hasn't suffered at all—*yet*."

Jameson leaned forward, the tip of his index finger pressed into the ink blotter atop his desk. "You'd best remember who you're talking to, my dear. Bobby doesn't know who you are. I made sure of that when I had you change your name. It'd destroy him. I'll not have it."

"Try and stop me," she seethed. She stood, clasping the edge of his desk with both hands. "Not only will I confront him, I'll tell the whole world who you two really are."

Jameson bolted from his seat. He mastered his composure, matching her icy scowl. "You'll regret it as long as you live. That's a promise. And as you well know, I always keep my promises. I strongly urge you to rethink this matter."

"Jameson, I strongly urge you to go fuck yourself!" She turned on her heel and marched out of the office, slamming the door behind her.

Ross shook his head. "I was afraid of this."

Jameson stared at his closed door. "Call and have the plane readied."

***

Had Jordan known about the rape, he might have tried harder to change her mind about driving over to confront him. That was reason enough for Farin to forestall giving up one of the two remaining secrets she kept hidden. Once she arranged a press conference, she would tell him. Not before. Never again would she rely on someone else to save her. This time, she would save herself.

Jordan gnawed the inside of his cheek as he drove. "Jameson's probably called him already."

"This isn't exactly something to discuss on the phone."

"He says Bobby's sick. Maybe he's right. Maybe he doesn't remember."

"I'll jog his memory."

"You should have slept first. What's it been? Two days?"

She flipped down the visor and inspected her features, thankful her uncut rage had adequately staved off closer scrutiny. Unhealed patches of yellow skin framed her left eye socket. "I haven't had a good night's sleep since I was ten. Another day won't matter."

He navigated the Jaguar onto Bird, then right onto Granada some blocks down. "There must be another way."

"I'm sure there is, but I've waited long enough. Did you know today's Friday the thirteenth?"

He frowned and glanced her way. "I never pegged you as the superstitious type."

"I'm not. I'm just looking forward to pulling Jason Voorhees's mask off once and for all."

When they pulled into Bobby's driveway, they found a limousine parked out front.

"It's Jameson," Jordan said.

She nodded at Charles, who waited in the driver's seat. "Told you it wasn't a phone topic. Park in front of the limo so they can't leave."

"You sure you wanna do this? Bobby's your friend."

Her features stiffened. "You don't know what you're saying."

"He didn't do it on purpose."

"Whose side are you on?"

"I just want you to find peace, Farin. This isn't how we get there."

She leaned over and kissed his cheek. "Let's get this over with."

Figuring their visit would be a short one, Jordan left his keys in the car. He exited then raced after Farin, who had jumped out the moment he killed the engine.

The anticipation of entering Bobby's home left her nauseated. Her face, wrists, and womanhood ached in sympathetic psychosomatic reaction to the memory of the assault. She hesitated, then pushed open the heavy wooden front door without knocking.

The inside looked as though a group of vandals had broken in and trashed the place. Papers were strewn everywhere. Furniture lay scattered in disarray, some overturned, some smashed or torn or ripped. Broken shards of glass covered the floor, crunching beneath their shoes.

Jameson squinched on the couch, his son quivering in his lap. He looked small and defeated as he stroked his son's golden hair. "Don't do this, Farin," he pleaded, cradling his son. "It's worse than I thought. He's off his medication."

Mixed emotions confused her as she stood before them. She sailed a sea of hatred, fear, and somehow, even sorrow as she beheld the pathetic sight. The two men huddled together, alone in a shattered home, alone even with she and Jordan standing before them, unsure of what would happen next.

Bobby's body convulsed. Sweat dripped from his face. Beside him, Jameson wept openly for his boy. Farin recognized that pain. She understood the loss tethered to it. The difference was, Jameson had lost nothing...yet.

A lifetime of tortured dreams won in the end. She refused to feel sorry for this pair. Had either one of them given her an ounce of consideration?

She moved closer, staring into Bobby's glassy eyes. "How could you?"

He looked distorted, unshaven, and dirty. Blinking, he gazed at her in disbelief. "Farin?"

She hissed through grit teeth, "Didn't Daddy tell you I was coming?"

Bobby scurried to his feet. He swayed as he licked his fingers, then smoothed his hair in place. "Are you here to stay?"

"No!" she said, recoiling. "I just didn't want to miss the look on your face when I confronted you...*James!*"

"Wha...what did you say?" Bobby's mind wrestled with the vague recollection of having temporarily adopted that moniker at some point, in another time, another life. He rattled his head. Something warned him he should be taking his medication. Why had he stopped?

"You killed my father!" Farin sobbed, releasing upon him years of blame and betrayal. "Didn't you think I'd find out who you were?"

He squinted in confusion. Then, near-recognition. "Farin...*O'Conner*?"

"James Wellingham! We were *friends*! I trusted you!"

Bobby looked back at his father. "Dad?"

Jameson's head dropped as Farin's nightmares and his own entwined. The toil of a lifetime slipped inexorably away. "I tried to stop her, son."

For a moment, the fog lifted. Bobby was a straight-thinking, sober, and very frightened man. He bent forward, clutched his stomach, and screamed in agony. "It's her! Why didn't you tell me?"

Jameson's lips parted to speak.

"Your dad says you're crazy," Farin spat, taunting him. She inched forward, leaning down level with his ear. "He says you're on medication. Is that how you live with yourself? Is that how you sleep at night?"

When Bobby straightened, she shuffled backwards. Her flats slipped on a piece of debris. When she fell, Jordan caught her from behind.

Bobby staggered forward as the murky memory from a long-forgotten evening flooded his awareness. Kelley O'Conner. They told him he had killed the man, but he remembered nothing except bent metal, broken glass, and blood. He had watched the accident from somewhere else. Only later had he learned the man who died had a child, a daughter, a girl. He loved that girl, he thought as his mind slipped away once more. "I'm sorry, Farin O'Conner."

"Tell it to my father! To my mother!" she railed bitterly.

Jordan repositioned his stance atop the debris as Farin moved out of his arms. Bobby lunged forward and shoved him back, his eyes again hazy and unclear. "What are you doing here, Jordan?"

He moved, and answered, with caution, fearing the danger lurking in the depths of Bobby's psychosis. "I didn't want Farin to come alone."

"That's not it." Bobby rocked on his feet. He wagged an accusing finger in Jordan's direction. "You're trying to take her away from me again! You've *always* tried to keep us apart!"

"Calm down, mate, all right?"

Bobby's eyes flickered with desperation. He clutched the sides of his head. "I'm sorry, Jordan. I'm not myself right now. You should go. Take

Farin and go—*now*."

Jordan inched sideways, his hands empty and up. "It's okay. We can help. No one here wants to hurt you. We're your friends, remember?"

Farin spun around, aghast. With a steely glint, she eyeballed Jordan, then glared back at Bobby. "The hell we are! We are *not* your friends, Bobby! I wish you were dead!"

Eyes glassy and far away, he smirked as he knelt down and fished out something from beneath the couch. In his hand, he held a worn snub-nosed .38 caliber revolver. The serial number had been filed down, then burned off with acid. Masking tape held its grip together. The Saturday Night Special was impossible to trace. He had made sure of that when he paid a local roadie who made most his money black-marketeering and dealing drugs over eight hundred dollars for the weapon.

Jameson rushed to his feet. "Where did you get that thing? You aren't to have firearms!"

Bobby snickered. He fixed his eyes on the couple before him, inclining his head toward his father. "I knew Jordan would find out. I knew she'd tell him. But I'm prepared."

Hands raised before him, Jameson backed away. His son waved the gun around the room, his finger resting intermittently on the trigger. "Relax, son. No one's going to harm you."

Bobby scratched his head. He surveyed the living room. "I'll have to get someone in to clean up before you move in."

Farin froze in place, terrified as Bobby swung the handgun in the air. Out of the corner of her eyes, she saw Jameson creep up behind his son as if to disarm him. Unfortunately, Bobby saw him, too.

"Leave me alone!" Bobby roared, clouting his father in the temple with the butt of the pistol. The blow knocked Jameson to the floor. With a single grunt, the old man lapsed unconscious.

Farin screamed. Jordan rushed to her side.

"Oh, is that the way it is?" Bobby snickered again, his mouth twisting into an evil grin. "It's okay, darling. You can kiss him goodbye."

Farin stammered, "C-calm down, Bobby. We can t-talk about this."

"About what?" He grabbed her bicep and ripped her from Jordan's arms, yanking her to his side. He stroked the gun against her face. "You don't love me anymore now that you know I killed your dad? Would you feel better if I, say..." he lowered the weapon at his father's still form, aiming straight for the heart "...evened up the score by killing mine? After all, he lied to both of us."

"Bobby, *no*! P-please!" Farin's body quaked inside his grasp. "He's your father!"

"Don't *ever* tell me no!" he bellowed, repositioning the gun against her jaw. He cocked the pistol. "Never tell me what to do or what not to do! *Understand*?"

"Enough now, Bobby! Leave her alone!" Jordan demanded.

"*You* shut up!" Bobby pointed the gun at Jordan's face.

Unceremoniously, he pulled the trigger.

Time and motion reversed, collapsing all about them, as several events simultaneously occurred.

The full metal jacketed 190 grain slug exploded from the brass cartridge the moment the hammer struck the primer. Farin's nose filled with the pungent combination of gun powder, burning cordite, and sulfur. The report assaulted her from inches away, the ear-splitting discharge nearly deafening her, leaving a solid ringing in her ears.

When the bullet struck his forehead, Jordan's body jerked. The back of his head exploded outward, leaving behind a five-inch hole across the left side of the back of his skull. Gore and brains sprayed outward in a macabre cone shape, spattering and spraying the walls, papers, floor, glass, and furniture. He crumpled bonelessly, landing with improbable force, sprawling on a carpet of shattered glass. His arms and legs were bent at uncomfortable angles. Blood trickled from his left temple. It pooled beneath the back of his head.

Bobby's arm dropped, setting Farin free.

"*Noooo!*" Farin dashed to Jordan's side. She crawled toward him, the broken glass slicing her knees and shins. Her flats slipped off her feet as she lifted his head onto her lap. "Oh Jordan, *no*! *Jordan!*"

Blood poured from the wound like a faucet with a broken spigot—warm like hot chocolate with the consistency of milk. The contents of his skull spilled out as she rocked him.

Farin rubbed absently at her forehead, then stroked Jordan's sticky hair and face. Blood covered her hands and soaked her clothes. "Jordan, please," she begged through her tears. She saw no spark of life in his opened eyes. He did not jerk or gasp for breath. His body looked wrong somehow, smaller.

Bobby stood before them, a look of terror on his face as Jordan's blood trickled toward his Italian leather shoes.

"You killed him!" she shrieked. She sobbed, eyes fused, as she lowered her forehead onto Jordan's. "You killed them both."

Stepping forward, he dropped the revolver and sank incoherently to the floor. "Drag him out of the car!"

His words sounded muffled, as if she wore earplugs.

"They might be able to bring him to!" He pointed across the room. "Look! He-he wasn't wearing his seatbelt."

Farin lowered Jordan's head back onto the blood-soaked floor, stood up, and ran.

Bobby bawled behind her, "It wasn't me! The light was green! I *know* the light was green!"

She leapt into the Jaguar, covering the keys with blood as she started the powerful engine, popped the clutch, and sped away. Her knees bled, the deep cuts little more than a distant itching sensation as her blood mixed with Jordan's and pooled on the floor mat. Smears and swipes of crimson contrasted the brilliant white, hand-stitched leather steering wheel, seat, gearshift knob, and dashboard.

When she found fifth gear, she mashed the accelerator to the floor. She swiped at her forehead, then glimpsed her bloody hands. Blood caked beneath her nails. It splashed up to her elbows. Her dress could have been wrung-out like a towel.

She sped to Key Biscayne doing ninety. The tires screeched in protest at every corner, though she managed to stay in her own lane most of the time. A persistent sound echoed through her compromised ears. Rhythmic in nature. She strained to identify it, praying the car would make it to her destination. Moments later, she realized it originated from inside her. With the release of every breath, she let out a long, slow moan through her tight lips. Breathe and moan, over and over. She could not stop.

Tears flowed as she screeched into Chris's driveway, smashed the Jaguar into the bushes out front, and exited the vehicle, leaving the door open behind her. The chime warned she had left her keys behind. Her ringing ears could not hear it.

A trail of bloody footprints lay in her wake as she rushed up the steps, slipping twice before she reached the door. She pressed the doorbell several times, then sank to the ground, pounding furiously on the door, leaving fist-shaped marks in sticky blood on the lacquered cherry and brass. Her bleeding knees, shins, and tops of her feet made tiny pools of blood beneath her calves, flowing in slow, thin, snaking tendrils across the porch.

From inside, she perceived voices. Someone had heard tires squeal. Someone had heard a noise like a car crash. Someone raced through the house.

Julie gasped as she opened the door and saw Farin perched against the door jamb, hysterical and blood-soaked. "What happened? Are you *okay*?"

A bubbly cry escaped her lips.

"Chris! Call an ambulance. *Hurry!*" Julie crouched down to inspect Farin's hands, arms, face, chest, and abdomen. As her hands came away from Farin's dress, bile rose in her throat. Had something ruptured from Farin's surgery in France back when she had lost her baby? She glanced at the Jaguar and saw through the still-open driver's side door the formerly pristine white leather interior covered in blood. "Oh *Farin!*"

Chris appeared behind Julie, a portable phone to his ear. The look on his face defied description as his eyes widened in horror.

Julie inspected Farin's body in fearful desperation. "I can't find where she's hurt!"

"Chri-i-is." Farin panted between sobs. "Have to...Lockhardt...Bobby's house...J-Jordan's dea-a-a-d..."

Her words vanished into a slow, high-pitched, wailing moan.

CHAPTER 33

*T*HE QUIET, EERIE SCENE FRIGHTENED *her. There came no rumbling, no stirring from the brown station wagon nor from that of the Porsche. No moan, no cry for help, nothing but the maddening hiss of a song on the radio.*

... a long, long time ago
... I can still remember
... how that music used to make me smile ...

All the traffic lights turned red. Liquid fog ebbed and flowed. It pooled at her bare feet, restricting her vision. To her right, an unearthly orange glow backlit the curtain of mist.

A long green Jaguar raced into view. It careened at impossible speed into the other two cars. Its impact sent a fountain of blood up through the ceiling of fog. Red, tendril-like fingers climbed higher, never returning to the earth. The crumpled cars before her burst into flames.

... now for ten years we've been on our own
... and moss grows fat on a rolling stone
... but that's not how it used to be ...

The radio stopped playing.

The murky winds carried no other sounds to her ears. In a sudden vacuum, a complete absence of sound, the fire consumed, red and orange flames raged, destroying everything. It burned red, to orange, to yellow, and finally to a deep azure blue. It returned to the pavement in a shower of sapphires, pooling like liquid and seeping back into the earth like a mirage. The fog rolled back in, noiselessly covering the newly pristine roadway.

***

Farin huddled in an overstuffed chair of the artificially darkened hotel room, sheathed in black. Numb and humming disjointed, random notes to a soulless tune, she held a copy of her mother's letter as she waited for the front desk to call. She was ready. Ready to reemerge. Ready to right the wrongs. Ready to leave Florida forever.

Her hair lay damp and untidy about her shoulders. Moist, puffy eyes demanded she forgo an attempt to make up her face. Friends and family would understand. The public's anticipated scrutiny did not bear consideration.

The funeral was set for noon. The press conference for two.

Given the tasks she had completed in the last seventy-two hours, she marveled over her ability to remain anonymous. Jameson had doubtless spared no expense trying to locate her. Then again, with her newfound understanding of his character, she figured he had spent that time completing tasks of his own—not the least of which would include paying off local authorities. She had seen the news reports, the frenzied speculation, and the claim that a botched burglary had resulted in Jordan Grant's tragic murder.

The police sought her for questioning.

There won't be a cover-up this time, Jameson. You'll pay for everything.

Twin manila envelopes lay atop the rumpled bedsheets, their contents identical—DMV records, an obituary notice, photocopied pictures and letters, and one VHS tape. A third envelope rested in safe keeping. It contained the originals of these items, along with the ruined clothes she had worn the night Bobby assaulted her. She would retrieve them in due time. She had more than enough to commence the chain reaction.

Her mother had been savvier than she realized. At Jameson's behest, Ross Alexander had authored two letters over the course of a decade. The first offered assistance. The second, an ultimatum. Despite bitter rage and illness, Beth had discarded neither. Instead, she had added them to her collection, which included an empty liquor bottle she had purloined from the wreckage of Bobby Lockhardt's Porsche, the obituary notice she had paid to run in the paper, a copy of the original police report that had mysteriously vanished into thin air, and photographs of both vehicles taken at the impound lot.

A thorough photo examination would reveal two nearly identical sets of images. In the first, taken by Beth the morning after the accident, the Porsche's California license plate was clearly visible. She had included shots of a tequila bottle lying on its floorboard, half-sheathed by a brown paper bag. In the second, taken by the police department a day later, the floorboard was empty and the license plates had been removed.

Beth had left her daughter little more than a moribund legacy when she passed. The sole personal item among the overwhelming pieces of evidence had been a handwritten letter. It offered an account of the facts surrounding the aftermath of the fatal event Jameson Lockhardt believed he had expunged. Woven between its virulent accusations and condemnation over the handling of her husband's death were heartfelt pleas for absolution.

> *I hope one day you can forgive me for driving you away. For making you feel less than you are. For my abandonment of you when you most needed me. I've loved you with the deep ache of a fractured heart—a wife too injured to heal, a mother too weak to parent, a woman too fearful to speak. Perhaps when you have children of your own, you'll understand. I pray God gives you the courage I lack so you may one day do what I cannot.*

Farin had read her mother's words a dozen times since she checked into the Sonesta Beach Resort on Key Biscayne two days ago.

The pages brushed against her stocking-clad legs as they slipped from her fingers. She stared at and past them with blurry eyes, then rose and returned them to the envelope addressed to Dale Eastland in Los Angeles.

She hoped the tape would not end up in the wrong hands once she gave it to Miles Macy, but prepared herself for the possibility. Perhaps no one would recognize her battered body as it looked after the rape. She had barely recognized her own swollen face in the bathroom mirror that night. It humiliated her that the only way to ensure her safety was to grant a member of the press first access to the evidence. If her gamble paid off, it would mark the sole instance where she had benefited from her fame.

As for her career, it was over. She wanted no part of the cold, ruthless world Jameson had opened up for her. The last three and a half years had taught her a bitter lesson: success was a game that mocked its most rewarded participants.

The shrill of the telephone chased away the silence of the room.

A friendly desk clerk greeted her. "Your car's here, Miss Wellingham."

"Tell them I'll be down in a minute."

"Yes, ma'am. I see there's also a message here for you. Please hold."

Tinny music filled the line.

... I met a girl who sang the blues
... and I asked her for some happy news

... but she just smiled and turned away ...

Jordan's death played like an old movie, the surreal event a spotty black and white horror flick projected onto the screen of her memory. At its grisly conclusion, the film strip circled and slapped against the recesses of her mind.

The idea she would never again see his smiling face or feel his arms around her seemed impossible. They had spent extended time apart before but had always found their way back to one another. No other possibility made sense. Too many things remained unsaid and undone between them.

Though she remained focused on her final chore, the funeral would test the fault line between her grief and the pursuit of justice. No matter. Today, she had only two goals: stay safe, and get to the press conference. Her own goodbye would come later, privately, and only after she dealt with the business at hand. Today's dismal rituals were a parody. A show for the public, their friends, and his grieving family.

... I went down to the sacred store
... where I'd heard the music years before
... but the man there said the music wouldn't play ...

She had made two calls since Friday—both on Sunday morning. One to Ben, and one to the *Miami Post*. While she had expected to get Miles Macy's voicemail, it surprised her no one picked up at Ben's. Maybe they were screening calls. Either way, the only message she left was for Miles, asking him to arrange the press conference. Part of her feared Jordan's family would blame her for what happened. And if they did not, they should.

... and in the streets the children screamed
... the lovers cried and the poets dreamed
... but not a word was spoken
... the church bells all were broken ...

For the last eight months, she had fooled herself—and maybe only herself. Convinced a steady transformation had taken place, she had believed she could overcome her problems. Her marriage had shown promise. Her health had improved. Her career fired on all cylinders. But holed up in a hotel room, fearing for her life, she had come face-to-face with the truest part of herself and did not like what she saw.

In stolen moments between mourning Jordan's death and plotting her next move, she realized what no one had dared tell her. Or maybe they had and she had refused to listen. She needed help. She harbored inside her perhaps the most destructive of all addictions: grief.

From the day her fathered died to the morning Jordan traded his life for her peace of mind, its insatiable craving had filled her being, ensuring misery for not just herself but for those around her. A cunning foe, it demanded sympathy and a steady diet of self-pity. As long as those within her sphere saw nothing more than an emotional cripple, she need never worry about being held accountable for her mistakes, and she was free to make them.

She massaged her hairline as she waited for the clerk to take her off hold. Her eyes ached from days of sobbing. Her ribs throbbed. Her lungs burned. They were gone—every one of them. Her parents. Jordan. Chase. Melody. Never had she felt more utterly alone. She wanted to scream, but needed to be strong. For the first time in her life, she would be.

... and the three men I admire most
... the Father, Son, and Holy Ghost
... they caught the last train for the coast
... the day the music died
... and they were singin', Bye, Bye ...

She hung up the phone, unconcerned she would miss the waiting message and too preoccupied to wonder how there could be a message for her at all.

She stood and surveyed the room to ensure she had not forgotten anything, then snatched her purse off the bed. After a moment's hesitation, she dug through its contents and retrieved a black velvet ring box. She had intended to return it to Chris many times but, like so many other things, she had failed to follow through.

With steady hands, she lifted the top and gazed at the perfect sapphire within, still puzzled by its purposed symbolism. She snapped the lid shut and placed the box on the desk beside the telephone. Odds were good he would refuse to take it back anyway.

She gathered the envelopes from the bed and double-checked their contents. The first one had Miles Macy's name scribbled on the front in ballpoint pen. This would stay with her until the press conference. The second was addressed to Mr. Dale Eastland in Pasadena, California. In more legible handwriting, the reverse side of the package read, "For safe keeping. Open in case of emergency." She would stop at the front desk on her way out and drop this one off, along with mailing instructions.

Tasks complete, she switched off the hotel entry room light, opened the door, and stepped out into the corridor.

... and we sang dirges in the dark
... the day the music died ...

A large bouquet of jonquils sat outside her door, a black ribbon tied around its crystal vase. No card was attached.

THE END

About the Author

Heather O'Brien lives in Nevada with her husband. She enjoys music, travel, cooking, documentaries, and research.

To learn more, or to read an excerpt from book two in the Music is Murder saga, *A Fate Worse Than Fame*, visit: www.booksbyheather.com.

Iconic Moments in Music History

The 1800s:

February 19, 1877 — Thomas Edison invents first recorded sound

November 8, 1887 — Emile Berliner invents Gramophone

1887 — Columbia Records founded.
It remains the oldest surviving brand name in recorded sound.

The 1940s:

July 1940 —1st Pop Music Concert

September 10, 1940 — South Hallsville School bombing

October 1, 1943 — Birth of Vinyl Records

October 12, 1944 — The Columbus Day Riot

The 1950s:

1951 — Alan Freed popularizes term "Rock'n'Roll."

March 21, 1952 —1st Rock'n'Roll Concert

October 7, 1952 — American Bandstand airs

July 9, 1955 — "Rock Around the Clock" hits Billboard Charts

November 21, 1955 — Sam Phillips sells Elvis to RCA

February 3, 1959 — The Day the Music Died

May 4, 1959 — 1st Annual Grammy Awards

The 1960s:

April 4, 1960 — Motown Records is founded.

The 1960s (**cont.**):

April 25, 1960 — Payola Investigations

November 1961 — Phil Spector's "Wall of Sound"

October 24, 1962 — James Brown at the Apollo Theater

August 30, 1963 — Introduction of the Cassette Tape

January 1, 1964 — Top of the Pops first airs

February 9, 1964 — The Beatles on Ed Sullivan

July 20, 1965 — Dylan Goes electric

September 15, 1965 — 8-Tracks introduced

June 16, 1967 — Monterey Pop Festival

August 27, 1967 — Beatles manager, Brian Epstein, found dead

August 15-17, 1969 — Woodstock

December 6, 1969 — Altamont

The 1970s:

October 4, 1970 — Janis Joplin joins the "27 Club"

November 8, 1971 — Stairway to Heaven is released

April 7, 1973 — Mirage plays the Speakeasy Club

December 10, 1973 — Hilly Kristal opens CBGB

December 19, 1975 — Stax Records closes

October 20, 1977 — Lynyrd Skynyrd plane crash

April 22, 1978 — Bob Marley's One Love Peace Concert

July 12, 1979 — The Day Disco Died

Iconic Moments in Music History (cont.)

The 1980s:

August 1, 1981 — Video Killed the Radio Star

1982 — Hair bands

October 1, 1982 — first CD is released

March 25, 1983. — Michael Jackson moonwalks on VH1 Music Awards

March 5, 1984 — Jordan Grant signs with Lockhardt Sound, Inc.

January 28, 1985 — We Are the World is recorded

July 13, 1985 — Live Aid concert

1987 — record labels consolidate to the "Big Six"

June 9, 1988 — Jordan Grant meets Farin O'Conner at Le Dome

August 6, 1988 — *Yo!* MTV Raps first airs

March 3, 1989. — "Like a Payer" video is released

July 21, 1989 — Milli Vanilli

August 29, 1989. — "Down Deep in Love" hits #1

The 1990s:

March 20, 1990 — Gloria Estefan bus crash

May 6, 1991 — Pro Tools released

November 24, 1991 — Freddie Mercury dies

November 30, 1991 — Mirage's farewell concert

January 26, 1994 — Chris Grant signs with Minor 6th Records

April 5, 1994 — Kurt Cobain dies

Iconic Moments in Music History (cont.)

The 1990s (cont.):

circa July 1995 — Suzanne Vega's "Tom's Diner"
used to test MP3 technology

November 14, 1995 — Jameson Lockhardt's retirement roast

March 9, 1997 — Hip-Hop rivalries

1998 — Graveyard Summer's debut album

December 10, 1998 — Big 6 record labels consolidate to Big 5

January 25, 1999 — Eminem's "My name is..."

June 1, 1999 — Napster

The 2000s:

June 11, 2002 — American Idol airs

April 28, 2003 — iTunes

January 6, 2004. — GarageBand released

August 5, 2004 — Big 5 record labels consolidate to Big 4

July 23-24, 2005 — the return of Lollapalooza

February 8, 2009 — Death Cab for Cutie's Grammy protest of Auto-Tune

The 2010s:

August 2, 2010 — "Jaded" released on Minor 6th Records

July 23, 2011 — Amy Winehouse dies

September 21, 2012 — Big 4 record labels consolidate to Big 3

www.ingramcontent.com/pod-product-compliance
Lightning Source LLC
Chambersburg PA
CBHW031155310726
48969CB00001B/88